MAXIMUS

MAXIMUS

A NOVEL

RICHARD L. BLACK

ENSIGN
PEAK

Library of Congress Cataloging-in-Publication Data

Black, Richard L. (Richard Lynn), 1953– author.
　Maximus / Richard L. Black.
　　pages cm
　ISBN 978-1-60907-985-7 (hardbound : alk. paper)
1. Romans—Fiction. 2. Jesus Christ—Fiction. 3. Judaea (Region)—Fiction.
4. Bible. New Testament—Fiction. 5. Rome—History—Fiction. I. Title.
　PS3602.L3252416M39 2015
　813'.6—dc23　　　　　　　　　　　　　　　　　　　　2014031146

Printed in the United States of America
Edwards Brothers Malloy, Ann Arbor, MI

10　9　8　7　6　5　4　3　2　1

For Marian Anne

CONTENTS

A NOTE TO THE READER

Many years ago I confided in a friend that I had an idea for a story about a Roman general in Judaea searching for truth during the time of Christ. Because I consider myself a student of the gospel of Jesus Christ, certainly not a scholar, my intention in writing this book was to study the gospel more deeply, become familiar with the time when the Savior walked the earth, and explore what it might have been like to witness the events of his mission. That research has helped me immensely to better understand the people and their time. I have made a great effort to be true to actual scriptural events and to the realities of the life people led at that truly marvelous period in the world's history.

All characters in this story are fictional except those taken from the King James Version of the Holy Bible. I have done my best to stay true to the characters in the Bible and have based their words on scripture. Citations for those passages are in Notes at the end of the book.

I have taken the liberty of embellishing three characters from the New Testament: Pontius Pilate, Caiaphas, and a man known only as a centurion, whom I have named Aurelius. I have done so only to help the plot development of this fictional story and without any intention of interpreting scripture. The story is purely my invention of what could have been said or heard or done by someone who could have witnessed or participated in the events.

I hope you find this story engaging and the descriptions of these events useful in gaining a broader perspective and appreciation for the challenges of the humble people in the meridian of time who chose to become disciples of Jesus of Nazareth. I'm not sure being a disciple today is any easier.

BOOK I

ROME

1

General Lucius Fabius Maximus rode an impressive dappled gray steed for the last few miles of the long trek back to Rome. He preferred walking with his men, but the walls of the great city were within sight, and he would be expected to display his rank as the great conqueror returning home. Word of the legion's arrival had preceded them, and he could make out frantic movement in the distance. The legionaries would soon be marching along the Via Sacra to the Forum, where thousands would be waiting to shower them with praise, flowers, and palms.

The men of the legion had put a thousand miles behind them since pulling up stakes in northeastern Gaul, and the weary legate had a thousand doubts about the continuing imperialism of the Roman empire. Almost two years of fighting fierce Germanic tribes had reduced his legion by a third.

Maximus looked back at his men. Like him, they were stretched to the limits of their physical strength. Many were wounded, but they were ordered in their ranks and walked proudly, holding the banners of the empire high, their shields forward and javelins straight. Over the years he had lost too many men advancing the avarice and self-righteous imperialism of Rome. He grieved for his men, but strangely, he also hurt for the loss of worthy fathers, sons, and brothers whom the men of the legion regarded as enemies because they fought to protect their families and cultures against Roman expansion. They were good men as well. He adjusted the scarlet cloak over his shoulder, raised his hand in salute to the revelers, and expanded his chest with a pride he did not feel.

His left calf bore a severe wound inflicted by an adversary's sword. Maximus looked at the backs of his dirty hands and studied the well-defined muscles of his forearms, made hard by years of wielding weapons. His right hand with its missing finger, another casualty of combat, rested on the wooden pommel of the saddle. He recalled the enemy's sword coming down, his own blocking parry not quick enough or accurate enough in the tiring hours of battle. The blade caught the outside of his hand just under the hilt of his sword. It wasn't until the battle was won and the adrenaline sufficiently spent that he realized the finger was gone, cut off at the lower knuckle. The foeman had paid for his brief success by dying instantly as Maximus spun and with full force delivered a backhanded counter blow to his enemy's exposed neck, cutting deep into the spinal cord. No one was a match for Maximus in close quarters combat. Many, too numerous to remember, had fallen to his sword and proficiency as a warrior.

Some conflicts, however, were seared into his memory forever. More troubling to the honorable general than the loss of a finger on a battlefield in Gaul was his loss of faith in the philosophies of the empire. He was indignant at the continuing subjugation of peoples. How many cultures did they need to crush and police? Greeks, Gauls, Jews—it never ended, with treasures of gold stolen, treasures of culture destroyed. The campaigns no longer made sense to him, but he kept those thoughts to himself. Voicing them would be treason. His wounds hurt, but his heart hurt more.

Maximus led his legion into the broad Forum to the boisterous ovations of the crowd, who showered the legionaries with flowers and placed palm fronds in their path. On the long stone steps up to the entrance to the Curia, meeting place of the Senate, stood the dignitaries of Rome waiting to honor them. Seated comfortably in an ornate chair and dressed in luxurious purple robes was the emperor Tiberius Caesar. Surrounding him were senators in white togas trimmed with wide purple borders. Maximus recognized his father among them but did not acknowledge him personally.

Tiberius held up his hand in greeting as the men of the legion approached, led by their valiant legate, who saluted dutifully.

"We have returned victorious!" General Maximus announced loudly, stopping his horse and sitting tall in his saddle with his disciplined troops standing like statues behind him.

As the people cheered, the soldiers pounded the hilts of their swords against their shields with renewed spirit. The long campaign was complete. Maximus's simple statement was all that was required today. Meetings with the Senate and the military council would begin in a day or two. The legate reined in his horse and turned to face his tired men and dismiss them with brief but heartfelt praise: "Well done, worthy Romans. Return to your homes." His words were greeted with cheers from the soldiers directed at their beloved general.

Maximus dismounted his horse, removed his brass helmet with its pretentious crest, and combed his fingers through his wavy, brown hair. He walked among his men, acknowledging their farewells. He wanted to drop in exhaustion as the mantle of responsibility he had endured for so long was suddenly lifted. But almost immediately the thought of another campaign began to weigh upon him. He knew the wheels of the empire never stopped turning. The rest of the afternoon was a blur.

2

Maximus stirred amidst stabs of pain from his bruised shoulder and his wounded leg. His feet were weary from the hundreds of miles of walking, and now his back ached from his having slept without moving for what seemed an entire day. After being relieved of the responsibility for a legion and a campaign he had shouldered for the last two years, he had laid down his head and slept soundly. Through the fog of waking, he saw two young women sitting on a bench at the foot of his bed, watching him. He didn't recognize his surroundings.

The one with dark hair addressed him in well-educated Greek. "My lord, we heard you stirring. What can we provide?" Without waiting for an answer, she knelt beside him to check his wounded leg.

Maximus propped himself up, leaning on his left elbow. "Did you do this?" he asked, pointing to the clean dressing.

"Yes, my lord. You fell asleep after bathing, and we thought it best to clean and bandage your wound then so as not to disturb you later," she explained.

"Where am I?" he asked.

"You are at the house of the senator Gaius Valerius. We collected you at his request shortly after your return and brought you here to rest."

He vaguely remembered entering the city, the crowds, the cheering, the Forum filled with nobles and plebeians alike. He recalled dismounting his horse and being met by two female slaves who had led him to this place, removed his armor, served him good wine, and escorted him to a warm pool of water to bathe. That was his last memory until this very moment that brought him the sunlit vision of two women dressed in white. The dark-haired one still knelt beside him. The quiet one with the large eyes remained seated and silent.

"My lord must be hungry?" the dark-haired one asked. "What may we bring you?"

He managed to croak, "Cool water." His gaze moved to the blue sky that could be seen over the balcony wall. "I'd also like fresh bread and grapes—lots of grapes." His tone was subdued and melancholy. The quiet slave left the room to run the errand as the other one continued to fuss over the dressing on his leg.

Maximus watched the sun brighten the transparent magenta leaves of the bougainvillea bush flowing over the wall of the balcony. He longed for delicate flowers and other beautiful things to be a part of his life again. He wanted a wife and children and a farm on which to raise and teach those children. Most of all, he wished for peace in his life.

Flashbacks of the battlefield recurred in his weary mind. They were in black and white, and they were always cold and dark, even if the battle had been fought on the hottest and brightest of days.

The fighting in Gaul had been fierce against the Germanic tribes' incursion. The legion had the upper hand militarily, but the enemy warriors were fighting for their homes. Their intensity reflected in their fight for wives, children, and the way of life they wanted to preserve. Their first attack came from the left out of the thick forest. They poured into the open meadow in a tidal wave of humanity. They had the benefit of surprise and the rising sun at their backs. The legion quickly turned and organized ranks to meet the massive onslaught. Shouting, screaming, and clashing of swords and shields echoed over the pastoral valley turned battlefield. Fighters on both sides clashed for two hours before the enemy began to fall at a faster rate than did the Romans. A seasoned warrior would fight with severe cuts and wounds: it was the nature of combat. In the heat of battle there was no time or place to stop and dress a wound or even tie a bandage around a leg or arm to stop the bleeding; a soldier would simply keep fighting for his life. Adrenaline combined with fear allowed warriors to fight on despite vicious wounds until they suddenly dropped from loss of blood. They either fainted or simply lay down with no strength to carry on; they were the dangerous ones.

Maximus's wound had been inflicted by just such a fallen warrior after the battle was already won. The foe immediately around him had been slain. Various singular conflicts raging within yards seemed mostly under control. Moving to aid a small group of his men, the legate looked down into the open eyes of a fallen enemy. He saw that the last breath of life had not yet escaped the bloodied warrior but discounted the foeman's ability to strike. Yet the warrior summoned his last bit of strength and, fueled by his hatred for the Romans, slashed with his sword at Maximus. The sword cut deep into his right calf, stopping only at the bone. Maximus howled and went down from pain and exhaustion. But battle adrenaline had not completely left him. He pushed himself to his feet and looked at the attacker lying on his back, completely spent but still alive. The attacker spat at the

Roman who stood above him. The black, bloody spittle dribbled down the side of his dirty cheek. He smiled as Maximus sliced off the top of his head with a powerful forehand strike of his battle sword.

Maximus was brought out of his stupor by the soft voice of the quiet slave: "My lord." The linen of her long white tunic rustled as she knelt beside him with a wooden tray holding a vessel of water, bread, and the grapes he had requested. He closed his eyes and took in the sweet smell of her feminine cleanliness, polar opposite of the smell of sweat, urine, and death that emanated from a battlefield. The dark-haired one smoothed from his callused feet the remnants of the long, dusty road. Too tired to talk or eat, he lay back and fell asleep.

◆ ◆ ◆

Why is she kicking me?

Maximus awoke groggily.

"Brother! Get up, you lazy swine!"

"Stop!" Maximus groaned, trying to roll away.

"I'll stop when you pull your lazy backside off your bed!" a masculine voice responded. Another thump had Maximus reaching for his sword.

"Get up, brother. Time to get back to work."

Maximus's vision and coherence finally returned. He found himself looking up at the looming hulk of Lartius Androcles, his *primus pilus,* leader of the first cohort of the legion and Maximus's closest friend. They had returned from battle together, and Androcles's foot was now firmly planted on Maximus's backside. "Get up! The Senate awaits your report."

Maximus, still groggy and stiff from his long night's sleep, propped himself up on his elbow. "Why do you look as fresh as the morning, yet speak with a voice of thunder?" He held both his hands against the sides of his head, squinting as the sunlight penetrated his fully dilated eyes.

Now in their thirtieth year, Androcles and Maximus had fought alongside each other since they were boys. Maximus came from the privileged families of Rome—his father was a senator, and his mother was from a leading senatorial family. He had enjoyed the best education and a comfortable childhood.

Androcles was from the Etruscan highlands. His father, Mamercus Lartius, had been a blacksmith, one of the best in the empire. Years before, Mamercus had happened upon a slave from the Indus Valley who shared with him a unique knowledge of metallurgy that made the blades of swords stronger and sharper. Mamercus soon found favor with the emperor Augustus for his improvements to the empire's weaponry. He could have lived near Rome and plied his trade closer to the military center of the empire, but he elected to stay in the highlands.

Androcles was the youngest of Mamercus's four sons. They had learned blacksmithing from their father. By the time he was ten years old, Androcles was wielding a hammer with the strength of someone twice his age, pounding out the various shapes of the swords and spears his father designed. His young arms developed the sinewy muscles that would become the massive, powerful arms he had now as a man.

"We go to the Curia today to make our report. The campaign was a great success, and you are to be honored—and we of the legion with you." Androcles beamed. "It's a great day."

As Maximus donned his purple-bordered white toga and prepared for the meeting with the Senate, he knew deep inside he no longer subscribed to the idealism of the empire. He had seen too much death and killed too many men who had fought valiantly for causes his own reckoning deemed more worthy than Rome's.

His fighting fire extinguished, he was physically and emotionally spent. He didn't have a plan for what to say to the Senate about the campaign or, more important, to his father, whose bidding he had unquestioningly done his entire life.

3

It was a good walk from the house of Gaius Valerius to the Forum. Maximus recalled seeing his father at the top of the steps of the Curia with a group of senators standing near the emperor two days before as he had made his brief report to the cheers of the crowd. After he made his full report today, he would be able to see his father and the rest of his family. His mother and two young sisters would be anxious for his return. He relished the thought of engaging in the normal activities of his family's household. His father often chastened him for not leading the typical life of a promising Roman legate and senator, residing in the city to make his name known and his legend grow. In that respect Maximus was more like his mother, who decried the pretentiousness of pampered life in Rome.

Maximus had no interest in self-promotion. He delighted in time away from the duties of a legate and the politics of the Senate. So much nonsense: ambitious men huddling around tables displaying different maps of the known world and debating the merits of capturing some section of a particular map for the betterment of Rome. Which section of the map made more sense? What peoples and resources did the empire need to feed its ever-increasing avarice and gluttony?

Maximus disagreed with continual Roman expansion. Something inside him had snapped some time before, changing his perspective. The urban mob loved the parades and the booty that came in from the wars, but thinking Romans didn't want more expansion, he reasoned. Now he saw only the insatiability of a handful of greedy senators who drove the war machine and subjected foreign cultures and people to the plunder, rule, and taxation of Rome. It was not the way he would have it. But there was no sharing his theories. As progressive as the ruling class of Rome perceived themselves to be, they had little tolerance for talk of peace and sharing resources instead of exploiting them.

The opinions Maximus had begun to formulate as a young boy made him euphoric at times. He could not come up with one negative aspect of his private philosophy. He believed that all mankind was genuinely good and, given the chance, would display that characteristic to strangers of other lands. Men went to war because of the greed of a few. He thought if you were the first to trust and the first to be generous, then like behavior would be afforded you. These were not thoughts worthy of an aspiring general. The culture of Rome demanded courage, vision, and belief in imposing its will, and it assured conformity by means of the sword.

Maximus and Androcles arrived at the steps to the Curia and began the ascent. The walk from the house of Gaius Valerius had been long enough for Maximus to subdue any thought he had of giving an honest report of his campaign. He was resigned to telling the senators what they wanted to hear: Rome had been victorious. Rome had solidified its hold on more territory and strengthened its stranglehold on its people and resources. He wouldn't put it just that way, of course. He didn't want to disappoint his father or let down his friend Androcles. He had to think of his men, who stood to gain a generous share of the booty for their efforts. He must leave the senators happy about their investment in the latest campaign, not puzzled and questioning. Maximus didn't care what they thought of him, but he didn't want to detract from the valiant efforts of his men. They had remained steadfast throughout the campaign despite a multitude of hardships. The weather had been constantly cold and wet. They ate mud with every meal, and cleanliness was a luxury. Fires for cooking were rare, food was scarce, and when they had it, too much of it was eaten raw. Battles were fierce encounters of mayhem. The enemy was neither disciplined nor organized, which removed any strategic advantage the legion might have had. There was rarely a frontal attack, and preparation was nearly impossible. It had been a spontaneous brawl for two years. The men remained dedicated and unified, and their grumbling was minimal. They followed their legate's orders without question. That was the reason the campaign was successful despite the tenacious foe. His men deserved the best report and the highest praise and honor Rome could bestow. Maximus would hold his tongue and serve his men as they had served him. The time would come soon enough to voice his true opinion. He trusted in the wisdom and understanding of his father. They would have a more honest and intimate talk soon.

"Maximus, my son!" Quintus Fabius Maximus ran down the last few steps to greet his son. The embrace was genuine and emotional. The battle-hardened son, although grateful to be home and see his father, lacked full emotion. So much killing had darkened the tender side of his soul.

"Father, your arms reassure me that life is worth living. There were times I lost faith in this reunion." Except for the graying of Quintus's shorter hair, they were a mirror image: father and son, the elegant and handsome senator, the chiseled and tanned legate.

"Come. The senators of Rome await you." Quintus motioned up the steps to the entrance of the Curia. Suddenly he turned. "Androcles, my son." He embraced Androcles with equal emotion. "I am overwhelmed you both have returned victorious and healthy." Quintus's tears flowed freely.

Androcles was like a son to Quintus. Marauding Gauls had killed Androcles's family years before. They had carried out a small suicide mission into the heartland of the empire, slaughtering every living thing in their path. His family and their farm had been purposely in the path of death. The leader of the Gauls had somehow discovered the trade of his father and wished to strike a blow to the military might of the empire by destroying its means to create superior weapons. The Gauls ruthlessly attacked the small homestead. The entire family was murdered and their bodies burned. The attack happened so fast that his brothers had had no time to defend their parents or themselves. They were hewn down mercilessly. Androcles was a young centurion then, away on his first campaign, when the massacre occurred.

That was the source of the unbridled fury with which Androcles fought. He carried his motivation around his neck in the form of a medallion his mother was wearing the day she died. It was the only possession from his family Androcles had. A few days after the Gauls' attack, a neighboring farmer and his sons buried the charred remains of Androcles's family in a mass grave. As they respectfully moved the disfigured corpses of Androcles's father, mother, and three brothers to bury them, the farmer noticed something unusual on the blackened chest of one of the bodies. He removed it, spat on it, and rubbed it between his fingers with his tunic. It turned out to be a disfigured gold medallion. He kept it safe for more than a year.

Androcles, upon returning to Rome and learning the fate of his family, immediately acquired a horse and traveled north at full gallop to his home. There was nothing left. Every stone and timber had been reduced to black rubble. He visited the neighboring farm to gain news of the destruction that had befallen his family. It was then that the farmer returned the misshapen medallion. Androcles recognized it immediately as his mother's. It was the last time he ever shed tears for the dead. From that day forward he wore the medallion on a leather cord around his neck. He clutched it in his fist before each battle, his gaze distant, cold, and fierce. Many good warriors fell by the sword animated by that deformed lump of metal. In the years that followed, Maximus became his brother, and Quintus his mentor and father.

"Come, you lions. The emperor awaits." Quintus walked proudly between them, his hands on their shoulders.

The three men entered the chamber, and as if on signal, the low buzz of important men discussing critical issues was suddenly silenced. The sight of Quintus entering with the two soldiers froze them. A wall of white stood to cheer the returning warriors. Quintus stepped back and added his applause. Maximus and Androcles stood numbed and embarrassed. Even the emperor was standing in their honor. Androcles smiled from ear to ear. For the first time in many years, Maximus forced himself to hold back tears, tears not of gratitude and pride but of sadness, loss, and confusion.

The voice of a herald rang out above the applause: "Lucius Fabius Maximus, honored son of Rome and general of the legion!"

The cheers grew louder. "Lartius Androcles, primus pilus and deputy commander!"

The volume of cheering once again spiked, then slowly returned to silence as the emperor Tiberius approached the two men. They bowed and knelt.

"Arise, noble sons of Rome," Tiberius said emphatically. "We are equals here." He stretched out his arms with his palms upward, signaling the two men to stand tall and look into the eyes of their dignified admirers. Then in a very nonimperial way he embraced them both as brothers of privilege and honor, a gesture many in the Senate had never before witnessed. More applause, then the senators quieted and with a rustle of togas took their seats. The emperor turned and walked to his seat. Quintus led the two honored guests to a space opposite the emperor. They were directed to cushions on the first level of the rectangular chamber. Quintus went to his assigned seat, sat down, and waited with great anticipation for the report of his sons.

The herald announced, "Maximus, you have returned with news of the success and expansion of the empire. The senators of Rome await your report." It was his cue to speak and then face the inquiries of this powerful group of men.

Maximus made his father proud. He praised the strength and endurance of his men. He endorsed the vision of the leaders of Rome. His speech ended to a thunderous roar from the throng of senators. Quintus cheered and clapped loudly, beaming with pride at the speaking ability of his son. Maximus's description of the battles was exciting. He had a way with words that would serve him well in the future. He gave direct answers to direct questions, and his report was without guile or self-serving pride. He selflessly gave credit to the obedience and duty of his men and the example of his worthy captains, deflecting all personal praise. His value as a general, leader, and citizen of Rome rose significantly. After his report, the senators held the legate in the highest esteem.

Androcles could hardly contain his excitement. This could translate into a large reward and maybe an assignment of his own as a legate. While the senators cheered, Androcles stood and embraced his friend. They stood side by side, accepting the accolades of the Senate. The emperor remained seated but looked upon them with favor and pride. Two slaves came forward to place the traditional laurel wreaths on their heads; they bowed graciously to receive the honor. Then the two soldiers were escorted from the chamber into an anteroom to await Quintus.

Androcles slapped his friend on the back. "You gave us favor with the gods. You were masterful, my brother," he beamed at Maximus.

"It would be more important to have found favor with the senators, my friend. They are the ones who make the decisions that affect us."

"Yes, but the gods influence the thinking of the leaders," Androcles countered. "The gods can invoke the feeling of generosity upon the senators and influence our entitlement."

"But the senators approve the allotment and regulate the disbursement. I would still lean toward pleasing them," Maximus responded sarcastically as he ate grapes from the wooden bowl on the table at the center of the room.

"You did well, my brother, but your true thoughts border on treason. You must keep them to yourself," Androcles cautioned his friend quietly. He and Maximus had spent many nights during the last campaign discussing the gods. Androcles was aware of his friend's internal struggle. He didn't come right out and say he didn't believe in the gods, but his guarded words betrayed his heart. Maximus thought man had control of his destiny and that the gods were bystanders. Androcles couldn't grasp Maximus's thinking: "It places too much power with men. Man cannot use such power well; only the gods can manage universal power."

They had debated late many nights, never coming to agreement. Androcles didn't mind his friend's unconventional thinking—in fact, Roman culture encouraged it—but Androcles understood things on a simpler level. He believed in the power of the gods and had no wish to offend them with his own inventions and explanations. Maximus did not advocate a new ideology; he just didn't agree with the Roman ideological and political machine. That was good as long as Maximus shared his thinking only with Androcles. The danger lay in his sharing his thoughts with someone less trustworthy. Betrayal of confidence had played a large part in the progression of many men who had sought the power, wealth, and comfort of the title of senator.

Maximus had been born into the bloodline of senators, but he no longer wished to find advancement in the Senate. The success of the recent campaign had led him to believe that his next assignment would be another campaign, possibly in the east. Though the plebs had no appetite for the spices and foods and fabrics of the eastern lands, the *nobles* did, and the Senate's order would be to conquer the will and might of another culture. The objective would ostensibly be metal ore and precious wood and the taxes that could be collected. But the real mission would be for spices and fabrics. Rome had no need for spices other than to satisfy the peculiar tastes of the wealthy. Expending the lives of Roman citizens and killing men in a far-off country to possess luxuries was immoral. What self-serving god would inspire such a campaign? These were thoughts Maximus dared not share even with Androcles.

Maximus and Androcles grew impatient at sitting quietly in the anteroom. Androcles sipped the wine that had been provided. Maximus sat on a bench, his back against the cool stone wall, and closed his eyes. He longed to be away from this formality. The accolades did not assuage his restlessness to distance himself from the heart of the Roman empire. There was still much to do this day. There would be individual inquiries to learn the specifics of the campaign. Military strategists in the senate would want to know what Maximus had learned about the enemy and if they had experimented with any new stratagem that had proved worthy of teaching to other legions. The war machine that drove the Roman empire fed on dealing death.

Quintus finally entered the room. "My sons," he exclaimed. Holding out his arms, he embraced first Maximus and then Androcles. He slapped each on the back heartily. "You make an old father proud. Sit and let us talk for a moment." He motioned toward the stone benches. "We're finished." He smiled at them both. "No more inquiries today. Your report was without reproach. The senator Gaius Valerius would like to talk with you sometime soon but not today. You're free to go."

The words *free to go* held a different meaning for Maximus. He was glad there would be no more reports today. He was tired, but he would have preferred to answer all the inquiries at once and have it over with. Maybe there wouldn't be another day? He could only hope. "So we can just leave? Go home?" Maximus asked his father.

"Perhaps tomorrow." Quintus answered cautiously. "I will ask Gaius Valerius to speak with you first thing in the morning. Now go, both of you." He glanced at Androcles, who was grinning from ear to ear. "Enjoy your night in Rome." He handed each of them a small purse full of coins. "This should carry you through for the time being."

Androcles was bold enough to open the purse. In it he saw a generous number of gold coins, sufficient aurei to fulfill any desire he might have for many nights. Maximus embraced his father. He had no intention of spending the coins.

"Now off with you two. Leave before a further demand on your time is required." Quintus escorted his sons to the steps outside the Curia and held up his right hand in salute as they walked down into the Forum. He sensed he had a difficult talk forthcoming with his son and was certain he knew the subject of that discussion. He turned, dismissing such difficult thoughts, and began pondering the business of Rome once again.

Androcles was like a child, giddily clutching the bag of coins as if it held the keys to the empire. "There's nothing we can't do tonight with this. There must be fifty coins in here." He shook the bag and slapped his good friend on the shoulder. Maximus winced as the friendly blow hit the bone in his shoulder injured by the blunt end of a stone battle-axe.

"Androcles, my friend," Maximus smiled at his loyal companion, "I'd prefer to go home and rest. I feel I could sleep another two days."

"You have been swinging swords with your men for months now," Androcles reasoned with Maximus. "Come swing a cup with them. They will love you all the more."

"Androcles, you are surely the firstborn son of Bacchus, the great god of celebration. Tell the men how proud I am of them." He took five gold aurei from his purse. "Use this to provide food and drink and whatever pleasure it will buy sufficient to dull the senses and help them celebrate the good battles they waged. Repeat my report about them to the Senate—I meant every word. Make my apologies for not being with them. I am sorely tired, my friend, and have a lot on my mind."

Androcles looked at him inquisitively but did not question his decision. "I will do what you ask, my brother. You are most generous. The gods be with you and give you strength." Androcles once again pounded his heavy hand on the tender shoulder of his friend. Maximus was anxious to part himself from the giant warrior and enjoy a quieter evening alone.

When Androcles finally found his men, perhaps a hundred had gathered. Some legionaries were off into the countryside, reuniting with families and neglected farms. Many had gone directly to infirmaries with mortal wounds, grasping onto a few more days of life. Some had died since arriving. Some were simply unable to fight any longer, victims of heinous wounds, blindness, loss of limbs, and other incapacitating afflictions. They had retired to whatever home they had left or whatever family they could muster to care for them. These were the effects of battle that loyal citizens of Rome did not discuss, senators denied, and Maximus had poured out to Androcles under the moons of many nights in the hills of Gaul.

4

As Maximus walked toward the house of Gaius Valerius, he visited once again the ghosts of his thoughts, the ones that had haunted him and he had ignored for far too long. He revisited the visual horrors of battle, the worthy lives lost on both sides, the causes for which they fought, and the vain effort to exert control over another people. There were other points he had unsuccessfully argued with himself. Killing and conquest would ultimately not serve the best interests of the empire; sane gods certainly couldn't support that kind of behavior. It went against everything he felt to be true about human nature. As a young student he had pondered and studied Aristotle's writings—how men should best live and the virtues of character, magnanimity, courage, gentleness, and self-mastery. Maximus absorbed Aristotle's writings and philosophy like a sponge; they had become part of him and his character.

He remembered a conversation he'd had with his teacher on the subject of moral virtue: How could a warrior display moral virtue and still do the treacherous bidding of the empire? How could a community of people, or on a greater scale, two countries, work together for mutual happiness and goodness? Where did the goodness inherent in man originate?

He recalled his teacher's failure to answer his heartfelt questions: "Why do I feel good when I do something good for my mother? Why do I feel bad when I disobey the wishes of my father? Why do I feel protective toward my sisters? Why do I feel hollow and cold when I fight with other boys, even if I win?"

The teacher had tried to explain that these were natural feelings but was unable to explain why they were natural. Then he shook his head and told young Maximus he shouldn't question the ways of the gods. Neither should he question the emotions inherent in man: they were the same powers that drove a wolf to kill for food or a horse to run. Maximus said he believed man to be superior to animals. The teacher tried to convince him that these were not things given for man to understand, that man just reacted to outside forces, including the forces of the gods.

"Then the force to do good comes from what god?" young Maximus would ask. "That is the god I want to worship," he would say. "I don't want to worship a god that makes men fight or cause harm or evil to other men."

The teacher, overwhelmed by Maximus's questions, had instructed him to think in more established terms in the future, to watch his tongue, and to be cautious where he voiced such troublesome thoughts. They could bring unwelcome consequences.

Maximus thought the teacher a coward for his unwillingness to stretch thought into understanding. He never did get an answer to his inquiries, so he manufactured and applied his own, which became his personal code. That was why over the years he found himself increasingly in conflict with traditional Roman philosophies.

Apart from his teacher, Maximus talked only to his wise father and patient mother about these feelings and later to his best friend, Androcles. His father seemed to understand his son's thinking but was more a sounding board, offering little advice or guidance. He answered Maximus's questions with other questions, inspiring him to continue to ponder and study and challenging him to formulate his own answers, because his questions required answers his father didn't have. His mother simply told him to choose his gods wisely and be loyal and true to his choice. That made the most sense to Maximus: "Be true to the best gods, the gods that inspire man to do good things." That had satisfied him as a boy but was not definitive enough for the now almost thirty-year-old general.

Maximus knew Androcles had listened to his theories much as a stump listens to falling rain. Androcles thought Maximus spoke heresy and cautioned him to keep his dissident and confusing thoughts to himself. "The gods would be displeased to know your innermost feelings. Let the gods do what they will with you. Fate, fortune, famine—it's their choosing. You should make offerings to invoke their protection and mercy."

Maximus didn't have the heart to accuse Androcles of being a simpleton. His friend could think what he wanted. It was his right, as it was Maximus's right to think and choose for himself. He hadn't figured out who the good gods were and to which ones he should pledge his ultimate fealty. It wasn't logical for him to pledge allegiance to statues, something created from the interpretations of man and the embodiment of arrogant gods. Rome, perhaps, had it wrong.

The ghosts kept him awake most of the night.

5

Liora ran back to the village as quick as her long legs could carry her. She was oblivious to the water sloshing out of the goatskin bag slung over her shoulder. The shawl covering her head fell around her shoulders, exposing her long, dark hair. Running wasn't the most acceptable behavior from a young lady in a small Jewish community, but Liora had never concerned herself with appearances. So she ran. She was at the well to fetch water for the house when she heard the glorious news: Jesus was returning!

Liora enjoyed her simple life in Magdala. The residents of the dusty village on the western shore of the Sea of Galilee made their living primarily from the sea, and they also benefited from trading with travelers of various cultures who journeyed along the Via Maris, the Way of the Sea, a highway that ran from the coast northeastward to Damascus. Many others worked small holdings in the countryside. The humble homes and shops lining the road were a blend of angles, shadows, and flat roofs embraced by clear blue skies.

Like a desert whirlwind, Liora stormed into the house and

hurriedly transferred the remaining contents of the goatskin bag into the cistern used to store water for the household. "David," she shouted breathlessly. "Where are you?" She could hardly contain her excitement and spilled water on herself and the dirt floor in her haste.

"I'm here," David answered as he walked through the archway that led to the opposite side of the house. "Why are you shouting?"

David was Liora's twin brother. He worked in the blacksmith shop connected to their mud-brick dwelling. He had learned the craft from their father, Menachem, who had died over a year before, leaving his son and daughter alone. People said he died of old age, but it was the cruel weight of heartache that had finally crushed his long, good life.

Liora and David were the last two of four children born to the highly respected Menachem and his wife, Anna, in their old age. Twins of any kind were a rarity, so Liora and David were the subject of much talk and speculation in the superstitious community of Magdala. Because he was male, much was expected of David, even at a young age; much less was expected of Liora, though she had entered the world first. She had grown from a gangly little girl into a graceful and beautiful woman. Jewish custom kept her from associating too closely with boys, but as her beauty blossomed in her early teens, her brothers constantly ran interference with the boys in Magdala who not so subtly vied for her attention. Liora had always remained aloof, not responding to any inducement for companionship, to the frustration of many a would-be suitor.

Liora tied her hair with strips of colored cloth and leather. At times she dared to adorn it with flowers in season, causing the women of the town to think her proud, which was entirely opposite her true character. She shared with her twin brother, David, the olive skin and piercing green eyes of their mother. She had also inherited from their late mother the ability to think clearly and express logical opinions on complicated issues. Her outspoken nature many times found her at odds with the opinions of the local rabbi, who believed that interpretation of politics, law, and religion should come from patriarchal elders; women should remain silent. Like her mother before her, Liora did not subscribe to that belief or succumb to the pressure of the elders. She never had the opportunity to learn temperance from her mother, however. Her father allowed Liora to speak her mind freely and found it all but impossible to correct her, as the logic of her opinions was frustratingly sound. Menachem had loved that trait in his cherished wife, so he indulged his forthright daughter.

David was hard working, quiet, and soft-spoken like his father. He would ponder his opinions before he voiced them or just hold his tongue and avoid the conflict that would arise from voicing a dissenting opinion. When David was old enough to walk, his father began to teach him the craft of blacksmithing, which Menachem had learned as a young boy from his own father in Jerusalem. The trade had been in the family for generations. David had worked hard to improve his skills. Now he was considered a master craftsman.

David and Liora's mother had died giving birth to them. The sadness that overtook their father then never left him. As Liora grew, she looked more and more like her mother, and as her personality unfolded, she displayed the same outspoken persistence. Menachem doted on the twins, especially Liora, because of her resemblance to their mother. As their father grew older, his two older sons, Nahum and Hanan, took responsibility for the family business. David worked closely with his brothers, and they helped him master the craft of their father.

Menachem spent most of his declining years studying

scripture. When he had the energy, he would meet with the various elders in the synagogue to debate points of religion and discuss the political issues of the day. Liora nurtured him by washing his feet each evening before she served him supper. She would check on him later to be sure he was covered for the night, tidy up the scrolls he had strewn about, and blow out the oil lamp he used for light.

The final undoing of Menachem had occurred one cold evening a year and a half before when news reached him that his two oldest sons had met an untimely death on a trip to Bethsaida. Within the week Menachem simply let death overcome him.

Liora and David continued to live together in the house, managing on the income David produced from blacksmithing. Fortunately for David and Liora, his command of his craft, learned at the feet of his father and refined through the patient instruction of his older brothers, resulted in their having a respectable living.

On one of their short but infrequent journeys north to visit their aunt and uncle in Capernaum, Liora and David were drawn to a crowd of people surrounding a rabbi preaching on a hillside. As they stood and listened, an unexplainable feeling came over Liora; the comforting warmth of goodness and truth flowed through her as this tall rabbi spoke. Everything he said aligned with her simple logic and open heart. His words echoed and reinforced the words her wise father had taught within the humble walls of their home. Liora bowed her head at that same moment and prayed, asking God to confirm to her the truth of what she was hearing. She was overwhelmed with a peace and warmth that surged through her body. David saw the change in her countenance and reached to give her assistance. All she could do was smile back at him.

Liora willingly became a follower of this rabbi known as Jesus of Nazareth. He spoke with a clarity and authority she had never previously experienced, and she had received her own witness of his teachings.

The Nazarene continued preaching in Capernaum and other places in Galilee. When Liora went to the well that morning to fetch water, she heard the other women talking of this Jesus. One woman had recently heard him teach. She spoke of the throng that now followed him everywhere he went. His popularity wherever he preached had stirred the animosity of the Sanhedrin, the ruling assembly of the Jews in Jerusalem.

The woman by the well said that she had witnessed with her own eyes Jesus restore sight to a blind man. Just hearing her tell the story brought Liora to tears—tears she couldn't explain, tears that came from a place deep in her soul. The tears further confirmed her belief in the teachings she had heard in his presence, and they also confirmed her belief in him.

The last thing she heard when she so excitedly ran off to find David was that he was coming! He was returning to Capernaum the day after tomorrow.

"David, we must go!" she pleaded. Her tired brother had been working all day in hot weather next to a hot fire with hammer, bellows, and anvil. He had no energy even to think about an impromptu journey to Capernaum, and he had work to do.

"Sister, I know the desires of your heart, but you ask too much of me," he protested. "You don't even know that he will preach. What if he's simply passing through? Then what would you do?" he asked.

"Follow him!" Liora answered without hesitation.

"You could be following him right back here to Magdala. If he is heading to Jerusalem, he could walk right down this very road." He gestured to the well-traveled dirt highway no more than a stone's throw from their door.

David turned back to his work. "You are a foolish girl. You would walk away from your responsibilities here to be among thousands just to get a glimpse of him. We could barely hear him the last time." He turned resolutely and walked away.

"David!" she exclaimed in frustration. "You felt the power in the words he spoke that day. You know what he says is true. You know how he made us feel. Either we are believers or we are not!"

"We can be believers and still be responsible to our duties here, sister," he responded without facing her, too tired to engage in another losing argument with his determined sister.

"I'll go by myself!" was her defiant retort. As much as she loved David, he could be so stubborn at times that she found him unbearable. She resisted the urge to follow him and resume her pleading.

Liora began to prepare for the trip to Capernaum. Even though she had not convinced him yet, she was certain she would win him over. Besides, David had been working hard lately and could use the break. He would see the wisdom in getting away.

"What time are we leaving tomorrow?" It was David's voice.

"What did you say?" Liora turned, not sure she had heard him right.

"I said, What time are we leaving tomorrow?" David repeated.

Liora ran to him and threw her arms around his neck. "I love you, brother!" she exclaimed.

"Yes, I know. I really do need to get away for a few days," David admitted.

Liora grinned.

She bounced around the house. The chores were no longer chores. She had to remember to find the hair comb her father had given her mother. She wanted to give it to her aunt, her mother's sister, who lived in Capernaum. She had found it in a small box of her mother's belongings. Her father had purchased it in Jerusalem long before David and Liora were born. Liora had plenty of keep-sakes from her mother, and she knew her aunt would appreciate this one. They were always welcome at her aunt's home, even though Liora knew their visiting was an inconvenience. The gift of the comb would be proper.

She wondered if they would see Jesus, or better yet, have a chance to hear him teach. He usually stayed in the house of one of the men they called apostles who lived not far from her aunt. Perhaps they could find the house and wait outside. The woman she met at the well said that sometimes the crowd was so large and pressed so close to him that he had to be taken out on a small boat onto the sea, from which he could preach to the multitude on the shoreline. She said the Nazarene spent time discussing important points of the Law with the leaders of the synagogues. The woman also told Liora stories of Jesus constantly healing people wherever he went. This had the effect of increasing his popularity and the size of the crowds that followed him. Liora got emotional just thinking about him. Tomorrow couldn't come soon enough. She wanted to run all the way to Capernaum.

The next day broke clear and crisp. Liora woke early after a restless night of anticipation. It only remained to pack some food and water, bridle and load the donkey, and secure the house. If she could get David to move a little faster, they would be in Capernaum by midday. She looked forward to embracing her aunt, presenting her the comb, and seeing her younger cousins, Sariah and Esther. They always had so much fun together. David would enjoy fishing with their uncle and two cousins, Lamech and Seth. Fishing was their trade. It was hard work for those who made a living at it, but for David it was a welcome relief from the heat and hammering of blacksmithing. His uncle appreciated the extra help, and David's strength made the grueling work of hauling in the net much easier.

"David, what's taking so long?" Liora called back into the house. David was slow at everything. In contrast, she was like a desert whirlwind, stirring up everything in her wake. David was deliberate and thoughtful. His methodical attention to detail, a trait that he inherited from his father, served him well as a blacksmith.

"I'm checking the fire one last time, and I wanted to take the extra rope to our uncle. I know he can use it on his boat," he called back.

"Well, hurry, please. I want to get going." Liora stood impatiently, the donkey's lead rope in her hand. David finally appeared with a cloth satchel tied at both ends and the rope slung over his shoulder. He secured the door to the house and joined Liora to begin the walk to Capernaum. She was already smiling.

The road wound inland from the shoreline of the Sea of Galilee. Between the lake and the road they passed small family dwellings and were treated to the scent of bougainvillea, oleander, and wildflowers of every kind. Palms, sycamore, and wild fig trees grew beside the highway, offering intermittent shade and softening the heat of the day. For most of their journey, the road wound through rocky brush and grassland under the full sun.

David and Liora talked of many things as they walked: their father, their brothers, fishing, blacksmithing, friends, and extended family.

Liora told David something she had heard spoken of by the women at the well. She said the talk amongst the disciples, and the subject that truly vexed members of the Sanhedrin, was the rumor that Jesus was the Messiah."

"What do you mean, Liora?" David asked.

"Some say he is the long promised Messiah. One or two even whisper he is the Son of God in the flesh," she replied.

"How can that be? He's from Nazareth. His father was a carpenter," David argued.

"David, I don't understand it either, but I believe it. That day in Capernaum when we heard him speak, I prayed to know if what he said was true. David, I received a witness in my heart that day." Tears welled up in Liora's eyes. "The feelings I have about him—the feelings we both have—are not made up. They are real. He is different from anyone we have ever seen. When he speaks of the prophets, it's as if he knows them personally. He interprets their words with authority and deep understanding and then explains them so ordinary people can understand them better." A familiar warmth welled up in her chest. She knew that the things she had heard and felt were true.

David was touched by her words. He too had later prayed and received a witness about this unique rabbi, but he had questions. Maybe they would be answered for him on this visit.

Liora was excited for her aunt Naomi to dote over her. Her aunt was the closest thing to a mother she knew. She was of an age to need another woman to confide in, one she could trust with her secrets. She had a variety of female friends in Magdala but none to whom she felt comfortable opening her soul. Her aunt would listen intently and ask questions that would have Liora confiding even more. She wanted to talk with her aunt about finding a husband. Liora had rejected her father's attempted introductions, and now he was gone. The responsibility for finding a husband for her rested now on David. She had thought about it almost constantly for the past few months, but she was reluctant to discuss it with her brother. That was one of those sensitive subjects on which she hoped her aunt would share wise counsel.

David was overwhelmed with his work as a blacksmith. He wanted to talk to his uncle about his cousin Seth returning to Magdala to work with him and learn the trade. Another option would be to move the foundry to Capernaum. Their aunt and uncle had invited them to move to Capernaum when their father died, but they had stubbornly insisted on staying in Magdala to prove their independence. They matured immensely, having to deal with the daily struggle of life on their own, but lately David had questioned their decision. He had not discussed the matter with Liora, however, because he wasn't sure how she would react.

David sensed Liora was starting to feel the need to be espoused. It was difficult for a young woman without a father or mother to get proper introductions to acceptable suitors, and he was finding it a difficult task to provide one. As obedient as Liora was to the Law, this was an area she felt differently about, and she would want to have a say in the choice of her husband. David hoped during this visit they could ask their aunt and uncle's guidance on these matters.

◆ ◆ ◆

Their arrival at the house of their uncle and aunt was celebratory. Even though they lived only a morning's journey away, their visits were too few, and their cousins delighted in their company. Sariah, the oldest daughter, was a year younger than Liora and the first to see them approaching. "Mother!" she yelled, "David and Liora are here." She took off running toward them, not waiting for her mother's response. "Liora, David!" she shouted as she ran. Upon reaching them, Sariah and Liora hugged and giggled. David smiled as Sariah reached for him and hugged him affectionately too. The three of them laughed together. Esther, the younger girl, age eleven, and her mother, Naomi, were not far behind. Esther ran and leapt into David's arms. He lifted her high into the air, causing her to scream with delight. David's arms felt like iron to her.

Naomi walked as fast as her short legs would carry her, the

hem of her robe kicking up dust from the road. "My precious children, what a surprise," she said as she hugged and kissed each of them on the cheek. She held Liora by the shoulders. "My child," she said looking into her eyes, "you are the living image of your mother from head to toe. Your eyes are the same color and full of the same mischief." Tears streamed down Naomi's face into the corners of her smile as she thought about her beloved sister. She hugged Liora again tightly and then waved for them to follow her back to the house. "We have fresh bread and honey in the house," she said over her shoulder. "The men went out early this morning, so they'll return soon. They will be excited to see you—especially you, David." She raised her hand as if pointing back to him. "They will enjoy your help in the boat." She laughed heartily, which made the four cousins laugh. David pulled the donkey along, Esther perched on top. Liora and Sariah walked together hand in hand, already whispering the secrets that girls whisper between themselves.

When they reached the house, Liora and Sariah followed Naomi inside. David lifted Esther off the donkey, letting her hang on his arm as if it were a tree limb. She squealed with glee but finally dropped to the ground and ran into the house. When David finished unloading the animal, he led it to a small wood-railed enclosure attached to one side of the house. There was a cistern of water and a pile of hay that it quickly began to nibble.

Rather than go inside to the talking and giggling of the women, David made the short walk to the shoreline to await the return of his uncle Jershon and his two cousins, Lamech and Seth. Lamech, the eldest son, was three years senior to David. Lamech was married and worked with his father as a fisherman. Seth was six years younger than David and had arms like an oak. Despite being just fourteen, he had the stature of a warrior. He had visited David a year before and helped him with a small project. Seth had wielded the heavy hammer as if it were a light stick and made it sing loudly as he crashed it down on the forming anvil. David couldn't help but admire his natural strength. He wondered again if his uncle would consider letting Seth come home with him for a season to learn blacksmithing. He would worry about that conversation when it arose. For now he was content to watch the fishermen at various tasks on the beach.

Small waves lapped at the shore. He counted nearly twenty boats either pulled up on the shore or moored in the shallows. He found shade under a poplar, sat down, and relished watching the men at work. Some repaired nets; others repaired sails. Some boats had already returned, the men hastily loading and carrying baskets of fish to tables where others sorted. Inside large, open stalls covered with palm fronds, carpenters cut wood, pounded nails and dowels, and planed upturned boat hulls. It was a noisy place, active and smelling of fish. Seagulls hovered on invisible currents of air and gathered on boats, piers, and roofs everywhere. Two small boys threw rocks into the water and ran back and forth to break up the flocks of standing birds. From his vantage point under the tree, he saw the same scenes repeated up and down the shore. He marveled at the industry of the people and the sea that provided the bounty to support so many of them. This seemed a much more appealing lifestyle than pounding iron next to a hot fire all day. He stretched out his legs and closed his eyes. Sleep quickly overcame him.

"David!" Seth shouted his name and kicked the bottom of his foot. "Get up, cousin. There's work to do."

David awoke a little disoriented but grinned broadly at seeing his young cousin. He reached his hand upward to Seth, who grasped it and nearly yanked him out of his sandals. "Whoa, brother. You'll tear my arm off!"

David stood and opened his arms to embrace his cousin. Seth

reached around him with both arms, embracing him and at the same time lifting him off the ground. David gasped as the air in his lungs was forced out.

"Come on, cousin," Seth said as he set David down. "Father spotted you sleeping and told me to kick sand on you. If you'll help unload our haul, you'll see what real work is like." He shoved David and took off running toward the boat.

David chased him all the way to the boat that was nosed into the beach at the shoreline. They were out of breath and laughing. David's uncle stood in the middle of the boat, separating the fish from the net and draping it in folds over the side. He had girded up his tunic to expose his muscular legs. Except for the gray in his uncle's beard, it was hard to tell Jershon from his son Lamech, who was working next to him.

"David, my son," his uncle said cheerfully, not stopping his work for an instant. "It's good to see you."

"It's good to see you, uncle," David responded. "You are still better looking and work harder than the lump of fish bait standing next to you." He smiled toward Lamech, who promptly plucked a fish from the pile at his feet and hurled it at David, hitting him squarely in the chest. An enthusiastic Seth splashed water on David, who caught him by the wrist. As Seth pulled back to escape his cousin's iron grip, David let go, and Seth fell headlong into the water. Everyone laughed.

Jershon kept working. "My sons, your mother wants us home for the midday meal. We have a lot of work to do. Seth, take your cousin to fetch the baskets, and let's begin unloading."

David and Seth walked back up the beach to fetch as many baskets as they could carry.

David felt a happiness and security here with his uncle and cousins that he never felt at home. He realized that in coming to Capernaum he had let the burdens, responsibilities, and daily decisions of life imperceptibly pass to his uncle. David quickly returned to being a twenty-year-old son of a strong, worthy, and wise father in the person of Jershon. He was more at peace than he had been in many months.

Jershon kept his arm around David's shoulders the entire walk back to the house. David relished the attention. His uncle gave him advice and direction and encouragement for the future. His aunt made him feel like a prince, nearly smothering him with affection and attending to his every need.

The midday meal was joyous. Lamech's wife, Raisa, was with child and would give birth soon. David thought she was beautiful. She and Lamech were deeply in love, as evidenced by the attention they lavished on each other. Lamech acted more like a servant than a young patriarch as he quickly took care of any little thing she requested of him. Soft-spoken Raisa had a glow about her. David watched her quietly and longed for a wife just like her.

"David, you need to get a full night's sleep. We are headed to the eastern shore tomorrow for a long day of fishing. I hope you can keep up. We hear that fish are schooling there, and we expect to come home with a large catch."

Before David could respond to the challenge of his uncle, his aunt broke in. "Oh, stop the talk of fishing. David didn't come here to be a slave on your fishing boat." She stood and poured more wine into her nephew's cup. "These two children came to visit and rest, and you want to put them to work as if they were servants." She playfully tapped Jershon on the back of the head as she passed.

Liora and Raisa talked intimately as they prepared the midday meal. Raisa placed Liora's hand on her stomach to feel the movement of the baby. Liora had little knowledge of childbirth. Her aunt Naomi had spoken plainly to Liora and Sariah on their last visit about the intimacy of consummating a marriage and bearing children. Liora pondered these things quietly at times. There was so much more she wanted to ask. When Naomi had shared those intimate womanly details, Liora realized how much she missed not having a mother. She longed to become a mother herself. She was envious of the attention paid to Raisa and wished that her aunt would encourage Jershon to help David arrange an introduction with a suitable young man. Liora would talk to her directly about it as soon as the opportunity presented itself.

6

Sunrise found Maximus in the ornate courtyard of Gaius
Valerius's house eating a hearty breakfast.

"Maximus! My dear young man." It was the booming
voice of the rotund senator. He entered the courtyard and sat
down next to Maximus at the table with a great release of air
from his lungs and the popping of overburdened joints in his hips
and knees.

"Thank you for your generous hospitality, Senator. The ac-
commodations have been glorious. I hope my staying here hasn't
inconvenienced you," Maximus said politely.

"No, not at all. This is just a little place I keep for special
guests," Gaius answered. "I assume your good father mentioned
that I wanted to speak with you."

"Yes. I have been curious what you wanted to talk about. It
has occupied too much of my mind," Maximus said with a smile.

"As well it should. It is understandable a young man would
want to know what fate the gods have in store for him, especially
when that fate, many times, lies in the hands of mere mortals."

Maximus interpreted the senator's words as an expression of modesty. "That is the lot we've chosen, sir."

"Yes, Maximus, it is. But there are times when a good man has the opportunity to change his course."

"Change course?" Maximus hoped he was the good man Gaius referred to.

"Sometimes the gods place circumstances and the desires of one's heart at a crossroads. At that point a well-prepared man can take the better road." Gaius looked straight at Maximus.

Maximus's heart leapt. "Forgive my boldness, sir, but what does the emperor desire of his legate?"

"Our good emperor Tiberius is supportive but had little to do with this decision," Gaius responded.

Maximus's heart sank. "My father?" he asked nervously.

"No."

"Is he aware of it?"

"Yes, and he approves. The assignment, my son, is the result of a request of mine." Gaius straightened up in his seat. "I have the greatest respect for your father. He has sired a fine son. I have watched you since you were a boy. You have obediently carried out your duties without complaint or second-guessing. You moved forward with confidence, whether you agreed or not, and accomplished the things asked of you better than all the other military leaders at Rome's command."

"You flatter me, sir," Maximus interjected.

"No, my son. I speak the truth. I know the difficulties you have faced in years of fighting in foreign lands. I don't think the citizens of Rome understand the life of a warrior. We sit and get fat on the bounty of good food and wine—all supplied to us by the blood of good men like you, Maximus." He squeezed Maximus's shoulder with genuine affection and respect.

Maximus was speechless. After a few moments of silence he managed to blurt out, "What is your request, Gaius Valerius?"

For the better part of an hour the senator spelled out a most intriguing assignment. Maximus had a thousand questions. Gaius had a thousand answers. Maximus was most definitely at a crossroads. He wondered if he was as prepared as the senator thought he was.

Gaius stood at times and spoke as if he were giving an oration to the entire Senate. Maximus sat quietly, listening intently. He had always been cautious and distrustful of the pompous senator, but their lengthy discussion had shown him that Gaius did have in mind the best interest of the citizens of Rome. He too was tired of the conquests, the bloodshed, and the loss of the best young men in the empire. Maximus didn't share his innermost thoughts, but he felt Gaius understood him in principle. The senator was masterful in his description of his vision of the future for the empire, the peaceful melding of cultures and trade, the sharing of philosophy and invention. He felt the emperor Tiberius was sympathetic to these ideas and hoped he would live long enough to promote some of the progressive policies they had discussed. Gaius expressed again his great respect for Quintus, Maximus's father. They laughed together about the loyal and impetuous Androcles. A new bond was struck. A new campaign was launched.

"Then we have an agreement, my son?" Gaius Valerius put out his arm to grip Maximus's forearm in the formal manner. Maximus smiled and sealed the agreement. They embraced as mentor and student, father and son.

7

David was dressed and eating before his uncle and cousins appeared. He looked forward to fishing. He enjoyed being out on the water in the company of his family. As a blacksmith he spent the entire day at home alone. He would break for the midday meal that Liora prepared and then after a short rest return to work until sundown. His life was filled with work and loneliness. To spend a day working with others and being able to talk and laugh—the thought of it invigorated him.

"Good morning, good nephew," his uncle said as he entered the room. "Eat up. You will need all the energy you can muster today—it will be a long one." Jershon took a small loaf of bread from the wooden bowl on the table. He combined it with a small slab of raw honeycomb, poured a cup of water, and sat down to eat.

Seth stormed into the kitchen full of life and mischief. Lamech was last, walking tiredly and expressionless. A good night's sleep had obviously escaped him. His eyes were dark, and he shuffled like an old man as he entered the kitchen.

Jershon watched Lamech prepare his morning meal. "Should

we leave you with the women today, my son?" he said with a smile. "I'm sure David will be a suitable replacement."

"No, my father. I will be fine," Lamech quietly responded. Jershon left it at that.

"We have a long sail this morning to the eastern edge of the sea. If we are fortunate and God looks favorably on us, we might be home early, depending on the direction of the winds." Jershon tore off another large piece of bread.

The meal was simple. Not much was said. Jershon read a passage from the Torah as the boys finished their morning meal. Prayers were offered to bless their efforts, bless their home, bless their wives, and most important, bless them with safety as they sailed across the treacherous and unpredictable sea. Naomi arose just before the men left. She hugged each one, reserving a tender hug and kiss for her husband, whom she loved dearly. She would worry and pray for them all day, as she did every day. Too many fishermen over the years had left home never to return, lost to the capricious winds of the sea. It was the lifestyle her husband had chosen and a reality she had learned to live with.

As the men departed, Naomi began her ritual of prayers: praising God for his bounty and asking blessings for the safety of her husband, sons, and nephew. She called down the power of God upon her daughters and pleaded for the safe birth of her grandchild. Today, especially, she asked God to guide her as she counseled her niece, Liora, whom she sensed carried a burden of uncertainty in her life. She finished her prayers and cleaned up after the men's breakfast. It would be a couple of hours before the girls awakened.

The men walked quietly in the early morning darkness to the boat. They had taken time the day before, as they did every day, to repair and refold the net. Jershon's sons complained of the extra work after the long day fishing, but they understood the wisdom of having everything prepared for the morning. They always enjoyed a headstart on many who left the preparation for the morning.

Lamech loaded the food and water Naomi had prepared and inspected the boat thoroughly. He checked the hull, tested the stiffness of the mast, and raised the sail to check again for tears or rips. The sail was sound. He lowered it again and folded it neatly in the bottom of the boat. David watched with pleasure as they smoothly went about their morning routine, helping when he was asked and learning as he observed. Jershon always said it was better to repair and prepare on shore than in cramped quarters on a choppy sea. It was even more disheartening to see fish escaping out of a hole in a net that had gone unchecked. Or worse, having the fish surround you and be sitting in the boat repairing bad netting, unable to cast. His routine and attention to detail were the reason he was one of the most successful fishermen in the area.

It was easy work launching the boat with the extra help of burly David. The boat was soon in the water and pointed away from the shore. After a short prayer, Jershon sat ready at the raised tiller. Lamech manned the ropes of the sail. David found a seat in the bow of the boat and tried to stay out of the way. From the shallows, Seth pushed the boat to deeper water and then climbed into the stern, sitting on the small bench opposite his father. Jershon lowered the tiller as Lamech raised the sail. It snapped taut in the mild breeze and caused the boat to plow forward. The day had officially begun.

"Settle in, boys," Jershon said. They sailed eastward into the rising sun. The wind picked up as they entered deeper water, and they made good time to the area Jershon had chosen to fish. David pulled his thick outer robe around his shoulders as the sun withheld its warmth behind the eastern mountains.

Back at home, the girls awoke and joined Naomi around the

hearth. Giggling and talking about marriageable men in the village started early. Raisa lumbered out a few minutes later, both hands resting on her stomach. She looked tired and pale. The girls helped her sit down. Naomi gave her a warm, damp cloth to wash her face and hands. "The time is almost here," Naomi said as she placed her knowing hand on the taut belly of her daughter-in-law.

"Yes, I believe so," Raisa responded as she shifted her weight in the chair to find some comfort. Naomi, with the help of other women in the village, had prepared the needful things for the birth. Women with special skills would assist when the baby finally came. The three girls did what they could to make things more comfortable for Raisa. Liora was excited at the thought of being present for the birth. She had firmly made up her mind to stay in Capernaum for a season, though she had not yet discussed that decision with David.

As the morning wore on, it became obvious that things were progressing quickly toward the birth of the baby. Naomi prepared the bed and sent Esther to summon the women who had agreed to help. Sariah began heating water, and Liora sat with Raisa.

The sun was at its highest point in the sky when the little boy took his first breath, which was followed by a high-pitched cry announcing his birth into the world. The baby was cleaned and swaddled and placed in his mother's arms against her breast. His grandmother, two aunts, and cousin Liora sat close by with tears in their eyes at the miracle of life.

Liora was exhilarated to have witnessed the birth. She had so many questions she wanted to ask her aunt. As she sat quietly in the warm room admiring Raisa, she wondered when her own time would come to be a mother. Lamech would be so surprised when he returned, as the birth had not been expected for another week. Liora had been in Capernaum only a day, and already so much had happened.

About the time Lamech's wife was giving birth to their son, Lamech and the others were hauling in the net for the final time. Flipping and squirming fish filled the boat, denying the four fishermen proper footing to pull in the heavy net. It had been risky to sail to the eastern side of the lake on rumors. Jershon was a cautious fisherman, but he had felt good about attempting this particular run and was now flashing a satisfied grin at their good fortune. He stood at the stern of the boat, watching the three strong boys pull in the final fold of the net and then as a group fall laughing among the slippery fish.

"Set sail, Lamech. Let's go home," Jershon ordered. Lamech managed to find footing and pull the lines that raised the sail. The wind was coming from the southwest, which allowed them to tack against it to return to Capernaum. Jershon held tight to the tiller as the fully loaded boat slowly responded to the pulling of the sail and leaned heavily over in the wind. Lamech adjusted the sail, the boat straightened, and they began cutting a deep path through the water.

"David, we will have to invite you more often. You bring us good luck," Jershon said. David smiled and raised his hand in acknowledgment. He had silver scales all over his body and smelled of fish. He was tired, thirsty, and hungry, but he had enjoyed every minute of the day. Hard work was so much easier when you didn't have to work alone. Maybe he would become a fisherman. He sat among the fish and leaned against the hull of the boat with his arm over the side. He could see the distant shore and the high mountains on the far horizon to the north. The promised land was a beautiful place.

Seth fell asleep in an instant, his head resting on the bulkhead of the boat. Lamech held the lines to the sails, making small pulls and releases as the wind changed direction. He thought of his tender wife and silently prayed for her comfort and well-being. Jershon had a strong arm on the tiller, keeping the tension tight against the pressure of the oncoming water to steer them home.

David closed his eyes against the afternoon sun. The heat of midday was more bearable than the hair-singeing heat of the foundry, and the occasional spray of water misting his face was joyous. Soon the hypnotic surging of the boat lulled him to sleep.

Jershon could see all the boys from his position at the tiller. David had been a huge help and had actually worked harder than his own sons. David never paced himself for a long day; he worked full speed all the time. It was almost tiring to watch him. Seth had become an enthusiastic and competent fisherman. Jershon was confident Seth would be successful on his own at this point. He directed his gaze at his eldest son, Lamech. What a joy Lamech was in his life. Surely Lamech was thinking of his sweet wife, Raisa, and anxious to be at home with her. He should probably counsel him to consider a livelihood that kept him safer and closer to his wife. Lamech worked hard and never complained when days grew long and they worked far into the night. But his special attachment to his wife could defeat him in this line of work. The land held a better future for him. He would bring up the matter with Lamech at an opportune time, perhaps the approaching Sabbath. Jershon recited a simple prayer for their safe arrival home.

8

aximus was ecstatic about the new campaign. What Gaius Valerius had proposed involved Androcles too. It would challenge and expand the skills of both of them. He hoped Androcles would be as enthusiastic as he was. There was still much more to learn, and the senator had promised to talk to him again later that day. For now Maximus had plenty to consider.

"Brother!" Maximus heard a shout from the front entrance to the courtyard. He turned to see the muscular Androcles entering. "I saw Gaius Valerius. He said he'd just met with you. What did he have to say?" Androcles inquired. "Something you want to tell me about?"

"I certainly do, but you should probably sit down." Maximus pulled his chair close to Androcles and repeated what Gaius had told him.

"Maximus," the senator had said, "about a month ago an emissary from Judaea presented himself to the emperor Tiberius. He carried with him a message from the prefect of Judaea, who is Pontius Pilate. Because Pilate happens to be a cousin to my wife, Tiberius assigned the issue to me for resolution. I met Pilate once long ago. He aspired to be a senator but displayed indecision and was passed over for more capable men. But he comes from a powerful family. His uncle had access to Tiberius and gained his confidence and his ear. Because of that, Pontius was appointed prefect in the Roman province of Judaea."

"Judaea is an interesting place. Do you know of it?" Gaius leaned toward Maximus and raised his eyebrows.

"I know where it is but know little about the country or its people, senator," Maximus responded.

"Well, it doesn't matter. It is far away and, frankly, offers the empire little in terms of assets, but strategically it lies north of Egypt. The Jews are a troublesome people. They are bound together by the worship of a god they call Jehovah. They claim royal lineage through an ancient progenitor they call Father Abraham. They look down on anyone who is not of the lineage of this Abraham. You and I, Maximus, would be known to these people as Gentiles, which is a derogatory term as far as I can tell. They have an arrogantly superior view of their race and culture."

Gaius stood and arched his back to stretch. "Being under Roman rule must really get under their skin," he chuckled.

"The territory has several parts. Galilee is in the north, named for a small sea in its midst. In the south are Judea, Idumea, and Samaria, which make up the province we call Judaea. Our friend Herod Antipas rules Galilee, and the prefect Pontius Pilate governs Judaea from Caesarea on the coast of the Great Sea. Inland is Jerusalem, the center of all Jewish religious activity." The senator walked around as he spoke, posturing and looking to the sky occasionally as if he were addressing a crowd in an amphitheater. *The consummate showman*, Maximus thought.

"What I find fascinating about this people is there is no apparent order of government other than the religious precepts to which they rigorously adhere. They are ruled by their priests, who are members of the Sanhedrin. As I understand it, this is a group of older religious leaders who have risen in rank to this position. Rome maintains a modicum of control over this body by reserving the right to appoint the high priest. The current one is a man named Caiaphas."

Gaius sat down next to Maximus. "I have done some research on this Caiaphas," he continued. "He was appointed by the previous prefect of Judaea, Valerius Gratus, and given authority over the Sanhedrin as well as charge of the Jewish temple in Jerusalem built by King Herod, the father of Herod Antipas, who is now tetrarch of Galilee."

Gaius looked at Maximus to make sure he was paying attention. Maximus met his gaze, wondering where this history lesson was leading.

"Pilate communicates to us that the high priest, Caiaphas, came to him with a group of religious leaders to ask for intervention by Rome." Gaius stood. "Here's where the story gets interesting. The Jews subscribe to an ancient belief in a person they call the Messiah. Their prophets have spoken and written about this Messiah over the ages. Our Jewish advisors in the Senate tell us that this Messiah is predicted to come in glory and power, like the great legate Maximus with his legion, and rescue their people from all oppressors. The gods know these people can't fight for themselves. History tells us the cities of the Jews have been sacked and the Jews enslaved by every people in the region. I can see where they would need to create a god called Messiah to deliver them." Gaius laughed sardonically.

"Caiaphas and his counselors told Pontius Pilate that there is a Galilean, a man known as Jesus of Nazareth, who people claim is this great Messiah. The funny thing is that Pontius Pilate seems genuinely concerned that this Jesus is some sort of god in the flesh! I think this Caiaphas is a sorcerer and has infected his mind." Gaius gestured as if dismissing the overreacting Pontius Pilate. "He is still weak." The senator sat back down in disgust.

"The emissary tells us that this Jesus is the son of a simple carpenter. He has become a popular rabbi, so popular that two opposing political factions among the Jews have actually united in their efforts to thwart him. They have rallied the support of the Sanhedrin to ask Pilate for Rome's help in stopping this Messiah, this carpenter Jesus." Gaius laughed out loud. "No wonder these people can't defend themselves. They fear carpenters." He laughed louder. "The emissary goes on to say that this Jesus has a following of thousands. Everywhere he goes they follow him like cattle."

For the first time since Gaius began talking, Maximus asked a question. "Is he armed?" He went on. "Does he carry weapons of war? Are these thousands they refer to a legion of warriors?"

"No, his weapons are his words. His followers are a mix of men and women, young and old, of the common classes. They sit at his feet in meadows and on hillsides listening to him preach. They crowd into the synagogues to hear him debate the Law with the Pharisees and Sadducees. The emissary reports that this Jesus confounds the experts with his knowledge and reason. They constantly challenge him, but he quiets them and at the same time infuriates them by speaking with clarity and boldness on the stickiest points of the Jewish law. He challenges them on their understanding of the ancient laws and proves them foolish in their interpretation. Maybe I should have him brought to Rome to help me argue my theories," Gaius said with a chuckle.

"Does he incite rebellion against Rome?" Maximus asked.

"No, the emissary says he speaks only of peace."

"With respect, what is the problem the high priest takes to Pontius Pilate, and what compelling argument does he make to cause Pilate to send an emissary to the emperor requesting assistance? Why doesn't he just command a cohort to hunt this Jesus down and throw him in prison?"

"First of all, my young friend, Pontius Pilate isn't man enough to command a cohort to relieve themselves at a latrine. And second, as the emissary admits, this Jesus hasn't done anything to warrant punishment by Rome."

"I'm confused, sir. If this Jesus hasn't broken the Law and isn't subversive, if he is just a popular rabbi with a new interpretation of the Jewish religion, why would Pontius Pilate think he is a threat to Rome?" Maximus queried.

"Logic would tell us that he isn't. But there is a peculiar element to this story." Gaius paused, and his tone became serious. "Thirty or so years ago King Herod was told the same fable of this Messiah. Our Jewish advisors inform us that members of a priestly caste in the east who were skilled in astronomy visited Herod in his court to inquire about a child born during that time who was to become king of the Jews. They told Herod they had seen the child's star in the eastern heavens and had traveled some distance to worship him. Herod asked the chief priests and scribes where this boy-king could be found. The priests informed him that one of the ancient prophets, a man named Micah, said Bethlehem would be the birthplace of the future ruler of Israel. Herod deceitfully asked these men to find the child so he himself could worship him. It isn't known whether the magi found the young child because they never returned. So Herod ordered the murder of all children under the age of two in Bethlehem and the surrounding area. He was always fierce in eliminating his enemies or those he thought would become his enemy."

Maximus wondered what all this had to do with him. "So the story of Herod killing the children is true?" Maximus asked.

"Yes, it is," Gaius replied.

"This Jesus," Maximus asked. "How old is he?"

"Good question," Gaius said. "If he is about thirty, he somehow escaped the purge. But the more important question is, Does this carpenter's son have the potential to evolve into the legendary Messiah? Is his strategy to pose as a peaceful rabbi, gather an army right under our nose, and when his numbers are sufficient, overtake our cohorts?

"Then you believe Pontius Pilate?" Maximus asked.

"Maximus, let me share something of my burden. The empire is like a large octopus whose tentacles stretch far and wide. The work of the Senate is to be sure that even when the tentacles are stretched to their maximum length, they still nurture the body that gives them life. The loss of even one can affect the balance of the whole. We have to make sure the body stays intact and the tentacles remain strong and firmly attached. Tiberius has asked me to attend to one of our tentacles. Now I could be patient and let this run its course. Nothing may come of it; it may be only the paranoia of a weak leader. But if I do nothing and this Jesus really is the Messiah spoken of since ancient times, and it all escalates into an action against the empire—I stand accountable. I stand accountable to Rome," he repeated. "If you, Maximus, were the commander of the cohorts in Judaea and this army arose and slew you and your men because of my inaction—may the gods have mercy on me!" Gaius raised his arms to the heavens. "Your ghost, Maximus, would haunt me to my death."

Maximus contemplated the senator's words and realized he spoke wisely. "The fastest way to Judaea is by sea. It would take a month or more to gather troops, set sail, and render assistance to the forces already established," Maximus added. He could see that somehow he was going to be a part of the senator's plan.

"Yes, I agree," Gaius said. "The land route would take far too much time."

"So you have decided to honor Pontius Pilate's request."
Maximus was trying to discern what was in Gaius's mind.

"I don't see this as honoring a weak man's request. I am
simply looking after the assets of Rome."

Maximus resigned himself to leading the campaign to Judaea.
"When do we leave?" Maximus stood.

"Tomorrow," Gaius answered emphatically, looking at the legate and waiting for his reaction.

"Tomorrow?" Maximus said incredulously. "It will take a week
to gather the men and another week to rearm. The ships, the
supplies—" he stared at the senator, not believing what he was
hearing.

"My son, you have sat patiently listening to me describe the
problem. Now sit patiently and listen to the plan."

Maximus obeyed. His mind was spinning with all the things
that would have to be done in a short time.

"Maximus," Gaius Valerius began, "I have discussed this with
Tiberius, and we have agreed you are to go to Judaea and meet
with Pontius Pilate, but we are not sending additional soldiers
with you." He stopped to let the words settle in.

"What do you mean, not sending soldiers?" Maximus asked.

"Exactly what I said, Maximus. We are sending you as an
emissary. We would like you and Androcles to investigate this
Jesus and the situation in the country. A member of the military
council has reported that an Egyptian merchant ship is sailing
late tomorrow, directly from Ostia to Caesarea. He has arranged
passage for the two of you." Maximus had not been able to conceal his shock at this new direction. "My son, I know you have
a multitude of concerns and questions. We will talk more this
afternoon."

For the first time Maximus could remember, Androcles sat

dumbfounded, not a word coming out of his mouth. Maximus smiled at his friend's bewilderment.

"When do you meet again with Gaius Valerius?" was all Androcles could muster.

"He just said later this afternoon." Maximus stood and put his hand on the shoulder of his friend. "My brother, my petition to the gods has been answered."

"*Your* petition, brother," Androcles retorted, "not mine."

Maximus could understand the consternation of his friend. After all, he was the consummate warrior, and this was unfamiliar ground. Androcles was used to slash-and-burn diplomacy. In past campaigns, when the opportunity presented itself to avoid a conflict and reason with the enemy, he would accompany Maximus to the table, but he always had one hand on his sword, not trusting the craft of negotiation and compromise, the skills that saved men's lives. Maximus was confident that Androcles would reason through whatever internal conflict he was having. If he couldn't, then Maximus would make the voyage alone. It was as simple as that.

"So, my brother," Maximus asked, "are you coming with me?"

Androcles turned to face his friend. "I'd rather be heading to Gaul with a thousand men armed with sharp swords than go with you on a long boat ride to godforsaken Judaea."

Maximus knew by that response that Androcles had made his decision: they were off to Judaea together.

9

With the help of David, Jershon and his two sons made short work of unloading the fish and taking care of the necessary preparation for the next fishing day. Seth put a few of the best fish into a basket for the first meal of the Sabbath that evening. They picked up their belongings and began the short walk home.

"Father," shouted Esther, who ran toward them on the sand. "Raisa had her baby today . . . a little boy." She turned toward Lamech, who had not fully registered the news he was hearing. "Lamech, you are a father." She hugged her older brother.

Lamech dropped what he was carrying and began running to the house. Esther ran after him. Jershon, David, and Seth laughed and, despite the hard day they had had fishing, followed at a quickened pace. When they arrived at the door, Naomi was there to tell them to be quiet: Raisa and the baby were sleeping. Naomi gave Jershon the affectionate and joyful hug of a new grandmother. Lamech sat on the floor next to his wife and new son, staring in disbelief, a single tear running down his cheek as he realized his life had changed forever.

Preparations for the Sabbath began before sundown. Tomorrow was a day of rest. The men cleaned themselves up for the first meal of the Sabbath. Jershon blessed the two loaves of challah bread. The meal was eaten with particular reverence in gratitude for the birth of the baby. Jershon shared news of the successful fishing that day and how blessed they were to have David and Liora with them. They spoke in soft tones as Raisa slept most of the evening. She woke up once when the baby fussed and began to feed him. The family congratulated her and Lamech briefly, but Naomi protectively rushed them out. They all looked forward to a day of rest from their labors. Tomorrow they would worship, eat, rest, and spend time together. There were so many things to talk about.

Sabbath tradition in the household was for Jershon to read from the Torah or the Prophets. As a family they would discuss their deep-seated beliefs. Jershon made sure his family honored their obligations under the Law of Moses. Within the walls of their home, however, they could question any doctrine or law. Jershon, due to his diligent reading and study, was very knowledgeable about the Mosaic law. On days the weather kept the fishing boats ashore, Jershon often visited the synagogue and sat with the elders to be taught.

"My children," Jershon began, "God has blessed us. Raisa has borne our Lamech a son. Be mindful today of the great hand of God in our lives." His eyes were moist with tears of gratitude. Naomi leaned over and hugged her good husband. She too was aglow with the joy of a new grandson. The small house was filled with the spirit of humility and the tender love of a grateful family.

Liora sent the conversation in a different direction. "Uncle, what think you of this Jesus of Nazareth?" All eyes in the house were suddenly directed at her, and then at the same moment all turned to Jershon, awaiting his response.

Jershon and his family had not long before encountered a large group of people by the seashore. Curiosity drew them closer, and they discovered the crowd was listening intently to a man who appeared to be a rabbi. He spoke in a kind yet authoritative voice and taught of God. His message was delivered with a clarity that pierced each of them to the core of their souls. Transfixed by his message, they stood and listened for an hour. When he finished, a group of attentive men, a couple of whom Jershon recognized as fishermen, surrounded the rabbi and escorted him away. Most of the crowd followed as they departed. Some people remained, speaking in muffled tones about what they had heard. Jershon and his family, deeply moved by what they had seen and heard, quietly walked back to their home.

Over the ensuing weeks, they individually pondered the experience and the feeling of inner warmth they felt in that rabbi's presence, but nothing further had been said about what had occurred that day. They learned this was the Jesus of Nazareth they had heard of. The children hesitated to ask their father about him because his preaching seemed to be controversial in Capernaum. The Sanhedrin in Jerusalem was not favorably disposed toward people who praised him, but the number of his followers grew daily.

Now Liora asked the question for all of them. Finally Lamech found courage and repeated, "Yes, Father, what do you think of this Jesus of Nazareth? It is said he is the Messiah." A palpable silence fell as this inquiry hung in the room.

Jershon could feel all eyes upon him, and he pondered whether he should guard his words or speak plainly. He knew that eventually his family members would speak openly of their experience by the shore that fateful day. He concluded that his feelings had been suppressed too long. "My beloved family, we have always had the privilege to speak freely in this home. God allows us to think for ourselves and choose for ourselves. He has graced us with laws to add discipline and order in our lives. He has been patient and protective of the children of Israel, as I have been with you." He smiled broadly at everyone. "Jesus of Nazareth," Jershon said. Palpable warmth ran through him as he spoke the words. "Liora, blessed be ye, daughter, for helping this old man break silence about this Jesus of Nazareth." Tears streamed down his face to the wonderment of his family. Naomi put her hand on the rugged hands that were folded in his lap. She began to weep quietly. Sariah moved to sit at the feet of her father, placing her head next to the folded hands of her parents. Then Esther, tears streaming down her face too, stood by her mother with her arms around her mother's neck. Liora could not hold back her own tears. Lamech, Seth, and David tried valiantly to hold back their own emotions, but the strong feeling in the room manifested itself in the moisture in the eyes of each of them.

"My children," Jershon managed to say in a voice that broke, "I have studied the Writings and the Prophets. I have spent hours on my knees, beseeching God to give me wisdom and understanding in this matter. I have listened intently to the discussions that circulate in the streets and in the synagogue. I have witnessed firsthand the animosity demonstrated toward him by Pharisees and Sadducees. Their mutual fear of his popularity has united those vipers." Jershon paused and then announced with his face toward the heavens: "He is who they say he is. He is who we know he is. He is the Messiah!"

Jershon's words stunned the family. He looked each of them in the eye. In that instant they shared silent witness of what each one knew to be true.

Liora and David had encountered him a few months before. Liora knew immediately that this man was more than a rabbi or even a prophet. His understanding of the works of God came from a personal knowledge. David took a little longer to admit to himself that this rabbi was different. He and Liora had discussed it many times. One night David abruptly stopped his prayer of recitation and prayed the words of his heart. His answer was received in the tears that overcame him as the warmth of truth manifested itself like a burning ember in his soul. Immediately he confided to Liora that he had the same feeling about Jesus that she did. He could not deny the witness he received about Jesus of Nazareth but was still uncertain about what exactly he should do about it.

When Jershon and his family had chanced to hear Jesus preaching on the shore that day, Jershon had listened intently. At one point his eyes met those of Jesus. Their spiritual exchange shook him to the core. Even though he was standing quite a distance away, the voice of Jesus was so clear it was as if he were whispering in his ear. Jershon knew.

The rest of the family had their own witness as Jesus continued to teach. Not a word was spoken as the family walked home. They knew they had been in the presence of more than just a man of God. Nothing was said from that day on until Liora's question broke the dam of silence and emotion.

A contemplative silence continued as they pondered the magnitude of their mutual admission. Jershon finally spoke. "My children." He looked from left to right at each of them. "My blessed Naomi." He looked affectionately at his wife and caressed her tear-streaked face. Then he looked upward, as if he were seeing a vision, and spoke: "It has always been prophesied to the house of Israel that Messiah would come, a king from the house of David to restore Jerusalem and the temple and conquer the great oppressor. Man has always interpreted the prophesies of God in the limited terms of men, in the way men understand the world around them, which is not necessarily the way God sees the world. Moses, Isaiah, Jeremiah, and all the Writings speak of the coming of the great Messiah, but, my beloved family, the scriptures don't tell us when or in what manner the Messiah will appear. No one would have imagined that young Joseph, after being rejected by his brothers and sold into Egypt, would be raised in Pharaoh's inner circle and become the savior of his father, Jacob, and the very brothers who had betrayed him. An abandoned baby from the house of Israel is raised by a princess of Egypt and became that Moses who led the children of Israel out of bondage." He looked again into the eyes of his children. They were riveted by his words.

Jershon continued. "We are infants when it comes to understanding the ways of God. Is it beyond the power of the God of Israel to create the Messiah out of a mere carpenter from Nazareth?" He let the words sink in. "If anyone doubts that, they doubt the very existence and power of the God who created them." He shifted his position in the small wooden chair in which he was sitting. "My children, our entire existence is based in the belief of Jehovah and his daily direction in our lives. That direction, in all cases, comes from the mouth of our prophets. The irony is that our people have stoned and killed the prophets over the ages, prophets who carried the message of adherence to the laws and the will of God, not to the laws and the will of men. I see the same pattern being repeated now. Another prophet has been brought to our people. He is the most important prophet of all, and the leaders of the Sanhedrin would just as soon stone him as listen to his message. It is as incomprehensible as if the ancient children of Israel had wanted to stone Moses because he said he could lead them out of bondage."

"Father, is he the Messiah who will come with a sword and deliver Israel once again out of bondage, as we have been taught?"

Sariah asked boldly. The attentive eyes on Jershon were now wider in anticipation of his answer.

He looked directly at his eldest daughter. "My lovely Sariah, I have read the words of the ancients concerning him. Not one thing has he done that contradicts what is written. Seeming contradictions are issues of interpretation. We have always thought that the Messiah would come with power and authority, wielding a sword and slaying the enemies of Israel. He certainly has come with power and authority, but he wields the righteous sword of justice and truth, not the sword of the great warrior the children of Israel have led themselves to believe would come." Jershon released his gaze from his daughter and looked again around the room.

"Up until this moment we have not discussed him within the walls of this home; we need to change that. We all have heard of the great works he has done. We all have experienced a personal witness of him. We can be either disciples of the Messiah or disciples of the Sanhedrin."

No one in the family had expected such an ultimatum from their patriarch. They began to think of the consequences.

This Sabbath day was unique for Jershon and his family. There was a new purpose in their worship. The Messiah was with them. He was to teach at the synagogue that day. They would go as committed disciples of the Messiah, sit at his feet, and be taught.

10

aximus and Androcles sought out Gaius Valerius to tell him of Androcles's decision and discuss the details of their departure, but the senator was nowhere to be found. Maximus coaxed Androcles into coming along with him to secure a few provisions.

As they were walking away from the senator's guesthouse, a familiar voice hailed them from an approaching coach. It was Gaius. "Gentlemen," he shouted, "it appears you leave us."

Androcles and Maximus stopped in their tracks. "We are just walking back to the city," Maximus responded.

"You look to be dressed for battle," Gaius said, motioning to the swords at their sides.

"We are soldiers. We dress like soldiers," Androcles responded.

Maximus added, "With the assignment at hand, we felt it wise to acquire some supplies and prepare."

"Always thinking ahead, as a legate should," the senator chuckled. "Maximus, it is no wonder you are successful at your craft. My friends, there are plenty of days ahead to prepare."

"But you said we leave tomorrow," Maximus protested.

"Indeed you do. Passage has been arranged on an Egyptian merchant ship, as I told you, Maximus. It will embark after midday tomorrow. In the morning you will travel by coach to Ostia. However, you are traveling light. There is very little to prepare."

"Yes, no legion," Androcles quipped.

"No legion is necessary, my good commander." Gaius squeezed Androcles's massive bicep. "I am glad you have agreed to the campaign," Gaius said to Androcles when they were seated back in the courtyard.

"I am not sure I have agreed, but I am accompanying my general." Androcles was bluntly honest.

"Well, good," Gaius said. "We could send you back to the north to police the Gauls in the cold," he joked, "or you can accompany, as you say, the good general here to sunny Judaea. I doubt you will lose any blood there." The senator smiled.

Maximus looked over at his friend, raising an eyebrow to caution him about any further complaint, serious or not. "But surely we will need provisions for the long journey."

"Yes, you will, but that has all been arranged. You remember Tatius Lucianus?" Gaius asked.

"Yes, he is a good friend of my father," answered Maximus.

"He has been arranging clothing, bedding, provisions—everything you could possibly need. Your passage on the Egyptian ship includes sleeping quarters and food for the duration. I have prepared a letter that you will carry under seal designating you as emissaries of Rome and personal messengers of the emperor Tiberius. You will not be traveling as Roman soldiers. Although you, Androcles," he said as he hit him playfully on the shoulder with his fist, "will find it hard to hide your battle-scarred Herculean look."

Androcles smiled.

Gaius continued. "The letters are for any authority of Rome you might encounter before reaching our friend Pontius Pilate. We want the two of you to appear to be common men of Judaea. You will leave your weapons and clothing with me until you return, and wear the wool robes of the Jews. A staff will be your weapon of choice, and as for your well-groomed faces, you must begin growing beards immediately."

Now Maximus opened his mouth to protest.

The senator held up a hand, stopping the comment before it left Maximus's lips. "You will do your best to become Jews, or at least to look like them. This is a mission of peace, but you must keep your identity a secret. It will allow you to gather the information we seek."

Androcles had already decided to somehow take his weapons; they were as much a part of him as the leather necklace and amulet he wore. That piece of protection would not be left behind either.

Maximus waged a valiant battle to remain silent but politely observed, "With all due respect, sir, we know nothing of Judaea or the customs of the people. How can we possibly blend in?"

"A good question, my friend," Gaius said. "You will go to school."

"School?" Maximus asked.

Androcles bristled.

"My friends, I can't think of a better thing to do while you are captive on the high seas. Can you?" Gaius continued. "The emissary who brought us the request from Pilate will be traveling back with you. His name is Ezra. He will be your guide and teacher. It could take three weeks or so with favorable winds to sail to Caesarea. Plenty of time to learn what you'll need to know about being a Jew."

The thought of being confined to a ship for that long was one challenge Maximus had not considered.

"Ezra is a Jew and of the cherished blood of their ancestor Abraham. He has lived in Judaea all of his life. He is an extremely intelligent man and understands the Roman point of view. He has worked closely with both your prefect Pontius Pilate in Jerusalem and Herod Antipas, tetrarch of Galilee. Ezra is the only other man aware of your mission and is sworn to secrecy on his life." Gaius stood. "You have the entire journey to talk. Consider all the things you should know to be successful in your mission. Discuss everything with Ezra—the smallest detail could be beneficial to you. Ezra also has knowledge of this Jesus character. It is most important that you learn everything you can about this carpenter. What drives him? What is his goal? Is he quietly gathering an army to overthrow us, as Pilate fears? I want to know about his generals and captains and the people in his inner circle. I want to know his confidants. I want to know where he is getting the treasure to supply and feed this army, if indeed there is one. If he is this great Messiah the Jews talk about, we need to beat him from within."

Gaius looked off into the distance as if seeing a larger plan. Then he turned and looked directly into Maximus's eyes. "Don't underestimate the importance of what you are doing, Maximus. These are the kinds of actions that save your soldier's lives before they are asked to sacrifice them. If we can conquer a foe before he becomes one, then we avoid a war. I don't necessarily believe all of Pilate's claims, but as I said before, to ignore them would be irresponsible."

Maximus and Androcles listened intently, not knowing entirely how they would meet the senator's expectations.

"My sons," Gaius continued, "I trust your good judgment. You are the best qualified for this assignment. I am confident you will do what is prudent for the empire and the citizens of Rome. You always have, and this will be no different." Gaius Valerius stood and bade them good-bye, saying Tatius Lucianus would collect them later in the afternoon.

Maximus and Androcles remained seated and pondered for a few moments the intricacies and challenges this campaign could bring.

"I'm not leaving my sword!" Androcles said emphatically.

Maximus remained silent. A thousand thoughts swirled through his head, the primary one being what to do during so many days on a ship.

11

Jershon and his family entered into a dangerous covenant to be disciples of Jesus. That commitment could bring them under the scrutiny of representatives of the Sanhedrin and the potential threat of being ostracized from the mainstream Jewish community of Capernaum. Jershon was a man of integrity. He knew in his heart that this was the right course and the correct commitment, regardless of the consequences. What man or group of men could possibly dissuade him from following the bidding of Jesus? What punishment would be greater, the punishment of man or the consequences of denying the Messiah? The answer was easy for Jershon. He believed Jesus of Nazareth was the promised Messiah. He was uncertain about the challenges discipleship would bring, but that didn't matter.

Liora was ecstatic. She had never doubted her own feelings about Jesus, but to have the confirmation of her beloved uncle compounded her resolve. She was anxious to go to the synagogue and listen to him teach. Now she wanted to stay in Capernaum. How would she convince David to leave his work for a season and stay with her? How would they sustain themselves? They couldn't ask their aunt and uncle to take care of two more adults. Should she follow Jesus wherever he went? Should she make herself known to him? Could she? Or would the men he called apostles hedge her way? Should she strike out on her own as a disciple with the group of Galilean women she had heard followed Jesus everywhere? A cluttered onslaught of feelings and emotions ran through her mind, the type of confusion that could not be sorted out in the normal manner with prayer and meditation. She needed a confidant, someone she could talk to other than the family, which potentially had an agenda for her future. Even though her uncle had extended patriarchal permission for the family to be disciples of Jesus, Liora needed more. She would listen intently to Jesus's teachings and follow her heart.

Liora was eager to go to the synagogue; it would be another hour before the family left. She decided to leave early. Her cousin Sariah told her that each time Jesus came to the synagogue on the Sabbath, the crowd grew larger. People struggled to get as close to him as possible. She had heard that people came from long distances. Some brought afflicted family members, hoping to place them in his path that he might stop and heal them or simply to get close enough to touch the hem of his robe, which was said to produce the same results as the touch of his tender hands. The miracles he performed were becoming legendary. There were stories of healings taking place many miles away from Jesus just because someone simply believed he had the power to heal them. These things swirled in Liora's head constantly. She wrestled with the comprehension of more than just the miracles, but the reality was that the Messiah was among them. It was more than she could fathom. She had to understand this on her own terms.

It was not acceptable for an unaccompanied woman to strike out on her own, but that was what Liora was contemplating. She was certain her aunt and uncle wouldn't allow her cousin Sariah to accompany her in following Jesus on his journeys. The only option was to persuade her brother David to come along. He, however, was driven by his work. He had had a difficult time leaving the foundry in Magdala to visit Capernaum. What made the decision easier for him was the opportunity to work with his uncle and cousins on their fishing boat. It would be hard for David to consent to following Jesus from place to place and give up his livelihood.

Liora donned her veil and headed for the door. She wanted to be among the first to arrive to assure a place within the small building. "I think I will go to the synagogue early," she said softly to her aunt and uncle. They both looked up at her with questions in their eyes but did nothing to stop her. At length Jershon's approving smile released her to go. David and Seth thought to follow but remained immovable as she walked purposefully alone out of the house.

Outside the air was mild, and the wind was briskly blowing off the lake. She gathered her robe and veil tightly around her and proceeded down the dusty road to the synagogue. She walked straight ahead, weaving through the uneven streets and alleys. On the main street she sensed a commotion and slowed her pace. To the right was the synagogue; to her left, approaching her, was a large crowd of people. Leading them at a measured pace was Jesus. She froze in her tracks. To his left and right and slightly ahead of him were the trusted ones she recognized from seeing him previously. They were walking calmly but in a protective mode, running interference as needed with people pressing too close to their Master. He was talking, turning his head to the left and then to the right, probably answering questions being asked by the men following close behind.

Liora pressed against the wall of the building where she

stood. She was transfixed as the group led by Jesus came closer. She decided to let them pass and then fall in behind. The crowd was large, and the street narrowed at the point where Liora stood. One of the men walking beside Jesus smiled and gently placed his hand on her arm, causing her to walk with him rather than being pressed by the throng of disciples. She looked down in modesty, but it was hard not to realize she was walking within an arm's length of the Messiah. She could hear his tender voice as he spoke. She stole a quick glance to her left and met his eyes. He smiled kindly, and in his eye was a spark of lightning that pierced her. She couldn't maintain eye contact, and she looked down at the road ahead of her. It felt like a warm blanket had been wrapped around her from head to toe. Her knees were weak, and she felt she would faint and stumble any moment. The kind man who had led her forward sensed her weakness and put a gentle hand on her elbow, giving her support. It was the only thing that kept her from wilting to the ground.

Liora was pushed along at the front of a human wave. One of the first to enter the synagogue, she sat down on the women's side near the raised platform at the front. On the men's side, Jesus and the men called apostles gathered their robes about them and sat down. Jershon had told Liora he was acquainted with the burly apostle who sat at Jesus's right. He was a fisherman from Capernaum, and his name, she remembered, was Simon. Her uncle said that three or four of Jesus's apostles were fishermen from Capernaum. They had left their boats and nets to follow the Messiah. She wondered how they sustained their families. The one known as Simon whispered something to Jesus, who was now sitting reverently as the synagogue filled with worshippers.

The stone benches around the inside walls filled quickly. Soon people were taking seats on the floor. At the back of the synagogue, opposite the teaching platform, was a heavy curtain that could be opened to allow people outside to look inside. Many whispered and pointed as they caught a glimpse of Jesus. Liora spotted Sariah outside and caught her eye. Her cousin flashed a girlish smile, envious of the choice seat Liora had inside the synagogue.

The congregation was absolutely silent as the rabbi rose to begin the Sabbath worship. Liora bravely looked at Jesus. He appeared to be just another Jewish rabbi, humbly bowing his head with his eyes closed.

BOOK II

THE GREAT SEA

12

Tatius Lucianus met Maximus and Androcles that afternoon to give them the meager supplies for their journey: Jewish clothing and a satchel they could sling over their shoulders. It held a blanket and a couple days' ration of bread and dried fish. Tatius told them they wouldn't need much for the trip as quarters and food would be provided for the entire journey. Tomorrow they would meet the emissary in Ostia who would be traveling with them. Before leaving, they would change into the required disguise. Tatius then led them to one more meeting with Gaius Valerius.

"Maximus, Androcles," said Gaius, "I want you to enjoy your voyage. In the past you have always been called upon to engage the best men of foreign cultures in battle. You have the charge this time to engage in something entirely different. Learn about these people. Live their culture. There is no specific time set for your return. You will report back by courier who this man Jesus really is and what validity Rome should place on the concerns of the prefect. We want to know specifically if he is a political or military threat. Gauge the climate of the people and mingle as best you can with them. We also want an assessment of the rule of Pontius Pilate and our client-king Herod Antipas. We need to know if they are effective leaders and if the system we have in place is working well and generally obeyed. As soon as you feel you have the information the Senate is seeking, you are free to return home. You will both receive a healthy reward as well as some real time away from the business of the empire, not simply a handful of days, as has been the case this time."

Gaius gave them a scroll under the seal of Tiberius stating their identity and authorizing their travel should they encounter any resistance from Roman authorities during their journey. He handed each man a purse of money. He also gave them a letter to present to Pilate, instructing him that any request denied General Maximus would be a denial of the wishes of the emperor himself. The senator knew that Pilate's desire to have Rome think well of him would guarantee Maximus and Androcles the best of care and respect. Lastly, Gaius saluted them both. "May the gods be with you."

Androcles stuffed his sword and dagger into the satchel.

"My good commander," Gaius said, seizing Androcles's arm. "You are posing as a citizen of Judaea. I doubt you will be able to keep your cover wielding such glorious weapons, particularly a sword with the shield of Rome emblazoned on its hilt."

Androcles looked at Gaius to gauge the seriousness of his words.

Gaius continued, "You are not to be discovered as Roman citizens and soldiers of Rome."

But Androcles could not stop clutching the weapon. He couldn't remember a time when he'd been without a sword. For him it was like giving up a body part. He simply could not do it.

Maximus interjected, "I understand the need to appear like

harmless Judaeans, but even they carry weapons, especially when traveling."

Gaius stared at the two for a moment and then sighed. "Just the daggers," he conceded, "and keep them well concealed. No one in Judaea will have daggers the likes of yours. In fact, I have a better idea. Tatius will find daggers suitable for your journey. Leave your weapons with me. I will give them to you upon your return." It seemed a reasonable request. Androcles reluctantly parted with his weapons. It was visibly painful for him.

Early the next morning they met Tatius Lucianus, who had arranged a coach to take them to Ostia, a trip that would take most of the morning. Androcles was uncomfortable at being weaponless for the first time he could remember. But even more uncomfortable for them both were the unfamiliar robes Tatius had supplied and which they were now required to wear.

When they arrived in Ostia, the port was bustling with all manner of cargo and culture and ships flying under colorful banners of the various regions that bordered the great sea. The coach, pulled by anxious and tired horses, turned down the main road that paralleled the docks. The organized commotion of loading and unloading cargo continued without interruption, the workers not giving much notice to the coach passing by, much less the people hidden inside. Tatius directed the driver to a vessel humming with activity. It had two tall masts and was the largest ship in port. Tatius pointed it out and said, "Your new home." It flew the standards of Egypt. Sailors clad only in white loincloths streamed in and out of the ship like ants of an anthill, carrying sacks of grain and pottery storage urns. A stern Egyptian soldier shouted orders and epithets to the scurrying crew.

The coach turned left down a narrow side street just past the ship. Tatius directed the driver to a group of buildings hidden from direct view of the dock. He wanted Maximus and

Androcles to disembark out of view of the sailors. Even though they were dressed as Jews it would raise suspicions if they were seen getting out of the ornate coach. Once hidden from view he told them to exit the coach and he would return and find them. The coach pulled away and Maximus and Androcles were left alone. Their usual confident demeanor had somehow departed. They were both self-conscious in their new clothing.

A small group of Roman soldiers suddenly rounded the corner and approached them on the street. Maximus and Androcles deferentially moved aside, turning their backs and concealing their faces. One of the larger men brushed against Androcles a little too hard, forcing him into a stone wall. Androcles wanted to wrestle his dagger away and slit his throat for the calculated insult. Maximus grabbed his friend's arm, pulling him away from an unnecessary conflict.

Androcles complied but silently fumed as the arrogant soldiers passed. "I'm not sure I can do this," he said quietly.

"Yes, you can, and you will," Maximus responded. "Would you say that if we were facing an enemy of ten times our strength?"

"No, but that's different," Androcles answered.

"No, it isn't, my brother. We will constantly be outnumbered and harassed in this campaign. Our sword and dagger are our wits and the strength to hold our tongue," Maximus counseled his friend.

"I haven't trained well with those weapons," Androcles admitted.

"Then it's time to start." Maximus slugged his friend playfully to drive his point home. "In the meantime, don't forget how to use your real sword and dagger. I am sure there will come a day when they will desperately be needed."

"My faithful brothers!" A kind voice hailed them from down the street. It was that of an elderly man dressed in a drab gray wool robe. Despite his appearance, Maximus noted that he moved toward them with the confidence and air of a nobleman. A dark cloth draped over his head and shoulders partially covered a head of graying hair. His long full beard was speckled with gray, reddish, and black hair. On his shoulder he carried three poles with a sack slung on the end of one. "You stand out like two palm trees in the desert." He smiled broadly and lowered the poles and the cloth sack to the ground. "We must change that as soon as possible." He spoke the perfect Greek of a noble Roman. Maximus and Androcles were caught off guard by his engaging manner.

"My name is Ezra." He held out his hand in greeting to each of them. They shook it warily. He continued to speak in a subdued tone. "I have been commissioned by our mutual friend Gaius Valerius to accompany you on your journey to Judaea. I am the emissary who was sent by Pontius Pilate. Gaius told me you would know who I am and the reason I have come to Rome." He looked at them directly, expecting an answer.

Maximus finally spoke. "Yes, we know of you and welcome your company. Please accept my apologies for our lack of manners, sir. My friend Androcles and I are not used to looking like this." Maximus looked down self-consciously at the clothes he was wearing.

"That's obvious," Ezra said with a broad smile and hearty laughter. "I apologize. Do not judge my laughter as disrespect. It's just that the two of you have the self-conscious look of being dressed like women. Let me assure you both: on the surface you look like common Jews, but your bearing is still that of Roman soldiers. We need to work on that." His eyes twinkled.

Ezra cautiously looked about, then bade them follow him a short distance down the street to a secluded area behind a wall overgrown with vines. He reached into the sack, producing two plain daggers and handing one to each of them. Androcles hefted his carefully and began to relax.

"I brought these as well." He handed each man a staff. "They are customary for travelers, and in a pinch they can be a crude replacement for the swords I know you are pining for." Each staff was about six feet long. Made from dried hardwood that had been cut to the proper length and smoothed with the sharp blade of a knife or hatchet, both had several knots and seemed well worn. Androcles could not see any likeness to a sword in the staff, but he could certainly see that if properly used, the long staff could cause a lot of damage in a battle. He was feeling better.

Ezra continued. "I cut these myself and had them worked with oil and fine sand to age them a bit. It would appear odd if you both carried new staffs. We don't want to do anything to draw unnecessary attention."

Maximus was impressed with Ezra's eye for detail. They had a lot to learn, and he would be a good teacher.

"There is one important thing we need to do." Ezra paused as he sized up both of them with his aged brown eyes. "Give you different names. I can't continue calling you Maximus and Androcles. After seeing you both, I think I have made a good decision. Maximus, you will be known as *Jacob*. Androcles, we will call you *Levi*. They are good, strong Jewish names." Ezra looked at them, pleased at the names he had chosen. "If this ploy is going to work, you need to leave everything Roman on the docks today. You—" he tapped the back of his hand on Maximus's chest, "need to become Jacob, and you—" he did the same to Androcles, "need to become Levi. We will have plenty of time on our voyage to create lives and stories for each of you and teach you the comportment of a modest Jew."

Jacob was starting to like Ezra and feel more comfortable about the task ahead. Ezra was skillful and unassuming. His attention to detail would be critical. Maximus judged they were in good hands.

"I have one more thing for you." Ezra bent to retrieve something else out of his sack. He came up with two folded pieces of cloth, one a grayish blue and the other a dark brown. He handed the gray one to Jacob and the brown one to Levi. "Head coverings," he announced. "Better to help you look the part. Wear them like mine." He watched, amused, as they struggled to get them just right on their heads and draped over their shoulders. He helped each of them make the final adjustments. "There," he smiled, "we are ready to go!" Ezra chuckled with satisfaction at his two charges. "Now come."

Ezra picked up his sack and staff and in a fluid motion turned and walked toward the wharf. Jacob and Levi followed obediently. They both felt less self-conscious with the head coverings. It gave them a sense of warding off curious stares.

Ezra walked confidently at a fast pace toward the Egyptian ship. He turned his head a couple of times to be sure his charges were close behind. Jacob and Levi had to pick up their normal pace to keep up with the energetic old man as he dodged and weaved through the hectic crowd surrounding the dock.

A burly seaman carrying a large chest and smelling of hard work bumped into Jacob. "Watch your step, Jew!" he barked.

Levi wanted to smash him with his fist. Jacob once again hustled his friend along and smiled that the surly workman had identified him as a Jew.

They continued to follow close behind Ezra, who stopped about fifty yards short of the Egyptian ship. There wasn't much activity on the dock next to the ship, which was mostly loaded and nearly ready to set sail. Slaves were moving quickly about the deck arranging rigging and cargo. Two officials stood by the gangplank chatting quietly with the Egyptian soldier they had seen earlier as he checked what appeared to be documents.

Ezra spoke softly to Jacob and Levi. "As of this moment you are no longer Romans. You are Jews. You walk like Jews. You talk like Jews. You are humble and nonconfrontational, no matter what anyone may say or do to you. You will pray when I pray and how I pray. You will eat what I eat and not eat what I tell you not to eat. We will keep to ourselves and talk quietly at all times. I will teach you some short phrases in Hebrew as there will be times when you will need them on this journey. Your use of Greek should be very limited. In addition, we must draw no attention to ourselves. Egyptians don't like Jews."

Ezra stopped for a moment. "It's a long story. I will tell you the whole of it one day. They don't like Romans much either. If they discover a Roman on their ship disguised as a Jew, as superstitious as most mariners are, they will most likely feed you to the fish." Jacob and Levi laughed. Ezra didn't. "For now, just be careful to stay away from them as best you can."

Jacob thought Ezra sounded like a general issuing orders before a battle. He listened intently to the instructions. He knew his life might depend on it.

"Remaining inconspicuous may be a little difficult on a long journey like this in a relatively small space," Levi quietly observed.

"Judging by your size, Levi," Ezra smiled, "remaining unnoticed could be a challenge for you, but you must be as inconspicuous as you can."

Ezra looked over their shoulders and into the distance. "Your friend wants to wish you well."

The two Romans turned and followed his gaze. A hundred yards down the wharf they could see Tatius standing by the coach, looking in their direction. Tatius stood beside the coach, his right forearm across his chest with his fist covering his heart in the honored salute of Roman soldiers.

"Do not salute him back," Ezra cautioned. "Leave all things Roman here." He emphasized his point by pounding his staff hard on the wooden dock as he turned toward the ship. Levi slowly and defiantly raised his staff into the air to acknowledge the salute by Tatius Lucianus.

Jacob looked at Levi. This was not the flamboyant and boisterous send-off for legions heading to a campaign, but it was an honorable one. They watched as Tatius stepped into the coach and the horses pulled away quickly. Jacob and Levi turned to follow Ezra. Levi clutched the amulet around his neck—the medallion that had been his mother's. He would never part with that piece of Rome.

The two younger men followed Ezra up the wooden ramp and onto the deck of the ship. Sailors and slaves were double-checking rigging and lashing cargo that remained on deck. Others stood at various positions waiting for commands. All of them looked curiously at the robed passengers. Jacob and Levi followed Ezra to a point forward near the bow and out of the way. A small ledge there could be used as a bench. They sat down and, like the crew, stared at the captain to anticipate his orders, even though they had no duties.

"Raise the gangway! Push off," the captain bellowed. "To sea, men!" A cheer went up, and everything and everyone seemed to go into motion at once. The gangplank was pulled aboard and secured to the side of the ship quickly and efficiently. Workers on shore untied the large ropes securing the ship to the dock at the bow and stern. Sailors collected and coiled the ropes on deck. About ten men standing on the dock placed the point of long staffs against the side of the ship and began to push it away from the wharf. As the ship drifted slowly out into the harbor, commands were heard from below decks. Oars from portholes on either side of the ship began protruding like legs of an awakening centipede. The men on deck remained poised at their stations.

An order was barked to the oarsmen below. The ship responded with a perceptible turn as the rowers on one side pulled and the rowers on the other pushed. Then both sides began to pull in unison, sending the ship straight into the outer harbor and away from the crowded dock. Jacob marveled at the crew's ability to work together to move the ship in the exact direction commanded.

"Hoist sail!" shouted the captain on deck. Men worked ropes, and the large square sail hanging from the center mast began to unfurl. Another smaller, rectangular sail was hung from a diagonal mast facing forward on the ship. Ropes were lashed and pulled tight as sails snapped taut upon catching the light afternoon breeze. The two large tillers flanking the rear of the ship were manned. The captain and the sailor who appeared to be his second in command stood by the rail, watching each movement of the bustling crew on deck. The oars, as if on cue, disappeared into the bowels of the ship, and soon the ship was gliding smoothly and quietly through the center of the channel and out into the blue waters of the sea.

Chatter ceased as each man became consumed with his duty. The captain stood with a satisfied look as his ship surged forward. Jacob felt a slight spray on his face and smelled the warm salt air. He caught the sense of what drew men to the sea, the adventure of the horizon. There was an odd quietness about setting out on a ship, different from the sounds of men walking, armor clanking, and horses and oxen plodding down a stone or dirt road heading to battle. There was a muffled reverence to the sounds of the ship cutting through the water and the wind rippling through the broad white sails. Jacob remarked that there was no dust, and Levi finally smiled.

A few men double-checked ropes securing cargo on the deck; others adjusted ropes attached to the great sails. The captain and his officers took their seats between the tillers. Everyone settled in for the long voyage ahead. The ship tilted slightly as the sails became taut under the sudden strain of the wind when they reached open water and tacked southeast. Jacob understood they would follow the coastline to Messina for a couple of days before entering the waters of the Great Sea. It would take about three weeks to arrive at their destination in the port of Caesarea in Judaea.

Jacob, Levi, and Ezra had no duties during the long journey. Their assignment as passengers was to stay out of the way and not interfere with the workings of the ship. They inspected the small quarters below that had been assigned to them, but Jacob and Levi refused to be penned up below decks. They told Ezra they would find a place on deck out of the way where they could sleep and pass the time. Ezra cautioned them against staying on deck and bringing too much attention to themselves. A quiet but heated debate ensued, and Ezra knew he would not prevail. He resigned himself to sleeping below each night and teaching his two students in full view of the crew during the day.

They left their meager belongings below and returned to the bench-like protrusion near the bow. The noise of the wind and the sea splashing off the bow of the ship allowed them some privacy in talking. No one could hear their conversation, even a few feet away from the Jewish imposters.

Ezra counseled Jacob and Levi not to stare at the sailors. "Do not return their gaze. We must remain as invisible to them as possible. Mariners by nature are very superstitious. We do not want to give them any reason to distrust or fear us. Be sure you keep your daggers hidden in your robes. Don't display anything that might attract attention." For that reason he told Levi to keep his amulet under his tunic. Their staffs must always be stowed in their quarters below. It would not be a good idea to allow a staff to roll across the pitching deck and interfere with the work of any of the crew—that could be deadly.

After a long silence Levi asked Ezra, "Who do they think we are? We are obviously the only passengers aboard."

"The captain knows me as an emissary from Judaea to Rome. I am returning with two of my countrymen who are acting as my escorts." He pursed his lips at Jacob and Levi and continued. "We have paid a fair passage, and the captain has a vested interest in my safe arrival in Caesarea—he will receive a bonus if I do."

"You mean *our* safe arrival?" asked Levi.

"No," said Ezra. "The bonus applies only to me. You two are ballast to him." Jacob and Levi didn't hear any humor in Ezra's response and took him at his word. "I am sure the officers and crew have been informed of our purpose here and should pay us no heed. But it is still our duty to remain in the shadows, as this normally is strictly a cargo ship, not a passenger ship. They are doing us a favor."

"That large sailor standing next to the captain with the scar down the side of his jaw does not look very friendly," remarked Jacob. He was referring to the first officer of the ship, who followed close upon the captain's every footstep.

Ezra replied, "His name is Akhom. He is the son of an Egyptian nobleman. He will soon captain his own ship. His authority on this ship should not be questioned. Do not trifle with him. He is in charge of the discipline of the mariners and the slaves. If we are attacked, he will serve as strategist and commander. I suggest you take every precaution to have as little interaction with him as possible."

"Attacked?" Jacob asked with eyebrows raised. "By whom? I thought this was a merchant ship." He shielded his eyes from the intense sun.

"Sea people . . . pirates," Ezra said. "Just like highway robbers. Though I doubt that in your journeys with your legion you had to deal with robbers. But out here," Ezra waved his arm along the horizon, "we are alone and vulnerable. We are a limited number of men and subject to the attack of those who want the cargo this ship carries."

"Who are these pirates?" Levi asked.

"They are not your typical foe, my son. They could be from anywhere. They run loose through all the seas, and many have no official allegiance; they answer only to the captain they serve."

Jacob and Levi both knew of such robbers and pirates, but the thought of their interfering with this journey had not crossed their minds.

"What's the likelihood of our encountering pirates?" Jacob asked.

Ezra looked at Jacob directly and pulled slowly on his thick graying beard. "We sail alone without military escort. We are laden with cargo, as evidenced by the deep draft on this ship. I would say the chances are high." Ezra's voice was matter of fact. Jacob and Levi looked at each other and shifted uneasily. Once again they longed for the swords they had been forced to leave behind. Ezra gazed nonchalantly at the seagulls trailing the ship.

After a little more small talk, they opened their satchels and ate some bread and dried fish. During the meal Ezra gave them more instructions in a subdued voice. "Speak only in Greek to the crew. Respond only to requests or commands, and be sure your responses are direct and to the point. Do not engage voluntarily with any of them. The less conversation the better."

He pointed a crooked finger at each of them and lowered his

voice still further. "I know you are both proud men and deserving of the high status you have earned in Rome. But on this ship your status is different. Here you are common Jews. In this world you are nothing. Do not stand up straight—especially you, Levi—and do not look them in the eye; they will sense your confidence. Always speak softly and keep your eyes downward to avoid needless conversation and confrontation. I know this will be hard for you, but it is for your safety and mine."

Their supper finished, the three men stood talking quietly near the railing. Levi idly tossed a crumb of bread to a trailing gull that snagged it midair and quickly flew sideways to avoid the harassment of others in the flock.

Suddenly a shout came from the stern of the boat. "Jew, is your food supply so plentiful that you feed the birds that beg in the wake of our ship? Perhaps your stores are sufficient to give each of us an extra ration!" It was the surly Akhom. "We should throw you to the hungry sharks that follow us. Perhaps you're as expendable as the bread you discard so carelessly." The large Egyptian menacingly approached the three Jews. Levi instinctively reached for the hilt of his short sword, which was not there. Reality hit him at the same time as an internal surge of adrenaline. *A Jew. I am a Jew. Not a Roman centurion. I could cut this arrogant Egyptian down and throw him overboard in the blink of an eye, but I must sit here in humility.*

Levi could feel the burning gaze of both Ezra and Jacob. In perfect Greek he responded to the imposing figure standing before him. "I apologize, sir. My intent was not to be wasteful or offensive. Forgive me. I am not familiar with the ways of mariners." Levi wanted to explode but lowered his head and remained still.

The display of deference caught the surly Egyptian off guard. He had expected a fight from the large, muscular Jew. *These people are weak, even the big ones,* he thought. *At least they know their place.* He drew his sword for effect. "You've learned your station well. Now learn some manners, or the next time I will make bait out of you." He swung his sword around threateningly, then skillfully sheathed it. He looked down contemptuously and walked off in disgust. Ezra and Jacob finally exhaled.

Ezra spoke first. "Well done, my son. You are learning quickly, but better yet to avoid the attention in the first place." He placed his dark bony hand on Levi's knee.

Levi could hardly contain himself. "Barbarian," he muttered under his breath. "That one will be shark food if he challenges me again."

"Be sure that doesn't happen, my brother," Jacob said as he slapped his friend good-naturedly on the back. "I don't want to have to step in between you two."

Levi leaned forward on the rail of the ship to dissipate some of the energy flowing through his body as a result of the confrontation. The cool spray and heavy sea air helped calm the warrior in him. Levi didn't doubt his ability to destroy the big Egyptian. But he doubted his ability to deal patiently with the bullying that was sure to come during the rest of the journey as a result of his display.

The afternoon passed into evening and then into the black darkness of night. A fire was lit in the cauldron near the center of the boat, and two torches fore and aft were the only sources of light. The moon and stars were hidden behind an overcast sky.

The three passengers went below to their assigned sleeping quarters. It was cold, dark and damp, and foul smelling. Ezra found his place, pulled his robe and blanket over himself tightly, and was asleep within seconds. Jacob and Levi grabbed their bedrolls and went back up the wooden stairs to the deck. A small crew of six manned various lookout points on the deck; two of them held the tillers steady. Jacob, always listening for useful information, had overheard earlier that a change of guard would be made during the third and fourth watch.

No one challenged them as they laid out their blankets in the same place they had sat most of the day. It was cooler on deck, and the air was fresher. They had spent many nights sleeping on the cold ground during campaigns; this was no different. The two men positioned themselves head to head close to a bulkhead to stay out of the way. The hissing noise of the ship slicing through the water and the creaking and groaning of the masts and rigging were constant and somewhat soothing. Sleep came slowly, but it finally came.

Levi had to restrain himself to keep from seizing the foot that awakened him with a swift kick in the small of his back. Fortunately his mind reasoned out the situation before his body reacted.

"Get up, Jewish swine!" cursed the large Egyptian as he loomed over Levi. "Move before my men trample you." Levi quickly rolled over and collected himself as Akhom walked off, yelling commands at the bustling crew now on deck. He saw that Jacob was already standing against the rail on the opposite side of the ship. Jacob was always the first up at camp, anticipating the enemy's attack.

"You could have spared me the rude awakening," Levi chided his friend as he rolled up his blanket.

Jacob laughed. "I didn't see him coming," he said.

"You, surprised by the enemy's ambush? I find that hard to believe." Levi smiled.

"I was not paying attention. Besides, the noise of the sea and the crew moving about were distracting," said Jacob. Levi noticed the sails had been repositioned to take advantage of the changing morning winds. It was toward the end of the fourth watch, and the activity on deck was fast and furious. Levi was amazed he'd heard nothing before the ignominious kick to his backside had wakened him.

It occurred to Jacob that he would have to figure out a way to get some exercise. He was used to walking some distance in the morning and again early in the evening as a way of getting away from the decisions of battle. But there was no getting away on the small deck of this ship. A walk would be thirty paces in one direction and then another thirty paces back. Weeks on this ship with such limited movement would paralyze him. He hoped the gods would send favorable winds.

13

After a while Ezra emerged from the bowels of the ship and walked forward. He stretched his arms wide and with head held high breathed deeply the pungent sea air. Ezra had obviously slept well and was used to travel on ships. Jacob couldn't say the same of himself. He was out of his element in more ways than one.

"My brothers," Ezra said with a slight grin, "it's time for prayers. Follow me, and do everything I do."

They had already discussed the need for prayer. It was part of the Jews' tradition. Ezra explained the prayer and demonstrated the movements they should make with head and hands. "You will improve as the days wear on but for now just follow along. They won't pay any real attention to us, nor do they understand our traditions, so they won't know if you are making a mistake, but they will be able to sense your intent. Be focused while praying with me. Our people are focused when we pray." Neither Jacob nor Levi was familiar with prayer. The prayers of Roman soldiers were more curses or warnings: "By the gods!" or "May the gods be merciful." Levi, Jacob was sure, gave the gods no thought at all.

Since the murder of his family, he had shown contempt toward every god.

Ezra moved toward the bow of the ship away from the crew and stood erect, facing the rising sun. Jacob and Levi followed. He pulled his head covering over his head and glanced at the two of them. The three men stood with heads covered and bowed. Then Ezra began to chant softly in Hebrew, which neither of them understood. He made a palms-up motion with his hands, and at his subtle encouragement they followed suit. Ezra continued chanting and looking to the sky as if he could actually see someone looking back. Jacob and Levi kept their heads bowed, one eye on Ezra to anticipate any movement of body or hands they would have to imitate. Ezra's chants sounded more like a song than a speech, his voice lilting up and down as he recited the prayer. Jacob had no idea what he was saying. What would you say to a god if you wanted to tell him something? Or ask him something? He assumed Ezra's prayer was a recital from memory, but at times it sounded like he was actually talking to someone, perhaps even pleading. Soon Ezra put his hands reverently together. Jacob and Levi did the same. Hands were raised upward to the sky, then slowly lowered and folded on the chest, then palms outward and up again, then folded. Finally a long silence with hands crossed and folded over their chests. Ezra touched the shoulders of Jacob and Levi to indicate that the prayer was finished. They retreated to the same area where they sat the day before to begin the long day. Jacob wondered again how he was going to get some exercise. Levi was like a stabled horse that wanted to break down the gate and run. He kept moving his feet. Jacob saw he was going to have to address their restlessness.

Food was brought up from below: bread, dried fish, and some fruit, which surely wouldn't last for the entire voyage. A sailor placed a small basket of food at their feet. Not a feast but enough to satisfy three men. Ezra took the bread and broke it, handing a piece to each of them. They ate in silence.

After a time Ezra spoke. "*Gentiles,* that's what we call everyone who is not of the house of Israel. It's not a derogatory term; it's just a word we use. We are knit together with the golden thread of a long history of tribulation and trials, from the days of Adam and Eve to the great patriarchs Noah, Abraham, Isaac, and Jacob, who later was named Israel. It is a rich heritage."

Jacob and Levi stared at Ezra blankly. The thought of learning all the Jewish gods was daunting. But it was something to distract them from the daily boredom of the voyage.

"Let's get started, shall we?" Ezra said.

Ezra began from the beginning, telling them of Adam and Eve, the first parents of all humankind, and of their sons Cain and Abel and the murder of Abel by Cain. Jacob and Levi found the story interesting. The Jewish gods seemed human, at least. Ezra explained that these individuals were not gods in the Roman sense. They were prophets and patriarchs of the large Jewish family.

After their midday meal, Ezra told them of Noah and the great flood. Jacob was taken aback by a god that would destroy his people out of anger; in that sense the Jewish god seemed no different from Roman gods. Ezra explained that the flood was a cleansing. "The children of God had become evil and no longer heeded the warning of the prophet Noah. In fact, they mocked everything he said and did. Jehovah decided to make a fresh start. But being merciful, he promised mankind that a purging by water of such magnitude would never happen again."

"So your God Jehovah made a mistake?" Jacob observed.

"No, not a mistake," Ezra clarified. "He destroyed children who had become so evil there was no turning them around. In his infinite wisdom, he made a new covenant to future generations.

The Jewish God is a covenant God. He makes promises with us based on our ability to obey his laws."

"Why are the gods so controlling and demanding of people?" questioned Levi. "It seems they want complete obedience but give little in exchange."

Ezra intently scrutinized the men before him. *They are so naïve,* he thought. They had grown up in a pagan environment with little or no understanding of their own gods, let alone the one true God. Romans considered themselves such an advanced race, yet they couldn't see that their true gods were the sword and the gold they stole with it. They would not understand fealty to a true God when worldly riches were not the reward. They invented mythical gods to justify behavior contrary to godliness. He shook his head in frustration. He had to remind himself that his job was not to convert Jacob and Levi but to give them a basic understanding of the Jewish way of thinking and aid them in their disguise and mission.

Ezra regrouped. "Let's not discuss *God* philosophically. I merely wish to provide you with a basis for understanding my people."

Jacob preferred philosophical discussions of God, such as those he'd had with his mother when he was a youth. He could tell Ezra's knowledge of this Jehovah was far greater than he was choosing to share. Jacob decided to find time alone with him to have a deeper conversation.

Ezra's comment seemed to satisfy Levi, who nodded his head and was ready to proceed. Ezra sensed, however, that Jacob was reasoning on a far different plane. He decided to filter out the details and stick to the surface level of Jewish history. What was important to the mission of these two Romans was understanding the claims of Jesus of Nazareth, whom they were tasked with investigating, and why these claims were of such concern to Pilate, whose directive they were following. That might prove to be the simpler path. Ezra realized he would have to keep Jacob on track and fill in the details when opportunities presented themselves.

"Jacob, Levi." Ezra addressed them directly and quietly to avoid any curious ears. "Your mission is clear. You are emissaries from the emperor Tiberius to investigate a threat to the Roman prefecture of Judaea. This threat is in the form of a man named Jesus of Nazareth, the son of a carpenter. On the surface this mission may seem straightforward. However, there are details to the story that don't add up, even for me. I am Jewish, and I have my own ideas about what is being professed by him and his followers, who call themselves disciples. He is not the rebel leader Pontius Pilate would have you believe. He is a peaceful man with peaceful teachings, but he commands with an authority that is almost palpable, and I can understand why Pilate is concerned. Pilate is a weak ruler but is a kind man when it suits him and is somewhat sympathetic to the Jews over whom he rules; he has even aided in the improvements to our temple. But when he perceives threats to his power, he overreacts. Even though having the ear of Rome and the friendship of the son of a powerful senator should be confirmation to him of the security of his status as prefect, his fear overcomes his reason."

Jacob interrupted, "What makes Pilate so afraid of this carpenter's son? Are these disciples armed? Are they plotting against Pilate and Rome?"

"Legitimate questions, my son." Ezra put his hand on Jacob's shoulder. "You and your good brother, Levi, will have to answer them for yourself."

Ezra checked their immediate surroundings with a sweeping gaze under his heavy eyebrows. He arose, gesturing for Jacob and Levi to remain seated. He looked out to the sparkling horizon, contemplating his next topic of discussion. He inhaled deeply the fresh sea air and then returned to sit with his charges.

He began his tale. "Long ago in Jewish history, thousands of Jews were enslaved and put to work building the land of Egypt. A great Jewish prophet named Moses was raised from an infant as an Egyptian, but when he grew to manhood, he discovered his true heritage, and it became the driving force of his life. He was eventually called by Jehovah to obtain from Pharaoh the release of his countrymen so they could return to the land of their inheritance—the land of Judaea, as we know it. I will spare you the story of Moses's negotiations with Pharaoh. Suffice it to say that with the aid of Jehovah, Moses ultimately prevailed, and Pharaoh let the children of Israel leave Egypt.

"Moses led thousands of Jewish men, women, and children out of Egypt. It was a monumental undertaking. Almost as soon as Pharaoh granted them leave to go, he sent his armies after them, whether to collect them or destroy them, we will never know."

Levi interjected, "What happened? Did the army overtake them? Did they do battle?"

"You are a curious student, Levi. That is good. It will aid in your understanding." Ezra smiled at the large man sitting cross-legged to his right. "Moses guided the massive throng to the borders of the Red Sea where the soldiers of Pharaoh caught up with them. Moses called upon Jehovah for deliverance a second time. Miraculously, the waters of the sea parted, and the children of Israel crossed to the other side on dry land. When the armies of Pharaoh pursued them, the sea consumed them, every one." Ezra paused to let the scene sink in. He knew this story to be absolutely true. He felt that Jacob and Levi would more than likely accept it on the basis of its similarity to stories told of the feats of Roman gods, but it didn't matter to Ezra whether the two Romans believed him or not.

Jacob asked, "What did the Jews do then? How long did it take them to arrive in the land of their inheritance?"

"They immediately got down on their knees and thanked God for delivering them," Ezra answered. "The story of their journey to the land of Israel is a little more complicated."

"As are all journeys," Jacob noted.

Ezra looked at Jacob with a twinkle in his eye. "Yes, Jacob, as are all journeys." He continued. "It was forty years before the children of Israel entered the promised land."

"Forty years?" Levi exclaimed.

"Yes," responded Ezra. "It seems incomprehensible, but it's a long story."

"A forty-year-long story, no doubt." Levi laughed. "So what took this god Moses so long to make the trip?"

"Moses was not a god. He was a prophet, whose actions were directed by the Jewish God, Jehovah. During their forty-year sojourn, Moses was directed by Jehovah to climb a mountain known as Sinai. There, Jehovah met with Moses face to face and gave him stone tablets engraved with the Ten Commandments, which he wanted the children of Israel to obey. The children of Israel had lived in Egypt for so long that many had adopted Egyptian gods and pagan forms of worship. They had forgotten the traditions of their fathers. Jehovah wanted to purify his people and bring them back to the fold, so to speak."

"Why didn't he just swallow them up in the Red Sea along with the Egyptian army?" interrupted Levi. "That seems to be your Jehovah's temperament."

"That is an interesting observation, Levi," Ezra rejoined, "but you'll recall that Jehovah had made a new covenant with the children of Israel."

"Was that why it took forty years to arrive in Judaea?" Jacob asked. "Forty years of purification?" he added.

"Very perceptive, Jacob. You are correct. Paganism had so infiltrated the people that Jehovah needed time, once again, to purge his people. It was another generation that finally arrived at the promised land. Sadly, Moses wasn't among them. Ultimately the Ten Commandments he carried down from Sinai became the basis of the Law of Moses. These laws are still adhered to today and fiercely defended."

"What are these ten commandments?" questioned Jacob.

Ezra smiled at his student's inquisitive nature. He recited the commandments as they were written, without embellishment or explanation. When he had finished, he said no more. He looked at Jacob and Levi, gauging their thoughts. They both had seemed to check off each commandment and weigh it in their minds as Ezra recited it.

"Simple, logical, and straightforward," Jacob responded.

"Yes," answered Ezra. "They are simple and to the point. Frankly, any man or nation would be better if they adhered to these fundamental laws." Ezra saw Jacob and Levi nod in agreement.

Levi commented, "'Thou shalt not kill.' How does your Jehovah justify war?" He was thinking of all the men he had killed for Rome in battle.

"Jehovah doesn't justify war, my son." He put his hand on Levi's muscular forearm. "War is a tool of the devil."

"Does he justify killing?" Levi pressed.

Ezra weighed what really was behind Levi's question and proceeded cautiously. "A lot of Egyptian soldiers were killed when the Red Sea came back together after the children of Israel passed through. However, I am not qualified to answer your question as it applies to all situations." Ezra turned his glance to Jacob, whose eyes were locked on Ezra, waiting for a deeper explanation. "God gives man life; therefore, only God can take that life away."

"That's not good enough," Levi blurted out. "Sometimes there are men that need to be killed." Jacob knew Levi was referring to his family having been ruthlessly killed by marauders, whom Levi thought should be dealt with in the same way. He determined to inform Ezra of Levi's experience in private.

Ezra asked Levi, "Are you speaking of revenge?"

"Justice!" Levi declared.

Ezra leaned back and sighed. "That is an interesting dilemma. Again, my son," he looked at Levi, his eyes heated with thoughts of some past enemy, "I am not qualified to answer that for you. I can only tell you that man does not look at things through the eyes of God. Perhaps if we could," he continued, "we would be able to make better decisions and understand God's reasoning for his actions."

Jacob spoke. "I think the gods are fickle and self-serving."

"With all due respect, my son, if a god is God, vacillation would not be in his nature. Jehovah has a purpose for his children. Jehovah requires obedience to simple principles, as would any leader of men. Obedience begets order, and order begets progress. Certainly a man of your position understands that truth." Ezra looked directly into Jacob's eyes and saw agreement. "God is entitled to be demanding of his children—in a way any loving parent would be. And God is entitled to jealousy." Ezra closed his eyes, raised his face to the sky, and quietly recited: "'Thou shalt have no other gods before me. Thou shalt not make unto thee any graven image, or any likeness of any thing that is in heaven above, or that is in the earth beneath, or that is in the water under the earth: Thou shalt not bow down thyself to them, nor serve them: for I the Lord thy God am a jealous God . . .'"

He kept his face toward the heavens for a moment, then lowered his head and looked deep into Jacob's eyes.

Jacob stared back at his mentor, realizing Ezra was an incredibly intellectual and spiritual man. He could learn a lot under his tutelage. "That would put Rome and Judaea at odds about the nature of God."

"Yes, my son, the most basic of all, and the first of many differences." Ezra smiled at Jacob, enjoying his inquisitiveness and wishing he could ask Jacob more about his understanding of God, but he felt that question would be best reserved for another time.

"You speak of your Jehovah as if he were the one true God," Jacob challenged.

"He is," Ezra answered without hesitation. His conviction was so strong that Jacob hesitated to argue.

"Jews, move your lazy bones from the deck of my ship! Do these masts remind you of the shady olive trees of your homeland?" Akhom had suddenly taken an interest in them. "Get below. This is not a barge floating a great river at sunset while royalty eat sweet dates and abuse wine." His hand was on the hilt of his sword, and it appeared he was willing to run it through anyone who disobeyed his command. Levi gathered his robe about him and stood with Jacob and Ezra. He had the fleeting thought to reach out and crush Akhom's larynx with one hand.

"My good man," Ezra politely rejoined, choosing diplomacy over conflict, "thank you for your patience with us. We were relishing the fresh air and the smooth sailing of your skillful crew. We could indeed have thought we sat under a welcoming tree in our homeland. But we do not want to interfere with your duties in any way. We shall honor your wishes and go below for a time. However, our passage here does not require imprisonment below decks. We shall return when it is more prudent." Ezra assumed that Akhom knew they had paid a hefty passage, almost a ransom, to be passengers on his ship.

Ezra motioned for Jacob and Levi to follow him. Levi had to exercise exceptional restraint not to glare into the eyes of Akhom and silently challenge him. He was not afraid of this chest-pounding Egyptian. The three men slowly descended the ladder to the lower deck. It was hot and smelled of unclean humans and spoiled food. They found their sleeping area and made themselves as comfortable as possible. Jacob put his back to the hull of the ship and stretched out his legs. He looked at Ezra, who seemed content. Levi was boiling. "You won a battle without drawing a sword," Jacob commented to Ezra. Ezra smiled as he lay down in a pile of fresh straw without saying a word.

14

Jershon and his family were anxious to hear the discussion of a text from the Law. As usual, the women sat on one side of the synagogue and the men on the other. The rabbi began with the usual prayers, but instead of reading from the Torah or the Prophets, he asked carefully worded questions to entrap Jesus. The representatives of the Sanhedrin sat with smug looks on their faces, waiting for Jesus to say something inconsistent with their interpretation of the Law. Jesus answered each question masterfully. He left no doubt about his knowledge and deep understanding of the Law and the Prophets, and he left his questioners with no opening for dispute. After an hour of intense questioning, they were visibly uncomfortable as they shifted in their seats, avoided his direct gaze, and did not make a rejoinder when he spoke of things peculiar to them. To his enemies he was just the carpenter's son and a thorn in their side.

Two hours sped by like ten minutes. His stories were captivating, his delivery smooth and polished. Toward the end he was asked where he received his authority. His answer, "From my Father," caused some to hiss and some to think he was speaking of Joseph. Others understood his response perfectly. He then bowed his head and offered the most amazing prayer Liora had ever witnessed. He truly spoke with God. He prayed that the members of the congregation would come to an understanding of the truth. Liora bowed her head and felt indescribable warmth overtake her. Tears streamed down her face, and she became even more determined to be a true disciple and follow him wherever he went.

Interestingly, it was Jesus who dismissed the congregation, not the rabbi. His authority seemed superior to any elder in attendance. Willingly or not, they deferred to him. Liora immediately found her brother, David, and hugged him. His embrace was reassuring. Sariah was weeping, and she and Liora held each other for some time. The walk home was contemplative for all of them.

They arrived to find that Lamech had prepared the midday meal while he stayed at home to tend Raisa and the baby. The conversation turned lively as they discussed the events at the synagogue. Their mutual conviction had been strengthened at hearing Jesus teach again.

"I was struck by the inability of the elders to find one flaw in his teachings, even when it disagreed with the rabbis' interpretation," said Jershon. "He was so easy to understand, but it was apparent the emissaries of the Sanhedrin refused to accept the logic of his words. Why do they insist on continuing their complicated ways?"

"Power," David responded. "If they accept his teachings, they lose power."

"You may be right, David," his uncle said. "They have certainly lost a degree of power over our family already. But God is not about wielding power over people. Obedience to his law protects us from the disruption of the adversary in our lives. Power is an imagining of man, with the aim to get gain from other men.

God does not need the riches of this earth; he created them. His riches are measured in the goodness and worship of his children, whom he will someday gather into the comfort and protection of his arms."

"Will he gather all of us, Uncle?" Liora interjected.

"Of course, my dear. Who would be excluded?" Jershon asked her.

"Gentiles?" Liora questioned.

"The gathering always refers to the children of Israel, the twelve tribes, Liora."

Liora lowered her voice. "I can't see Jesus not gathering everyone." She stopped, not wanting to be confrontational.

Lamech blurted out, "Do you think Jehovah is willing to gather Gentiles, the likes of the heathen Romans?" He leaned forward in agitation, his comment introducing a sudden gloom.

"My son," Jershon interjected, "I still wish retribution and judgment on Rome for the tyranny they have brought to our land. But I also believe with all my heart that Jesus is the Messiah that has been promised. How he will rectify the injustices they have inflicted upon our family is a mystery to my simple mind, but Liora has a point." He gestured for Liora to approach. She moved to take his hand and sit at his side. "My lovely daughter—you *are* my daughter—your understanding is beyond ours. I believe his message is clearer to you, blessed one." He stroked her long hair gently. Liora looked up and smiled, then turned and kissed his hand. "Jesus comes to teach his chosen ones, yet he heals whoever asks him for healing. I believe that is the greater message. It reminds us to be patient with our oppressors."

Jershon approached Lamech, who got to his feet to receive the embrace of his father. "It is too easy to fall into the ways of the adversary and stir up anger about things over which we have no control. This anger will chase out the spirit that embraces us today. Be calm, my son. You will join us the next time he teaches, and you will know of what I speak." Jershon held Lamech by his shoulders and looked at him proudly.

The family finished their meal with no further discussion, each contemplating the things that had been said. When Liora could see that her aunt Naomi was finished with the food and the dishes, she approached her quietly.

"Aunt Naomi, can we have a private talk soon?" Liora whispered in her ear.

Naomi embraced her niece. "Of course. Today is a good day. Would you like to sit under the tree across the way?" Liora smiled and walked to the large tree across the road. Naomi followed her shortly, carrying a blanket for them to sit upon.

"What is on your innocent mind, my child?" Naomi began.

Liora looked away, and the tears streamed down her face.

"What is the matter, my child?" Naomi implored as she put her arms around Liora. Liora's tears turned to sobs. The memory of her brothers' death, the thought of her father dying soon afterward, and lacking a mother for all her growing years had opened a cavernous wound in her heart. Her desire to be married and her longing to be a true disciple of Jesus and follow him wherever he went were all too much for her. Her thoughts tumbled out of her like rocks breaking from the precipice of a waterfall. Naomi just held her, saying nothing, understanding most of it.

After a while Liora wiped her face with the sleeve of her robe. She laid her head in Naomi's lap, wanting to nap instead of talk. Naomi remained silent, knowing more words would come.

"We want to come live with you, Aunt," she finally blurted out, speaking for both herself and David, whom she had not yet consulted. "We have been so stubborn in our ways and now are caught up in a life full of work and loneliness. We should each be having a family, like Lamech and Raisa. But we have isolated ourselves from the world and might as well be slaves to a cruel master." She began to sob again. "Who would have me now? I am old and undesirable."

Naomi chuckled. Liora raised her head and looked at her, confused by her aunt's reaction.

"Look at you, Liora. You are the image of your mother. You are a radiantly beautiful young woman, and yet, you are a difficult woman for a man to approach with confidence. I was going to have a talk with your uncle about this and how we might help you find the right man. We need to think of David too. We should have a plan to introduce both of you to worthy spouses."

"I don't want to be introduced to my spouse in that way. I want to choose him myself," Liora said defiantly.

"Why am I not surprised by that?" Naomi sighed. "Your poor father didn't stand a chance when he met your mother. He was like a fish, leaping into the boat to avoid the struggle; it was the smartest thing he ever did. He would never have chosen her on his own, though. He didn't have the courage."

Liora sat up, wanting her aunt to tell her more.

"Your mother was just like you: headstrong and full of curiosity and life. She knew what she wanted; nothing could get in her way. It caused her a lot of trouble as a little girl and more as a young woman. Your father, God rest his soul, was the best thing that ever happened to her. He never tried to corral her. I have never seen a man more in love with a woman; they were the perfect match." She smiled as a tear escaped from her own eye.

"Tell me more, please," Liora begged.

"We could talk for days, my child." Naomi smiled at her niece.

Suddenly Liora got up. "Wait here," she said and ran to the house. She returned in a moment, carrying her mother's comb in her hand. She handed it to her aunt, who looked at her in puzzlement. Naomi took the comb and held it to her chest, weeping softly.

"You should have this." Naomi tried to return the comb.

"No," said Liora, "you keep it. Mother would want you to have it. There will be a time in the future—you can return it then." Naomi smiled broadly and reached out to hug Liora and give her a warm kiss on the cheek.

"So how do we find you a man as good as your father?" Naomi asked.

Liora smiled back. "I want to find him. You just tell me what to look for," she said.

"If only it was that simple, child," answered Naomi. "It's not a list you carry with you and check off with every boy you meet. You have to *know*."

"How will I know?"

"You will meet him at the most unexpected time and in the most unexpected place. He will smile at you, and your heart will melt—and you will know. You must be careful not to stare when that happens!" They both laughed. "My child, we are people with a long history. I only hope when that moment comes, the man is worthy of you, a man of Israel, a man of goodness and tradition, a man your brother and uncle will approve."

Liora hugged her aunt tightly. It seemed like a good time to confess her next concern.

"I want to follow Jesus, Aunt." Liora looked up with serious eyes.

"I thought it was obvious that our whole family was following Jesus," Naomi replied.

"No, *follow* him," Liora clarified.

"Oh," was all Naomi could say. There was a period of silence as Naomi processed what her niece was saying. "That would be a question for your uncle, my child. We should discuss this with him. Have you talked to David about it?" Naomi inquired.

"No."

"What are David's feelings about moving to Capernaum?"

"David is excited. He talked about perhaps moving his blacksmith shop up here." Liora wasn't being entirely frank, but she wasn't being untruthful either. David had mentioned that he wanted to talk to Seth about blacksmithing. She and David would have to have a more formal discussion and then approach her aunt and uncle with a plan.

"We should talk more at the appropriate time," Naomi said. "Now, about this man." She looked at Liora with one raised eyebrow. They both laughed. They talked till almost sundown on a myriad of subjects: love, marriage, intimacy, childbirth. All the things Liora had been curious about. The air began to get a little chilly as the sun went down and the cool air from the lake approached. They had decided to move back to the warmth of the house when Sariah called from the front door.

"The baby's awake. You're going to miss your chance to hold him."

Liora and Naomi both rose to their feet, embracing each other one more time.

15

After they passed through the narrow strait at Messina and into the Mediterranean Sea, it was a new experience for Jacob and Levi to look around and see nothing but water. Their life had been roads and trails through valleys and mountain passes. They had often set up camp in a protected valley or in the foothills of great mountains, always thinking of the strategic advantage and defense of their location. But out here there was no strategic advantage; you could be attacked from any side and have nothing to put your back against. Jacob deduced that the only thing you had in your favor was the wind and the speed of your ship. Ezra said it could sometimes take half a day or even longer for a faster ship heading in the same direction to overtake you, but it was just a matter of time before it ran you down—there was no escaping. The only positive result of a long pursuit was the extra time you would have to prepare for battle. If a ship were concealed by fog or was sailing toward you, your preparation time could be cut to minutes.

The days at sea wore on, but the conversations with Ezra were invigorating. After a few days of prayer, neither Jacob nor

Levi needed to follow his lead. They had memorized the prayers and the motions. Presently they prayed like native Jews and could have fooled anyone. Ezra taught them more of the geography of Judaea and the distances between the cities.

"My homeland is a humble one, and I see no persuasive attraction for Rome," Ezra said. "We have no great resources. We have salt, fish, sheep, goats, and olive oil. Our only strength is our unity, forged by millennia of religious trials. We are not a military threat. We've been run over, sacked, and enslaved by every neighbor we have." Ezra chuckled. "You realize that Rome holds our entire country captive with mostly ill-disciplined and locally raised auxiliary troops and a single detachment of cavalry? Hardly enough to put down any significant organized rebellion. Pontius Pilate knows that. This is why he loses sleep over this Jesus. Any man who proves his ability to unite thousands of Jews, regardless of the reason or motive, could be a real threat to Roman rule. But I maintain that Jesus is more a threat to established Jewish rule than he is to Rome."

Ezra stood to stretch. Looking south, he exclaimed, "A ship!" He pointed toward the horizon. Jacob and Levi stood to look. It was an overcast day with the sea lightly rolling, but on one of the peaks they both saw the ship far in the distance.

"It looks like it is heading in the same direction we are," Levi observed.

"Yes, it is!" came a booming voice from behind them. It was Akhom. "We spotted it a day and a half ago. It could be coming east from Carthage, but it seems to be maintaining a consistent speed and distance from our ship. That ship has more sail than we do, and if its captain was worth his salt, he could have outrun us long ago." Akhom approached the trio standing in the bow.

"Is it that he carries more cargo and is heavier laden than our ship?" Jacob spoke his first words to Akhom, wondering why the Egyptian was suddenly confiding in them.

"No, the haze cleared briefly yesterday afternoon. One of our lookouts climbed the mast and said it appeared she was sailing high out of the water. She's no merchant," Akhom said ominously, then walked away as suddenly as he had appeared. He returned to the stern and engaged the captain and two of the crew in an animated discussion.

Jacob and Levi exchanged a knowing glance. Levi finally said what they all were thinking: "Pirates." Ezra gathered his robe about him and sat back down. Jacob and Levi stood at the rail, watching the rogue ship until the rolling of the sea and concentrating through the haze made them both a little queasy. They sat down next to Ezra, wishing he would voice an opinion. He said nothing.

Distracting thoughts of the other ship subdued conversation for the rest of the day. Just after sunset Ezra went below. Jacob and Levi followed but only to get blankets. They were sleeping on deck tonight.

No one objected to the presence of Jacob and Levi on deck. They settled in their usual spot and found relative comfort near some large coils of rope. They wrapped up in blankets, and Levi was asleep in minutes. Jacob, however, watched the activity at the stern of the ship to get a clue to the sailors' strategy if there was a threat. Four lookouts had their eyes locked on the horizon. Akhom and the captain sat with their heads close together, but the noise of the wind on the sails and the prow slashing through the water drowned out their conversation. Akhom spoke to one of the slaves, who immediately extinguished the fire in the small metal cauldron between the stern and the mainmast. Then he doused the small torches that burned at both the bow and the stern of the ship.

Jacob noted the full moon as he looked out on the rolling sea and was captivated by the silver and black rippling of the water. The fire and the torches made their ship visible to the ship that was stalking them—if it was stalking them. Jacob looked southward to see if he could glimpse the other ship's fire or torches. All he saw was blackness on the horizon. The only thing that distinguished the sea from the sky was the sparkle of silver streaks as the moon reflected its light on the water. He pulled the blanket around him and lay back down. If it was pirates, he should get some rest. The mind of the Roman legate was plotting his own strategy.

Jacob tossed and turned all night. What little sleep he got was interrupted prematurely by a commotion and racket he couldn't identify before he was fully conscious. It was the sound of men shouting and running on the deck. He leapt to his feet. *It must be the changing of the watch,* he thought. The sky was a dark blue. He leaned on the rail to steady his wobbly legs and saw in horror the cause of the commotion.

During the night the phantom ship had pulled close to the Egyptian ship and was now parallel with it. It was evident it was not a merchant ship. The lookout was correct: the draft on the ship was high, and it was lighter and therefore faster. No markings or banners identified its origin. The sails were trimmed to match the speed of the Egyptian ship. Sailors were constantly adjusting ropes. Jacob saw the prow of the boat was equipped with a large wooden unicorn, whose horn was an oversized metal spear close to the water line and extending twenty feet forward. Jacob knew about Roman military ships equipped with brass ramming beaks to sink enemy ships. But the spear on the pirate ship was too far above the waterline to sink a ship. Jacob deduced it must be for impaling ships, so the pirates could board and take the valuable cargo that would be lost if the ship sank. Oddly, Jacob remembered that as a boy he had speared fish with his uncle in a shallow brook by his home. After spearing the fish, they clubbed them to death with a mallet. He assumed the same concept was in operation here.

The ship was close enough for Jacob to see the crew clearly and hear their voices. They spoke in an unrecognizable tongue but were definitely preparing for attack. By rough count, a hundred or more dark-skinned men, dressed in odd clothing of different shades of gray and black, manned the ship. They wore black turbans and carried long spears with swords and knives and secured in wide leather belts draped over their bodies. Many were leaning against the rail, calmly looking back at him. Jacob remembered that Levi was sleeping nearby and kicked his backside.

Levi finally stirred on the third kick. He leapt to his feet and out of long habit reached for the sword that wasn't there. "What's happening?" he shouted to Jacob.

"We're being attacked. Pirates," Jacob answered.

Levi disappeared below deck.

The Egyptian sailors armed themselves with swords and shields from under the raised area where Akhom and the captain were seated. A sailor handed Jacob two swords and two shields. He said something in Egyptian and from his hand gestures, Jacob understood that everyone was expected to fight. He threw off his outer robe and reached for his dagger, which he realized he had left below. Just then Levi came running with both daggers. He had removed his robe and cut off his tunic just above the knee. He handed Jacob his dagger, and Jacob did the same thing, cutting off the lower portion of the cumbersome tunic to give him better movement of his legs. They took the sashes from the robes and made tight belts to secure their daggers.

Hurriedly they picked up the swords and wooden shields that had been laid out on the deck. Levi almost laughed out loud at the wooden discs. He put his arm through the leather straps; the shield barely covered his forearm from knuckles to elbow. It was no more than half the size of a Roman battle shield, but it would have to do. Jacob waved the sword back and forth, twisting his arm in every direction to gauge the sword's weight and center of balance. The blade was of an inferior steel and rusty from lack of use and storage in the salty environment of the ship. Fortunately, it was about the length of his Roman short sword.

The pirate ship was not rushing their attack, which gave time for the Egyptian crew to prepare to defend the ship. Akhom, now in full battle armor, was yelling orders with one eye on his men and the other on the enemy ship. He motioned to Jacob and Levi. "I have instructed the old man to stay below; he will be a nuisance in battle. You two must fight. If you fight like your Jewish countrymen, you won't be much good to me, but we are outmanned and need every healthy man who can carry a sword. Stay behind my men and support them where needed. Try to carry yourselves like soldiers—your lives may depend on it." Akhom walked away.

Jacob and Levi looked at each other and shared a nervous grin. Jacob said quietly, "Here we are on a peaceful mission to Judaea, and we find ourselves in the middle of another bloody campaign. My wounds haven't healed from our last one." He reached down to ensure the bandage on his lower calf was secure. Despite the care the two women at the house of Gaius Valerius had taken in dressing the wound, it was still swollen and tender.

Levi bent down to tighten the laces on his sandals and cut off the excess leather. He had learned a hard lesson as a young soldier about tripping over loose sandal laces. Never again did he go into battle with loose sandals and long trailing laces. Sword in hand, he reached with the other hand to grasp the amulet from under the front of his tunic. He stood tall with the amulet in his fist—calm and ready.

Men at the stern of the enemy ship wrestled with a gangplank secured on one end to a mast-sized post. The other end swung free on a boom secured with ropes. It would be swung over the deck of another ship and lowered for boarding. It was apparent the pirates' strategy was to ram the Egyptian ship, relying on the forward motion of the two ships to position them side by side and close enough to swing the gangplank over. Jacob saw Akhom position most of his men toward the stern in anticipation of the point of entry being the swinging gangplank. *He's been in battle before,* Jacob thought.

A shout rang out from one of the pirates, and in an instant the threatening ship turned sharply into their path. The angle they took would cause the spear to penetrate the forward third of their hull. As quickly as the enemy changed course, the Egyptian captain shouted an order, turning their ship away from the attack. Because of the heavy cargo onboard, however, the response of the Egyptian ship was slower and the angle was not as sharp. The pirate ship rammed the front of their boat, but the massive spear missed and went forward of their prow. The two ships collided with a loud wood-crunching shudder, and crews on both ships were thrown onto the decks as if they were wine goblets falling on a bumped table.

Jacob and Levi, anticipating the blow, squatted and gripped the railing to maintain their balance, popping up quickly when the ship leveled out. The enemy's gangplank was expertly swung over and dropped with a crash, lodging itself in the rails at the stern of the Egyptian ship and firmly secured by spikes protruding from its bottom. A wave of arrows from the pirate ship was ineffective as the Egyptians ducked down behind the near railing. A shower of spears followed next, for the most part sailing harmlessly over their heads or sticking into the side of the ship, but a few spears did hit their mark, downing at least three sailors. The pirates yelled a war cry and stormed the gangplank into the waiting swords of the Egyptians. The first few enemy attackers were hewn down, but they came too fast and were too plentiful. Eventually they spilled onto the deck of the Egyptian ship. Akhom was in the forefront, swinging his sword and inflicting fatal blows. Levi made his way to the stern with Jacob right behind him. The gangplank lodging fully extended at the stern of the Egyptian ship kept the two ships from drifting side to side, which prevented the enemy from boarding at any other point.

Jacob saw that the contest was turning into a land war on their deck. The enemy archers were wreaking havoc now as seamen were focused on repelling the boarding force and not on protecting themselves from the arrows. Only three Egyptian soldiers were armed with bows and arrows. Overall the Egyptian force was outmanned almost two to one. The outcome of the battle didn't look good.

The attacking horde poured onto the deck freely as Akhom and his men retreated toward the mainmast in the middle of the ship. Levi claimed his first three victims in rapid succession, hacking, parrying, and blocking with his shield and thrusting forward. He was too fast and skilled for the pirates, who relied on numbers and brute force. Levi cut through the attackers like a scythe through wheat.

Jacob found himself shoulder to shoulder with Akhom. With shields up, they pushed their attack into the face of the onslaught, slowing the forward motion of the pirates and holding firm amidships. Egyptian sailors were falling at an alarming rate. The defenders were as untrained as the attackers. It was a close-in battle of hack and slash, in which strength in numbers usually overcame.

Jacob saw out of the corner of his eye pirates coming in from behind him and Akhom. He turned and fought them off. He broke the outstretched arm of one attacker with a blow of his dull sword, sending him to the deck screaming. With a swift backhand he slashed the exposed neck of another pirate and then crouched and thrust a deathblow to a third as the enemy foolishly lifted his sword with both hands to strike a downward blow against Jacob. Akhom turned just long enough to see Jacob drop the three attackers to his rear.

Levi managed to exchange his inferior Egyptian shield for that of a fallen enemy. It happened to be a Roman shield of leather and brass, obviously booty from another attack. With the larger, more familiar shield guarding most of his upper body, Levi became invincible. He spun and slashed in the small space of the deck. He pushed two of the pirates over the side of the ship with the sheer force of his arm and massive body strength. The enemy began to fall at a faster pace. The Egyptian soldiers had returned to the stern and kept almost a third of the pirates from crossing over the gangplank, effectively reducing the odds against them.

The Egyptian sailors now had the pirates surrounded. The forward mariners had held, and Akhom, Jacob, Levi, and a small group of seamen were slowly crushing them from behind. Within minutes every pirate aboard had been slaughtered. A cheer went up as the fighting stopped.

The pirates remaining on their own ship quickly attempted to disengage the gangplank. Without thinking, Levi climbed onto the raised gangplank, charging over bodies and moving courageously toward the pirate ship. Akhom followed. The remaining Egyptians and Jacob were not far behind. Out here the battle had to be decisive. Neither side would take any prisoners.

The pirates fled the stern of their ship to avoid the incursion led by Levi. They gathered to defend themselves at the bow. Levi,

Akhom, and Jacob led twenty or so Egyptians into the retreating enemy with renewed vigor.

Within minutes it was over.

Bodies of dead and wounded men were strewn over the decks of both ships. The surviving Egyptians raised their swords and shields in a victory shout. On the bow of the pirate ship, Akhom looked at Jacob and Levi for a moment and then with his shield bumped each of them on their heaving chest in a gesture of respect.

Akhom shouted to his men, "Clean up this pigsty, and let's get moving! We have cargo to get to Caesarea!" He raised his sword to salute his men, who gave another victory shout. Jacob and Levi followed him back across the gangplank.

After a land battle, victorious Romans engaged brutal men, called stickers, to comb the battlefield for wounded enemy soldiers. They would thrust sharp javelins through the survivors' lungs and heart to ensure the death of the entire enemy force. It was little different at sea.

Akhom's men scoured the enemy ship for loot. They claimed the fresh water and food stores and found a chest of coins and gold, which they took back to the captain. The bodies of dead and wounded pirates on the Egyptian ship were thrown overboard. The dead Egyptians were gathered on deck and sewn into blankets with their personal belongings and a small ration of food, then with ceremony and great respect lowered into the sea. The wounded were taken below and treated. After much hard work, the heavy gangplank was disengaged and the pirate ship set ablaze with all the dead and wounded pirates still aboard. The smaller front sail of the Egyptian ship was trimmed, pulling them away from the burning boat. Screams could be heard as wounded pirates were burned alive; some managed to roll overboard to a watery death. Battle was a grisly thing on land or sea, and Akhom showed no mercy.

The crew stowed the weapons and began washing blood off the deck with buckets of seawater. When everything was in order, the captain set course and the main sail was trimmed and secured. They could see the black smoke rising on the horizon from the burning ship for a long time as they continued their journey eastward. Levi had picked up a sharp Roman short sword from one of the fallen pirates. He reluctantly gave up the shield and sword to the sailors collecting weapons. He satisfied himself with the thought that they were within his grasp should they have another encounter.

The strain of the battle on Jacob's leg had caused the wound to open slightly, and it was bleeding. He had suffered a cut on his right forearm, which he did not remember getting. Something or someone had hit him on his tender shoulder, and that was causing him the most pain. Levi appeared to be untouched, except for the blood spattered on him from head to toe. Until he washed with a couple of buckets of water, it wasn't clear whether any of the blood was his own, but it wasn't. For all his aggression in the fight, he had come out of it unscathed.

Ezra had remained below during the fight, as instructed. Now he returned to the deck. Upon seeing Jacob and Levi, he embraced each one. No words were exchanged. Then he led them in a reluctant prayer. Jacob and Levi wanted to rest, but they understood the need to keep up the deception. Their ruse was open to serious question, now that their skills as warriors had become known. Jacob observed Akhom and the captain talking and looking curiously at them.

16

After the experience with Jesus in the synagogue and the long talk with her aunt, Liora set her course. Jershon refused to allow her to follow Jesus on his journeys, but she was so determined that he reluctantly gave her permission if her brother would accompany her. David resisted at first, preferring to stay and fish with his uncle and cousins. He hoped that after a few days Liora would reconsider or make friends in the camp who could offer her sufficient protection and thus allow him to return to Capernaum. After all, these were disciples of the Messiah, not robbers and ne'er-do-wells.

Sariah coaxed her parents into letting her go as well, but Jershon made them promise they would return after a week to report on their experience. The next day Jershon, Lamech, and Seth were up early to fish. Liora, Sariah, and David spent the morning preparing to leave. Sariah and Liora gave Naomi a tearful hug. They kissed Raisa and the baby; they would miss him most. Naomi and Esther stood in the road outside the door and waved for as long as they were still visible.

Sariah had learned that Jesus and his apostles were staying at a farm not far from Capernaum and they would be traveling to Bethsaida on the northeastern shore of the Sea of Galilee, about the same distance northeast of Capernaum as Magdala was southwest. Within a few minutes, they met a crowd of people on the road just outside Capernaum. Maybe as many as two thousand people were sitting in a field, waiting. One of the disciples told them that Jesus had gone to visit a family with a seriously ill daughter and he would return soon to continue on to Bethsaida.

They had waited no more than thirty minutes when the crowd began to murmur at the sight of Jesus emerging in the distance from a cluster of dwellings. A buzz went through the crowd as the report of Jesus healing the sick girl was passed along. Liora smiled at Sariah with anticipation of the things they might witness in his presence. The walk was slow, hot, and dusty but didn't deter them.

At about noon the crowd of disciples stopped beside the lake in a large grove of olive trees that provided plentiful shade. A large number of people waited to refill their water bags at a well nearby. Jesus and his closest associates sat on an outcropping of rock not far away. Liora led David and Sariah closer, so they could at least observe him. A small group of children ran noisily up to him. The men around Jesus tried to ward off the giggling children, saying that he needed to rest. Jesus signaled to his friends to cease discouraging the children. Liora heard him say, "Suffer the little children to come unto me, and forbid them not: for of such is the kingdom of God." He walked among the children, touching their heads and brushing their tender cheeks. He smiled a wonderful smile, and Liora heard him laugh. He finally sat down on the ground among the children. They sat in his lap, leaned on his shoulders, and snuggled into him, relishing his affection. He talked to them quietly for some time and then sent them happily off.

Liora pondered the meaning of what she had witnessed, deducing that the kingdom of God must be full of children. It made her wonder if she would someday have her own children. She would take them to sit at the feet of Jesus, who would touch their faces and laugh with them. The thought pleased her.

David pointed out to Liora the contemptuous Jewish elders who were sitting in a group by themselves, talking quietly.

"They slither after him like snakes, waiting for him to say something that will allow them to strike," Liora said with disdain.

"These same men were at the synagogue yesterday," said David. "I don't understand their attacks."

"They question his authority, David," Liora replied. "It's not obvious to them, as it is to us. They want proof. They've seen him perform miracles; you'd think that would be proof enough of his authority."

The three new disciples made themselves comfortable and ate some of the food that Naomi had prepared. Liora could not take her eyes off Jesus. After talking with the children, he spoke with a few of the disciples near where he was sitting. He smiled, apparently at ease with the people. It seemed everyone wanted to be near him and talk to him. Liora was satisfied watching from a distance, hoping he might preach to all of them at some point in the journey. He returned to his apostles and lay down near them in the grass to rest. Liora thought how tired he must be. He had no peace or rest even among those who loved him, yet he always appeared to be of good cheer, willing to stop and talk to people or bless them. *What an amazing man,* she thought.

They rested for about an hour, and then Jesus arose to continue the journey to Bethsaida. It took a few minutes before Liora, Sariah, and David even started to move, so great was the mass of people stretched out along the narrow road. The dust the crowd kicked up was stifling.

At Bethsaida, Jesus and his apostles disappeared into a house. The disciples found shade among the olive groves and set up camp. They would wait until Jesus moved on or found a place to preach to them. Liora, David, and Sariah settled under a small shelter David made of some dead branches and a blanket that gave them additional shade and some small degree of privacy. They were willing to wait, whether for an hour or days, to see and hear Jesus again.

17

Jacob awoke about sunset. Someone had dressed the wound on his forearm and rewrapped the wound in his calf. He started to sit up, but the deep bruise in his shoulder gave him considerable pain. He watched as the bodies of three more Egyptians who had succumbed to their wounds were being lowered into the sea.

He and Levi had estimated that twenty to twenty-five crewmen had been slain in the attack. That was close to half the number who had sailed from Ostia. It took about ten sailors to man the sails and keep the ropes in order on deck. The rest were likely oarsmen. Jacob realized the journey across the Great Sea, sitting at the feet of Ezra discussing philosophy and Jewish culture, had suddenly turned into a vigil for the enemy, whoever they were. The remote possibility of an attack had become a reality, and Jacob wondered whether they could sail all the way to Caesarea without being attacked again. They hadn't even sailed far enough to be south of the island of Crete, where most pirate attacks occurred. It seemed that for most of his life he had been on the lookout for one enemy or another. Could a man find anyplace in the world where he need not worry about the threat of some enemy?

"Jacob!" Levi shook his friend. "Wake up."

Jacob rolled over, careful not to lean on his injured shoulder. Levi and Ezra were sitting up, and Akhom had joined them, sitting on a low wooden stool. Darkness had fallen, and the fire had been restarted in the cauldron. The torches fore and aft burned brightly once again. Fresh fruit and meat still steaming from the flame were set on large plates next to them. Jacob sat up as Akhom poured wine from a goatskin bag into goblets he had brought from the captain's table.

"You fought like lions today, my Jewish friends. I am reluctant to say it, but we owe our victory to you both." He proposed a toast, and they all drank. Jacob savored the taste of the excellent wine. "Tell me where you learned your skills," Akhom said.

Jacob answered, "We've spent some time in Rome. The soldiers were kind to us."

Akhom laughed. "You could teach the Romans a thing or two. They fight no better than the rabble of pirates today, and they have less passion." He laughed again.

Jacob glanced at Levi, silently warning him to hold his tongue, and then changed the subject. "Thank you, sir," Jacob said respectfully.

"Eat, my friends." Akhom gestured toward the trays of food.

Ezra spoke. "Thank you for your generosity, Akhom. The fruit should satisfy our hunger. The meat would be better distributed among your good men. They fought a valiant battle today too." Sharply disappointed, Jacob and Levi looked down at the large chunks of steaming pork, their mouths watering.

"Very well," said Akhom. He summoned one of his men to remove the meat. "My Jewish friends, thank you for your bravery today. If there is anything I can do to make your voyage more comfortable, please let me know."

Ezra, Jacob, and Levi smiled and nodded their gratitude.

Akhom stunned them with his next comment. "Did you go to Rome to learn to fight so you could return to your homeland and fight for the new king of the Jews?"

Jacob and Levi stared at him.

Ezra spoke up. "What do you speak of?" he asked.

Akhom adjusted his position on the stool and set his wine goblet on the deck. "I have been plying the waters of this great sea for a long time. Half a year ago I was in the port of Caesarea. I heard a story there about a man named Jesus, a Galilean, I believe." Akhom paused. "Surely you have heard of him?"

Ezra remained silent.

Akhom continued, "Supposedly he works some kind of magic to heal blind men and lepers. The merchant who told me the story said he saw these things with his own eyes. I told him I thought he was drinking too much wine. Then he told me that this Jesus could turn water into wine. I asked the man if Jesus could join us on the next leg of our voyage. That talent would come in handy." Akhom laughed again.

Ezra chose his words carefully. "I have heard of this Galilean, but some of the claims seem exaggerated. I can assure you, my two companions and I have not left Rome to obtain employment with a new Jewish king, although the thought of a new king of Israel is amusing." Ezra baited Akhom with his next question. "Why would this Galilean think he could become king of the Jews?"

Akhom leaned forward. "The merchant in Caesarea said that in Jewish lore there is a story about a messiah, I think he said, who would save the Jews from all oppressors. And it's about time." Akhom laughed. "If my knowledge of history serves me right, and with all due respect, your country has been mostly under the control of your enemies, Rome being the latest. I can see where a rumor like that would get the attention of a lot of people." Akhom picked up his wine goblet and took another drink.

"What do you think, Akhom?" Ezra asked.

"I don't think anything," Akhom answered, "but it would serve the Romans right to be thrown out on their ear."

"Do you think there is any truth to this merchant's story?" Ezra probed further.

"He is a trusted friend of the captain. The captain asked him how this new king would manage to seize power. He told us that Jesus was from the house of David, whatever that means, and has the birthright claim to the throne of Israel. I can't see that strategy working with Rome." Akhom laughed loudly as the wine began to take effect.

Ezra looked upward, closed his eyes, and in Hebrew softly recited: "'Behold, the days come, saith the Lord, that I will raise unto David a righteous Branch, and a King shall reign and prosper, and shall execute judgment and justice in the earth.'"

"Another prayer, my friend?" Akhom asked.

"No, just a prophecy from one of the ancients," Ezra said dismissively.

"Well, good luck with your new king." Akhom laughed heartily, toasted his new friends one more time, and then retreated to his perch at the stern.

Jacob and Levi breathed easier and looked at Ezra. "What an odd place to get your first morsel of information, my sons." Ezra smiled.

"What was that prayer you murmured?" asked Jacob.

"Not a prayer. An ancient prophet named Jeremiah spoke of the advent of a king from the loins of David." Ezra sensed Jacob wanted a more complete answer. "David was the youngest of eight brothers in ancient Israel, yet he was chosen by Jehovah to be king."

"So your God chose the king?" questioned Jacob.

"Yes," answered Ezra. "David was favored of God."

"Did God just come down and tell the people that this David was to be king?" Jacob asked.

"Jehovah made his choice known through his mouthpiece, the prophet Samuel," answered Ezra.

"And the people accepted the word of this prophet?"

"Yes, Jacob. There were times when the children of Israel were very obedient to Jehovah, and other times when they were not so obedient."

"So why doesn't Jehovah just come down now and tell the Jews that Jesus is to be their new king?" Jacob asked.

"That's a fair question, Jacob. For centuries the prophets have been telling of the coming of the Messiah. The question begs for an answer: is this Jesus of Nazareth the chosen Messiah?" Ezra let the thought sink in. "Recently there has been a man, a prophet among the people, named John. He doesn't fit the usual Jewish perception of a prophet, however. He mainly lives alone, spending most of his time preaching in the wilderness of Judaea rather than in the synagogues. He has gathered quite a following of more humble folk and has begun baptizing them in the River Jordan. Interestingly, I have been informed this John is a cousin to Jesus. In fact, I heard a report that he even baptized Jesus. John has publicly denied the title of Messiah—Jesus has not. The problem the Jewish rulers have is Jesus's lack of denial about being the long-promised Messiah." Ezra paused to take a drink of wine. "It is complicated, but I can understand the threat he poses to the Sanhedrin and the high priest. I believe they are the impetus behind the paranoia of Pontius Pilate and Herod Antipas. An ancient prophet named Isaiah told the Jewish people long ago . . ." He once again closed his eyes and recited from memory: "'Therefore the Lord himself shall give you a sign; behold, a virgin shall conceive, and bear a son, and shall call his name Immanuel.'"

"But this man's name is Jesus," Jacob argued.

"Yes, it is, but the Hebrew word *Immanuel* means 'God with us.'" Ezra opened his eyes to gauge Jacob's reaction. Jacob appeared perplexed. "There's another point of interest that I'm not sure has been considered by the religious authorities in Jerusalem. If indeed Jesus of Nazareth is the *God with us,* or the Son of God, then who would dispute his right to the throne?"

"You have a point, but that claim would be difficult to prove," Jacob rejoined.

"Perhaps, perhaps not," Ezra said. "Regardless, my sources in Galilee tell me that both his mother and father claim their lineage from the house of David, so either way, the qualification for the throne is met."

"You sound like you are trying to convince me of the reality of the threat to Rome, Ezra," Jacob said.

"I'm not trying to convince you of anything, my son. I am just giving you information to help satisfy the mission from your emperor." Ezra leaned back. "Let's finish the bounty you earned from our host and retire for the night. We can talk more tomorrow."

They ate the rest of the fruit and bread on the tray. Shortly, Ezra congratulated them both on getting Akhom to befriend them, then excused himself and went below. Levi complained to Jacob about the lack of meat, but they maintained their identities and went to sleep craving roast pig.

18

The next few days on the open sea proved uneventful. The danger of pirates diminished as they neared Caesarea. They saw two ships heading west, which meant they were getting close to port. Perhaps one more day. Akhom continued to give his three guests extra rations of wine and fish. Occasionally he talked with them. Jacob found it challenging to discuss the affairs of the world, philosophy, battle, and Rome without sounding like a Roman, but it was good practice. Akhom engaged Levi in a conversation about swords and sword making and was enthralled by Levi's knowledge of metallurgy.

Toward evening Jacob saw Ezra standing near the prow of the ship staring off toward the horizon and thought it might be a good time to talk with him privately about questions that had been brewing in his mind. As Jacob approached, however, he could see Ezra's eyes were red and tears were streaming down his cheeks. He immediately apologized for disturbing Ezra's private thoughts.

"No need for apologies, my son," Ezra said without turning. "Sometimes men yoke themselves to the cruel past like an ox to a cart of stones. It is sometimes difficult to unyoke and look further out on the horizon."

Jacob understood perfectly.

"You have a question you want to ask?" Ezra said.

"Many, but perhaps now isn't a good time. I'll leave you to your thoughts." Jacob turned to go.

"No, at times my thoughts pull me to the bottom of the sea. Perhaps your questions will redirect them."

The two men found a comfortable place to sit, and Jacob looked directly at Ezra, who seemed to have aged suddenly.

"You haven't told us much about yourself or your family," Jacob ventured.

Ezra hesitated. "You add a stone to my cart," he finally said with an ironic smile.

Jacob again apologized. "I'm sorry. I didn't mean to bring up a sensitive subject."

Ezra wiped the tears from his face. "My family is a pleasant memory, but aspects of it cut like a dagger." He regained control of his emotions and began speaking freely.

"I am a simple man from Jerusalem, my son. Being Jewish is not so much a religion as it is a way of life. It is thrust upon you as you leave the womb of a good Jewish mother, as mine was. It is not a designation you can just walk away from, no more than you can walk away from being Roman. I am proud of my heritage and the traditions of my fathers. I am Jewish; I will always be Jewish. I was a member of the Sanhedrin, which is comparable to your Senate in Rome. I was young, my wife . . ." His voice trailed off. Jacob placed his hand on the forearm of his mentor. Ezra looked up at Jacob, his eyes filled with tears. It was a few moments before he could speak. He continued in a broken voice. "My beautiful wife, Miriam, was the joy of my life. She made hard days bearable and good days better. But she was never able to conceive. Whether that was God's wisdom or simply fate, I cannot say.

"My lovely Miriam grew ill one summer and by the coming winter was taken from me." There was another long pause. "I spent many an hour on my knees in the great temple talking to God, trying to reconcile myself to that loss. My heart had been taken from me and trampled. I could not heal. Although I didn't know what direction I should go, I knew I couldn't continue as I was, and I resigned my position in the Sanhedrin. For the longest time I remained alone and away from society—you might say I was a hermit. I became angry, and soon my talks with God were different. I complained and blamed and finally cursed God. I was not strong like the ancient prophets Job and Jeremiah, who dealt with a life full of tragedy and remained faithful. I began hating my God. I ultimately fell prey to the lure of drunkenness to ease my pain and anger.

"One evening after too much wine, even for a drunk, I ventured to a nearby grove of olive trees. I cursed God at the top of my lungs and vowed vengeance, whatever form vengeance toward God takes, and drank until I passed out. When I finally awoke, I was lying on my bed. I was in clean sleeping clothes, and there was a bandage on my head where I had hit it against the stump of a stubborn olive tree when I fell. I tried to sit up in bed but was unable. I turned my head to the side of the bed where my Miriam used to lie. I kept my eyes closed, hoping that when I opened them she would be there. What I saw eventually was a dirty young boy in ragged clothes sitting on the floor with his knees tucked under his chin and leaning against the wall of my chamber. I asked him who he was. He said his name was Uah-Er-Meri. He was an orphan who had been sleeping outside my house for some time. My feeble wine-laden brain deduced it was an Egyptian name.

"I prepared a place for Meri to sleep next to the hearth inside the house. From that day forward he became my son. The arrival of Uah-Er-Meri saved my life," Ezra said as he looked off into the distance. "Uah-Er-Meri became Benjamin. He is about your age, Jacob. He is strong and intelligent like you." Ezra gave Jacob a tender smile.

"Does he live in Jerusalem with you?" Jacob asked.

"No, he lives in Alexandria. Remember, he is Egyptian. Together we own a shipping business of five ships that ply the Great Sea to ports like Caesarea, Piraeus, Ostia, and Carthage—war permitting. We also own two Nile barges that allow us to trade with Benjamin's countrymen far to the south. It has been a peaceful time, and in the last few years things have gone very well for us."

Jacob stared incredulously at Ezra. "How often do you see him?" Jacob asked.

"Not often enough," Ezra answered, "but I intend to change that."

Jacob had a myriad of questions he could not resist asking. "Did you raise him Jewish or did he maintain his Egyptian heritage?"

"A man's home is in his blood. Benjamin is Egyptian. Even though he went to Jerusalem as a young boy, Egypt is in his blood. I respected his decision to take a wife and have a family in Alexandria. You," he pointed a craggy finger at Jacob, "Rome is in your blood, and you will always be a Roman, despite our best efforts to disguise that fact." He playfully rubbed the back of his hand on Jacob's new beard, and they laughed heartily. "We don't choose our home; it chooses us. You will choose to live in Rome because that is the home of your birth. Sometimes extraordinary events are thrust upon us and we change our inbred allegiances, but that is rare. For example, the Jews of Alexandria are mostly descendants of the Jews who were born in Egypt before the exodus with the prophet Moses. Some never left; some returned. Some Jews generations later than those who actually returned to the promised land returned to live in Egypt. Egypt was still somehow in their blood." Ezra looked at Jacob. "I don't think there is anything that could tear you away from Rome, is there?"

The question caused Jacob to ponder what extraordinary event could cause him to change his true home. Philosophically he had already moved, but Ezra was right: Rome ran in every vein of his body. Jacob answered no to avoid further discussion.

"Tell me more of your Jewish god—Jehovah," Jacob requested.

"I don't know if I can give you the answer you seek. I really think you want me to justify why *you* should believe in him, and that is a very personal thing."

"Exactly," said Jacob with excitement in his voice. "It is a personal thing. People should have a personal relationship with the gods they believe in, not walking around in fear of them. I consider the relationship I have with my father. People should have that kind of relationship with their god. It seems the gods men invent are tyrannical and selfish and give nothing in exchange for the devotion they require. Fate, good or bad, is simply credited to the gods. Men make most decisions themselves and suffer the consequences of those decisions. The gods didn't make the pirates attack us. None of us on this ship did anything to bring that upon us except take a voyage. Nevertheless, we met them and suffered the consequences. In Rome it would be said the gods weren't with us, or the gods must have been displeased, or any number of other reasons why it was the doing of the gods. I just don't believe that gods meddle that much in the affairs of men."

"Maybe you wouldn't make a good Jew," Ezra said. "Jews believe that everything that happens is directed by Jehovah. And in their history that's how it is recorded. But Jews are a peculiar people—we arrogantly believe Jehovah is Jewish. But I have always thought that even if he is Jewish, if indeed he is the one true God, then he would treat all men equally, love all men equally, reward or punish all men equally.

"Jacob, in the synagogue I studied the dealings of Jehovah with the children of Israel. He did favor them, guide them, chastise them, and love them, just as any earthly parent would do with his own children. We can ask, Why would Jehovah pay so much attention to the Jews? Well, they were the only ones who believed in him. Think about it. The Greeks have their own gods, as do you—the Romans. The Egyptians have their gods. The cultures farther east have their gods. So by default, he became the God of the Jews, the only people left who believed in him. When Moses led the children of Israel out of captivity in Egypt, many of them didn't know Jehovah. They continued to worship the Egyptian gods they had grown up with. That is why they wandered in the wilderness for forty years. They refused to fully accept Jehovah, so in that harsh wilderness he dispensed of the generation of nonbelievers, and then when the new generations accepted him, he led them into the promised land."

"You sound convinced that Jehovah is the one true God," said Jacob.

"I know he is. Where the Jews get it wrong is in thinking he belongs exclusively to them. I believe he is the God of *all* people." Ezra placed his hand on Jacob's shoulder. "I believe he is *my* God and *your* God too, Jacob, but you have to discover that for yourself."

Jacob wanted to believe Ezra but knew he was right: he would have to find out for himself. "And this Jesus of Nazareth that we have been sent to investigate?" Jacob asked. "Do you believe he is the Son of God?"

"Jacob, if God wanted to have a son and send him to walk

among us in the form of a Jew, do you think he has the power to do so?"

Jacob didn't ponder long. "A god I could believe in would absolutely have that power," he answered with conviction.

"It appears you will soon have an opportunity to search these things out for yourself," Ezra continued. "You must promise to tell me what you discover about this Nazarene as well as about God. You will always be welcome in my home, Jacob."

"Thank you, Ezra," Jacob said. "I question my life sometimes. It is so very different from yours. You have worked hard, and I believe God has blessed you."

"I have been most fortunate. You know, God is willing to bless a Roman legate posing as a Jew, as well." They laughed. "He knows you're a Roman, but he also knows the intent of your heart. Of all the things I have learned about you, Jacob, I have learned you have a good heart."

"I certainly haven't done anything worthy of a blessing from the Jewish God," Jacob said.

"You think that because you are Roman?" Ezra asked. "Jacob, you honored your mother and father and did the bidding of your leaders. You are an honorable man. God does not hold men accountable for laws they have not been taught. The Jews are obedient to the Law of Moses. What do you know about the Law of Moses, Jacob?" Ezra asked.

Jacob shook his head, indicating he knew nothing.

"That's my point exactly, Jacob. God doesn't expect you to keep the Law of Moses; it has never been taught to you. I know you are a man of good intent and you treat your fellowman with respect and kindness. Those are godly traits. That is behavior God blesses." Ezra smiled at his student.

Jacob felt warmth envelop him from head to toe. It was hard to hold back the tears caused by more than fifteen years of battle.

Something Ezra conveyed about this God rang true to his heart. This was a God he could understand. This was a God he could love and worship. This was a God who could heal him.

"I sincerely hope you find what you are looking for," Ezra commented.

"Those are many things." Jacob laughed.

"The most important is finding the true God and a good wife. And you are on the path to encounter both," Ezra said.

"How can you be so confident I will find them?" Jacob asked.

"You are a man who seeks the truth. You are also a man with great discernment. God will bless you, Jacob. You will find what you seek."

19

For two days in Bethsaida, Liora, Sariah, and David saw little of Jesus. David insisted they camp near where the River Jordan flowed out of the Sea of Galilee. Perhaps they could buy some fish from the many fishermen who worked the area.

As the three sat talking, they noticed a small group of men emerging from a narrow alley of the town. One man appeared to be leading another man. As the group approached a marshy area near the river, Liora exclaimed excitedly, "It is Jesus." She rose and walked rapidly toward him with Sariah and David in tow. When they were a few yards away, David caught Liora by the arm, cautioning her to maintain a respectful distance. They sat down in a small grassy area within earshot of Jesus and his companions.

Jesus stood face to face with the blind man, holding his hands in his own. He bent forward and addressed him quietly. The apostles stood close by, listening intently to the words Jesus spoke. Suddenly Jesus leaned closer and spat into both eyes of the blind man. Liora and Sariah looked at each other curiously, then turned back to watch events unfold. Jesus placed his hands on the man's forehead, covering his eyes. He raised his face skyward and appeared to be praying aloud. When he had finished, he asked the blind man, in tones clear enough for Liora and the others to hear, if he could see. The blind man gazed about hesitantly. With a smile he said, "I see men as trees, walking."

Jesus once again placed his hands on the blind man's eyes and bade him look up. This time the man's sight was fully restored. He fell at Jesus's feet, weeping and thanking God. Jesus blessed the man and told him to go home, but not by way of the town, and cautioned him not to tell the people what had occurred.

The old man walked away with renewed confidence. Jesus pulled his headdress over his head to protect him from the intense sun, bowed his head briefly as if in prayer, and returned with his apostles the way they had come.

Liora and Sariah had their hands over their mouths in astonishment, tears running down their faces. David was speechless. They had witnessed a miracle and there was no denying what they had seen and heard. Their conviction was sealed. As Jesus and the apostles disappeared down the alley, Liora, David, and Sariah sat in silence, trying to assimilate what they had experienced.

It was a long time before the three could talk to each other.

David finally asked, "What does this all mean?"

Liora spoke boldly. "It confirms that he is who he says he is. He is the Messiah. As your father said, Sariah, he is not the Messiah the people look for; he brings power of a different kind. He does not enforce his message with a sword. Yes, he is here to rescue us, but in a way I can't fully put into words. I need to know more."

David agreed. "This is more than I had anticipated. I know what I saw, but I also feel confused."

They spent most of the day in the meager shade of a struggling oleander bush. They ate a small amount of food and talked quietly together. The experience of the day had lifted them but at the same time seemed to drain their energy. It was almost too much to contemplate.

Late in the afternoon they observed people moving from different places they could see from their camp. People were gathering their belongings and walking toward the town. Liora, David, and Sariah decided to join them. As they neared the main road and merged with the crowd, word was passed along that Jesus and his apostles were going to a hill outside Bethsaida and Jesus was going to address them. The three new disciples were excited at the prospect of hearing Jesus speak.

Eventually they reached their destination, and Jesus greeted the crowd. Even though Liora was sitting more than fifty yards away from him, it seemed as if he was right beside her. His gentle voice penetrated the air as clearly as it penetrated each heart. His message was simple and needed no interpretation by learned rabbis.

Jesus spoke for almost an hour. Every word went straight to her heart. He taught the people about dealing with oppression and tribulation. He taught them about prayer and praying in secret. She marveled at his knowledge and the authority with which he spoke. How could anyone not believe this was the Son of God? Liora reasoned that if God was indeed his father, Jesus would have similar traits and characteristics and know his father's will. Liora had never thought of God having a body of flesh and bone, but she now believed he did.

David and Sariah listened with open hearts and were filled with the warmth of his words. Doubts that any of them might have harbored were dispelled. His admonishing his listeners to be perfect, as his father was, seemed a monumental task. But

Liora understood that it was a lifetime of improvement; her father had taught her that. He had taught her that Jehovah was patient and long-suffering, and the stories he related about the children of Israel illustrated that truth. Liora knew logically that no one could become perfect overnight, but if one truly sought the kingdom of God every day, as Jesus admonished them, then perfection would be the result. She had always thought her father was perfect, and the stories he'd told Liora of her mother made her perfect in Liora's eyes too. Jesus's message was about creating a life filled with service to others and forgiveness. All the building blocks of the kingdom of God were laid out plainly. Liora understood more fully what her father had taught her. She wept in gratitude for the knowledge she had gained today.

Jesus concluded his sermon with a blessing on the disciples and prayed for all of them. He took his leave, his apostles following, and returned to the town to retire for the evening. As he walked through the crowd of people, he stopped to touch and pray for various afflicted people in his path. Liora was certain he healed those he stopped to talk with. It was truly an amazing day. If they returned to Capernaum now, they would have been fed for a lifetime.

BOOK III

JUDAEA

20

The final run into Caesarea was a quick one. Their easterly direction kept the ship at an attitude to take advantage of the strong wind generated from the desert of the African continent. It blew generously the last two days, filling the sails to capacity and even causing the ship to list. Standing without holding onto something proved difficult, and uninterrupted sleep was impossible.

Ezra reiterated to his two students the power of the Sanhedrin and the political and religious divide between Pharisees and Sadducees. Ironically, Jesus of Nazareth had brought the two sides together—he was fast becoming their common enemy. Behind closed doors, they rejected his claim to authority but were reluctant to challenge him directly. They watched him like a hawk and followed him everywhere, listening to him expound his new message. They listened for any doctrinal aberration to accuse him of heresy. Many of the Sanhedrin resorted to allying themselves with Rome to paint him as an enemy of the empire. That is how Ezra became involved.

Jacob was fascinated with the dynamics and couldn't wait

to encounter Jesus and observe his tactics. It would be easy to discover if he was a genuine threat to Rome or just a personal threat to the ruling Jews. Men with greater knowledge can strike fear into those less learned, especially if they teach a nontraditional philosophy and are able to sway the opinions of multitudes. It seemed to Jacob that this was exactly what he would find in Judaea.

During the voyage from Rome, Ezra had taught Jacob and Levi more prayers and Jewish customs. He cautioned them against making any close friends and helped them devise a story about their Jewish roots in Egypt as a cover for their un-Jewish look and language. Because it was said that many disciples who followed Jesus had left home and livelihood to do so, Jacob and Levi would profess to be disciples of Jesus to avoid any undue questioning about their presence in Judaea.

At sunrise they spotted Caesarea in the distance. Ezra informed them it had been built by Herod the Great. Soon they could see the aqueduct taking water into the city, much as the great aqueducts did in Rome. The port was bustling, and the city was sprawling.

The captain brought the Egyptian ship swiftly into the wharf and Ezra, Jacob, and Levi began to gather their belongings. Akhom met them at the gangplank.

"My friends, it has been a pleasure to know you. If all Jews were like you three, perhaps we could have a stronger peace between our countries." Akhom laughed. "Once again, I extend my gratitude to you, Jacob, and Levi, for your valor in our conflict. I did not know that Jews could produce such skilled warriors. Ezra, you should be safe walking the streets of Jerusalem with these two at your side. By the way, would you like the swords and shields you captured? You earned them."

"We are not in need of them, I assure you. They may serve

you in the future, but I petition God you never have to use them."
Ezra answered for his friends.

The men bade one another farewell, and the three Jews
made their way from the ship. Jacob and Levi followed Ezra into
the bustling city, where merchants shouted in languages Jacob
could not understand as they bartered for goods to fill ships and
caravans.

Ezra led them toward two Nabataeans sitting at a table. One
wore a turban accented with colorful jewels, and his silk robe of
orange and red was emblazoned with unique patterns. He spoke
energetically to his companion, waving arms laden with great
bracelets of gold.

The flamboyant Nabataean smacked the table with his fist,
disturbing the coins he was counting, and stood up. "Ezra, my
old friend!" he bellowed. "What wind brings me such wonderful
company on this hot day?"

The two friends embraced while Jacob and Levi stood by,
surprised once again at the network of connections and friends
that were Ezra's.

"My good friend Iqbal, I would like you to meet my traveling
companions, Jacob and Levi."

"Are you in danger, my friend?" Iqbal asked. "With these two
at your side, no one would think of harming you." He sized up
the two men standing beside Ezra. "Where are your weapons,
gentlemen?" he asked. "I can provide you with swords of the finest Damascus steel. Or perhaps you prefer the smaller Roman
short sword. I have a supply of those as well. They are good for
sticking rats in the alley but not very effective in a real battle." He
laughed. Levi held his tongue.

"You always want to make a deal, my friend," Ezra said. "We
are not in the market for swords today but would like to secure
passage to Jerusalem in one of your caravans."

Iqbal scratched his cheek through his thick black beard. "We are transporting a large shipment of wheat in a caravan leaving in three days. You can travel with them. I will arrange for three camels, a small tent, and food to sustain you for the journey. But of course there would be a small fee," the cagey Nabataean observed.

"Yes, my friend. We will pay you in advance," replied Ezra.

The deal was struck after the customary bargaining, and Jacob paid the fee from the purse given him by Tatius Lucianus.

"You carry Roman money," Iqbal said.

"Yes," replied Ezra. "We have traveled from Rome."

"What took you three to Rome?" he asked.

Ezra gave a careful answer to the curious Nabataean, not offering any expanded explanation. "We have been on a diplomatic mission."

"I saw our esteemed leader and your friend Pontius Pilate at the bazaar just yesterday," Iqbal remarked offhandedly.

Ezra made more small talk. He and Iqbal finally shook hands and bade each other farewell.

Ezra led Jacob and Levi down the street. When he was sure they would not be overheard, Ezra addressed his two companions. "That was valuable information Iqbal gave us. We might be able to arrange a meeting with Pontius Pilate here. If that is possible, and we can determine that Jesus is still in Galilee, as we've heard, then you could travel directly there and save the detour through Jerusalem."

"How do we secure a meeting with Pilate?" Jacob asked.

"Leave that to me," Ezra said. "Why don't you walk back to the dock to find a place to wait? I will join you shortly," he instructed his two companions. He started to walk away and then thought of one more thing. "There are more soldiers here than in Jerusalem. Be sure you avoid them and don't do anything to bring attention to yourselves." He turned then and strode off confidently, his staff clicking on the cobblestones.

Jacob and Levi walked back toward the docks. On their way they purchased food in the bazaar. Greek was being spoken everywhere, so no one seemed surprised at their use of that language. Beginning to feel somewhat more at ease with their new look in their new country, they took their food and walked leisurely to the dock. They noticed four auxiliary soldiers on the wharf, so they veered away from them, continuing down the rocky incline away from the main street and sat on some flat rocks near the sea. Other people were also eating and enjoying the mild day.

The soldiers were talking to two Jewish men. Jacob kept one eye on the soldiers, whom, because of their appearance, he suspected had been recruited by the Romans from among the Hellenized residents of the area. Suddenly a soldier shoved one of the Jews to the ground. His companions responded with raucous laughter. As the other Jewish man bent to help his friend stand up, another soldier kicked him, sending him toppling to the ground as well. The soldiers guffawed. The two Jews, wanting to avoid further trouble, stayed on the ground, despite the soldiers' taunting them to get up. Jacob and Levi had seen such behavior all too often among auxiliary troops. Too often undisciplined, such troops frequently acted like thugs, terrorizing other inhabitants, who would never fight back for fear of further punishment. Jacob had punished soldiers under his command who behaved in such a way.

Soon the soldiers lost interest in the two men and walked along the road toward Jacob and Levi, stopping just above where they were sitting. Jacob kept his back to them and encouraged Levi to do the same. The soldiers stood above them about twenty yards away and made loud, disparaging remarks in Greek about the Jews' dirty beards and dirty robes. Their crude language could be heard by everyone on the small beach. It was obvious the soldiers were trying to pick another fight.

A woman sitting not far from Jacob and Levi finally could take no more and stood, humbly asking them to stop. The soldiers went silent for a moment, then laughed and peppered her with demeaning remarks and more foul language. The woman turned away. Then one of the soldiers climbed down the rocks and seized her head covering. Throwing it aside, he grabbed a handful of her hair and roughly jerked her head back.

"Who are you to talk to us that way?" he yelled in her face.

The woman was visibly terrified, and tears freely streamed down her face. The others on the beach sat frozen, unable or afraid to go to her aid. The soldier stood within a few feet of where Jacob and Levi sat. Observing the unkempt soldier's drunkenness and the stains on his uniform, Jacob had finally had enough and decided to intervene, but Levi spoke before he could move.

"Leave her alone," Levi said in Greek. "She has done nothing to you. Go in peace."

The soldier released his grasp on the woman's hair and turned to face Levi. "And who are you to tell me to do anything, Jew?" He spat at Levi's feet.

"I am her friend," Levi said. "We have come to enjoy a small meal in this peaceful place. Go in peace."

Jacob was surprised at the quiet restraint with which Levi confronted the soldier. Jacob had had something else in mind entirely.

The soldier stepped closer to Levi. The strong stench of wine and stale sweat made him all the more obnoxious. "Friend," the young soldier mimicked Levi, "I suggest you shut your filthy Jew mouth and stay out of my business."

Levi stood up. The soldier took a step back as he sized up the giant standing before him. "Your job is to keep the Roman peace," Levi said softly. "This woman poses no threat to you or anyone else. You and your drunken threats to weak people are an embarrassment to Rome." He glared at the soldier threateningly.

"What do you know about Rome, barbarian?" the soldier challenged Levi.

"More than you do," Levi answered.

The soldier reached blindly for his sword, but before he could get his hands around the hilt, Levi planted a massive fist squarely in his face, sending him tumbling unconscious backward onto the sand. Levi took the sword and the dagger out of the fallen man's belt, then shouted at the three remaining auxiliaries, who were standing motionless above him. "This drunken boy is unworthy of the weapons of Rome. Give him a sword when he grows up and understands who his real enemy is." Levi turned and with all his strength heaved the sword and dagger out into the water. He stood shoulder to shoulder with Jacob, looking upward at the three soldiers and waiting for their attack. But it never came. They were either too shocked by what they witnessed, too drunk, or simply too cowardly to engage the two large, muscular Jews. Instead, they walked off, leaving their dazed companion lying on the sand.

"They'll be back with reinforcements," Jacob said. "We must go."

Levi agreed. They gathered their things and clambered back up to the main road. The auxiliary soldiers were nowhere to be seen. The handful of people on the beach followed Jacob and Levi up the hill. They scattered but not before thanking them and warning them to hide or, better yet, leave Caesarea entirely. The woman mistreated by the soldier approached Levi, tearfully expressing gratitude in a language he didn't understand but that sounded something like the Hebrew of the prayers he had learned from Ezra.

He uncomfortably accepted her thanks and then in Greek urged her to leave quickly before the soldiers returned. She scurried off.

"Well," said Jacob, "we've done exactly what Ezra told us not to do. We've drawn attention to ourselves, and we've definitely engaged the enemy." He was surprised at his own choice of words in referring to Roman soldiers as the enemy.

Levi and Jacob took off running. Suddenly Levi stopped in his tracks and grabbed Jacob by the arm. "We shouldn't run. That will just draw more attention to us, plus we need to wait for Ezra. He won't know where we are."

"You're right." Jacob paused for a moment. "The ship. We can return to the ship. The soldiers won't find us there. We can watch the street that runs along the wharf from there, and when Ezra returns, he will be easy to spot." Without a word the two walked quickly back down the wharf to the Egyptian ship they had arrived on.

The crew was still unloading, but Akhom was gone. The sailors greeted the two returning Jews with smiles. Jacob explained that they had become separated from Ezra and asked if they could wait onboard out of the way. It seemed a logical story, and the sailors allowed them to board the ship. They sat near the bow below the bulkhead. They wouldn't be spotted easily there but could watch for Ezra.

An hour passed before Levi spotted their mentor far down the wharf, walking slowly toward their ship. He was looking from side to side, wondering where his friends were.

"Let's just wait till he gets closer rather than risk being discovered by someone looking for us," Jacob said.

Soon Ezra was within hailing distance. Jacob stood and

waved his arm to get Ezra's attention without shouting. Ezra saw Jacob and walked briskly toward the ship. Jacob motioned for him to board. Ezra sighed and walked up the gangplank to where the two men sat.

"What is this all about?" he asked, standing above them with his staff firmly at his side.

Jacob and Levi looked up at him like two puppies caught stealing meat from the table. Jacob sheepishly began to tell their mentor the story.

Ezra looked at his two contrite students and laughed. "So it was *you* they were talking about in town." He smiled broadly.

"What did you hear?" asked Levi.

"An old friend took me to Pontius Pilate—he is indeed in town, just as Iqbal said. While I was there, a courier arrived to notify him of an incident on the beach near the wharf. My first thought was the two of you. The courier said two Jews had attacked four Roman soldiers near the docks, leaving one dead on the beach and the others running for their lives.

Jacob and Levi looked at each other and began talking at once.

Ezra held up his hand. "One at a time," he said.

Jacob deferred to Levi, who recounted the whole story. "The soldier is not dead, but when he wakes up, he will have a serious headache for a while," Levi concluded. Jacob nodded in agreement.

Ezra sighed and sat down beside them. "I assure you this won't be the last time you witness the darker side of Roman occupation. It will be difficult for you not to interfere, but you mustn't. You must both be patient and avoid trouble, even if it comes and sits in your lap. If you don't, you jeopardize your whole mission."

Jacob and Levi both lowered their eyes and apologized.

"You need not apologize to me, my friends," Ezra continued.

"I probably would have beat them black and blue with my staff had I witnessed that kind of behavior. But we both know that the only way occupational forces can exert control is by intimidation, even at the expense of the innocent. It boosts their courage and self-esteem. What they don't understand is that it solidifies the hatred their enemy has for them and bonds the enemy together. This story will be passed around as an example that Jews can gain the upper hand if they choose. That kind of story terrifies the Romans. You two are ultimately guilty of treason against the emperor and the citizens of Rome." Ezra let the comment settle in before he smiled.

"This is probably a good place to hide for a few hours. We are meeting tonight with Pontius Pilate. I suggest you tell him exactly what happened today."

"Why should we tell him?" Levi protested.

"Because you two are most recognizable, and two of the soldiers who witnessed the incident are guards at Pilate's palace. It will soon come out that you were involved. You should tell your story truthfully and preempt any accusation," Ezra admonished.

"But the soldiers will lie. That will put us in jeopardy," Jacob objected.

"Jacob, have you so soon forgotten who you are? You are a legate of Rome. You come here with the highest credentials under the express authority of the emperor. Despite your disguise Pilate knows exactly who you are. Your word will be taken over that of drunken foot soldiers."

"Nevertheless, it is imperative you maintain your disguise," Ezra reiterated. "A Roman would never get as close to Jesus as you two need to get. Only a Jew will be able to follow him from place to place for any length of time without raising suspicion. Otherwise, you could have come as you really are. It would certainly be less complicated. I hope you understand."

Jacob nodded.

"It is bad enough that you may have compromised your identity to these Roman soldiers. We will have to make sure Pilate takes measures to hold their tongues."

21

Under cover of darkness, the three men ventured from the ship to the palace of Pontius Pilate, carefully avoiding any further encounter with soldiers. At the gates stood two guards with long spears. Jacob and Levi pulled their head coverings down low over their brows as Ezra introduced himself and his companions, stating that they had an appointment with the prefect. One of the guards acknowledged him and opened a creaky wooden gate. They stepped into a large courtyard lit with many torches. A Jewish man in a white robe met them and escorted them to the chamber where Pilate waited. Two more guards stood at attention at the entrance of the private chamber. Ezra and his two companions walked in without hesitation.

They entered a large chamber with tables and chairs placed haphazardly about. More men with white head coverings were seated in a group around one of the tables. Pilate sat in his *curule*, flanked by two guards. Ezra walked up to him, stopping just a few feet away.

"Welcome, my good friend Ezra," Pilate boomed, extending his hand. "These must be the decorated Romans you have

brought with you." Ezra winced at Pilate identifying Jacob and
Levi as Romans in front of so many dangerous ears. The guards
at Pilate's side looked curiously at the two large Jews standing in
front of them. Some of the Jewish elders sitting off to the side of
the chamber studied the three men with curious stares.

"My good prefect." Ezra inclined his head slightly. "I was hoping we could have this discussion privately." He looked around at
everyone now openly staring at them.

Pilate looked about. "Perhaps you are right." He immediately
commanded the dozen or more people to leave the chamber. The
two guards at his side didn't budge. "These two," Pilate motioned
to the guards at his side, "can be trusted."

"Very well," Ezra said. "May we be seated?"

"Yes, of course."

Ezra sat on the stone floor with his legs crossed. Jacob and
Levi sought cushions and sat, flanking Ezra. Jacob thought it odd
that they would sit at Pilate's feet like schoolchildren. Jacob's first
judgment agreed with what Ezra had shared with them during
the voyage: he did appear weak and self-conscious. Probably that
was why he sat in a high chair and kept the two guards at his
side. The senators in Rome were less pompous.

"You have made good time on your journey. I didn't expect
you for another month," Pilate began.

"We were able to secure passage quickly, and the winds were
generally favorable." Ezra engaged in the small talk.

"So this is the mighty General Lucius Fabius Maximus I have
heard so much about." Pilate made a limp gesture toward Jacob
and Levi. "And your bodyguard?"

Jacob didn't like the tone of Pilate's voice. He took a deep
breath and slowly lowered his head covering to expose his
full head of hair and chiseled face covered with a scruffy
brown beard. "This is my good friend and deputy commander,

Androcles. He is not a bodyguard; he is my friend and equal. He shares the risk and commitment to the success of our mission." Ezra admired Jacob's directness and diplomacy.

"I see," Pilate said. "A general and a commander—Rome has taken me seriously for once," he laughed. "When you first entered, despite knowing who you are, I was wondering why Ezra had brought with him two ordinary Jews." He laughed, but no one joined him.

"Rome takes any potential threat to the empire seriously, governor. They have sent the best," Jacob said confidently.

"Yes, they have, Lucius Fabius Maximus. I know your father— I met him once in Rome. Gaius Valerius introduced us. Both are great senators," Pilate said condescendingly.

"It is under the direction of the good Gaius Valerius that we are here. He has given us explicit instructions." Jacob reached into his sack for the scroll given to him by the senator. He handed it to Pilate.

Pilate took a couple of minutes to read over the scroll and then handed it back. "You will be given every assistance you require, I assure you."

"You are most gracious," Jacob replied. "We have been fortunate in meeting you here in Caesarea, as it may save us a great deal of time. If you could tell us where this Jesus of Nazareth currently travels, we will be on our way as soon as possible."

"My sources tell me he is in Capernaum, a small city on the northwestern shore of the Sea of Galilee. At last report he was thereabouts preaching and gathering forces," Pilate replied.

"Forces?" Jacob questioned.

"Well," Pilate said as he adjusted his position in the chair, "he has become more popular with each passing day. My informants tell me he talks of a new kingdom. They tell me his followers call him Messiah and refer to him as king of the Jews. Members of the Sanhedrin complain to me almost daily that he blasphemes their religion by intimating he is the Son of God, which they consider a crime punishable by death under their law. Frankly, I don't care much for the Sanhedrin; they are a self-serving group and seem threatened by this Nazarene, but I take what they tell me under advisement. You well know that one reason Rome succeeds in bringing foreign lands into the empire is that we let the people rule themselves. We stay out of their religions and their internal workings. We are there solely for the taxes and other wealth to be collected for Rome. As long as the people stay in order, the system works fine. But when I hear rumors of a messiah, or king, or whatever this Nazarene calls himself coming into power, I have to be concerned for the security of Rome, especially as his forces increase. I don't care about the charges of blasphemy—they don't concern me. What causes me unrest is potential peril to Rome."

"I understand your unease, governor," Jacob nodded, knowing full well that Pilate was concerned more for himself than for the good of the empire.

Pilate added, "There has been a disturbing development recently, and I am wondering how far it might resonate. Word recently came to me that Herod Antipas, tetrarch of Galilee, imprisoned and then, at the request of his new wife, beheaded a Jewish prophet named John the Baptist. It is said that many Jews thought John was the long-awaited Messiah. Surprisingly, multitudes followed that rough, uncultured man—he too preached of a kingdom to come. I am further told this John the Baptist was a cousin to Jesus. It was reported that John flatly denied being the Messiah, instead maintained there was one coming more powerful than he, referring to this Jesus of Nazareth. Most of John's followers now follow Jesus like sheep following a trail of green grass. I am concerned that the death of this John the Baptist will solidify these zealot Jews and bring them to an armed uprising.

Jews are fickle and dangerous people, present company excluded."
Pilate smiled weakly at Ezra.

"The matter appears complicated. What of the reported miracles?" Jacob asked Pilate.

"Many have been reported. I think they are fabricated by his followers to increase his legend and inflame the Jews with a false confidence. The Jews will seize any hope of liberation." Pilate stood impatiently. "It's not wise for this Jesus to be talking about a new kingdom, professing some godly power, and gathering sizable support in the face of Rome. You two are here to investigate what I have heard and bring me the truth. I don't trust the Jews, and I don't trust what this Nazarene is up to. I need to hear the truth from the mouth of a Roman."

"We will do our best to bring you a truthful report. The sooner we leave the sooner we can return with that in hand," Jacob replied.

Pilate sat down wearily and addressed Ezra. "Is Iqbal the Nabataean an acquaintance of yours?" he asked.

"Yes. We have paid him to join a caravan that leaves for Jerusalem in three days. If Jesus is in Galilee, as you say, it is better my friends go there directly. I will change the arrangements tomorrow," Ezra said.

"Good luck getting that horse thief to give back any of your money." Pilate laughed.

"I am sure Iqbal will accommodate us," Ezra responded curtly. "Thank you for your concern."

"Is there anything else I can do for you?" Pilate asked.

Jacob spoke. "There is one small issue." He glanced at Ezra, who nodded. "There was an incident earlier today at the wharf." Jacob recounted the incident to Pilate.

Pilate guffawed. "That is a story those auxiliaries won't be repeating—being bested by two upstart Jews. I should do them

the favor of telling them they were defeated by a decorated general and a deputy commander of Rome. That would at least make
them feel better about their failure." He pounded his fist on his
thigh, his laughter echoing throughout the chamber. "These
young auxiliary soldiers need to be taught a lesson occasionally,
and they learned one today they won't soon forget. I assure you
there will be no retaliation." He dismissed the three men with a
wave of his hand. The two guards escorted them promptly to the
front gate. They could hear Pilate laughing in the background.

Outside Jacob and Levi looked at Ezra for direction. "Friends,
I hoped for better hospitality from Pilate, but it appears he has
forgotten his manners. It looks as if we sleep under the stars
tonight."

22

The next morning Ezra arranged with Iqbal for Jacob and Levi to accompany a caravan traveling to Damascus. The caravan would head northeast to meet up with the main trade route at Capernaum.

The jovial Iqbal marked notes on his scroll and with animated hand movements gave directions in Arabic to a worker, who scurried off to do his bidding. "My friends, everything will be ready when you return. But don't be late. My caravan leader is a very impatient man and will not wait for you," Iqbal warned.

Ezra thanked his friend, and the three left to buy food at the bazaar. They found a small grove of trees nearby where they could eat. Ezra sat cross-legged against the trunk of a gnarled olive tree. "Your adventure begins, my friends," he said as he took a drink of water.

"I think we have had sufficient adventure already," responded Jacob.

"Indeed, it has been an interesting journey so far," said Ezra. "I must caution you both again," he said, leaning forward for emphasis. "You will witness many injustices. I suggest you avoid any future conflict and walk away if it comes to you." He looked at both of his students. "Do you understand?"

Jacob and Levi nodded in agreement.

"It will be hard for you at times. You are good men, but you alone cannot fix what is broken in my country. Gather your information. Report it truthfully to Pilate and to Rome. If you choose to question Roman leadership, that is your prerogative, but do it with words, not with weapons." Ezra leaned back against the tree and closed his eyes. With a sigh he said, "It will be good to go home."

The three spent the remainder of the morning resting under the sparse shade of the tree. At the appointed time they met back up with Iqbal, who greeted them with the enthusiasm of an old friend.

"Come, I want you to meet my business partner and the man who will lead your caravan." Iqbal led Jacob and Levi, with Ezra trailing, to meet Alhasan, a tall Nabataean with piercing eyes set deep in a weathered face. He had no time for small talk and merely nodded to the group when he was introduced. He continued to secure cargo on an uncooperative camel.

Iqbal led Jacob and Levi to a camel that was sitting languidly, chewing its cud. "Have you ever ridden a camel, my friends?" he asked. "You will find them pleasant traveling companions, but never turn your back on them." He laughed loudly, exposing yellowed teeth. He gave the two quick instructions on mounting and dismounting and some one-word Arabic commands for handling the camels. He showed them how to secure their belongings to the rear or side of the wood-and-cloth saddle.

"Alhasan has packed the food and tents on the other camels. He will supply you with the necessities as the journey progresses. It should take about three days to reach Capernaum. When you decide you have reached your destination, let Alhasan know, and you can go your own way."

Besides himself and Levi, Jacob noted about a dozen men, two women, and two small boys traveling in the caravan. Four of the men worked with Alhasan securing cargo to the twenty or more camels resting nearby. Jacob determined they would heed Ezra's counsel to keep to themselves and not interact with their fellow travelers.

Alhasan whistled, and the men barked orders to the camels. They reluctantly struggled to their feet. It was time to go.

Iqbal handed Alhasan a small package, which he tucked safely into a pocket on the side of the saddle on his camel.

"My friends, enjoy your journey," Iqbal said as he scurried by to attend to other business.

Jacob turned to Ezra. "So, now we part, teacher."

"It is time. My work is done," Ezra replied. "You have been good students. I wish you well and hope you find what you are looking for." Ezra smiled at Jacob and Levi, and they each embraced Ezra affectionately.

"Will we see you again?" Jacob asked.

"If your journey should take you to Jerusalem, I hope you will find me. You have a home there with me," Ezra replied. He grasped Jacob by the arm, looked him in the eye, and said, "Don't forget your prayers." They both laughed, but Jacob knew Ezra was not joking. He warmly embraced his mentor once more, then Ezra raised his staff in a final salute and walked away.

Jacob and Levi struggled to climb aboard their respective camels and were able to hang on as a handler gave the command for the camels to stand. It wasn't the most comfortable seat, and Levi thought of jumping off and walking. They both settled into their saddles, adjusting their robes and the cloth and leather beneath them. The handlers passed up the reins, and the caravan was off to the slow rocking gait of the beasts.

For the next two days, the caravan proceeded uninterrupted, stopping only for sleep and water. Jacob and Levi kept to themselves, not engaging with the others in the caravan, as Ezra had instructed.

Just outside of Cana, at Alhasan's order, the caravan came to an unexpected halt. One of the handlers trotted back, telling the travelers to move their camels to the side of the road. Jacob could see a cloud of dust in the distance. As the cloud got closer, he made out a large group of men on horseback coming toward them. His first thought was of brigands. Were they being attacked in the open by a band of armed robbers? He reached for his missing sword and settled for resting his hand on the small dagger tucked in his sash. He exchanged glances with Levi, who was doing the same. He instinctively began to assess the terrain and look for high ground and cover. The men on horseback appeared to be riding at a leisurely pace and in rank two by two, not in the wild gallop of an attacking horde.

As they came closer, Jacob realized it was a cohort of auxiliary soldiers, probably raised in Caesarea and passing through the tetrarchy of Herod Antipas. His chest tightened as they approached, their breastplates and helmets reflecting in the sun. The leader held up his hand as they arrived at the front of the caravan. One of the soldiers rode over to Alhasan, who remained seated on his camel. A conversation ensued, and Alhasan handed the soldier a scroll, no doubt papers authorizing their travel. The soldier looked over the papers carefully, then handed them back. There was more conversation, then he rejoined his men, raised his hand, and the mounted soldiers slowly rode forward. They were about fifty strong; the soldiers stared the travelers down as they passed. Jacob and Levi were careful not to make eye contact with any of them. Jacob could feel condescending eyes upon him and struggled to maintain his composure. He himself had been in similar situations, policing foreigners in strange lands, validating travel papers, and enforcing occupation by intimidation. He was seeing the other side firsthand. It came full circle to him why he and his men had been so hated.

The auxiliaries passed without incident, and Jacob breathed easier. Alhasan once again sounded the order to move forward, and the caravan slowly lumbered back into motion.

Two hours passed, and the caravan came to a small rise. As Jacob reached the summit, before him was the full view of the Sea of Galilee. Many in the party paused to take in the wonder of the large blue lake cupped in the palms of surrounding hills; it was beautiful. Alhasan continued forward without pause. He whistled sharply and with fervent hand signals urged the company to keep moving. It was approaching late afternoon, and he wanted to make the shoreline of Galilee before nightfall.

Dusk brought them to the outskirts of Capernaum. Levi quickly set up the tent, and Jacob retrieved the night's ration of food. After eating, they decided to take advantage of the bright moonlit night to inspect the seaside town.

The small fishing fleet was idle on the pebbly beach. The evening was warm and the water calm. The moon rose in the east, leaving a silver streak across the lake. There was a certain peace about the place that appealed to Jacob. They completed their tour and went back to the camp for the night.

In the morning, the caravan was up and on the move early. Levi gathered their belongings while Jacob said good-bye to the camel handlers.

"You leave us?" said the deep voice of Alhasan.

Jacob and Levi turned to see the tall Alhasan standing behind them.

"Yes, our journey ends here." Jacob extended his hand in friendship.

An uncomfortable moment passed before Alhasan clasped Jacob's hand. "We will pass by here again with the coming of two new moons," Alhasan said. "If you choose to journey back, you are welcome to join us." He lifted his arms and with palms up, bowed his head as if blessing them, then walked away.

Jacob turned to Levi. "Let's go find him." They strode confidently into Capernaum, walking leisurely through the dusty streets. The low houses and buildings were constructed of dark gray basalt, which increased the heat in the narrow streets. A soft, warm breeze met them as they came out of the maze of buildings onto the hard rocky beach. The boats were already long gone, off for the day's fishing. Two men were repairing the hull of one overturned boat; another was mending nets that hung on a large wooden frame. A few men sat idly on makeshift chairs in open shelters where the counting and processing of the day's catch was done. They would be busy later in the afternoon when the boats returned. Two racks, made of poplar branches laid across a waist-high framework, approximately six feet wide and extending some fifty feet, ran parallel to each other and held hundreds of fish drying in the sun. The air was filled with the smell of fish.

Jacob continued on to the water's edge. He wrapped his robe around himself and stepped into the shallows up to his knees. The cool water was refreshing. He held his staff in the crook of his arm and removed his head covering. After dipping it into the water and wringing it out, he wiped the sweat from his face and neck. He wanted to throw off his robe entirely and bathe. Jacob swished his sandaled feet in the water to rid them of the built-up dirt and grime. Levi did the same, then kicked water on his friend. Jacob hurriedly moved away, certain that a wrestling match would shortly ensue; he didn't want to make a scene their first day in Capernaum. Like a big kid, Levi chased Jacob out of the water, kicking water on him again. The two men scraping the hull of a fishing boat nearby stopped to watch in amusement.

Jacob approached the two weathered men and spoke to them in Greek. "My name is Jacob. This is my friend, Levi." The shorter men looked up suspiciously at the two formidable strangers speaking to them in Greek. "We have come a long way to seek Jesus of Nazareth. Do you know where he can be found?" Jacob asked.

The men looked at each other. Finally one responded, "Where do you come from?"

"Egypt," answered Jacob.

"News of Jesus has traveled far," the thinner, more muscular one said.

"Do you know where he can be found?" Jacob repeated.

There was a pause as the fisherman laid his metal scraper on the hull of the boat. "He and his many followers have caused quite a commotion with their need for food and shelter. They come down here to the shore and get in the way. I have heard that Jesus went north to Bethsaida and many, like a trail of ants, have followed him—we have enjoyed the peace and quiet of their absence. I hope they stay a long time." He looked at his companion and laughed, revealing sparse brown teeth. "Are you disciples too?" he asked.

Jacob weighed his answer. "We are just curious."

The man picked up his scraper and returned to his work. "You've come a long way merely to satisfy curiosity."

"How far is Bethsaida from here?" Jacob asked, ignoring the sarcasm.

"If you leave now, you could be there before sunset." The fisherman spat, then resumed his scraping, dismissing the strangers.

Jacob and Levi made their way to the main road.

"We should have stayed with the caravan," Levi said as he adjusted the satchel over his shoulder.

"How were we to know he wasn't here?" Jacob responded. He followed Levi as they began walking north on the dusty road.

"We haven't talked much of home," Jacob said, trying to make conversation as they strode along, staffs in hand.

"Our home has always been a long road to a battle somewhere," Levi responded. "We've spent more time on campaigns in the last fifteen years than we've spent in Rome." Jacob sensed a bit of melancholy in Levi's voice as he added, "I'm not sure where my home is anymore."

"You seem like you're enjoying yourself," Jacob observed.

There was a pause as Levi thought for a moment. "I do feel a little more at ease . . . as long as we don't sail into the path of any more pirates. However, I don't think I will ever get used to not carrying a sword," Levi said. Jacob laughed.

"You have a stick now." Jacob rapped Levi on the shoulder with his staff. Levi turned, and the sparring was on. Both men grabbed their staffs and, with boyish grins and hands spread wide, began jousting for position. The staffs clacked and banged together as each tried to connect with a friendly body blow. They kicked up sand and dust and danced around, laughing and exchanging friendly insults. Jacob got his legs briefly tangled in his long robe, which wasn't ideal for close-quarter combat. In adjusting the material, Jacob took his eyes off Levi for an instant. Levi saw his opening and pounced, tackling his friend to the ground. They struggled and laughed in each other's grasp. Jacob finally broke away and jumped again to his feet. He stopped dead in his tracks just as Levi retrieved his staff and swung it around, popping Jacob on the shin. Jacob winced but his attention was fixed on a small crowd of men that had appeared over the rise a short distance away.

The men walked, peacefully encircled around a taller man who was talking and moving his hands gracefully for emphasis as he walked.

Jacob stood up straight, forgetting about the sting and bruise he would certainly see on the front of his leg tomorrow. "It's him," he said quietly.

Levi rolled over and collected himself to his knees, following Jacob's stare. A cloud of dust arose behind the smaller group of men. Hundreds of people following the men suddenly came into view, looking like an army cresting the hill.

"It's him; it's Jesus," Jacob repeated excitedly, still frozen in his tracks.

The mass of humanity was about two hundred yards off. Jacob and Levi dusted themselves off and proceeded along the road toward them. He wanted to make sure Jesus and his men didn't duck into a building before he could get a closer look. As the mass of people got closer, Jacob and Levi stood against a stone wall and waited. Jacob counted about ten men immediately surrounding Jesus. These must be the apostles he had heard about. As they got closer, he could hear their voices. Jesus occasionally nodded his head and smiled.

Jacob's eyes were fixed on Jesus; he appeared happy and at peace. He moved with an air of confidence and authority Jacob had seen in men of power in Rome—but without the Romans' flamboyance and arrogance. He could immediately see why men would be drawn to him. He wore a white tunic and a simple brown robe and headcovering that gave him relief from the hot sun. He was dressed as humbly as the men he walked with. He had a full beard, and his long, dark hair framed his tanned face. Jesus passed within a few feet of Jacob and turned his head.

Their eyes met for a brief moment, and Jacob felt himself transfixed by the most kind and crystal clear eyes he had ever gazed into. Jesus smiled warmly and acknowledged the stranger leaning against the wall. Jacob felt weak; warmth flooded his soul, and tears began forming in his eyes. He instinctively knew this was no rebel or warrior. This was a humble man of peace. The feeling was overwhelming, as if he had been immersed in a warm bath.

Jesus and the apostles moved on, and the horde of people began passing quietly: men, women, and some children. This was certainly not the making of an uprising. These were ordinary people, not warriors. Many smiled at Jacob as they walked by. Most walked with heads bowed silently in reverent contemplation.

Jacob and Levi fell in with the walking crowds, and followed them back through the town and to the shore again. The fishing village was soon flooded with people, and the thin shoreline once again returned to being a makeshift camp. Jesus was nowhere to be seen, having escaped, no doubt, to the residence of friends somewhere in town. Jacob and Levi walked through the people back to the waterline and sat on the hull of a small overturned boat, watching the spectacle of humanity gather.

The afternoon wind picked up and the people, sensing Jesus was not returning to preach, began to seek shelter away from the shoreline. Many moved into the surrounding countryside seeking the protection of the hills west of town. Jacob and Levi stayed on the beach with the few who remained. Fishermen were starting to return from their day's work. Many of them were under full sail until they neared the shore, where the fishermen beached their crafts, securing them on the rocky shore.

23

Jacob and Levi watched the hard-working fishermen as they unloaded the day's catch into large baskets. Within an hour, about a dozen boats lined the shore and were in various stages of unloading fish or drying and repairing nets. Jacob looked out to the horizon and saw a small speck of sail approaching and sensed something was awry. The sail, small and irregular, was not raised to full extension on the center mast. As the boat got closer, he could see that the mast had been broken and what was left was lashed together and holding up a tattered sail that caught just enough wind to drive the heavily laden boat slowly ashore. The boat moved sluggishly, like a large piece of driftwood on the water. As the craft came to within fifty yards of shore, a sudden shift in the wind collapsed the sail, and the boat was suddenly dead in the water. Two men manning the small craft stood and began waving their arms frantically. Jacob thought he could hear them calling out.

The fishermen on shore looked up but seemed hesitant to help. The boat was held offshore by the uncooperative wind and the lack of sail sufficient to harness it. It was obvious to Jacob that the boat was under duress as the two-man crew continued waving for assistance. Jacob and Levi stood and looked around to see if one of the fishing boats would shove off and set sail to lend aid—no one moved. The boat drifted to within thirty yards of the beach, but the water was too deep to walk out with a rope to help. The two men were obviously shouting for help. The wind shifted again and began to push the boat south along the shoreline and further out into the lake. Something had to be done immediately or the boat and the men in it might not make it to shore. Jacob could now see clearly that the mast had been snapped in half, and the boat was at the mercy of the offshore wind. Before Jacob could make a move, however, Levi had shed his robe and tunic and, clad only in a loincloth and sandals, run into the water.

A crowd had gathered upon hearing the cries of distress coming from the boat, but they stood and watched rather than attempting to rescue the imperiled fishermen. When Levi ran past them and into the water, they pointed and gasped and began to chatter loudly among themselves.

The fickle wind shifted again, and the boat momentarily stopped its drifting offshore. Hard-swimming Levi reached the boat within a couple of minutes. Jacob dropped his staff and removed his robe. He girded his tunic around his waist and walked into the water, shouting encouragement to his friend. Levi reached the side of the boat and with one hand grasped the side rail. A conversation ensued, which resulted in one of the men handing the end of a rope to Levi, who began swimming back to shore. Jacob couldn't believe Levi actually seemed to think he could tow the heavy boat back to shore, but the wind had subsided and he was making slow progress. Jacob removed his own tunic, threw it onto the beach, and dived into the water. In a short time he had reached Levi, who was straining to swim with the rope in his hand, pulling the boat slowly along. Jacob grabbed the rope as well and with renewed energy, they both worked to tow the boat to safety. They could hear the encouraging shouts of the small crowd that had gathered along the beach. Still, no one launched another boat or ventured into the water to assist.

After a few minutes of exhausting swimming, Jacob's feet reached bottom. He yelled at Levi, who was still swimming. Levi stopped and stood on the bottom in about five feet of water. They both dug their toes into the muddy, rocky bottom and made better headway. Jacob jokingly said to Levi, "Ezra would tell us we are drawing too much attention to ourselves." They both laughed. When the water was only waist deep, two other men waded out to help them tow in the boat the rest of the way.

Once the boat was secured, Jacob and Levi stepped aside as people began to help the fishermen from the boat. Jacob remembered Ezra telling him about the conservative customs of the Jews, that their culture wasn't as comfortable with the uncovered body as Romans were, so they retrieved their tunics and robes and, despite being soaking wet, dressed. There was a commotion near the disabled craft, and Jacob saw that the men were struggling to remove from the boat a man with a bloody bandage around his head. Impetuously, Levi moved forward and scooped up the young man from the grip of the unorganized effort. He cradled him in his arms and looked for direction from an older man who jumped down from the boat. The crowd parted as the older man grabbed Levi by the arm and guided him toward the town. Jacob fell in behind them with a young boy who was weeping as he trailed the older man closely.

The older man spoke rapidly as they walked. Neither Jacob nor Levi could understand a word he said. Jacob finally addressed the old man in Greek and asked how they could help him.

The old man apologized and introduced himself as Jershon

and in somewhat halting Greek began to explain the circumstances. "Our sail went slack, then without warning, a strong gust of wind filled the sail and snapped the mast." He motioned to the man Levi was carrying. "My son was hit in the head when the mast fell. My younger son, Seth, and I have been struggling for hours to get to shore." The old man looked apprehensively at his eldest son cradled limply in Levi's arms. "He has lost a lot of blood." He reached out for the dangling hand of his wounded son and pointed Levi down a side street. "Our home is nearby." Jacob could hear the emotion and helplessness in the old man's voice. He walked up beside him and put his arm around his shoulder for comfort and support. "Thank you, young man," Jershon murmured quietly as he walked rapidly, his head down.

Jershon led them down a narrow street for about fifty yards, bringing them to a weathered doorway where he bolted inside and began calling out instructions. Levi followed him inside, carrying the wounded man. From outside the doorway, Jacob heard a scream. He entered the humble home and a short, rotund woman, her hand over her mouth, was crying and hastily clearing a spot for Levi to place the man. A small girl entered the room and started to cry as she clutched the older woman.

Levi laid the man on a low bed as a young woman came out from the back of the house into the room. At the sight of the bloody man lying on the bed, she released a tearful moan and collapsed to the floor. The older couple together gathered her up and leaned her against the side of the bed.

The older woman then carefully removed the wrapping from the man's head and gasped. She began to shake and sob; it was obvious she would be no help in assessing the wound and dressing it. Jacob had seen plenty of bloody wounds in the battlefield so he stepped in, knelt at the man's side, and asked in Greek for warm water and rags. Jershon repeated Jacob's request in the language that sounded somewhat like Hebrew, and the older woman collected herself and scurried off, the younger girl close behind. Jacob removed the rest of the bloodied dressing and turned the man's head to the side to get a better look at the cause of the bleeding. There was a deep, ugly four-inch gash behind his left ear. He was most likely unconscious from the blow and now weakened from blood loss. Jacob lifted the torn flap of skin behind Lamech's ear and, with his finger, carefully felt around the deep cut. He was encouraged upon discovering that the skull had not been fractured. He would clean and dress the wound, and they would have to wait for him to regain consciousness—Jacob hoped for his family's sake that he would.

He washed the wound clean with warm water and patted it dry. Naomi collected herself enough to prepare a poultice of ground herbs to dress the wound. Jacob placed it gently over the cut, then began wrapping Lamech's head with a clean cloth to secure the poultice and cover the wound. When Jacob finished, Naomi stepped in and washed her son's face and neck, covered him with blankets, and made him comfortable in the bed. Raisa, who had fainted earlier, had come to and was sobbing quietly in the arms of Jershon, who was trying to comfort her. Jacob and Levi stood aside uncomfortably, not knowing what to do.

Jershon said gratefully, "I apologize for my earlier rudeness. Thank you, my sons, from the bottom of my heart. Our family will always be grateful."

Speaking in Greek, Jershon introduced his family to Jacob and Levi: Naomi, his wife; his younger son, Seth; and his younger daughter, Esther. He explained that the injured man was Lamech, his eldest son, and introduced his daughter-in-law, Raisa. She stood, tears streaming down her face and expressed her gratitude in the language they soon learned was Aramaic.

Jacob and Levi nodded politely and smiled. She knelt at the side of her husband and held his seemingly lifeless hand.

"Please, tell us your names and where you are from." Jershon gestured to Jacob and Levi, inviting them to sit down on a bench near the entry.

Jacob was more nervous than he had been a month ago in reporting to the emperor Tiberius and the Senate in Rome. He timidly began. "My name is Jacob. This is my brother, Levi. We have recently traveled from Egypt. We arrived in Capernaum just this morning."

"Your timely arrival is our good fortune." Jershon smiled and clapped his hands. "Please, you must stay and eat. Do you have lodging?" he asked.

Jacob and Levi looked sheepishly at each other. "No, we are just passing through," Jacob quietly responded.

"You must eat and stay at least one night with us. I see by the crowds that the rabbi has returned. There will be no place to sleep. You must stay with us." Jershon was emphatic.

Naomi came forward and with tears in her eyes, she thanked them and looked longingly at her motionless son.

"He should be all right," Jacob tried to assure her. "I have seen wounds like this before; they are not serious. He will sleep awhile and will wake up with a sore head, but he will be fine."

"How do you know this?" Jershon asked.

Jacob thought quickly, calculating his answer. "I have seen wounds like this on ships. They bleed profusely, but the wound in your son's head isn't that deep, and the bones are not damaged."

"Do you work on ships?" Naomi asked.

"We have recently traveled on ships," Jacob answered, not wanting to lie. "We really don't want to be any trouble to you. We are glad to have been able to help you today," Jacob said, trying to change the subject.

"You are no trouble to us. We owe you our lives. A meal and a night's lodging are small payment," Jershon said. Turning to Naomi, he inquired, "If the rabbi is back, where are Sariah, David, and Liora?"

"I don't know," Naomi replied.

"The rabbi?" Jacob asked. "You speak of Jesus?"

"Yes," Jershon answered. "Are you disciples?"

"No," Jacob answered. "We are just curious. We were on our way to Bethsaida and met him coming into town."

"Then will you be staying here for a few days?" Jershon asked.

"We haven't decided yet. We will probably head back to Jerusalem soon," Jacob answered.

"Well, you are welcome to stay here as long as you are in Capernaum," Jershon declared.

The front door flew open with a loud bang, and a crying, distressed young woman burst into the room. It was Sariah. "We went first to the shore, hoping to meet you coming home and heard that Lamech had been hurt," she sobbed, seeing him lying on the bed with his head bandaged. "Will he be all right?" she asked as she knelt down next to Raisa, hugging her.

"These men say he will be," answered Jershon. Sariah hadn't noticed the two strangers in her home. Jershon made introductions as Naomi tried to comfort Sariah, who was still upset at seeing her injured brother.

Jershon stood to embrace his niece and nephew, who were standing in the entry to the small room. "Jacob, Levi, this is my nephew David and my niece Liora." Jacob shook David's hand, then turned to Liora, standing in the sunlit doorway. He could see only her shadowy figure with the bright sun to her back. Liora shut the door behind her and pulled back her head covering. As Jacob's eyes refocused in the dimmer light, he was immediately struck by her beauty: her light olive skin, almond-shaped eyes, and high cheekbones were framed in long, dark hair flowing over her narrow shoulders. He didn't know whether he should bow or shake her hand. He couldn't make any words come out of his mouth, so he simply stared and smiled at her. Liora smiled at the two strangers as she entered the room, barely taking note of them—too concerned for the well-being of her cousin, lying on the bed with his head bandaged. She knelt beside Sariah and Raisa and asked what had happened.

Jacob turned to Jershon and said, "You have a large family, and we will be an imposition. We appreciate your invitation, but please let us make lodging arrangements somewhere else."

"Nonsense. There are no other arrangements to be made. You will stay here." Jershon was firm.

Jacob and Levi nodded in agreement, feeling like children being reprimanded by their father.

Jershon then recounted the story to everyone: how they set sail to come home, and the wind had turned fierce. Lamech stood to furl the sail. As he slackened the ropes, a sudden and severe gust of wind filled the sail, causing the mast to snap in half. The mast fell and the boom swung around precariously, hitting him in the back of the head. Lamech went down hard, falling inside the boat, fortunately. He was bleeding, but Jershon and Seth had to secure the sail and dangling mast before they could attend to him. The wind whipped the waves, almost capsizing them twice. Jershon tore a piece off the bottom of his tunic and had Seth hold it on the back of Lamech's head to stop the bleeding as he lay unconscious among the fish in the bottom of the hull. Jershon thought he might be dead, but Seth said he was breathing. The strong wind threatened to blow them to the eastern shore, but after thirty minutes or so it abated and shifted, and Jershon was able to rig a small sail to help them tack back toward Capernaum. Two hours later and fifty yards from shore, the poorly rigged sail failed and they were dead in the water, drifting eastward again. That's when they stood up and began hailing people on the shore.

Jershon knew they were doomed when the wind began slowly pushing them offshore again. He explained that the fishermen were reluctant to launch a boat to assist in a rescue, because too often, when one went out to help another on the choppy water, both boats would be lost. Jershon said he couldn't believe his eyes when he saw a man jump in the water and begin to swim toward them.

"Our fellow fishermen are watermen for sure, but they are boatmen. Swimming is not something many of us have learned to do," Jershon added for Jacob and Levi's benefit.

"When I saw a man swim up to the boat and gesture for a rope to tow us to shore, I was skeptical. No man could tow an empty boat to shore against the wind, let alone one with three men aboard and half-filled with fish. But I knew it was perhaps our only hope, so I handed a line to Levi here, who swam off as I secured the other end to the bow cleat. We actually began to move forward for a short time, and my hopes soared. But the wind picked up again, and Levi began to tire. That's when I saw another man swimming out to give us aid. That was Jacob, and between the two of them, they managed to pull us to safety. Then later, amidst the confusion on land, Levi stepped in and picked up Lamech, who is no small man, and carried him to the house. Jacob here," Jershon pointed to Jacob, "cleaned the wound and dressed it. We are truly fortunate that these two strangers happened into Capernaum today."

The family listened to Jershon's account with fascination. Seth was smiling, admiring the two muscular visitors sitting in his home.

Jacob and Levi were embarrassed, listening to Jershon extol their heroics in front of the family.

"Where were your oars?" Liora asked the question no one else had thought about. Jershon looked at his youngest son. Seth hung his head and explained he had taken the oars out the night before while cleaning the bottom of the boat and forgot to put them back. It was a mistake he sorely regretted and said would never happen again.

Naomi gathered the girls to prepare supper and left Raisa to tend to Lamech and her hungry baby.

Lamech appeared to be resting comfortably. They all trusted Jacob's word that he would wake soon; the mood in the house lightened and there was even a small bit of laughter coming from the kitchen.

David and Seth sat on the floor next to Jershon. Jacob and Levi sat back down on the bench by the door.

"Where did you learn to swim like that?" Jershon asked Levi.

"We had a lake near our home. During the hot summers when I was a young boy, each day my brothers and I would go with my father to swim after the work was finished. He was an excellent teacher, and we all learned how to swim," Levi responded.

"What work does your family do, Levi?"

"We are blacksmiths," Levi answered.

At this, David spoke up. "So am I. I have a small shop south of here in Magdala. I learned the trade from my father and brothers too." Levi smiled and nodded.

"I was thinking of talking with you, Uncle, about moving the business to Capernaum so we could be closer," David added. Jershon looked at David with his eyebrows raised.

"Well, perhaps we can discuss that later," Jershon responded.

David nodded sheepishly, embarrassed he had brought up family business in front of strangers but glad he had broached the subject with his uncle.

They heard giggling coming from the kitchen. David began to

ask Levi questions about blacksmithing. Jacob knew it had been some time since Levi had actually worked with his family. Under the circumstances, he hoped Levi wouldn't be put on the spot, but no sooner had the thought crossed his mind than Jershon asked, "Tell me more about your family, Levi."

Levi shifted uncomfortably on the bench and fiddled with his robe. Jacob tried to think of something to interject, but Levi calmly said, "They were all killed."

The mood in the room changed, and Jershon sat back, looked Levi in the eyes, and said, "I'm sorry, my son. I apologize for asking."

"You couldn't have known," Levi responded.

David and Seth stared at the floor, not wanting to make eye contact with Levi.

Jershon sighed heavily, then boldly said, "If I may ask, how did that happen?"

Levi sat quietly for a moment, looking straight ahead, and then he looked directly at Jershon. "They were killed by a band of marauders." There was a palpable silence in the entire house. Even the noise and banter in the kitchen stopped. Levi continued, "It was a long time ago. That's when I became brothers with Jacob. His father became my father."

David looked up at Levi from his seat on the floor. A tear formed in the corner of his eye, and he said, "My older brothers were killed by Roman soldiers."

Levi was stunned but managed to ask about the circumstances.

David composed himself and answered, "They were with friends in Bethsaida and were hacked down by two drunken soldiers in an argument over the shade of a tree under which they were sitting. Our father never recovered from the shock of the news. Within a week, he simply let death overcome him. I hold

Rome responsible for our father's death as well." The tears flowed freely down David's face. Jershon reached over and put his hand on his nephew's shoulder. David bowed his head sadly, remembering his loss.

Jacob felt he had been struck by lightning with David's revelation. He knew the murderers were likely Roman auxiliary soldiers, the likes of which they had encountered in Caesarea, but there would be no convincing David they weren't Romans. Then Levi did what Jacob thought was an amazing thing. He extended his hand and pulled David to his feet. They stood toe to toe, and Levi looked directly at David. "I know how painful that is for you, more than anyone here, but it's important to heal and move on." Levi then grasped David around the shoulders and embraced him. David hugged him back.

Jershon stood. "It appears we have much in common and much to give thanks for," he said.

The meal was served, and the family took seats on the blankets and cushions surrounding the low table. The family bowed their heads and joined their father in the traditional Jewish blessing. Jacob and Levi recalled the prayers Ezra had taught them and quietly followed along. When the prayer was concluded, Liora suddenly jumped to her feet and went back into the kitchen. She returned with a large urn filled with wine and began moving around the table, filling cups. When she leaned over Jacob to fill his cup, he glanced at her, trying not to be obvious. Her skin was like silk. Liora turned, and their eyes met for a split second. She inadvertently poured too much wine into his cup, and it overflowed onto the cloth in front of him. Seth and David laughed as Liora made a fuss trying to clean it up. Jacob stood to move out of her way.

Liora cleaned up the spilled wine as best she could, then faced Jacob to apologize. She looked into his eyes, and Jacob looked down at her, smiling broadly. She stared up at him, her mouth open to speak, but no words emerged. It was all she could do not to fall into him and lean against his chest. The words of her aunt rang in her head, and Liora knew. She quickly caught herself and brushed past Jacob back to the kitchen to regain her composure.

Naomi, who had been watching, followed. In the kitchen she wrapped her loving arms around her niece and whispered into her ear, "It looks like we have some work to do."

Liora smiled and looked into her aunt's eyes as tears ran down her cheeks.

Then they heard Raisa let out a short gasp. "He moved—his eyelids fluttered!" she exclaimed. Raisa had not left Lamech's side. She pushed the food away that Esther had set in front of her at the foot of the bed. Everyone gathered around Lamech. His eyelids fluttered again, then opened.

Lamech reached up and carefully placed his hand on his head behind his ear. "My head hurts. What happened?"

Naomi and Liora ran from the kitchen when Raisa shouted and knelt next to her. Naomi cried with relief and opened her arms to Jershon, who had walked over to stand by their son. Everyone was smiling and talking at once. Jacob and Levi were relieved that Lamech had revived. Levi noticed that Sariah was standing by him and had unconsciously clutched his arm with both of her hands. He looked down at her and smiled. She quickly let go of his arm and smiled back.

"God has been merciful," Jershon said as he raised his hands to the ceiling. He turned and spoke to Jacob, "You were right—he has returned to us with a good headache." Everyone laughed, and Jershon knelt to embrace his son.

A prayer of thanks was given, then Jershon explained to Lamech what had happened since he'd been knocked unconscious and embraced him again. Naomi brought a bowl of warm soup over for Raisa to feed Lamech and then, with fervent hand movements, signaled for everyone else to move back to the table. They all returned to their places and with renewed spirits began to eat and talk.

Liora knelt next to Jacob at the table and, smiling, leaned over and whispered, "Thank you."

Jacob smiled back. In the crowded space, Liora's shoulder touched his. It felt warm and wonderful—and she didn't move. The bread, soup, fish, and fruit tasted heavenly, and the company was delightful. Strangely, Jacob felt at home.

24

Jacob awoke abruptly. The house was quiet, and Levi was gone. He saw Raisa across the room, lying next to Lamech and nursing the baby, so he arose quietly.

As he stood, Raisa whispered, "They are gone."

Puzzled, Jacob looked down at her.

"The men have gone fishing for the day. Your brother went with them," she said quietly.

Jacob remembered that the night before Naomi and Sariah had prepared the food for the men to take, but he couldn't believe he had slept through all the movement and chatter that surely took place when they left in the morning. Jacob walked outside. The sun was still hidden below the eastern horizon and the morning was chilly. He decided to walk to the shore to see if perhaps they were still there. He arrived in time to see Seth standing on Levi's shoulders in the boat, double-checking the strength of the mast and boom they had replaced. David saw him coming in the predawn darkness. "Jacob, over here," he shouted.

Boats were already pushing off from shore and yet Jershon, even with the lengthy repair, was ready to push off as well. Seth finished securing the boom with Jershon shouting the last instructions, then jumped off Levi's shoulders.

"Why didn't you wake me?" Jacob asked Levi.

"You were sleeping more soundly than the baby, my brother," Levi answered, as the men laughed in unison. "I decided to go with them this morning and try my hand at fishing," he added.

"Can I go?" Jacob asked somewhat meekly.

"Four is already crowded in this small boat. Levi takes almost as much room as two men. I am afraid one more would be too much," Jershon answered. "We are only fishing for a short time today and should be back after midday. Stay at home and help the women tend to Lamech." Jershon instructed them to push the boat off the shore. The task was made easy with the efforts of the five men. Seth was the last to jump into the boat, and it floated off.

Jacob stood by himself in the shallows. "Did you remember the oars, Seth?" he shouted. Seth smiled and held them up for Jacob to see. Jacob smiled and waved. He felt like a little boy required to stay home from the hunt, a feeling he was not accustomed to. The rising sun was beginning to blanket the shore in yellow light. Jacob lingered on the beach for a few minutes, sitting on a large rock. When the sun crested the eastern mountains, he stood to head back to the house. He could still see the small boat with its sail unfurled far in the distance.

Upon returning to the house, Jacob found Naomi and Raisa bathing the baby in a small tub. The baby boy was voicing his protest, and soon Sariah, Esther, and finally Liora came out into the room to see what the fuss was about. Lamech lay asleep. Jacob found himself uncomfortably out of his element. The women went about trying to help as best they could. Liora and Sariah disappeared into the kitchen to prepare something for everyone to eat. They returned with bread and fruit.

"Where is Levi?" Sariah asked, already knowing the answer.

"He has gone fishing with your father," Jacob answered. Sariah offered him some bread. "Did you not want to go?" she asked.

"Well, I was asleep when they left," Jacob said sheepishly. "I caught them before they cast off, but your father said there wasn't enough room in the boat."

"I'm not surprised," Sariah replied. "It's a small boat, and Levi is as big as two men." She smiled.

"That's exactly what your father said," Jacob responded.

"Well, you'll have to stay home to wash clothes and make bread with the women today," Naomi said with a laugh.

"I'm afraid I am not very good at either chore," Jacob said.

"Then you are no different from the other men in this house," Naomi chortled. The girls giggled, and Naomi laughed louder. That little-boy feeling came over Jacob again.

"The men won't be gone a full day," Naomi continued. "I'm sure you can find something to do."

Lamech suddenly spoke. "Is there anything to eat? I'm hungry." Everyone gathered around him, and Raisa knelt to embrace him. He tried to stand up, but it was obvious he was still weak. Jacob reached him just in time to keep him from falling down. "Take it easy, my brother. I know your body is anxious to get going, but your head is saying otherwise. It's best that you stay put for a couple of days."

Jacob helped him lay back down on the bed. Naomi and the girls admired the tender way Jacob handled Lamech.

"I'll be fine," Lamech said. "I'd like to go meet my father when he returns today."

"If you're up to it, I'll help you walk to the shore," Jacob offered.

"Maybe we could all go," piped young Esther.

"That might be a good idea," said Naomi. "Let's get our work done quickly. We could all use some fresh air today."

Jacob ate, then went outside and busied himself cleaning out the small stable at the side of the house. He found some tools and repaired a part of the enclosure in which the donkeys were kept. He straightened up the area that was used for spare wood and rope and netting, then piled debris and manure from the stable into a cart. Esther directed him toward the town trash pile. He hauled two loads to the pile, then returned the cart to its place and stood satisfied, admiring his work. He decided he should go to the shore and bathe, as he was sweaty and dirty from head to toe. His sandals were caked with the muck from the stable and needed a good cleaning as well.

Jacob walked just out of town along the shore of the lake, looking for a private spot in which to swim. Jershon was right; the disciples who had followed Jesus to Capernaum were camped everywhere. He had to walk almost half a mile before he found a suitably private place to bathe. Seeing all the people waiting for another opportunity to be with Jesus reminded Jacob of the reason he was there. Being with Jershon and his family and meeting Liora had all but made him forget his mission.

Jacob enjoyed the swim and time alone. He washed his tunic and draped it over an oleander bush near the shore to dry. He laid the blanket from his satchel on the pebbly beach and considered a short nap, but his head was too full of divergent thoughts. He thought of his wise mentor, Ezra. He felt he had already come to a conclusion about Jesus even though his investigation had hardly begun. He pondered the peace and warmth he had encountered in the home of Jershon and his wonderful family. He had enjoyed immensely the simple work he had performed today; it brought a smile to his face. And then there was a ray of light that had pierced his heart in the form of Liora.

The great general Maximus lay beside the Sea of Galilee, far from home, without a plan, without weapons, without an enemy, and, for the first time he could remember, he was content. He lay back, closed his eyes to the glare of the bright sun, and smiled.

25

Jacob returned to the house feeling clean and refreshed. He longed to shave off the beard that itched and made him feel unkempt; it was something he would never get used to. When he arrived, he encountered Lamech outside, sitting in the warm sun on a small stool, leaning against the outer wall of the house. The women had changed clothes and were anxiously waiting Jacob's return so they could walk to the shore and wait for the returning fishermen.

Jacob helped Lamech to his feet. He gave Lamech his staff and told him to put his other hand on his shoulder for stability in case the dizziness returned. They started the short walk to the shore, the women following behind. Raisa wrapped the baby tightly in a lightweight blanket. Esther skipped ahead, spinning around occasionally to look at Jacob and smile. Jacob smiled back, which sent her off squealing.

They stopped under a large sycamore tree a few yards from the waterline and laid down blankets to sit on and wait for the men. Naomi quickly passed out some water and wine for them to drink.

Lamech was beginning to be more lucid and asked Jacob to retell the story of his rescue.

Jacob obliged, giving all of the credit to Levi.

Sariah asked, "Levi said he was a blacksmith. What does he make?"

Jacob weighed his answer. "He makes tools."

"Why was his family attacked?" Sariah pressed with genuine concern in her eyes. This was a more delicate question, one Jacob preferred to avoid, but all eyes were upon him.

"It was an ugly and sad thing and happened a long time ago," Jacob began. "Levi doesn't talk about it much, so I don't really know details. He has reconciled himself to his loss and is much happier now." In an effort to redirect the conversation, Jacob turned to Sariah and said, "You seem very curious about my brother, Sariah."

Sariah blushed, and Liora put up a hand to conceal a smile.

Jacob felt Sariah's discomfort and was instantly sorry for his teasing. "He is a good man, and despite his size he is as tender as a tame rabbit." As he spoke, Jacob remembered Levi viciously slashing through the attacking pirates on the Egyptian ship.

Naomi patted Sariah on the shoulder, and Liora and Esther smiled at each other.

Jacob wanted to talk to Liora but was so nervous he felt like a little boy in the company of adults, not wanting to interrupt. Then Naomi asked him about his family. He remembered Ezra's admonishment not to get involved with any of the crew on the ship, which would help eliminate too many questions. Jacob could see the wisdom in not getting involved with anyone; even a peaceful family like this could ask too many questions, and he would be forced to be untruthful—or make the slightest mistake and possibly expose his cover.

"My sisters and mother work on the farm at our home. My father is a diplomat," Jacob answered truthfully.

"A good Jewish family?" Naomi stated more than asked.

Jacob hesitated, then answered, "Yes, a good family," sidestepping the real question.

"And what do you do, Jacob—what is your craft?" Naomi asked. Lamech, Liora, and Sariah were intent on his answer. Esther was collecting small smooth stones from the beach and couldn't have cared less.

Jacob paused and then said, "I am a partner in a trading company. We have a handful of ships that transport cargo between Alexandria, Antioch, Carthage, and Rome."

"And you have a family? I mean, a wife and children?" Naomi pressed.

Jacob nervously laughed. "No, I am not married and do not have a family. I have been traveling a lot the last few years and haven't had time for a family." *That* much was not a lie.

Naomi simply exclaimed "Oh" with a satisfied grin and turned to adjust one of the blankets. Then she asked, "And Levi. Does he have a family of his own?"

It wasn't hard for Jacob to deduce the purpose of Naomi's questions—she had an eligible daughter and niece, and to her, Jacob and Levi represented two eligible Jewish bachelors. Their disguise was working too well. Jacob felt it was time to change the direction of the conversation.

Without answering Naomi, he turned to Liora. "I understand you and David have been following Jesus?" he inquired.

Liora, nervous that Jacob's attention had suddenly turned to her, stammered, "Yes, we have."

"How long have you been following him?" he asked.

"Only a week. We followed him to Bethsaida." Liora was

choking on every word and finding it difficult to speak under his attentive gaze.

"He has quite a following. His message must be compelling."

"Yes, it is." Liora's answer was clipped.

"Can you tell me about it?" Jacob probed, wanting to continue the conversation with her.

Liora looked to Sariah for help. Sariah was silent, not knowing how to answer either. "Well, he teaches a new message that goes beyond the Law of Moses, but mostly he teaches kindness to our fellow man. And tolerance. He loves children, and we saw him heal a blind man one day." Liora became animated as she related the story.

"So the stories of the miracles are true?" Jacob asked with some skepticism.

"We only witnessed the one, but I am convinced the other stories must be true," Liora said.

"After seeing what we saw, I believe all the stories we have been told of him," Sariah added.

Jacob nodded as he listened. "Tell me, Liora." Jacob directed his conversation purposely to her. "Why are the rabbis and the high priest so afraid of him?"

Liora shifted nervously. "My uncle says that they feel threatened. Jesus comes from the small village of Nazareth and was an ordinary carpenter. The members of the Sanhedrin don't believe he has any authority to teach the things he does." Liora paused to look up at Jacob, who was smiling at her. "Frankly, I think they are jealous that so many people want to follow him and listen to his teachings," she said, smiling warmly at Jacob.

Jacob recalled something he had heard from both Gaius Valerius and Ezra. "I am told Jesus is of the house of David and because of his genealogy alone would qualify for leadership in Israel."

Naomi interrupted. "You seem to be very knowledgeable, Jacob. Tell us why you became a disciple."

Jacob smiled. "I'm not sure I am a disciple yet."

"What do you seek, then?" Naomi asked.

"I seek the true God," Jacob said emphatically.

"As a Jew, Jacob, you know that the great Jehovah is the one true God," Naomi said. "Do you seek Jesus simply as a leader, or do you believe he is the Messiah?"

Jacob weighed his answer and after a minute responded. "I was not taught well in Egypt as a youth about the ways of Jehovah. I hardly qualify as a Jew." Jacob looked out to the water, not wanting to make eye contact with Naomi as he pondered how to answer her. "In trying to understand the nature of God, I am drawn to this Nazarene. In fact, when I saw him briefly yesterday as he came into town, my heart and mind were filled with an emotion I can't explain." Jacob was telling the truth.

Naomi responded. "We have all felt that, Jacob, and rest assured, we are not judges of your dedication to Judaism. We are your friends. We are constantly searching for truth as well." Naomi smiled at Jacob in a way that made him think of his own mother. He felt an emotion welling that he quickly controlled.

"I think I see them," Lamech announced, looking out upon the lake.

Everyone turned their gaze to the water and spotted the triangular sail on the horizon. All the fishing boats looked the same, but Lamech was sure it was his father's boat. They stood to get a better look.

As everyone edged closer to the water, Naomi approached Jacob. "I perceive you have a good heart, my son," she said.

Lamech stood on the shoreline, leaning on Jacob's staff and waving with his other arm. They could see Seth standing with one foot on the prow of the boat, waving back. Within a couple of minutes, the boat was fifty yards away and closing. In the heat of the day, Jacob had been itching to step into the water. He unceremoniously discarded his head covering and robe and waded into the water to help pull it ashore. As he stood in the shallow water, his tunic pulled up and gathered around his waist, Liora and Sariah both noticed the many scars on his legs, shoulders, and arms, taking particular note of the deep gash in the calf of his left leg. They looked at each other curiously but said nothing.

Seth threw a rope to Jacob, who secured it with one tight wrap around his hand. He turned and, with the rope over his shoulder, pulled the boat up onto the beach. Lamech walked over to help, but Jacob held up his free hand and cautioned him about exerting himself too much, and Lamech backed off. Seth anxiously jumped out of the boat, and David and Levi helped Jershon furl the sail.

"Levi was good luck," Seth blurted out. "We filled the boat with one cast of the net."

Levi jumped out of the boat and reached up to lend Jershon a hand. "Your father took us right on top of the fish. I had nothing to do with it," Levi responded.

Seth suddenly kicked water on Levi, who charged after him, and the two ran down the beach, Seth laughing uncontrollably. In short order, Levi caught him by the scruff of his neck, hauled him to the water, and pushed him in. Jacob and the family watched in amusement.

"We have work to do yet," Jershon admonished.

"Work, work. All you think about is work," Naomi said as she wrapped her arms around her husband. He laughed and hugged her back.

"Go on home, Jershon," Levi said. "Seth and I can prepare the boat for tomorrow. Jacob and David can help unload the catch."

"Are you sending me home with the women?" Jershon rejoined with raised eyebrows.

Levi laughed. "No, my friend," he said with a new familiarity. "We have enough hands. Go home and rest."

Seth stood by Levi as they pulled the net out of the boat to inspect it for damage and refold it for tomorrow. David led Jacob to retrieve baskets to unload the fish. Jacob smiled pleasantly at Liora as he walked past, which didn't escape the notice of both Naomi and Jershon.

Jershon held Lamech's arm as they walked back to the house. Liora and Sariah trailed, talking together and giggling, occasionally looking back.

"We have acquired two worthy sons," Naomi said quietly to Jershon as she walked beside him, leaning affectionately on his arm.

He looked down at her curiously and saw the twinkle in her eye—he knew what she was thinking. Smiling, Jershon whispered, "Woman, you plot like an anxious fox at the gate of the henhouse."

Naomi smiled back.

During the evening meal, David had a thousand questions about blacksmithing that he directed at Levi. Lamech was feeling better and cuddled both his wife and his son. Esther made both Levi and Jacob hold her up with their strong arms. She hung on as if she were hanging on tree limbs and giggled with delight. Jershon watched the interaction and wondered how in such a short time these two strange men had become part of his family.

"They have been sent by God," Naomi remarked, reading his thoughts.

"You certainly want them to be the answers to a mother's prayers." He nudged his happy wife.

"I believe they *are*," Naomi said with a cherubic smile.

"We are a long way from what you have in mind, my dear," Jershon cautioned.

"Yes, we have some work to do. You and David should talk to both of them soon," Naomi said, poking her finger playfully into his ribs.

Jershon flinched. "I knew somehow this would turn out to be my responsibility."

"Well, it is, and you need to take the earliest opportunity to talk to each of them and discuss arrangements," Naomi pressed.

"You are casting the net before the boat has left the beach, my dear. Be patient, woman," Jershon said as he put his arm around her and held her close. He had already considered the conversation he would have with these eligible men but knew there could be objections. It was apparent they enjoyed the company of Sariah and Liora, but that was no guarantee that they were in a position to be married.

He had some reservations. Jacob and Levi, on the surface, were good men with good hearts. Their background was still in question, and attempts to get them to reveal information were met with apprehension and contemplation before giving answers. By their own admission, their immersion in Judaism was incomplete. But that could be a factor of having lived in a foreign land with parents—Levi admittedly had none—who didn't adhere closely to the traditions of their fathers. That was a common occurrence. It was certainly plausible that they were both good Jewish men but were a bit removed from the commitment Jershon would like to see in husbands for his daughter and niece. That was not an insurmountable obstacle. He watched the two men as they interacted with his family members; they were both kind and gentle. He, like Naomi, had sensed immediately the attraction between Jacob and Liora, and Sariah was definitely not shy about her feelings toward Levi, who seemed oblivious to her.

What is a father to do? he thought. There was a lot of work to do, and it would all fall on him. He would pray for guidance tonight and have a long talk with his God. Then he would have a longer talk with Naomi tomorrow. But as he considered the circumstances, it seemed Jehovah had certainly placed the fish under his boat. He closed his eyes and gave a prayer of gratitude.

26

The next morning Levi again accompanied the other men fishing. Lamech was improving, but he was not well enough to go out in the boat all day in the hot sun. Levi was the first one up in the morning, causing Seth and David to stir and beating Jershon to the shore to prepare the boat.

Jershon was pleased with Levi's enthusiasm and work ethic. Was a second boat in the family's future? Quickly he put that thought out of his head. He didn't want his daughter married to a fisherman.

Jacob joined them on the beach for the launch, then watched them sail off in the gray of the early morning. He sat on the shore and pondered, realizing he and Levi needed to get back on task with their investigation of Jesus of Nazareth.

Jesus had remained sequestered with his apostles for a couple of days' rest, but rumor had it he was preparing for another outing. It had been easy to get comfortable with the hospitality of Jershon and his family. He was also enjoying Liora's company. He was smitten by her natural beauty, but he was even more impressed with her outspokenness and intelligent conversation. She had opinions about Jesus, the Jewish hierarchy, and the Roman occupation. Her points were sound and logical. She obviously thought deeply, listened intently, and intelligently processed the opinions of others. She reminded him of his mother—another strong and confident woman.

Jacob longed to talk to Liora privately, but it wasn't likely to happen. Jewish customs were funny that way. Ezra had told Jacob and Levi during their journey how proper Jewish families functioned to zealously guard the honor of their women. Young women of marriageable age were never allowed to be alone with young men, even a potential husband. It was such a different culture from the one in which he'd grown up. He lay back and closed his eyes, enjoying the warmth of the rising sun.

"Jacob . . . Jacob!"

Jacob dreamed someone was calling his name.

"Jacob!" Realizing he was hearing Liora's voice, Jacob sat up quickly and then felt dizzy as the blood suddenly rushed from his head. The sun was well over the eastern horizon. He was quickly losing his soldier's edge, falling asleep without a weapon and failing to hear someone approaching him. He scolded himself for being lazy and challenged himself to stay sharper.

"Jacob, were you sleeping?" Liora asked.

"Yes, I'm afraid I was. It's so comfortable and warm here on the shore." He couldn't believe his good fortune at being alone with her. Then he noticed Sariah and Esther behind her.

"When you didn't return, my aunt asked us to find you and take you something to eat." She knelt next to him, setting a basket on the ground. Her olive-colored head covering accented her large eyes. The warm morning breeze caused her head covering to fall back, revealing her long brown hair that glistened in the sunshine. She was no more than two feet away. Jacob noticed that her skin was soft and without blemish. Dark brows and long lashes framed her eyes. The sweet, clean smell about her filled his nostrils. He couldn't take his eyes off her.

She suddenly looked directly him. "Is something wrong?" she asked.

"No . . . no," Jacob stammered, trying to excuse his staring. "I guess I'm not fully awake." He wanted to reach out and pull her to him.

Instead, he invited Esther and Sariah to sit beside them. Liora set out a small loaf of fresh bread and unfolded a cloth full of grapes.

Jacob took the bread from her and deliberately brushed his fingers along hers.

Liora smiled.

Sariah observed the exchange. "Esther, come with me for a minute, down to the water's edge."

"But I'm hungry!" Esther complained.

"Take a piece of bread and come with me. I want to show you the most beautiful thing," Sariah said, coaxing her sister with her hand. Esther tore off a small piece of bread, leapt up, and ran to the water. Sticking her toes into the water, she screamed delightedly. Sariah caught up with her and led her down the beach a few yards. It was obvious to Jacob and Liora that Sariah was allowing them to talk privately.

Jacob spoke. "Thank you for the food. This is a nice place to eat breakfast."

"Yes, it's peaceful here when the fishermen have gone out and the sun is not yet hot," Liora said nervously.

Jacob could tell she was uncomfortable. He stood and extended his hand to help her to her feet. "Let's take a walk." Jacob wished he could continue holding her hand.

Liora, for her part, was hoping he wouldn't let go of her hand, but he did. They walked side by side, following Sariah and Esther at a distance.

Finally Liora said, "You and your brother are strange men."

"Strange?" Jacob objected, feigning offense. "How so?"

"*Strange* may be the wrong word," Liora laughed. "I'm sorry. *Different* is probably a better choice."

"I'll accept *different*," Jacob said. "But I still want you to explain what you mean," he added.

"You don't seem Jewish." Liora was direct.

Jacob suddenly wished he hadn't asked. They walked a few steps before she spoke again.

"Maybe it's because you're more Egyptian than Jewish." Liora looked up at him.

Jacob avoided eye contact. "Yes, Levi and I have lived elsewhere all our lives and have not experienced many Jewish traditions." He tried to change the subject. "It must be hard for you and David living alone in Magdala."

"It is," Liora responded. Jacob felt relieved, but then she said, "Despite his strength, Levi doesn't have the burn scars of a blacksmith as my brother does."

Jacob scrambled for an explanation. "His father taught him well, and he is extremely careful."

Liora pressed further. "What is it you trade in Alexandria?"

Jacob realized she had purpose in her questioning and now wished they weren't alone. He couldn't avoid answering, but he didn't want to lie to her, either. Once again, Ezra's caution about not becoming involved with people came back to haunt him. "A myriad of things, really," he hedged. "A lot of goods are traded between Alexandria, Caesarea, Rome, and other cities bordering the Great Sea."

"Yesterday when you helped pull in my uncle's boat—" Liora shyly lowered her head and her voice softened. "Forgive me for looking so closely, but I saw the scars on your legs and arms. You have what appears to be a recent wound on the back of your leg, and you're missing a finger. David told me that when Levi rescued them, they observed similar scars on his arms and back." She paused, hesitating to say the next thing on her mind but decided to plow forward. "David thinks they look like the battle scars of soldiers." She stopped walking and looked up at him with kind but questioning eyes.

Jacob hesitated, looking deep into the innocent gaze of her beautiful eyes, then led her toward a slightly elevated wooden wharf. He sat down with an audible sigh. Liora sat close beside him. Sariah continued to distract Esther, keeping their distance. Liora didn't seem angry—in fact, she seemed almost apologetic—but Jacob knew she was studying him and desired a truthful explanation.

"I'm sorry to probe, Jacob. I should mind my own business," Liora said as she lowered her gaze.

"It's all right. I understand your curiosity." Jacob breathed deeply and thought for a moment. "Levi and I *are* different. We have come out of nowhere and landed in your life. Yet in less than a couple of days your aunt and uncle have made us feel like part of the family. You all have been so kind and forthcoming. It's just difficult . . ."

"Are you uncomfortable with us?" Liora asked, brushing the hair away from her face with graceful fingers.

"No, you are all very easy to be with. It's just . . ." Once again he found the words wouldn't come. The silence lingered for a few awkward moments.

"Is something wrong?" Liora looked up at him with concern in her eyes.

"No, nothing is wrong, and yes, everything is wrong," Jacob

said as he looked down at his feet. "Perhaps now is not the time to have this conversation."

"Jacob, we all like you and Levi very much." She placed her hand on his forearm. Her touch sent a charge through him that almost made him gasp. Jacob closed his eyes and relished the feeling. He looked down at the contrast between her delicate hand with its long, thin fingers and his muscular, scarred forearm. He thought of the multitude of differences between them, and yet he hoped she wouldn't move her hand. He placed his hand on top of hers to assure that wouldn't happen.

"I like you very much, Liora." Jacob looked her directly in the eye and held her gaze. "I wish you could know and like me for who I really am."

Liora placed her other hand on top of his and looked up at him with gentle eyes. "Try me," she said.

He squeezed her hand. "Not today." He looked away as a wave of guilt overtook him.

Liora didn't object to his answer and, respecting his wishes, pressed no further. She threaded her arm through his and easily melted into his side, leaning her head against his upper arm and shoulder.

Jacob tilted his head toward her, delighting in the feeling of her soft warm hair on his arm and face.

Things had unalterably changed between them. He barely knew her, but he knew he was in love with this graceful, charming, and beautiful woman beside him. He was certain Liora loved Jacob, but how could she love General Lucius Fabius Maximus? He was fighting his emotions harder than he'd fought any foe he had ever met on the battlefield.

"Liora . . . Jacob!" Esther shouted, breaking the spell as she skipped happily toward them. "Look!" She held out a handful of wildflowers she had gathered.

Liora and Jacob sat up straight, but Jacob did not let go of her hand.

"How pretty," Liora said. "Let's take them home. Your mother will be so pleased." She stood and Jacob stood with her, still unwilling to relinquish her hand. Liora didn't object or pull away even when Sariah approached. They walked hand in hand back to the house.

Sariah followed behind, grinning widely.

At the house, Sariah and Liora quickly disappeared into the back, whispering excitedly.

Jacob chatted with Lamech and Raisa, who were tending to their new son.

"Lamech, do you feel like taking a short hike today?" Jacob asked.

"I would love to get out for a while. Being indoors is getting to me." Raisa punched him on the arm playfully. Lamech rephrased. "A walk in the fresh air would do wonders for my health." He smiled and kissed his wife.

"Good," Jacob said. "I'll wait outside." The day was still young but already proving to be a hot one. He was concerned that he had said too much to Liora. He wondered if, even now, she was telling Naomi and Sariah and they were continuing their guessing game about their mysterious guests—or was she keeping his confidence? He should have asked her to stay silent until they spoke more. They had made known their mutual interest, and he was sure that knowledge was being shared with Sariah and Naomi. It was no secret that Sariah carried a torch for Levi. Jacob smiled to himself thinking about it. Sariah made her feelings obvious; Levi was slow on the uptake, totally unaware. He wondered if the unspoken feeling between himself and Liora had been as obvious to everyone. Naomi was probably already planning their matches. He laughed out loud, then quickly sobered with the thought that it might be true. Naomi and Jershon had an eligible daughter and niece. Jacob and Levi certainly seemed like eligible Jewish men. The thought made him uneasy. He looked back toward the house. *Where is Lamech?* Jacob was restless to get going and clear his head. *I'm losing all self-discipline,* Jacob chided himself as he began to pace anxiously. *How did I get caught up in this so quickly?* He suddenly had the urge to escape.

Lamech finally emerged from the house. Jacob led the way up the road northward out of town. "Where should we go, Lamech?" Jacob asked.

"There's a path a short distance from here that leads to a hidden cove on the sea. It is full of large rocks and plenty of shade. Maybe we could wash the dust from our feet," Lamech replied.

"That would suit me," Jacob said.

"It's good to get out of the house. I'm going a little crazy just lying down all day and not being active," Lamech finally said. "Something certainly has the women all worked up this morning. Raisa and the others were all giggling and chattering at once." He added, "Perhaps she'll tell me about it when I get back."

Jacob grimaced inwardly. "Who knows what makes that happen," he responded.

"Well, you and Levi have certainly stirred things up," Lamech said.

"How so?" Jacob asked, already knowing the answer.

"You and Levi have stolen the hearts of my sister and cousin, but I am sure that's obvious to you." Lamech looked at Jacob and smiled. "The young men of Capernaum don't have a chance."

"Do they have suitors?" Jacob asked curiously.

"Not that compare to the two of you," Lamech responded.

"I don't think we're a very good match for such fine women," Jacob said.

"My father and mother think differently," Lamech offered.

Jacob was caught off guard. "What do you mean?"

"It's a small house, Jacob. A whisper only makes one listen more intently. It's difficult not to know what people are saying. My mother likes you two and is pressing my father to speak to each of you about a betrothal. But because they don't know you very well and know nothing of your families, my father has been resisting."

"Your father is right to be cautious," Jacob said, pulling a leaf off a dangling sycamore branch as he passed.

"I don't know you two very well either, Jacob," Lamech confessed, "but I feel you are good men with good intentions, and I think you would make good husbands."

"Well, you just keep your feelings to yourself, my friend." Jacob shoved Lamech in the shoulder. They both smiled and walked on.

Jacob felt a knot forming in his stomach. *What have I done? How am I going to get out of this gracefully if it escalates?* It appeared already to have progressed beyond a point of safe retreat. It would be hurtful, but he was sure if he told the truth to Jershon, he would decide that he and Levi would not make good husbands. After all, they weren't Jewish, and according to Ezra, marriage between a Jew and a Gentile was forbidden. He and Levi had not forced their way into the daily life of this good family, but circumstances had made it virtually impossible to refuse their warm hospitality. Jacob again scolded himself for his lack of discipline. He had lost focus and allowed comfort to dictate his actions. If he were this careless on the battlefield, it would cost lives and perhaps the failure of an entire campaign. He couldn't suffer this distraction any longer. He and Levi would have to move on tomorrow. Jesus was supposed to be leaving Capernaum soon, anyway, and they would follow him as they had planned. It would be best. Then a vision of Liora flashed into his head.

He closed his eyes and tried to expel it. It didn't work. He had breathed her in, and it wouldn't be easy to leave her. He crushed the leaf in his hand and threw it angrily to the side of the road. He would talk to Levi tonight.

Many times on campaigns, he had walked by himself, processing information and mulling strategic options. This was no different. The hike proved both calming and invigorating. His head was becoming a little clearer. He liked Lamech and appreciated what a good, committed husband he was. Raisa was beautiful, and Lamech was very much in love with her. His new family was paramount in his mind, and he thought only of their future happiness. Jacob wondered if he would ever have a family and be able to dedicate his life to them—the thought seemed so foreign. But that was only one of many battles raging inside of him.

Jacob was uncomfortable at the midday meal and found it difficult to make eye contact with Liora. This was all such an enigma. He just wanted to be gone.

Liora filled the wine cups, kneeling by Jacob's side. He turned to look at the graceful profile of this perfect woman, and his resolve vanished. He finished eating and excused himself. He walked outside, not knowing where to go or what to do. He wished that Levi was back and wished that he could talk to his father or mother, Ezra—anyone.

He walked westward of the village into the rolling hills a few minutes away and found a hidden meadow, where he sat down in the shade of a stand of poplar trees. Feeling very alone, he remembered Ezra telling them on the voyage about talking to his God. Jacob had never thought about talking to the gods; they were inanimate to him. He cursed them at times, as all Romans did, but never thought they listened to him. Ezra talked of this Jehovah as if he were a real person, someone who visited and cared for his people, directed them in times of difficulty, and gave them rules to follow. The God of the Jews required a high degree of fealty, but at least this Jehovah seemed to give things in return. *Maybe I should try to talk to him?* Jacob shook his head. *Why would a Jewish god listen to a Roman masquerading as a Jew?* The thought produced a sardonic smile. Ezra said Jehovah was the God of all men; he only favored the Jews because they believed and obeyed him rather than idols or other gods manufactured by men. Jacob had also heard that Jesus healed all manner of persons of their various afflictions, even a Gentile or two. *The God of the Jews must approve of such blessing and healing, so why can't I talk to him?*

He stood as Ezra had taught them to do when they prayed and bowed his head. After a few moments he began to speak quietly.

"Forgive me, God of the Jews, for presuming that you would listen to a Roman—a Gentile. My friend Ezra has recently taught me of you. He says he talks to you a lot. I consider myself unworthy to talk to you, let alone ask something from a god to whom I have not shown allegiance. I have been searching for the true God, and I have faith that you exist. It seems logical that you, in some way I don't understand, would be a man like me but much advanced. So I will talk to you like a man. I know this will be a one-way conversation, but if you will listen, I will be satisfied.

"Forgive me for the wrongs I have done. I have killed many men at the bidding of my country. Those actions now seem wrong to me, and I can no longer justify them. I have succumbed to sins common to man, but I have tried to be an honest and fair person. I have looked after my men as if they were brothers. I have made many foolish decisions in my life and want to make them right. I have been blessed with good health. I have been blessed with good parents and many fine things in this world. If they are

somehow gifts from you, I give you my sincere thanks. I am un-
deserving of these blessing on my own account.

"I have come to this land to investigate a man who is rumored to be your Son. I have seen him and felt his aura, and I
believe him to be a good man, not any threat to Judaea or Rome.
I have decided that will be my report to the people who sent me.
I struggle with the thought that he is your living Son, but I don't
understand all things.

"I have met a wonderful family who have been good to me.
One of them is a wonderful woman, a woman I believe I could be
happy with for the rest of my life. But I have been dishonest with
them, and I don't want to hurt or disappoint them. The world we
live in has made this all so complicated. I don't know what to do.
I am not strong enough to sort this out on my own. I need some
help and . . ."

Jacob could speak no more. His heart was full, and tears
flowed uncontrollably from his eyes. He wept like a small boy.
He couldn't remember the last time he wept so openly. He
thought of his good parents and sisters—and wept. He thought
of the sadness and ugliness he had seen in battle—and wept. He
thought of his brother, Androcles, and the needless and ruthless
slaughter of his family—and wept. He thought of Jershon and
his family—and wept. He thought of Liora and was totally overcome with emotion. He fell to the ground, burying his face in his
hands—and wept. Years of pain and sadness and regret came to
the surface.

Jacob looked to the sky and, through the tears filling his eyes,
pleaded, "If you are real, I need to know it."

The feeling started at his toes and crept up his entire body.
It was if someone were dipping him slowly into a vat of warm
oil. The feeling proceeded until it enveloped his entire body
in unmistakable warmth, comfort, and well-being. His arms

involuntarily folded themselves over his chest as if he were embracing himself.

He lay there, disbelieving what was happening. Then as quickly as the feeling came, it departed. Left exhausted, he seemed to melt into the ground. His tears were no longer tears of sadness and remorse but tears of joy and light.

After a time he was able to sit up. Something deep inside him recognized what he had just felt. He would never be able to deny it. He hadn't received answers to all his questions or specific guidance in the difficult issues he faced, but he received the most important answer of his life: there was a God, he lived, and he cared enough about Lucius Fabius Maximus to communicate with him. That was a knowledge that would help and guide him the rest of his life.

Jacob knew this wasn't the last conversation he would have with God. He longed to share his experience with others, but for now he would keep it to himself. The right time would come.

It took an hour or more before Jacob had the strength to stand and walk back to the house. It was late afternoon and he decided he would go back to the shore and meet the men when they returned from fishing. He arrived about fifteen minutes before he recognized the sails of Jershon's boat far in the distance. Jacob helped them land, unload, and prepare the craft for the next morning.

Jershon put his arm on Jacob's shoulder as they walked back to the house. "Are you all right, my son?" he asked. "You seem . . . pensive."

"Yes, I'm fine. Just a little tired."

"You look tired. Did you not sleep on the beach all day? We saw you lie down as we were sailing away." He laughed and patted Jacob on the back.

"I probably *should* have slept here all day," Jacob responded.

They walked in silence down the road to the house. Jershon and Jacob lagged behind Seth, David, and Levi, who had grown quite close. "I would like to talk to you privately, my son," Jershon said solemnly to Jacob.

Jacob looked at Jershon's weathered face; it glowed with the redness of being in the sun all day. His deep-set eyes were kind but seemed to look right through him. Jacob knew he could not deceive this good man and his family any longer and immediately came to a decision. "It will have to be tonight. Levi and I are leaving tomorrow," Jacob replied abruptly.

Jershon stopped walking and stared, shocked, at Jacob. "You're leaving? Where are you going?"

"We have heard that Jesus will be leaving Capernaum tomorrow, and we must follow him. We appreciate your generosity and hospitality, but it is time for us to take our leave." Jacob continued to walk, and Jershon took brisk steps to catch up.

"This is a surprise. I am certain my family will not take this news well. In a short time we have become accustomed to your company. You really have been a tremendous help to us. Surely Jesus will travel for a couple of days and return. You will certainly return with him, won't you?" Jershon was almost pleading.

"I'm not sure. Wherever he goes, we will follow him, and then we will go on to Jerusalem," Jacob said flatly.

"Whatever for?" Jershon asked.

"We have business there," Jacob said almost curtly.

Jershon knew he was not going to get a satisfactory explanation. He sighed and resigned himself to the unsettling news. Naomi would be devastated. He would have to think of a solution quickly.

As they entered the house, Jershon greeted his wife. Then he raised his hand. "I have something to announce." He waited for all to gather in the small room. "Jacob informs me that he and

Levi are leaving in the morning. We will enjoy our meal with them tonight and then say our good-byes."

A dead silence fell over the room. Levi looked curiously at Jacob, who looked away. Liora bolted from the room with Sariah on her heels. Naomi put her hand to her mouth, then turned to escape to the kitchen.

Seth broke the silence. "You can't leave, Levi. We were just getting used to fishing with four of us in the boat. I like coming home early every day. Since you've been helping us, the work has been much easier."

"I wasn't aware we were leaving so soon," Levi answered, looking hard at Jacob, who still would not look at him.

David spoke up. "I was hoping we could plan that trip to Magdala we talked about. I'd like to fire up the forge and have you show me some of the techniques you told me about. Will you be returning soon?"

"I'm not sure, David," Levi said. "Jacob and I haven't talked about our immediate plans." He shot Jacob a look and put a hard grip on his shoulder. "Why don't we go outside and clean up?" He almost forced Jacob out of the door. They walked a short distance before Levi spoke. "So what's the hurry, my brother? What happened while I was away? And don't we discuss our plans?" Levi was obviously irritated.

Jacob did not answer immediately. Then he looked Levi directly in the eye. "It's time to get back to the campaign, my brother. We are wasting time here. Our task is to investigate Jesus, make a report to Pontius Pilate, and then return home— not come here to Capernaum, live with a family, and fish. We have lost focus, Androcles." Jacob was emphatic.

"I'm Androcles now?" Levi responded.

"You have always been Androcles, and I am Maximus. Jacob and Levi are names we hide behind. They are as temporary as these wretched beards!" He pulled at his for effect. "It's time to remember who we really are and what we are here for and act accordingly."

Levi looked at his friend sternly. "So it's hit you that you love that girl."

"What girl?" Jacob snapped.

"What girl, indeed. Liora, you fool. You two haven't hidden your interest in each other from anyone. We laughed about it in the boat today, wondering when you would wise up and admit it. So something has finally made you admit it, and you want to run, don't you?"

Jacob looked at Levi and, without warning, shoved him forcefully away. Levi caught his balance and approached Jacob closer. "That's it, isn't it?" he shouted.

"I'm not running. I'm getting back to my duty, a duty I should never have left. We are not here to find wives, my brother!" Jacob retorted angrily.

"But you've found one, haven't you? And she far surpasses any woman you have met in Rome," Levi challenged. Jacob didn't respond and turned to sit on a nearby outcropping of rock. "We haven't forgotten our duty, Jacob," Levi argued. "The Nazarene is holed up like a hunted fox. Did you just want to sit on a log and wait for him to make a move?"

"That's what we do in battle, brother," Jacob blurted. "When the foe is entrenched, you wait them out if you can. You don't go into their village, make friends with their women, and go fishing with their men," Jacob said with disdain.

"What's wrong with you, my brother?" Levi looked at Jacob with a puzzled expression. "Why are you so angry? Did Liora reject you?"

"No, she didn't reject me, and nothing is wrong. It's time to be soldiers again. We are not part of this! We are not Jewish fishermen or blacksmiths. We are not part of this family. We are not two Jewish men hoping to be betrothed," Jacob hissed sarcastically. He held out his hands, pleading with his friend.

Levi sat down and let the air clear for a minute. He reasoned, "Why aren't we allowed to enjoy ourselves for a short time before resuming our mission? We've earned it. These people have taken us in because of their gratitude for saving their son and brother. We didn't seek them out. We have earned our keep—at least I have." He smiled and hit Jacob on the shoulder. "You've stayed home with the women. You're the one who's getting soft. Not me."

"Maybe we *have* earned it, but it's not right. If we stay another week or month, it won't be easier to leave." Jacob's voice was softer, but his mind was made up.

"You really are smitten, aren't you?" Levi teased.

Jacob looked Levi in the eye and in a serious tone said, "Yes, but nothing can become of it—*nothing!* Jershon said just a moment ago he wants to talk to me alone. Do you know what that's about? I will tell you—he wants you to marry his daughter and me to marry Liora. Naomi has already put a scheme in his ears that he is itching to execute." Jacob shook his head in exasperation. "That can't happen, Androcles—it won't happen!" He turned to look out over the sea and sighed heavily.

"Why can't it?" Levi asked.

Jacob turned, dumbfounded. "Have you lost your mind?"

"No, I haven't. In fact, I think I've finally found my mind, Jacob. I'm very fond of Sariah; she is a beautiful woman. I would much rather spend my future lying next to her in a soft bed at night in Capernaum than on the ground in some godforsaken country next to you and the cold steel of my sword." Levi picked up a rock and flung it disdainfully down the hill in front of them.

Jacob's jaw dropped. "You haven't even noticed Sariah!"

"I have noticed, and we have talked," Levi answered.

"Talked? How? When?" Jacob asked.

"In the early morning. She was up early to prepare the food for us to take in the boat even before I awoke. You have been sleeping like a baby; you wouldn't know. We have talked about a lot of things," he said, smiling.

Jacob turned away, shaking his head in disbelief. "You have made this even more difficult. We can't deceive these people any longer, Androcles! We are already living a lie, and we are only going to hurt them further." He wiped the sweat from his brow with the sleeve of his robe. "Why the Jews wear these hot wool robes I will never understand!" Jacob fidgeted in the robe and pulled the hem up over his knees to get fresh air on his legs.

"So why don't we just tell them the truth? Seth keeps asking me where I got all my wounds and scars. David thinks I'm a pretty careless blacksmith because of them." Levi laughed.

"Except none of your scars are burns," Jacob added. Levi looked at his friend curiously. "Liora and I had a talk today. She asked the same thing. Apparently our scars have been a topic of discussion. Liora said David noticed your lack of burns. I told her you were taught well and were very careful." He looked at Levi, and they both laughed.

"So what do we have to lose in telling them the truth?" Levi asked. "These are good people. They have taken us in, and I believe they have already accepted us for who we are."

"For whom they *think* we are." Jacob pondered Levi's hypothesis. "It's too dangerous, my brother. If one word got out about us, it would compromise our mission and put their family at risk."

"Exactly the reason we are safe, Jacob," Levi said enthusiastically. "They have all the reason in the world to keep the secret. They are already risking serious trouble from the leaders of the Jews by admitting they are followers of this Jesus. They wouldn't want to further admit they are harboring a Roman general and his deputy commander," Levi reasoned.

"That is precisely why we have to go, Androcles. Our presence in their home puts them at risk. Their culture may ostracize them anyway for their belief in Jesus, but that's a choice they have made. For them to appear to befriend the Roman conquerors is another issue. If your feelings toward Sariah are what you say they are, my brother, you will see there is no other choice for us. We have to go." Jacob looked down at his feet, not liking what he was hearing himself say—and wishing they had never got into this situation in the first place.

Levi knew Jacob was right but was unwilling to admit it. He was enjoying his time in Capernaum. This was the closest he had ever come to recreating a family. Seth and David had become like brothers in just a few short days. They were hard workers, and he enjoyed their company. Jershon was wise and demanded the best of his sons; he reminded Levi of his own father. He had not thought about his parents or brothers for a long time. It was uncomfortable for those memories to suddenly be thrust forward. He stood up and looked out toward the Sea of Galilee, inhaling deeply through his clenched teeth to regain his composure. After a few moments he turned back toward Jacob and stood. "Then let's leave now."

Jacob looked at Levi walking away and was confused by his sudden change of heart. "Androcles, wait!" he shouted after him. Levi stopped but did not turn around. Jacob caught up with him. "I think it would be rude to leave tonight. We must get back into our roles as Jacob and Levi, eat dinner with them, and bid them good-bye, as Jershon said. Then we will be free to leave early in the morning." Levi did not respond.

They walked silently back to the house. The women were busy in the kitchen preparing food. Jershon was reading from some yellowed scrolls. A noticeable melancholy permeated the house. The meal was served quickly, without conversation, and Jacob saw that Liora's eyes were red and swollen. His heart ached. Naomi retained her good humor, but it was obvious she was a bit distressed. Jershon ate in silence, which bothered Jacob the most. Jacob felt he had lost Jershon's respect with his hasty announcement. He tried to console himself with the fact that it was all for the best. Jershon would never let his daughter or niece marry a Roman, a Gentile. It went too much against their deep-seated beliefs. Jacob knew they would be doing the right thing in leaving, but he wanted Jershon to know it too. Jacob wrestled with the idea that he should have declined their invitation to a meal and a night's stay. The snub wouldn't have hurt them as deeply as Jacob suspected they were hurt now.

Naomi went to great efforts to make a superb meal, but to Jacob the food was tasteless. He ate out of politeness, not from hunger. Liora, who had sat next to Jacob during the meals, was on the other side of the small table, between David and Naomi. Jacob dared not look at her, but he figured she wouldn't make eye contact with him anyway.

When the meal was almost finished, Jershon spoke. "It has been quite a somber meal. We are all saddened by your sudden departure. We hope we haven't done something to offend you." Jershon motioned toward Jacob and Levi, then picked up his wine and took a sip.

"No, no, of course not. You all have been more than kind," Jacob responded. "We just need to finish the business we came for." He was immediately sorry for his choice of words.

"And what business is that, Jacob?" Jershon asked in a tone less kindly than he'd used with them earlier.

"We came to follow Jesus, sir, to learn more about him," Jacob weakly tried to make his words seem less harsh. "Jesus is here in

Capernaum, but he has been holed up like a hunted fox." Levi couldn't hold back a smile. Those were the exact words he had used earlier.

"Is something amusing, Levi?" Jershon asked in a serious tone.

Levi quickly lost his smile but could offer no explanation.

"We have enjoyed your company immensely," Jershon said, glancing at both Jacob and Levi. "We owe you a debt of gratitude for saving our son."

Jacob started to speak, but Jershon held up his hand. "Our hospitality has not continued out of a feeling of indebtedness, Jacob, if that's what you were going to say. The two of you have fit into this family, and in a short time have become part of us. It is no secret that we are all very fond of you." Liora and Sariah both squirmed in their seats and blushed. "We have been open and honest with you. We have shared our beliefs about Jesus. That in itself is a dangerous thing to admit, but you have earned our trust, despite the many things we do not know about you." Jershon's last comment hung in the air, causing Jacob some discomfort.

Jershon continued. "Jacob, I said to you today that I wanted to have a word privately. But let us be frank." Now Jacob was really squirming. "I understand your desire to be a disciple and follow Jesus; you said those were your intentions when we first met, so I am not surprised that you prepare to leave as he leaves. But I am sensing something deeper that you are not sharing with us, especially since you have indicated you will not return to us. That you have *business* in Jerusalem is acceptable, but that you would leave and not return is puzzling to me, my son."

Jershon's eyes softened as he looked at Jacob. Jacob stared straight ahead. Jershon sighed, shaking his head almost in disbelief at what he was about to say, then spoke softly. "It seems that since this family's commitment to become followers of Jesus, it has become easier to stray from other traditions we have long held firmly to." He looked at Naomi, whose eyes were wide in anticipation. "It is bold to speak so openly about this, but we are family, and we should not have secrets and speak in whispers. I believe what I am about to say will be no surprise to anyone sitting here. I propose a union between you, Levi," he motioned with his hand toward Levi, who sat stupefied, "and my daughter Sariah." Sariah lowered her head and seemed to want to pull her head covering over her face from embarrassment, but she sat still, eyes downcast. "I have discussed this with Sariah and her mother, and we believe you are worthy to be her husband." Before Levi could open his mouth, Jershon held up his hand, commanding silence. "And to you, Jacob, I propose a union between you and my lovely niece, Liora." Liora was so shocked she trembled. "I have spoken to Naomi and Liora about this matter also and have the blessing of Liora's brother." David was astonished at his uncle's openness but managed to nod his head in approval.

Jershon continued. "Jacob, it has come to my attention that you and Liora have made known to each other your feelings of affection." Levi glanced at Jacob with a bemused grin. "I know this is unusual to make these proposals in such a manner, but these are unique circumstances, and I believe my boldness is warranted." Jershon breathed out like a man who had been relieved of a heavy burden. "There, it is done," he said resolutely.

The room was silent and heavy. No one dared speak. Naomi was flushed and held her hands over her mouth. Everyone avoided eye contact. David put his arm around Liora, sensing she was about to faint. Then Esther's suppressed giggle broke the tension. Seth chuckled, then Lamech. Levi joined in, and then Raisa and Sariah began to laugh lightly behind their hands. Only Jacob sat expressionless.

"Do you all find this amusing?" Jershon said in a more light-hearted voice.

Finally, Jacob spoke. "No, it's not amusing. In fact, it is not funny at all." His tone was serious. The room fell uncomfortably silent again. In a calm but commanding voice, Jacob began. "Jershon, you honor us. We are honored by your proposal, but Sariah and Liora deserve better men than we are." There were immediate objections from Jershon and Lamech. This time it was Jacob who held up his hand for silence. "You have taken us in like sons. I don't remember a time feeling more at ease with people and . . . more loved. But we are not worthy of this honor." Tears flowed down Naomi's and Sariah's cheeks. Liora's heart ached.

Jacob continued. "In the spirit of openness that you have so graciously introduced, Jershon, I too must speak boldly. Our intention is not to hurt or offend, but Levi and I cannot accept your proposal." Liora slumped onto her brother's chest. "I cannot give you further explanation, and our decision to leave tonight may never be understood. The fault lies with us solely."

Suddenly Lamech set down his wine cup with some force. Everyone looked his way.

Jacob said, "I would beg you not to be angry with us, Lamech, but I can understand that you may be. We never intended to take advantage of your hospitality or feelings. But our explanation must remain unspoken for the safety of all of us."

Jershon stared at Jacob in disbelief at the rejection. The air was taken out of him, and he couldn't speak.

"You are good people—no, you are *great* people. God will bless you for your generosity." He looked at Jershon, aching to explain, but he was constrained by the discipline of the general he was. "Jershon, it is better you hold tightly to your traditions; they are good ones. Our continued presence would only further disrupt what you hold dear." Jacob suddenly stood. He looked down at the sad, confused faces staring up at him. "Jershon, Naomi, I beg your forgiveness. I beg forgiveness of all of you." He looked at Liora, who was quietly weeping in David's arms. "Liora, I especially beg your forgiveness. It is no secret I love you, but you deserve to be loved by a better and more honest man than I." With that he turned and walked out into the night. Levi soon appeared behind him. Without speaking they walked down the road. A mournful wail followed after them.

Levi had remembered to grab the two bedrolls with their meager belongings. He handed Jacob his bedroll, Jacob slung it over his shoulder, and the two men kept walking.

It had been an emotional day. Jacob's heart had been filled with his vivid realization of a living God; it was now equally empty. He felt as guilty as if he had lost a legion in fruitless combat with the enemy, only there was no enemy. None except circumstance and fate, both of them foes difficult to vanquish when they are against you.

They walked an hour before Levi spoke. "Why don't we stop here for the night?"

Jacob turned off the road and walked fifty more paces into a dark meadow. He stopped and threw his bedroll onto the ground and sat down.

Levi looked around, surveying their location in the dark gray of the night, determined they were safe enough, and sat down quietly. He had seen his friend and general in this condition before. Not all had gone well in the many campaigns they had fought together. They had suffered many setbacks—this had the feeling of one. He knew Jacob would have a restless night but eventually sleep enough to clear his head and talk in the morning. Levi rolled out his blanket and lay down. He never found it difficult to sleep and was soon breathing heavily, not to wake until the light of the rising sun touched his face.

Jacob brooded. He leaned against a rock and looked back at the city. He could see the glow of a few fires and torches. The moon had not yet risen, and the sea was black against the horizon. Everything was black. Juxtaposed with the influx of supernatural light and warmth he had felt earlier in the day, he was confused about how he could have moved so swiftly from one polar emotion to another. The general's thoughts were of duty and responsibility. The man's thoughts were of truth and honor. His entire life he had questioned the Roman gods—questioned the idea of God itself. Today he had received an unanticipated and convincing response to his prayer. It hadn't supplied him with all the answers, but he certainly had a solid witness of truth he could never deny. That was a start. He had found a woman he could be happy with for the rest of his life. Even though they had spoken little, there was a connection and feeling of closeness he had never experienced with anyone else. His life had been filled with the business of men and war; it was cut and dried, matter-of-fact, and at times brutal. No emotions were involved in his decisions as a general; they were purely strategic for the good of his men and the empire. Never was a decision made for his personal gain. Decisions were made from necessity and expediency. The consequence was life or death. Indecision was the road to failure. His decision process tonight had been driven by the general—strategic, precise, and carried out quickly to minimize further pain, suffering, and loss. But Jershon and his family, particularly Liora, were not the enemy; they were not a campaign; they were people he had come to love and respect. He began to question his actions. He was resigned to one thing, however: there was no turning back. He would move on, get the information required, and report back to Gaius Valerius. When he returned to Rome, he would sort out the internal confusion he had felt for some time, though it appeared *that* was only getting more complicated.

For now, he would honor the campaign and complete his assignment. He tried to relax but knew it would be a long night. When he was this restless, it was usually when he would be facing the enemy in the morning. This time the only enemy he had to face was himself.

◆ ◆ ◆

As soon as Jacob and Levi disappeared out the front door, Liora and Sariah ran into the bedroom, crying inconsolably. Naomi and Esther followed. Lamech and David stood together in an attitude of anger to discuss pursuing their recent guests.

Finally Jershon raised his hand. "Your emotions are blinding your reason, my sons. To pursue them would not be prudent. I believe what Jacob told us—their sudden departure has good reason. They are honorable men, and I will tell you, their intentions were never evil in any way. We should respect their decision. As in all things, we will eventually come to a fuller understanding."

Jershon could hear Liora, Sariah, and Naomi in the back room weeping and talking in indecipherable tones. He would leave them be. Women always seemed to have a better insight into matters of the heart. He pondered the implausible events of the past few days, his own acknowledgment of his belief in Jesus as the Messiah, the birth of a grandson, the near-fatal injury to his son Lamech, the sudden appearance of two strange young men who had quickly become part of their family, the idea that they could become husbands to his daughter and niece, and now their disappearance. It was all too much. He closed his eyes and spoke silently with God, pleading for understanding and guidance.

A frantic Naomi interrupted his prayer. "You must stop them," she pleaded. "They are young men who sensed our eagerness and are running scared. Surely you can reason with them." She was holding her hands over her heart as if to keep it from bursting out of her chest.

Jershon held out a calm hand to offer Naomi comfort and sympathy. She embraced her husband. "My dear, they are grown men. I do not have answers for you today. There is something Jacob wanted to tell us but couldn't, and the only way he had of communicating the conviction of his message was to depart. I heard in his words and saw in his eyes a resolute decision tempered by much thought. Jacob didn't make the decision to leave just a few minutes ago. He wanted to leave the first day when we invited them to stay and eat with us. But he had a greater wish not to offend us. We made it easy and comfortable for them to stay."

"Are you suggesting we enticed them and then trapped them?" Naomi said with a scowl on her face.

"No, my dear, but I remember how hard it was to leave your parents' home when we were courting. Your mother was a very good cook, and you, as you continue to be, were the prettiest thing my eyes had ever seen." He held her head to his chest as she wept less painful tears. "I think these two men came here on a mission they were unable to divulge. Jacob realized that they had lost focus and couldn't indulge any longer in fishing and sharing philosophy around the hearth. They sacrificed comfort and association with us to once again pursue what they originally came for."

"How do you know all this?" Naomi asked without moving from his embrace.

"I don't know, but I know their decision wasn't malicious," he said in a calm voice.

"We have two girls in the next room with broken hearts. You know as well as I do that there are no men in Capernaum or parts roundabout to compare to Jacob and Levi," Naomi said with exasperation.

"What did we really know about them?" Jershon asked.

"We know enough," Naomi replied.

"Enough for them to become husbands of our beloved Sariah and Liora?" Jershon asked.

"You yourself were convinced enough to make them a proposal," Naomi came back.

"Yes." Jershon let out a heavy sigh. "And perhaps they have done us a great favor in protecting us from our impetuousness and saved our daughters from greater pain."

"You may be right, but the pain each of them is feeling right this moment is exquisite." Naomi looked up into the tired face of her husband and stood to return to Sariah and Liora.

Jershon could only stare straight ahead, realizing he had no consolation for the acute emotions of disrupted love. He turned to his sons and nephew, who sat brooding on the far side of the room. "Lamech, do you feel up to fishing tomorrow? We could use your help."

"Yes, Father. I am well enough to go," Lamech said quietly.

Jershon nodded. "We should retire early and get our rest. There will be difficult days for a while." His voice trailed off. He quickly drained the last of the wine from his cup in the hope it would help him sleep. He pushed his meal away, no longer hungry.

The following day proved to be a long one for Jershon. He had not slept well, and he questioned his judgment of Jacob and Levi. He pondered the possibilities of the untold part of Jacob's story and had no answers for the questions posed to him by Naomi and his sons. Liora and Sariah were devastated. He had thought of staying home for the day to try to comfort them but quickly realized that would only make the day pass more slowly. Perhaps the activity and the fresh breeze on the sea would bring him some clarity.

Jershon prepared food for the men. Sariah had finally fallen asleep early in the morning, and he did not have the heart to wake her. There was little talking as Lamech, David, and Seth prepared the boat and set sail. Each knew his duty and did it quietly, but the boat soon proved too small for four somber men.

"Lamech, did you sleep well?" Jershon asked, trying to start a conversation.

"No, Father, the baby was fussy, and Raisa needed help. It was a long night." Jershon met his son's eyes, and they shared a look of understanding. Jershon turned to see Seth slouched in the bow of the boat, sound asleep.

"When there are no fish, there are no duties. Sleep well, my son," Jershon said to the sleeping boy.

By midday they had caught nothing. Each man showed increasing signs of fatigue from the long, restless night. Jershon surprised them all and set sail early for home.

The house was quiet when they arrived. The women were sitting in the main room talking when the men walked in. Jershon immediately noticed that they all had red, puffy eyes. The women abruptly resumed their duties, embarrassed that they had been discovered neglecting them. Jershon, sensing a resolution must be struck quickly, addressed them all. "My dear family, please gather round. We must talk," he said in a kindly voice. Naomi returned from the kitchen, drying her wet hands on a towel. Jershon embraced her affectionately, then in turn kissed Sariah and Liora on the cheek. They sat in chairs and on the floor around him.

"My children, we are all hurt by the departure of our new friends. Most troubling is not knowing the reason for their actions. Jacob and Levi entered our lives and immediately became part of our family." Jershon paused for a moment, wondering how best to proceed. "Perhaps we made a mistake—not in giving them our trust but in allowing ourselves to think these two wanderers would be content to stay with us." He looked directly at Naomi. "They were strong men, men on some purposeful journey. They were honest with us about the reason they were here: they came to follow Jesus. If that was their original intent, why would we not expect Jacob and Levi to follow him when Jesus left Capernaum for Chorazin today?" He let his observation sink in. All eyes were lowered. "I suspect they were informed of Jesus's departure somehow and that is why they left."

"But why did they leave so abruptly?" protested Lamech. "They left without warning, as if they had been offended by something," he added.

"I agree, Lamech," answered Jershon. "I would have expected a more cordial parting," he sighed, "but as I told your mother, they had also become attached to us and perhaps found it hard to express themselves. I suspect, my sweet daughters"—he looked at Sariah and Liora—"I suspect that Jacob and Levi have the same feelings you have. It's difficult for a man to know how to express feelings of love. We are like little boys in so many ways, and sharing our inner feelings with the women we love can be most difficult, even when we're older." Liora sagged into Naomi's lap and sobbed.

Sariah collected herself. "Will they return, Father?"

Jershon looked at his beautiful daughter, wanting to give her hope but at the same time wanting not to mislead her. "I don't know, daughter. I don't know." Jershon lowered his head, then raised it again. "I will say this. If Jacob and Levi feel about you the way I suspect they do, then they will come to a crossroads and decide to return. If they don't feel that way, then it will be better for you both that they have left."

Despite their claim of traveling from Egypt, there were things about Jacob and Levi that seemed more foreign than that story would account for. *Were they truly Jewish?* Jershon laughed to himself at the thought. Did his confession of belief in Jesus as the Messiah and the Son of God change things in any way? Did that make him less Jewish or more Jewish? If Jacob and Levi believed in Jesus as the promised Messiah, did that belief unite them with Jershon in some way that transcended their identity as Jew or Gentile? It was a puzzling dilemma.

"My children, our lives must go on. We must be content with what God has blessed us with. We must also be content with what God has chosen to take from us. Without Jacob and Levi, we might not be here as a family. Lamech might have perished without the help of those two valiant men. We all might have perished that day on the boat."

Everyone knew Jershon was right. Raisa leaned her head on Lamech's chest. Lamech held her tight and lightly kissed her forehead. Naomi shed a few more tears, but a peaceful spirit finally came upon them. Jershon lowered his head and began to pray.

27

J acob was up early, inquiring of the whereabouts of the Nazarene. He was told Jesus and his apostles would be heading to Chorazin that day. He and Levi gathered their belongings and started out early in order to stay ahead of the crowds of people that would certainly attend him. They took a position on a small hill overlooking the road and waited.

Two hours had passed when Levi shoved the dozing Jacob on the shoulder. Jacob abruptly sat up, a look of confusion on his face.

"He comes," Levi said, as if stalking an enemy.

They were too far away to see expressions but were close enough to witness Jesus's attention to each person who pressed upon him from all sides. His apostles tried in vain to create space around him, but it appeared Jesus enjoyed interacting with the disciples of all ages who constantly surrounded him. He picked up small children and held them for a moment. He touched the shoulders or heads of people who knelt in fealty as he passed.

Jacob and Levi resumed their journey to Chorazin, walking swiftly to stay ahead of most of Jesus's followers. They noticed crippled individuals and lepers standing in small groups on the roadside. One leper knelt on a blanket, his entire body wrapped with dirty cloth with just a slit for his eyes. Jacob motioned to Levi that they should stop nearby and then observe what happened when Jesus passed. A few minutes later, Jesus knelt on one knee beside the leper. He said something, and the leper held out his bandaged hand. Jesus took the leper's hand. The multitude began to block Jacob's and Levi's view, but not before they saw Jesus place a hand on the leper's head. Jesus bowed his head, and Jacob perceived that he was speaking, perhaps saying a prayer. After a moment, Jesus helped the leper rise to his feet, and he uncovered the man's head and face. As he did so, a gasp arose from the crowd, and animated conversation followed. The man could be seen embracing Jesus and then dropped to his knees before him. Jesus raised the man from his knees and whispered in his ear. The two embraced again, and then Jesus walked on. Many people passed by the leper and stared. Some paused to touch his shoulder or hand in acknowledgment or blessing. Jacob wanted to walk back to the man and see for himself, but he knew he would see a man healed of the dreaded disease, his normal life restored. If that were not the case, no one would have approached the leper, let alone touched him. Jacob looked at Levi, and both shook their heads in disbelief. They resumed their quick pace to Chorazin.

When the crowd arrived at the well in Chorazin, several people tried to offer Jesus water. He took a drink from one and moved to the shade of a nearby tree. The people gave way to allow him space to sit. When he was seated, they all sat down facing him. Jacob and Levi remained at a distance.

"Have you ever witnessed anything like this?" Jacob asked Levi. "These people adore him. I don't know how he can live this way, constantly being put upon by so many needy people."

"He's the son of a god, remember," Levi sarcastically remarked.

Jacob turned to his friend with an inquisitive look. "Do you believe that?" he asked.

Levi didn't answer immediately. "I have listened to Sariah talk about this man, saying he is the Messiah the Jews have awaited." Levi paused. "But I don't know what to believe."

Jacob smiled at his friend and looked back at the scene near the well. Jesus had begun teaching, and the people moved closer together. "Great orators in Rome aren't afforded such attention," Jacob said. "Look at this—these people are feeding on his every word. He holds them in his hand like an injured bird. They would follow him anywhere."

"Even to war?" Levi replied.

Jacob thought for a moment. "Yes, even to war. But we both know that is not what this man is about. He is about peace, about individuals changing themselves from within, not about inciting rebellion. He may be a threat to the leaders of the Jews, their priests and the Sanhedrin, but he is not a threat to Rome."

Levi weighed his next comment. "Jesus may not be a direct threat to Rome, but as you say, being a threat to the ruling class is indirectly a threat to Pilate and Herod, who regulate the affairs here. Rome prides itself in allowing the vassal state to continue to govern itself. It creates a workable relationship and tenuous trust between the two. But if the ruling class is threatened or feels compromised, is that a good thing for Rome?"

"I like the way you think, my brother," Jacob responded. "But do you think this is an internal revolution in the making?" His question was rhetorical. "There is no power play here. This Jesus doesn't seek anything; he doesn't even have what you would call a home. He's a wanderer, no more than a nomad with a message of hope for the poor." Jacob again motioned to the crowd below.

"These people aren't warriors. I'll wager most of them have never held a sword or a spear. They are fishermen and farmers. The roads he travels are lined with lepers and cripples. They are not conscripts or even the beginnings of an army. If this is a war, it is a war of philosophies."

"All wars are philosophical," Levi argued.

"I agree, but this is not a man looking for power or territory. In fact, he already has power and authority unmatched elsewhere in this country. I submit that even without legions and weapons he is more powerful than Herod and Pilate, or even Tiberius." Jacob leaned back on his elbows. "This man is not Hannibal, Levi."

"But is he the Jews' mythical Messiah?" Levi asked. "Jershon told me when we were fishing that the Jews look to the Messiah to conquer and crush the enemies of the nation. We Romans would certainly qualify as enemies."

Jacob sat up. "I don't disagree with you, but as I have thought about this, I wonder if we are the *real* enemy? Jershon also spoke about the different factions in this country that vie for control— the Herodians, the Pharisees, the Sadducees, the Sanhedrin. Ezra said the same. Those struggles are really no different from the power struggles among the factions in Rome and in the Senate. Everyone wants control."

Levi adjusted his position on the ground to take advantage of the shade of a small bush. "Jesus is beginning to control the people. I think that's what they are afraid of."

"Jesus has influence on the people who follow him, but he doesn't try to control them. Besides, as Ezra told us, the people here, the Galileans, are simple people, not like the people in and around Jerusalem. I wonder if his influence is as great among the merchants and the wealthier classes of Jews." Jacob ran his fingers through his scraggly beard. "Jesus teaches of peace, my brother, not discord—there is no guile in the man. The Sanhedrin and Pilate are afraid of losing control over the people, but from what we have learned, he is only teaching them to be good to each other, not to revolt against the government."

"So that will be our report?" Levi asked.

"I want to talk to Ezra about it first. Since Pilate will be in Jerusalem during Passover, we'll have to go there to report to him, but I want to sort this out with Ezra before we meet with him." Jacob stood to go and then paused. "First, though, there is a centurion I want to meet."

"A centurion?" Levi exclaimed, as he hopped to his feet.

"Yes, a centurion," answered Jacob.

Levi fell in beside his friend. "What are you talking about?"

Jacob headed back to the road that led to Capernaum. "Lamech told me about a centurion who lives just south of Capernaum. Apparently he is a kind man and somewhat accepted in the Jewish community. The soldiers he commands maintain a presence in the area but are fairly low-key and don't meddle in the affairs of the people. He and his soldiers are actually helpful in the community, assisting in construction projects and even occasional repair work on some of the fishing boats when they get bored. This centurion had an experience with Jesus that I want to verify."

"He had an *experience*? You don't want to be seen by soldiers in Capernaum—but you desire to meet with their leader?" Levi asked. Jacob continued to walk in silence, his resolve firm.

When Jacob and Levi reached Capernaum they stopped to ask two men where they could find the Roman centurion. They were given instructions, and Jacob walked on, Levi anxiously in tow.

They came to a tidy abode on the outskirts of town, bordering a wheat field. Jacob reached down and opened a short creaky gate and entered a small courtyard boasting flowers and an intimate seating area with two wooden benches under the shade of a latticed arbor. He called out, announcing their presence. "Hello," he said loudly as he walked toward the front door of the stone structure. A young Jewish boy came to the doorway and stared wide-eyed at the two large men standing before him.

"Is your master home?" asked Jacob.

The boy said his father would be returning shortly. Jacob thanked him. They would return later.

Jacob and Levi hiked a fair distance off and sat to rest in a nearby grove of trees. Levi immediately lay down and within minutes was fast asleep. Jacob couldn't help but smile as he looked at his friend. *A hard-working man with a clear conscience,* he thought. Jacob sat pondering the events of the last few weeks. Not far from his mind was the constant vision of Liora and her resonant beauty. He felt they were coming to the end of their mission. He wanted to talk to this Roman centurion, then journey immediately to Jerusalem, as he was anxious to meet with Ezra again, then make his report to Pilate. The thought of returning to Rome caused Jacob some dismay. He wanted to go home, to see his mother and sisters especially. He knew a report to the Senate and Gaius Valerius was mandatory, but he wanted no part of the business of the empire. How would he explain this to his father? He shook the disconcerting thought from his mind and leaned against the bulbous and knotty trunk of an ancient tree.

Within an hour Jacob saw a man approach the centurion's house. He was dressed in a common robe and tunic but was clean-shaven and did not have the bearing of a Jew. He sat up when the man opened the small gate and entered the garden. The little boy who had greeted Jacob and Levi ran from the house and leapt into the man's arms. The man picked up the boy and threw him in the air. Jacob heard a scream of delight from the child. The man caught him and set him lightly back down on the ground. The boy seemed to be saying something as he pointed directly at where Jacob was sitting. The man looked up briefly, then took the boy by the hand and walked into the house.

"Let's move," Jacob said to Levi as he stood and nudged Levi with his foot. Levi sprang to life, sitting and then standing in one fluid motion.

As they approached the gate, the same man Jacob had seen from a distance came out of the house and entered the garden. He had changed into a Roman tunic, a short sword dangling from the belt around his waist. He stood tall and didn't wait for the two strangers to speak.

"My name is Flacchus Aurelius," he said with an authoritative voice. Jacob could see the bearing of a seasoned soldier in the man and noticed his hand cupping the short hilt of his sword—*at the ready, like a true centurion.* Jacob came no further. "My son said two soldiers came calling. Are you those men?" he asked.

Jacob smiled. "Yes. May we have a moment with you, centurion?"

Aurelius looked at them quizzically, sizing them up but neither moving forward nor changing the stern look on his face. "You have the bearing of soldiers, yet you appear to be Jews. Many deserters travel this highway, men from various parts of the empire. Who are you?"

Jacob smiled. "Centurion, we are not deserters. We come in peace. Despite our appearance, I am the legate Lucius Fabius Maximus; this is my friend and deputy commander, Lartius Androcles. We are citizens of Rome sent to Judaea as emissaries on a specific mission. May we have a word in private with you?"

Aurelius eyed them with more curiosity. "Who is your father?" he asked, raising his powerful chin in their direction.

"My father is Quintus Fabius Maximus, a senator in the council of Tiberius," Jacob answered straightforwardly.

Aurelius looked at Jacob for a moment more, then dropped his hand from the hilt of his sword. "I admired your father. He was a good man." He stepped forward to shake hands with the two visitors.

"Thank you. He is still a good man," Jacob responded.

"I'm glad to hear he is still with us. Rome could use more men with reasonable minds like your father's." Aurelius smiled wryly. Jacob felt he had discovered an ally. Aurelius turned toward the house, peeked in the door, and said something in Aramaic. A moment later the young boy appeared with bread, honey, a flagon of wine, and three goblets. Aurelius invited his guests to sit on the benches in the garden. He offered them bread and poured them wine, which they gratefully accepted.

"So, gentlemen, you definitely have my full attention," Aurelius said, raising his graying eyebrows. "Please tell me about your mission and how I can be of service." Then he chuckled to himself. "Forgive me; I look at you and know how uncomfortable you must be in this disguise," he said, smiling broadly. "You could have fooled me, but you certainly didn't fool my son." He laughed out loud.

Jacob and Levi joined him. "What gave us away?" Jacob asked.

Aurelius took a swig of wine. "Look at you two. You," he pointed at Levi, "your fists could flatten a cow with one blow." He laughed again. "One of my men, who joined me recently from Caesarea, told a story of two strong Jews who beat up a friend of his. The friend was embarrassed at being bested by Jews and blamed it on his drunkenness. Is that perhaps an altercation that involved the two of you?" Jacob smiled at Levi. Then they laughed, and Aurelius joined them. The three of them toasted with the wine goblets and laughed heartily as Levi related the story of the encounter with the auxiliary soldiers in Caesarea.

They enjoyed conversing. Jacob relaxed, knowing he didn't have to measure every word he spoke. They explained their purpose to Aurelius, who nodded and seemed to understand Pilate's concern.

Jacob finally asked Aurelius, "What is your opinion of the man they call Jesus of Nazareth?"

Aurelius set his goblet down and took off his sword belt. There was a palpable silence, and Jacob sensed a great emotion swelling up in the proud man. Suddenly he looked Jacob in the eye and said with some disdain, "Have you tried and convicted him in your minds, as his fellow Jews have done?"

Jacob was taken aback at the change of countenance in the centurion and the accusation in his question. "No, we have not," Jacob answered firmly. "In fact, we think he is doing nothing wrong, and soon that will be our report to Pilate." Jacob looked at Aurelius directly.

The centurion began to soften, then said, "I had an encounter with this Nazarene." Emotion began to show in the form of moisture in the corners of his eyes. "For the past year, my men and I have followed his actions, but from my observation and the reports of my trusted men, he has done nothing but talk of peace and perform incredible works of good with the power he has." A tear ran down his cheek. "My own son . . ." Aurelius wiped the tears now forming in his eyes. "My son, Aaron, is a bright light in my old age. I should explain. His father and mother were servants in my home from the time I first arrived. I was told his mother was barren. Her husband passed away of an illness after she was miraculously with child. Aaron was born without a father, and I became like a father to him. I ignored my growing feelings for his mother as she would be cast out if she married a Roman—a

Gentile, as the Jews call us. The Jews are a peaceful people, but they can be unbending when it comes to their customs and harsh judges of those who don't comply. If you have followed Jesus for any length of time, you will know of what I speak."

Both Jacob and Levi nodded their understanding. Jacob felt the sting of his words more acutely as he thought of his feelings for Liora.

Aurelius continued. "We have carved out a good life here, a peaceful coexistence. Aaron and his mother are part of my household and are known as my servants, but they are much more than that. I love them with all my soul." Aurelius clutched his fist to his heart for emphasis. "Aaron was always weak and smaller than others his age. A few months ago, he became ill, nigh unto death with a fever and a palsy that could not be tamed. My heart ached for the pain he suffered. His mother sat by his side, constantly tending him and awaiting the day God would have mercy and take his life." He wiped more tears from his face and took another drink of wine. "I had traveled to Cana with a handful of my men, and we encountered Jesus and his multitude of disciples there. We observed him and the miracles he wrought there among the ill and afflicted. I have a good relationship with the elders in Capernaum, so I asked them to request that Jesus heal Aaron. I received word a couple of days later that the Nazarene was coming to my home. I quickly went out to meet the entourage to tell Jesus I was not worthy that he should come into my home and that if he but spoke the words, Aaron would be healed. I told him I was a man of authority also, and when I asked my soldiers or servants to do something, it was accomplished. I had only to command them and the deed was done; I didn't need to be present. I expected Jesus of Nazareth had the same type of power." Aurelius paused, holding his emotions in check. "The Nazarene smiled and looked kindly into my eyes, then he placed his hand on my shoulder. I felt a warmth run through me like the sun at midday. He said to me that he had not found so great faith, not in all of Israel."

Aurelius looked at Jacob and Levi with reddened eyes. "On returning to my home, my servants came running out with the news that Aaron had been healed." He again clutched his chest and looked at Jacob and Levi with humble sincerity. "He was healed, my friends, at the very hour of my conversation with Jesus. Aaron has been normal ever since." He wept freely.

Jacob let a moment pass, then placed his hand on Aurelius's shoulder. "That is why we are here. I wanted to confirm that story with you."

"It is true, my friends, every word of it," Aurelius stated quietly.

"Have you embraced Judaism?" Jacob asked.

Aurelius laughed. "Oh no, like you, I am a Roman, and that can never be changed. But my heart now believes in this Nazarene. He is who some say he is."

"The Son of God?" Jacob interjected.

Aurelius answered without hesitation. "Yes."

"The long hoped-for Messiah?" Jacob questioned.

Aurelius paused momentarily. "Yes, he is that too, but not in the sense that the Jews think. Jesus is certainly the king of a kingdom. But these members of the Sanhedrin are so caught up in their own importance and interpretation of things that they don't get it. They will do anything to silence him, including killing him. Not by their own hands, mind you, but by ours—Rome's. I don't know how they will do it, but that will be the outcome, my friends. I have studied the Jews over the years, and one thing has been made clear throughout their history: they have hounded, stoned, and killed many of their own prophets. They will kill this one too."

Aurelius paused to touch a nearby blossom, admiring its beauty. "The Nazarene is an outsider; he threatens the power structure and the very foundation they build their religion upon. I have lived with these people a long time, but I am removed enough from them to see things more clearly." He finished the wine in his goblet and poured more. "You seek a revolutionary, general? You have found one. Jesus of Nazareth walks more confidently and leads with more authority and effectiveness than any general I have ever known—with all due respect, sir." He motioned with his glass toward Jacob, who smiled. "His message is a revolution of peace—it turns the ruling class Jews on their ears. They have much to fear. The commoners follow him like bees to a fresh blossom. It's the commoners who wield the swords for Judaea, gentlemen. The ruling class interprets and enforces the laws, they don't brandish swords. When the Jews go to battle, the common man makes up the army, the same men who follow Jesus. But I'm afraid they will follow him to his grave without ever striking a blow against the enemy."

"Who is the enemy?" Jacob asked.

"The Jewish leaders themselves!" Aurelius shook his head in disgust. "One thing you should know about the Jews, my friends. They are good, hard-working, God-fearing people. They are strictly obedient to the precepts of their culture and religion. They keep to themselves pretty much. They tend to their families and look out for each other. They sacrifice greatly to make annual pilgrimages to Jerusalem for what they call Passover, an ancient ritual dating back to their great prophet Moses. I don't understand all of it." He waved his hand dismissingly. "I just know they are a disciplined and stern people. This Nazarene has taught them how to smile and serve others; he's different from the rabbis and priests who rule the synagogues with an iron fist."

Jacob pondered Aurelius's remarks in light of his experience with Jershon and his family. What Aurelius was saying coincided with Jacob's own assessment.

"I am boring you with my babble, my friends," Aurelius apologized.

"No, on the contrary, listening to you has been most interesting and enlightening," Jacob assured him. "My observations are in agreement with what you have said. And I thank you for sharing a most personal experience with us. It once again confirms my own feeling about this good man."

"He is more than just a good man, general. We both would be blessed to attach our allegiance to him. Of course, Rome would renounce us and the Jews would stone us. But there are worse things in this life." He laughed and Jacob laughed with him.

They sat in the inviting garden until almost sundown, talking of Rome and discussing the campaigns in which Jacob and Levi had taken part. Jacob judged Aurelius to be a good man and a loyal citizen of Rome, although he told them emphatically he had no intention of ever returning to Rome. He could never leave Aaron and his mother and confessed his growing sympathy to Jesus and his movement. He was not welcome in the synagogue but was welcome among Jesus's disciples. Aurelius's men did not share his beliefs, but they respected him as their leader. Jacob and Levi had made a new friend and found an ally in Aurelius. Their secret was safe with him.

The conversation with Aurelius brought the feelings Jacob had for Liora to the surface, producing a knot in his chest. As he contemplated departing Capernaum and Galilee for good, the thought of never seeing her again plagued him. He couldn't shake his vision of her, the sound of her voice, or how her soft hair felt against his shoulder. She had somehow infected him with an unfamiliar emotion. He thought of the difficulties Aurelius had shared when he told them of his reasons for not marrying Aaron's mother. He could not do that to Liora or Jershon and his family. He wondered if God had led him to her and what God would think if he simply walked away. He knew he would never find anyone to compare with her. He had to treat this like all distractions that came to him as a general in battle; he would let it go for now, compartmentalize it, and deal with it later. He found, however, that purging his mind of Liora was easier said than done. Right now he had a battle plan he had to stick to: they were off to Jerusalem. They would leave the next morning.

Aurelius directed them to a stable, where they secured horses to ride south to Jerusalem. They made an agreement with the owner for the horses and a supply of bread and dried fish and rode to the hills outside of Capernaum to make camp for the night.

BOOK IV

---◆---

JERUSALEM

28

I think I prefer the gentle ride of camels," Levi said as he dismounted his horse and stretched his stiff muscles.

The evening air was mild and filled with the sound of frogs croaking among the reeds edging the water. "Maybe we should camp a little further from the river. The insects are swarming." Levi swatted mosquitos off his arm.

They ate a supper of bread and dried fish and talked briefly of their voyage from Rome, laughing when they recalled Akhom's bewilderment at their fighting skills. For years, Jacob had slept out in the open with his soldiers. Eschewing the privileges of rank, he preferred his attendants carry extra rations of food and replacement weapons instead of the bulky tents, soft beds, and other trappings that generals normally packed on campaigns. His men noticed this sacrifice and respected him all the more.

Jacob let thoughts of Liora keep him up too late. Battlefield decisions were cut and dried, but he was finding that decisions of the heart did not always follow a logical path. He had enjoyed the comfort and hospitality of Jershon's humble home. He liked the fact that Liora slept a few feet from him in the next room. He knew she thought of him as she lay there. He wondered what she thought of him now. He rolled over, trying to push her out of his thoughts—it was harder than ignoring the mosquitos. He pulled his blanket over himself for protection. He would take Levi's counsel tomorrow and choose a camp farther from the river.

They awakened early, disrobed, and walked into the slow-flowing river to wash off the sleep and soil and sweat of the previous day. After drying off, they quietly ate bread and fruit and drank the rest of the wine Aurelius had sent with them. Aurelius had also supplied them with two Roman short swords and a sling. Levi was ecstatic with his new weapons. Aurelius had cautioned them about the robbers they could potentially meet along the way and had insisted that they be prepared. They stowed their meager gear, wrapped the swords inside blankets, and tied them to the horses. The daggers they had acquired in Ostia remained hidden in their belts.

They returned to the main road south and soon passed a caravan of Nabataean merchants heading north to Damascus, moving goods by camel. They were acquainted with Iqbal and Alhasan. The leader removed a small satchel from the saddle of his burdened camel. He offered it to Jacob—it was a package of dried meat. As he handed it to Jacob, he said, "It is the forbidden meat, but I know some Jews who eat it when no one is watching." He and his friends laughed heartily. Jacob accepted the gift. He and Levi were weary of dried fish and, unbeknownst to their Nabataean benefactors, they would enjoy the dried meat without sin. Each party bowed and shared wishes of peace and safe travels.

Jacob and Levi walked their horses slowly, enjoying the dried meat. The day passed quickly. They talked of home and what the future might bring. Neither of them had a clear vision of returning to Rome. Levi admitted to Jacob that he and Sariah had actually talked about a life together. Since the murder of his family, Levi had shut down all feelings of tenderness. That helped him greatly on campaigns and in battle, but closed-down emotions did not endear him to people. Jacob had noticed during the brief time they had spent in Capernaum that Levi had become less and less the hardened soldier. Jacob had seen his soft side and sensitivity return as Levi interacted with Jershon's family. He saw the joy Levi experienced when he played with Esther and mentored David and Seth. He hadn't seen Levi clutch his amulet in some time. It was obvious neither of them relished the idea of returning to Rome or to battle.

That evening, they spoke more intimately to each other than at any other time since they were young boys. They shared cares and concerns and possibilities for the future. Levi, in speaking of Sariah, mentioned how her smile reminded him of his mother's and how much his mother would have liked her. It was the only time Jacob could recall Levi mentioning his mother in any conversation. Levi said Sariah had asked him about his family. He had told her the story of their murders, and she had cried and sympathized with him. She had later shared the story of the murder of her cousins—the older brothers of Liora and David. It was a painful tale for her to tell and for Levi to hear. It was not his doing, yet he felt responsible for the killings. Levi admitted to Jacob that he was feeling emotions he had never felt before. It was cathartic and healing and drew the two friends closer together.

Jacob and Levi had witnessed experienced soldiers wounded in battle, crying with pain and remorse, crying out for their wives and mothers and sometimes their gods, weeping like the little boys they once were. It was a disturbing scene: grown men, their lives being violently drained away, clutching and crying out for the things that were most important to them. Battle had hardened the normal emotional responses in both Jacob and Levi.

Both admitted they had felt more human in the past few weeks than they had felt in years, an effect of their time away from battle and tender moments spent in the home of Jershon.

"I want to be a man like this!" Jacob said, clutching the robe on his chest. "A man that feels again, a man that doesn't avoid tenderness, a man that produces goodness, not one that sends men off to die." Jacob pounded his chest with his fist. Levi sat quietly. This was new ground for the two lifelong friends.

Jacob turned toward his friend. "I had an experience I want to tell you about." He shifted uneasily. "We have talked many times about the gods," Jacob began. Levi nodded in agreement. "I have struggled, brother. I have struggled with our gods. For all the in-telligence and knowledge Rome, Greece, and Egypt have brought into the world, we have adulterated the concept of God. We have invented gods for everything and every event. We have even bor-rowed gods and changed their names to suit us."

"We've been through this before, my brother." Levi sighed heavily.

"I know, I know," Jacob said, "but it still plagues me. I can no longer accept the gods of Rome. They have no place. They are not human."

"That's the point of a god, Jacob," Levi interjected. "They are *not* human. They are *gods*."

"I believe God has a form like ours, only with infinite glory," Jacob said with conviction.

Levi did not want to engage again in this endless and am-biguous debate, but Jacob looked him in the eye. "Somewhere, I believe, God has to have had experience as a human in order to understand the feelings and needs of mankind." Jacob shook his head, unable to quite form into words the thoughts in his head. "Levi, do you talk to God?"

Levi looked quizzically at Jacob. "What do you mean?"

Jacob became animated. "Have you ever talked to Jupiter or Neptune?"

"Well, I think when we boarded the ship in Ostia to come here I said something to Neptune." Levi smiled.

"But you didn't place your trust in Neptune, did you? You placed your trust in the captain and Akhom."

"You're confusing me—you're not making any sense." Levi shrugged his shoulders.

Jacob sat up straight. "Do you remember praying with Ezra on the ship?" Levi acknowledged he did. "He was talking to someone, Levi; he wasn't just reciting some verse. It actually appeared he was having a conversation with his God; it was personal. Do you remember hearing Jershon pray? He prayed humbly, sincerely. He spoke with his God, no, he pleaded with his God, expecting a response. Their prayers are different." Jacob looked off into the distance, his brow furrowed.

"I'm not sure where you are going with this, Jacob. So their prayers are different. So they think their God is human, more personal to them—so what? How does that affect us?" Levi asked.

"Because I believe this Jehovah is our God too," Jacob said boldly.

"He's a Jewish God, Jacob. He walks and talks with the Jews, not with the conquering Romans," Levi replied.

"I believe differently," Jacob responded.

"That's not surprising; you have for some time." Levi sighed.

"Yes, but before I could never define what I believed; I can define it now."

Levi leaned back against a large rock, getting more comfortable, and looked at Jacob, waiting for his explanation. Jacob stared into the small fire they had started. Levi could sense there was emotion welling in his brother's eyes.

"The other night," Jacob began, "I went out by myself and hiked to the top of the hill near Jershon's home. Something was working on me, an unknown, yet a comforting force. I felt compelled to address its presence. I did what I had seen Jershon do many times; I began a conversation with Jehovah. I talked to him like Ezra would talk to him, frankly and boldly. I asked questions. I told him my concerns, doubts, and fears. I confessed my sins and admitted my weaknesses."

Levi could see the tears running down Jacob's face.

Jacob continued, "I asked this God if he was real. I asked him if he cared about me—a Roman. I asked him if this Jesus of Nazareth was his son." The tears flowed freely now. "You're going to think I am foolish, brother, but I received an answer."

Levi sat forward, leaning on his knees. Jacob was struggling to talk. Levi had never seen his brother in such a state. He had seen the compassionate general mourn over the loss of soldiers in battle, especially those that had become friends. He knew of the deep feelings and passion that Jacob had demonstrated throughout his life. He had seen his friend in a myriad of difficult and sometimes gut-wrenching circumstances over the years. Levi had experienced many of them himself. But what he was now witnessing was different. There was a peace and serenity about Jacob. The anxiety and frustration of the battlefield that accompanied all leaders was absent. Jacob was calm and contented as he tried to explain his innermost feelings.

Jacob wiped the tears with the back of his hand. "It came over me like a warm blanket, and I felt a burning from within. It started here," he placed his hand on his heart, "and soon took over my entire body to the point where I had no strength. I felt the poison of evil running out of my body and being replaced with goodness and hope. All I wanted to know was confirmed to me in an instant. I collapsed on the ground, unable to move. I woke up sometime later and returned to the house. I was unsure how to tell anyone what I had experienced, so I kept it to myself." Jacob looked squarely into Levi's eyes. "God is real. Jesus of Nazareth is his son. He is not exclusively the God of the Jews—he is the God of all men, and his son walks among us, my brother." Jacob's eyes were red with emotion. Tears spilled down his cheeks and into his beard. "I don't expect you to believe me. But whether you believe me or not doesn't matter. I know what I know and can't deny what happened to me. It makes me wonder if I should stay in Judaea."

Levi digested what his friend was telling him. He could see Jacob was serious about what he was saying. It was making him uncomfortable and he didn't know how to respond. Levi admitted to himself he had felt a soothing peace as he observed Jesus. He sensed he was a good man, a special man. He had not taken the step his brother had in asking in prayer what it all meant. He was skeptical of all the gods. He couldn't fathom the meaning of a god walking among men openly. Levi's thoughts were more pragmatic: *Why does this Jesus allow the Jewish leaders to defame and antagonize him? If he is a god or a king, why doesn't he use his power to throw out the Jewish leadership and the Roman occupation at the same time?* There was too much that didn't make sense to his logical way of thinking.

Levi hadn't given any real thought to whether the Nazarene was the living son of a god. His job was limited to determining if the Nazarene was a danger to Roman rule. He had determined he was not; therefore, he considered his involvement finished. They were off to Jerusalem to make a report to Pontius Pilate and return to Rome for the same purpose. The campaign was coming to an end. It became apparent to Levi that Jacob was suggesting a continuing involvement.

It was incomprehensible to Levi's way of thinking. He

admitted to himself that he missed Sariah. She was different from any woman he had ever met. They had talked in private about many things, creating a bond of trust. It wasn't until he became acquainted with Sariah and her family that he gave any thought to a serious relationship with a woman or having a family of his own. His life was that of a soldier; he thought of nothing else beyond that. This campaign to Judaea had been a nice diversion, but it also opened his eyes to a life he never thought he could have. Suddenly Jacob was suggesting that it could become a reality. But he had left Capernaum and put life with Sariah out of his mind. Jacob's admission confused him. *Was he seriously thinking of staying and not returning to Rome?* Jacob and Liora had definitely shared a special attraction for each other. It would be understandable for him to want to stay with her. But this talk of Jesus and Jacob's confession of belief in him as a living god was more than Levi could process.

Jacob stared blankly into the fire, not expecting any response from his friend. The tears had stopped flowing but still streaked his dusty face. Before Levi could say anything, Jacob spoke. "They are going to take his life," he said quietly. "I believe what Aurelius told us. These zealot Sanhedrists will somehow put him to death, and unless they outright murder him they will have to lean on the authority of Rome to do their dirty work. We have to stop it."

His comments were interrupted by the sound of approaching hooves. Their attention was drawn to a group of about eight men approaching on horseback, seemingly foreign, certainly not Jewish. The men stopped about fifty yards away and dismounted, making a halfhearted attempt to appear like they were setting up a camp like normal travelers. The sun was still above the western horizon and the subdued orange light of the early evening bathed the rocky hills. Both Levi and Jacob watched their movements, sensing something about them wasn't right. Most travelers they had encountered along the way were poor. Most of them traveled on foot, though a few possessed a horse or donkey to carry their belongings. Women and sometimes children accompanied them. This was a band of men on horseback, traveling light. It was then Levi noticed the flash of a long, curved sword hanging from the waistband of a large, menacing man wearing a dark turban.

"It appears we may have unwelcome visitors," he remarked to Jacob, not taking his eyes off the intruders. Aurelius had told them they would encounter many foreigners traveling to Jerusalem this time of year to visit the temple for the high holy days of Passover. He cautioned them to stay close to the main road to avoid bands of robbers that frequented the highway, taking advantage of defenseless parties camped along the way. The men seemed more interested in looking at Levi and Jacob sitting on the ground by their small fire than they were in making camp.

"They are likely after our horses," Jacob said.

"Well, they will get nothing," Levi said as he stood and removed his robe, exposing his massive arms and strong legs in his short tunic. He faced the men. They handed the reins of their horses to a member of their band and moved to one side. Their intentions were becoming clear. Levi produced the sling given to him by Aurelius. He found a suitable stone and placed it into the webbing. He whirled it over his head and at the right moment hurled the stone toward the group of horses. It skipped through their feet, causing them to rear. Eyes wide, the horses wheeled, knocked the helpless attendant to the ground, and galloped into the nearby hills. Levi, in the meantime, loaded another stone in the sling and whipped it over the heads of the small band of men standing in disorder. It hissed over their heads, causing them to flinch and duck in response. Jacob had been watching in amusement. With one eye on the robbers, he retrieved the short swords from their bedrolls, still tied to the horses. He tossed one to Levi, who caught it by the hilt in one hand, the sling dangling from his other hand. Jacob removed his long outer robe, and both men tightened the sashes of their tunics to prepare for an attack.

Levi shouted a curse in Greek at the top of his lungs as he grasped the amulet around his neck in his fist. "By the gods, if you come to harm us, you will be sent back to your own god cut up in so many pieces he will not recognize you." He then brandished his sword. He lunged and sidestepped, twirled the sword over his head and brought it down fiercely onto his imaginary foe. To see him do it was intimidating and gave the viewer no doubt as to his skills and intentions with the flashing sword. He dropped to one knee and with both hands drove the sword into the ground in front of him with a force that would have pierced the body of any enemy. He bared his teeth and screamed in defiance at the robbers who stood still, staring at him from a distance in disbelief. There was complete silence. Jacob stood behind Levi, sword in hand. The only movement was the shuffling of the two horses that were suddenly skittish from the flailing movements of their master.

The thieves had chosen the wrong people to rob. The bandit leader turned to his men and with a slight wave of his hand signaled his men that the fight was over. They collected their remaining horses and rode off as quickly as they had come.

Jacob couldn't help but laugh. "Do you think they will return?" he asked.

"Yes, in the dark of night. We should make camp elsewhere, perhaps near another group of travelers to discourage them—and we should set a watch."

They hastily put out their small fire, gathered their meager belongings, and mounted the horses to move to safer ground. They returned to the main road and within a few minutes approached a flat area where several groups of people were encamped. They stopped a friendly distance from the largest group and made camp, kindled a small fire, and settled in for the night.

After a meager meal, they lay quietly on the ground, staring up at the night sky. "Did you expect a response from me earlier, before we were interrupted?" Levi asked.

"About what?" Jacob responded.

"About Jesus and Liora and Sariah and all the things you babbled on about."

"No—you're right, I was just babbling," Jacob responded. "But those things have weighed heavily on my mind lately. I want to be engaged in something that is not centered on killing and subjecting people to rule. We talked about this in Gaul; you know how I feel. My disdain for Roman expansion has not changed—I need to move on." Jacob once again became passionate in his speech. "My brother, I love Liora, but I realized that can't be. That's why I made the decision to leave abruptly—it just wouldn't work. I know how disruptive that would be to her family. They all may be followers of Jesus, but they are still Jewish. Those traditions run deep. I respect her too much to make her an outcast in her own community."

"Then take her to Rome, brother. Take her to your home. Your mother and sisters will embrace her. Your mother will convince your father that following your heart is better than following the conventions of Roman society. Your mother never followed convention. She was never caught up in the patrician lifestyle made available to her. She decided to follow her heart and live outside of Rome and its demands. She and your father made it work. And is your mother any less respected? No, she is not. She is beloved, looked upon in almost a higher state. When she accompanies your father to Rome, she is regal and elegant, and women look up to her because she is different and because she is her own master. She alone has decided the course of her life, not the fickle whims of the emperor."

Jacob laughed, "You are observant and wise in ways that constantly surprise me, my brother."

"Well, it wasn't very wise to challenge eight bandits. That could have gone a lot differently had they chosen to attack," Levi said.

"But they didn't. You convinced them without saying a word that it would not be prudent for them to move upon us. It was strategic and masterful."

"You flatter me, my friend—it was bold but stupid," Levi remarked.

"But it worked, and that's all that matters," Jacob said as he made himself more comfortable on the hard ground.

"So why don't you go back and get Liora and do something bold and stupid—that strategy might work too," Levi challenged.

Jacob simply smiled. "Let's first finish what we came here to do, and then I will think about being bold and stupid." He pulled the small blanket over his shoulders and rolled over, signaling the end of their conversation.

Suddenly a scream pierced the night sky.

Levi was up as quick as a cat, his sword in hand. Jacob sat bolt upright and then stood, tilting his head to determine what direction the scream came from. He retrieved his sword, and the two of them moved quickly and quietly toward the now-muffled screams.

Soon they could see a campfire in the distance. They could make out shadows of men moving around quickly. As they approached, they could tell it was the same band of robbers that they had occasion to meet earlier, this time picking on a weaker foe. One of them held a woman by the throat, attempting to stifle her screams. Two bodies lay on the ground motionless at his feet.

The other men brandished swords and stood guard over a small group of people nearby. Jacob could see now that it appeared to be three men, two women, and several children being held in a tight group. Levi and Jacob glanced at each other and with a few silent motions of their heads and hands devised a strategy. Levi began to circle around, staying outside of the small fire's light. Jacob moved forward slowly and deliberately. He carefully placed the sword in his sash behind his back, then moved into the light of the fire.

"Does someone need help here?" Jacob asked innocently. All eyes were on him as he approached slowly with his arms to his side. One member of the band of robbers met him at the edge of the light and held a sword out, pointing directly at him.

"Just leave, and we will cause you no trouble," one of the bandits said from his place with the hostages in the background.

Jacob didn't move. "I thought I heard a scream." Jacob looked around. "It appears you're already causing trouble here," he said.

The bandit took a couple steps forward, his large sword still pointed at Jacob. "This does not concern you, Jew. Leave now or you will become part of this," the leader rejoined.

"Oh, I think we're already part of it," Jacob said. A muffled groan came from somewhere in the background. Levi had grabbed the thief who was holding the woman by the neck and thrust his dagger into his heart from behind. The thief crumpled in a heap on the ground, and the woman renewed her shrill scream. As the bandit in front of him turned to see what was happening, Jacob in one fluid motion grabbed his short sword from behind his back, swung it forward, and caught the robber on the side of his neck, dropping him dead in his tracks.

The other robbers were confused with the sudden turn of events and the sight of Jacob and Levi walking confidently toward them, swords and daggers in hand. Making a fatal error in judgment, the bandits decided to fight instead of run. The bandits fought wildly but were no match for the skill and strength of Jacob and Levi. As they fought, the women were screaming and the children were crying hysterically. Within minutes, Jacob and Levi had dropped the other six men. When it was over, the two large Romans stood with blood-spattered tunics, looking down at the bandit leader, who had suffered an incapacitating wound. Jacob cautiously knelt down by his side. "Where are you from?" Jacob asked the man, who was struggling for breath.

"Damascus," was his feeble response.

Jacob looked him in the eye and held his sword up for the man to see. "I want you to get on your horse and ride back to Damascus. You tell your friends that it doesn't pay to ride into Judaea and attack innocent families and rob them. Jews like me take exception to that. I don't ever want to see you again." Jacob spat out the words.

The man shakily nodded his head in agreement, but before he could get up, Levi swiftly rammed his sword through the man's chest.

Jacob looked up in disbelief. "What?" was all he managed to sputter.

"I've disposed of an enemy that would soon return to do battle," Levi said defiantly. He was clutching the amulet around his neck. "These are the same type of scum that killed my family. They do not deserve to live!"

Jacob stood and looked at his friend, who was visibly shaking with anger.

"Look at these people they have attacked," Levi went on, motioning with his sword toward the family that was now huddled together, sobbing quietly. "They have killed their men and left a dark imprint on these women and children that will never leave them." He looked toward the sky. Jacob saw the tears streaming down his face in the moonlight.

Levi threw his sword on the ground and held up his bloodied hands. "I'm tired of the conflicts and the killing. I've had enough!" he cried out, bowing his head.

Jacob returned the sword to his sash and placed an arm on Levi's shoulder. "I'm tired of this too, my brother."

He stepped forward and hugged Levi. Jacob knew his brother was shedding tears held inside for a long time. Tears for his family, tears for comrades lost in battle, and even tears for the noble enemies he had slain out of allegiance to Rome. Jacob was witnessing his brother's discovery of remorse, humility, and penitence. He knew Levi had turned a corner and would never be the same. Jacob silently wept with him.

"Thank you. Thank you for what you have done." The patriarch of the family approached the two defenders. "We have traveled from Cana. My family is going to Jerusalem for Passover. If you are going to Jerusalem, won't you please travel with us? We can feed you. This is a terrible setback but we are determined to move on—we must," he said, clutching his hands together.

Jacob looked into the cloudy and pleading eyes of the old man standing before him. He reached out his hand and touched his arm. "I am sorry this has happened. I am glad we were nearby and could help. I only wish we had come sooner. We will help you clean up and stay with you for the remainder of the night, but in the morning we must move on alone. You will be fine if you stay on the main road. There are plenty of travelers for protection."

Jacob and Levi dragged the bodies of the robbers outside the camp and left them in a heap behind a small rise. They gathered the swords and daggers and purses of the eight men. They helped the two younger men traveling with the group to dig graves for their slain family members, who happened to be the husband

and teenage son of the woman who was being held by the robber when Jacob and Levi had arrived. She wept uncontrollably as the four men wrapped the bodies in robes and placed them in the shallow grave.

Jacob and Levi retrieved their belongings and horses from their nearby camp and returned to sleep with the mourning family. At sunrise, the women served them fresh bread and warm grain porridge covered with honey. The meal was excellent and filling. Levi took the best of the robbers' horses, handing the reins of the others to the man in the group who appeared to be the oldest. "Take these horses with you. Keep them or sell them in Jerusalem. They appear to be of good stock and should bring you a handsome profit. The swords and daggers are equally valuable, and I am sure there is a trader who will pay you a worthy sum for them." Then he handed the man the good-sized purse of coins the robbers had possessed. The man wept with gratitude.

As Jacob and Levi took their leave, the woman who had lost her husband and son rushed to Jacob and hugged him tightly. She had no voice left and was frail and drawn. She looked up into his eyes and hoarsely said something that Jacob did not understand, but he knew it was a blessing of sorts. Then she turned and hugged Levi. As she did so, she reached up, put her hand on the amulet around his neck, raised it to her lips, and kissed it lightly. She repeated the same blessing and gently placed the misshapen piece of gold back in its place against Levi's chest. He embraced her and kissed her on the forehead.

The two Romans walked away from the camp as the family called out blessings and farewells. They walked silently for some time along the main highway to Jerusalem, leading their four horses.

It was almost an hour before Jacob finally spoke. "You know, my brother, there's a place for soldiers who protect the innocent.

What we did back there was a good thing." He placed his hand on Levi's shoulder. Levi didn't look up. Jacob let the silence continue.

After a few minutes Levi responded. "I know what we did was good—and necessary. But it hit me that many of the enemies we have slain over the years had wives, mothers, and families like that woman who lost her son and husband. We have killed a lot of sons and husbands." He paused. "The men we killed last night deserved to die." He paused again. "But it's too easy for me to kill people. I'm weary of it. I think I understand now how you feel. Remember how I pined for a sword on our sea voyage? I felt naked without it. Now I am not sure I ever want to carry one again."

29

L ate the following day, the sun began its slow shift to the
west. The two Roman travelers climbed a steep and long
rise, pausing at the top to enjoy the view before them. Far
off in the distance they caught their first glimpse of the great city
of Jerusalem.

Smoke and dust arose from various points, telling of hearth
fires and the movement of thousands of people. It was not as
grand as Rome. The city was a mixture of low mud and stone
buildings and taller structures made of chiseled limestone.
Portions of the great walls surrounding the city could be seen,
walls built by King David and his son Solomon and later expanded by Herod. Jacob studied the city in the distance and
made out what he believed was the temple spoken of by Jershon.
It was surrounded by its own wall, and although it appeared small
on the far horizon, it was clearly one of the larger structures in
the city.

Next to the temple, Jacob could see the Herodian fortress of
Antonia. Its high towers that Aurelius had mentioned reminded
him that there was a garrison of Roman auxiliary soldiers in

Jerusalem, and they would, no doubt, encounter patrols regularly, especially with the influx of so many pilgrims. Jacob had become comfortable looking like an ordinary Jew and doubted the soldiers would pay them any heed.

Sight of the city filled them with adrenaline, and they rode on with renewed purpose. They hadn't talked about the upcoming meeting with Pontius Pilate. During the short journey, Jacob had formulated the report in his mind but wanted to talk to Levi about it. More important, he wanted to talk to Ezra. "How do you think we will find Ezra in this mass of people?" Jacob finally asked Levi.

"Good question. Maybe we should go to the temple and ask around. He said he was still friends with the high priest. Perhaps he would know where to find him," Levi answered, shifting his weight on the horse.

"That's a good idea. I want to spend some time with Ezra before seeing Pilate. Frankly, Pilate could still be in Caesarea, but I assume he will be in Jerusalem for these holidays. If he is still in Caesarea, we will stay in Jerusalem for a couple of days, then head to the coast. Perhaps we can secure passage on a ship home from there." Jacob's voice trailed off with his last comment.

Levi looked over at his friend. "So you have decided to go home?"

Jacob looked straight ahead. "I suppose," he finally said.

"You don't sound very convinced. After our meeting with Pontius Pilate, will we have any unfinished business?" Levi asked his friend with a smirk.

"There's always unfinished business at the end of a campaign," Jacob said flippantly.

"But I'm talking personal business," Levi responded.

Jacob reined up his horse defiantly. "What personal business?" he barked. Levi just kept moving slowly ahead on his horse. Jacob sat for a moment, then loosed the reins and dug his heels into the side of the horse to get him moving forward. When he came alongside Levi, he turned and said, "If you are talking about Liora, I might ask the same of you—what about Sariah?"

Levi kept his gaze straight ahead, not acknowledging the question. After a few minutes Levi turned to Jacob. "What about Sariah?" Levi snipped. "Neither of those good women would chain their future to a couple of Roman soldiers, especially not Liora. Her brothers were killed by Romans."

"They weren't killed by Romans like us," Jacob defended. "They were like those we encountered in Caesarea, auxiliaries from Syria or Macedonia or some other Greek-speaking area of the empire. I would bet on it."

"How do you plan on convincing them of that?" Levi shook his head.

"We don't have to convince them," Jacob said, flustered. "There is no need to convince them of anything—we're going home!" He kicked his horse to move ahead.

"What about Jesus? Will you stay and become a disciple?" Levi shouted after his friend.

Jacob again reined up his horse. "You have questions that I don't have answers for," he spat.

"If we go home, we go home as Romans: you the senatorial legate and I your primus pilus and deputy commander. Nothing changes," Levi said with a hint of melancholy in his voice.

"It's you . . . you're the one who wants to stay," Jacob exclaimed.

"No worse than you, my brother, but you won't admit it," Levi retorted, then kicked his horse and moved on. Jacob kicked his horse and caught up.

"Do you want to talk about this?" Jacob asked.

"No, not really," Levi answered.

"Brother, at some point we need to address this and make a decision. We will be expected back in Rome once we give our report to Pontius Pilate, and that could be in the next few days," Jacob pointed out.

Levi was silent. They passed an encampment of about twenty pilgrims resting alongside the road. Greetings and blessings were exchanged. Jacob had become comfortable with casual Aramaic exchanges. His accent drew a little attention, but the fact that he spoke even a few words of their language diminished the curiosity of the travelers.

They passed houses on the outskirts of Jerusalem, and people were becoming more plentiful. At the occasional rise they could plainly see more details of the great city. Small paths and roads broke off everywhere. It was easy to stay on the main highway, as it was wider and well rutted, very different from the stone roads leading into Rome. They were forced to make their way around the bustling people and carts that plied the road in and out of the city. Presently they passed merchants and beggars lining both sides of the road, peddling their wares or sorrows. The smells of pungent spices and open sewers hung heavy in the air. Smoke and incense intermingled with dust from the roads, creating a haze throughout the city. Everyone seemed to be in a hurry and there wasn't much space to maneuver with four horses.

As they neared the gates of the city, Jacob and Levi dismounted and led their horses through the throngs. They passed through a massive portal and intermingled with a sea of people. The temple was not far off, and Jacob led them toward its high walls.

Near the temple, the crowds increased and merchants were everywhere, their cages of doves and goats vying for buyers' attention. Boisterous men stationed at small tables exchanged money. The noise was deafening, people shouting for attention and bartering their wares. The temple of the Jews hardly seemed a respite for worship and contemplation.

Jacob spotted three men in robes similar to the ones he'd seen on the elders in Capernaum. He nodded to Levi, who took the reins of the two horses from Jacob so he could walk after them to inquire of Ezra. They stood with their arms folded, discussing something in low voices among themselves. Jacob approached them boldly.

He spoke in Greek, addressing the group respectfully. "Rabbi, I seek a man named Ezra, a rabbi who lives near here. I am a friend of his and seek his company."

All the men looked at him inquisitively.

"You are not from here," a short man with a long gray beard said.

"No, I am not, rabbi. We come from Capernaum," said Jacob.

The men continued to look at Jacob with blank stares. The old man continued. "Yet you are not Galilean." The man raised his eyebrows, inviting more explanation.

"No, rabbi, I am from Egypt." Jacob hoped his answer would end the questioning.

The man speaking furrowed his brow. "An Egyptian Jew," he said in a condescending tone, "coming to Jerusalem by way of Capernaum. That is most strange. And why seek ye this Ezra?"

"He is a friend," Jacob stated flatly, annoyed with their attitude and irrelevant questions. He straightened his shoulders and with a stern look in his eyes addressed the elders firmly. "Do you know him and his whereabouts, or not?"

The three men looked up at the large, apparently Jewish man before them and shuffled with discomfort. "Yes, we know him," one of them said. "If you will go out of the gates of the city and travel a short distance on the main highway you will see a grove of trees to your right. Just prior to that grove you will encounter a merchant selling colorful cloth. He acquires that cloth through his relationship with Ezra. His name is Tamur. He will lead you to Ezra."

Jacob bowed with respect and thanked them despite the contempt he felt. He returned to where Levi held the horses. Jacob could sense the three men watching his every step. "I think we've found him," Jacob said to Levi as he grabbed the reins of two of the horses. They led the horses back the way they had come.

When they had made their way through the crowds and beyond the city walls, Jacob walked beside Levi and told of his conversation with the elders. "It was odd the way they questioned me. You would think with all the pilgrims in Jerusalem that the presence of a stranger asking about someone wouldn't raise eyebrows."

"Perhaps they are curious about your interest in Ezra. Who knows how they feel about him. Ezra was someone of importance here at one time. Maybe they have reason to be suspicious of him," Levi observed.

"You're probably right," Jacob responded. "I found it interesting that they knew this merchant and his name—it didn't seem coincidental. As Ezra told us, these people know everyone's business. Maybe we made a mistake asking them about Ezra and alerting them to our presence."

"We're not going to be here long," Levi responded. "And you forget—once we meet with Pontius Pilate, we are Romans again. They wouldn't dare interfere with us or with Ezra."

In the distance, Jacob saw the grove of trees the elders had referred to. There were merchants along both sides of the road and with the influx of visitors, it was like passing through a bazaar. Jacob spotted a tent displaying colorful cloth hanging from ropes suspended from tall stakes. Under a flap in front of the tent sat a large man in a multicolored robe, different from the drab brown and gray robes they commonly saw. He was engaged in an animated conversation with two men sitting by him on a deep red rug. Jacob and Levi approached slowly, guiding the horses carefully through the crowd of people. As they approached the front of the tent the three men sitting on the rug stopped talking and looked up.

"We seek Tamur," Jacob announced.

The large man in the colorful robe stood. "I am Tamur," he said, smiling broadly at the two strangers.

Jacob put his hand out in greeting, and Tamur reciprocated. "My name is Jacob. This is Levi."

Tamur sized up the two men briefly, raising a bushy gray eyebrow suspiciously.

"We come from Egypt by way of Capernaum. We come seeking a man named Ezra. We are friends of his. We were told you could help us find him."

The mood instantly changed. Tamur laughed heartily, opened his arms, and embraced Jacob like an old acquaintance. "It's so like my friend Ezra to have friends with a foreign appearance and strange speech." The three men laughed together. Jacob and Levi joined them.

"So you know him," Jacob said.

"Of course," said Tamur jovially. "Come, sit, and join us in a drink. You look weary from the road, and thirsty." Tamur and his friends turned and sat back down on the rug.

They secured the horses to a nearby tree and returned to join the three men on the rug. Tamur gestured to a boy standing at the side who quickly ran into the tent and returned with two gold goblets that he placed on the tray in front of Tamur. Tamur filled them from an ample flask and offered them to his guests. The wine was cool and excellent.

"So tell me." Tamur motioned to them with his hands. "What

business do you two *Egyptians* have with my friend Ezra?" Tamur said sarcastically and enjoyed more laughter with his friends at the expense of Jacob and Levi. Jacob felt a curious liking for Tamur and sensed he could trust him.

"It's a long story," Jacob answered.

"We have plenty of time and we enjoy long stories. I am sure it will prove interesting," Tamur encouraged him.

Jacob considered being fully truthful but felt it best to be discreet. "We met Ezra in Rome. We traveled here with him a short time ago. Our mission is almost complete, and we want to meet with Ezra before we depart."

"Mission?" Tamur asked. "That sounds serious."

Jacob regretted his choice of words and searched for a rejoinder. "Our time here is complete," he said flatly. "We just have a few details to take care of, and meeting with Ezra is one of them." He hoped he would not be questioned further about his presence in Jerusalem.

Tamur realized he had made his two guests uncomfortable and was now more curious than ever. He offered them bread and fruit from another tray. Jacob and Levi ate hungrily.

Tamur finally said, "Ezra mentioned some time ago he was traveling to Rome at the behest of some powerful men. When he returned, we had occasion to meet again, and I asked him about his journey. He told me it was uneventful, that he had simply escorted two diplomats back to Judaea. I assume you two are the diplomats?" Tamur smiled agreeably at his two guests.

Jacob realized it was fruitless to hide behind half-truths. "Yes, we are the two diplomats. I would say our presence is inconsequential and our task was a small one, and it is now complete. Please forgive us for not being more forthcoming."

Tamur smiled at the two imposing men sitting before him.

"I'll wager your story is much more interesting than you let on." He laughed heartily and poured more wine.

"You come at an interesting time," Tamur continued. "Passover brings pilgrims from all parts of our land and many foreigners, not unlike you two. By the end of the week, there will be thousands of visitors. The streets will be filled with customers." He laughed again and his friends joined him. "We are fully stocked, thanks to our mutual friend, and look forward to the influx of new money." Tamur then dropped an interesting comment. "We hear this Jesus of Nazareth is coming from Galilee. He brings with him a multitude of followers, adding to the confusion of this week. The priests have their robes in a flutter over the arrival of this 'king of the Jews.'" Tamur's friends once again shared his laughter.

Jacob almost choked on his wine. A thousand questions came into his mind at once. He sorted his thoughts, then said calmly, "We heard of this Jesus during our time in Capernaum. He seems to stir up the people."

"He stirs up the Sanhedrin! What could be better?" Tamur asked. "Those vipers are afraid of their own shadows, let alone a man who professes peace and change within the Jewish religion. They are simply afraid of him."

Jacob chose his words carefully. "You seem to know something of this Jesus," he said.

"My good friend, we sit here all day at the crossroads of commerce and communication. I don't need to seek news—it just comes to me. I use what I can for my gain. After all, I am a humble merchant." He inclined his head with a wry smile then continued. "Jesus was here some time ago. He has friends, I understand, nearby in Bethany. When he visited the temple, he caused quite a stir, throwing out the moneychangers and merchants who had set up shop within its walls. I frankly don't blame him. I am not a devout Jew, but I think the temple should be a place of reverence and worship. It has taken on the appearance of a common bazaar. His cleansing of the temple precincts was not popular with the priests, and he has become less popular with them as time has progressed. I fear his arrival in Jerusalem might precipitate his arrest."

Jacob could see that Tamur was an observant and well-informed man. "Well, it will be interesting to see the reaction of the powers that be if Jesus does in fact come," Jacob said.

"Oh, I have it on good authority that he will come. Perhaps I should invest in some trumpets to signal the arrival of the king. That would surely disturb the priests." Tamur and his friends laughed. "It's an interesting phenomenon—he is popular with the people but not with the leaders. His popularity will prevent the priests from having him arrested publicly; that would cause a riot. And if you believe the stories about the miracles, especially the ones we have heard about him raising the dead with the touch of his hand, perhaps the priests are afraid he could take their life with the same touch." Tamur laughed again.

Jacob was enjoying the wine and the company but was getting anxious to meet with Ezra. "Tamur, you have been most hospitable. We appreciate the food and wine, and the conversation has been stimulating, but we are eager to meet with our friend Ezra. Can you point us to him?"

Tamur leaned back and gave a brief whistle. Immediately the young boy who had attended them emerged from the tent. Tamur gave him rapid instructions in Aramaic. The boy darted back into the tent and returned with a small scroll that he handed to Tamur. He opened the scroll briefly and nodded his approval, rolled it back tightly, and gave it back to the boy. "I have a list of items I was preparing to send to Ezra. Tzevi here can take you to Ezra and deliver my message at the same time." He beckoned young Tzevi forward. The boy stood tall, proud that he had been asked to run an adult errand and lead the two strange Jewish men.

Jacob and Levi stood. Tamur and his two friends stood with them. They shook hands and wished each other well. Tamur heartily embraced Jacob as if he was now a cherished friend. He whispered in his ear, "I sense your interest in Jesus of Nazareth is more than a passing curiosity. I am almost convinced myself to be a disciple, as I believe he is who they say he is." Tamur leaned back and held Jacob by the shoulders. "Go with God, my son, and give my blessing to Ezra."

Jacob was surprised at Tamur's comment and wondered what he had done or said to give him the impression of being deeply interested in Jesus. He simply bowed his head. Tamur returned the bow.

Tzevi had already collected the four horses and held them two by two. He tucked the small scroll in his waistband and walked ahead, Jacob and Levi following.

They continued along the main highway for another few hundred yards when Tzevi took a right turn down a side road. He looked back quickly to make sure the men were still following him. They weaved along narrow alleys and streets through a myriad of houses of various shapes and sizes, all of which seemed to share common walls. The heat reflected off the brown clay buildings as they passed. People moved aside obligingly as Tzevi and the horses approached. After endless twisting and turning through the labyrinth of dwellings, they approached a somewhat larger house off by itself, a small enclosure to the side where a donkey leaned his head over a well-worn railing. This was the house of their friend Ezra.

Tzevi approached the front door, knocked, and then shouted something in Aramaic. Jacob could hear a mumbled response from within the house and knew it was Ezra's gravelly voice. Another minute passed, in which they could hear what sounded like furniture being moved inside and more mumbling. Tzevi looked back at Jacob and Levi, and the three of them smiled.

Shortly the door flew open in a cloud of dust and out walked Ezra. Tzevi barely missed being struck by Ezra's staff as Ezra emerged.

"What do you want, young man?" Ezra asked loudly, apparently disturbed by the interruption to his day. Tzevi spoke again in Aramaic and handed Ezra the small scroll, which Ezra glanced at quickly. "Is there anything else, young man?" Ezra asked tersely. Tzevi smiled and stepped back, pointing toward Jacob and Levi, who stood beside the horses. Ezra looked curiously at the two large men, and then a beam of recognition came over him. "My sons!" he said loudly. He walked forward, his arms wide, nearly tripping over his robe in his haste.

Jacob handed the reins of the horses to Levi and stepped forward to meet Ezra. They embraced heartily. Jacob felt the frailty of Ezra's body. He had lost weight, and upon further inspection, it appeared his beard was grayer and his face drawn. Ezra turned and embraced Levi; he looked like a little boy in the massive embrace of the deputy commander.

"Jacob, Levi, my sons, please come in, sit down with me. We have so much to talk about." Ezra turned and pulled a coin from a small purse and handed it to Tzevi, who smiled with glee. "Thank you, my boy. Give my regards to Tamur. Tell him I will visit him after the holy days." Ezra raised his staff in dismissal. Tzevi ran off happily, clutching the coin in his palm.

Levi guided the horses to the enclosure and, in deference to the restless donkey, tied the four horses to the outside railing rather than leading them in. He grabbed some armfuls of the nearby dried grass and scattered it in front of the hungry horses.

They began munching contentedly. He followed Ezra and Jacob into the house.

Ezra's house was much different from what Jacob had expected. There were scrolls lying everywhere on the meager furniture and scattered about the floor. The home was a good size, but the disorganization made it crowded. Ezra immediately began to gather scrolls and pick up other things to make room for his unexpected guests. Jacob sensed Ezra was not quite himself. He seemed agitated and unable to focus.

"Sit down, sit down, my friends," Ezra said as he dumped a handful of scrolls into a wooden box in the corner. "Let me pour you some wine. You must be thirsty and hungry from your travels." He made nervous movements in ten different directions at the same time.

"No, thank you, Ezra," Jacob said. "We recently ate with your friend Tamur, who led us to you." Jacob and Levi stood, waiting for Ezra to sit down. It took a minute, but he finally quit fidgeting with scrolls and took a seat opposite them.

"It is so good to see you." Ezra laughed. "You are convincingly Jewish, my friends—look at you." He gestured to them with an open hand. Jacob and Levi smiled sheepishly. "How was your stay in Capernaum? Did you travel anywhere else? What brings you to Jerusalem? Are you done with your investigation?" Ezra fired off several questions, not waiting for answers.

Jacob started slowly. "Yes, our campaign is coming to a close. We are preparing to report to Pontius Pilate but wanted to meet with you first. We had hoped you would advise us and accompany us." Jacob paused. "Ezra, is something wrong? The man we left in Caesarea was calm and confident. With all respect, it appears that something is weighing heavily on you. Am I wrong, or can you tell us what it might be?" Jacob said, concern in his voice.

Ezra looked at Jacob directly. His eyes were clear and focused and he seemed to calm down. "I am excited to see you two. Nothing is wrong . . . but everything is wrong. I am better than I ever was. Before I tell you my story, tell me yours—I imagine it is exciting." Ezra smiled broadly with anticipation.

Jacob took a deep breath and began the tale. Levi embellished it. Two hours passed before they reached the final chapter and told of the encounter with the robbers and the last leg to Jerusalem. Ezra listened attentively, asking many questions and shaking his head in wonder throughout the narrative. Jacob purposely left out any mention of his attraction to Liora or his prayer and deep personal feelings about Jesus of Nazareth.

"My sons," Ezra began, "your time here has been short but you have learned a lifetime of lessons. I am so grateful for your safe return. I worried much about you over the last few weeks. I hoped someday you would come to my door unexpectedly, and unexpectedly you have, praise God." Ezra stood and hugged them both again. "You must be thirsty and hungry by now," he said as he moved to the back of the house. "I have some good wine supplied by our mutual friend Tamur. Fresh bread and cheese were delivered this morning. I have been too distracted to eat yet today, but now my appetite is voracious. Please join me." Ezra brought out a large wooden tray with bread and cheese. Jacob and Levi moved their chairs to the nearby table to partake in the impromptu meal. Ezra produced an urn filled with wine and set three gold goblets on the table. Levi picked up one of the goblets.

"Bounty from a pirate raid?" he asked as he raised the finely crafted goblet for inspection. They all laughed.

"No, they are an extravagant gift from my son, Benjamin," Ezra answered, "a small indulgence for a simple man." He poured the wine and sat with his friends to break the bread—then stopped. "Prayers . . . I assume you two have kept up with your prayers?" Jacob and Levi looked at each other. Jacob bowed his head and recited a prayer in Hebrew. Ezra never closed his eyes. He just stared at Jacob in wonderment. "You have me convinced," Ezra said when Jacob finished. "You have become part of the family of Abraham." He chuckled and raised his goblet to toast his friends.

Ezra questioned them about various incidents they had related. The three men relaxed into a friendly conversation.

As their visit wore on, Jacob observed that Ezra began to act more like the man he remembered from their voyage. "Ezra, it appears you are working on a project or doing some research." Jacob motioned toward the scrolls strewn everywhere.

"Oh yes, that," Ezra shrugged. "Yes, I have been doing some work lately." He began to move some of the scrolls around, pretending to organize. Jacob sensed his discomfort.

"What's the matter, Ezra?" Jacob asked directly.

"Well, nothing is the matter. It's just . . ." His voice trailed off. Jacob let him continue without further probing. "I have been doing some research from the writings of the prophets that I borrowed from the archive at the temple. I still have friends there." Ezra looked up at them. His eyes seemed red and swollen.

"What's wrong, Ezra?" Jacob asked again, furrowing his brow.

A tear leaked from the corner of Ezra's eye and ran down his cheek. He spoke with difficulty through quivering lips. "I know now with certainty it is He."

"It is who?" Jacob asked.

Ezra hesitated once more. He gathered his emotions and spoke softly and clearly a Hebrew word. "*Immanuel*," he breathed out.

Jacob and Levi shared a look of confusion.

"Immanuel . . . God with us." Ezra closed his eyes and wept freely. "Jesus of Nazareth. He is *God with us*. I have been reading from these scrolls and those are the words of Isaiah, an ancient prophet—I told you about this on our journey. He prophesied of the Messiah and called him by name—*Immanuel.* Since I returned from our voyage, I have been obsessed with this. I have spent hours reading and pondering, fasting, and on my knees praying. Everything I have read, seen, and heard. Everything that you have told me confirms what I feel and now know in my heart—Jesus is the long-awaited Messiah." Ezra folded his arms around himself as if embracing the truth and joy of his own realization.

Jacob could not fully comprehend everything Ezra was saying, but he knew what Ezra was feeling. He had had an experience similar to Ezra's. Jesus's holiness had been revealed to his heart too, but Jacob was reluctant to share his feelings. He thought for a moment. "We hear he travels to Jerusalem as we speak."

Ezra's eyes popped open wide. "He can't!' he said loudly. "They will kill him."

"Who will kill him?" Jacob asked.

"The Sanhedrin and the high priest. My sources tell me they meet daily to plot his death. If he comes, they will surely arrest him and press false and twisted charges against him. He must be stopped." Ezra stood and nervously began rearranging the clutter around him as if he could find a hidden solution. He turned swiftly and approached Jacob, seizing him by the shoulders. "*You* can stop this!" he said.

Jacob shook his head. "How can I possibly stop it?"

"You are here to meet with Pilate. The Sanhedrin can pass a sentence on someone, but they cannot carry out a death sentence. That requires the hand of Rome."

Jacob shook his head in bewilderment. "We will give our report to Pilate as he has requested, reporting the evidence that Jesus is not a threat to Rome. I can't be responsible for what the

Sanhedrin does or if Pilate rules otherwise; he is the prefect of Judaea. I cannot force him to any decision."

Ezra looked into Jacob's eyes with a renewed intensity. "How passionate are you about the evidence, my son?"

Jacob carefully considered his answer. "I know the evidence to be irrefutable."

"Irrefutable?" repeated Ezra.

"Yes," Jacob began, "I know what I saw and I also know what I feel. The evidence is irrefutable. However, I have not proven it by your Jewish scrolls and prophecies. I have seen it with my own eyes, Ezra." Jacob was reluctant to tell him about his prayer; it seemed too unbelievable to share. But Jacob thought, *Is that any different from saying you saw a blind man's sight restored or a leper healed? Was a direct answer to a prayer any less mysterious or believable?*

"Members of the Sanhedrin have heard reports of his miracles, yet they refuse to believe. Why do you believe?" Ezra probed.

"It's hard to explain." Jacob fumbled for words. "Because of things that have transpired, I just know in my heart," he finally said.

"'I will hide my face from them, I will see what their end shall be: for they are a very froward generation, children in whom is no faith.'" Jacob shook his head, not understanding Ezra's words. "It is from the fifth book of the great prophet Moses—the book of Deuteronomy. Moses saw our time and the evil of the children of Israel. A perverse generation, he calls us." Ezra closed his eyes as if in prayer or deep thought, then commented, "Jacob, you saw with your own eyes, but you believe because you have faith. According to God and the prophets, that is the most convincing and enduring kind of knowledge." Ezra paused and studied Jacob.

"What will you do with this newfound knowledge, my son?" he asked directly.

"I'm not sure what you mean," Jacob said quietly.

"You have a personal and intimate knowledge of the Messiah, my son. That knowledge requires action," Ezra said.

"It does?" Jacob raised his eyebrows.

"Of course, my son. Faith begets commitment; knowledge begets action. You have a newfound knowledge regarding Jesus of Nazareth. What is your plan? Are you a disciple? Will you follow him?" Ezra asked.

Jacob squirmed. "We have been following him," he responded, evading the real question.

"Not with the steps of your feet but with the actions of your heart," Ezra clarified.

Jacob knew what Ezra meant. His mission had kept him from having to make that decision. He would meet with Pontius Pilate soon and then report to Rome. He could catch a ship back to Rome soon afterward and forget everything that had occurred here in Israel, including Jesus of Nazareth and Liora.

In the ensuing silence, Jacob recalled when he came to the crossroads all young Roman boys encountered. Sons of poor families didn't have a real choice. They enlisted in the legions to fight for the empire because they had no hope of a future any other way. He, though, came from a wealthy senatorial family and had a choice to enter the armies of Rome or pursue an education at the feet of great teachers. He had soaked up knowledge from the great philosophers and orators like a dry sponge and wished to continue his studies. But his closest friend had coaxed him to choose a life with a sword in his hand. They were twelve at the time, and they had been fighting and killing men since. Jacob sighed deeply. How he wished he had made another decision. He didn't blame his friend. He blamed Rome.

"My son, you wrestle with yourself," Ezra commented in a soft voice. "There are two voices that talk to us constantly," he continued. "The voice of man and the voice of God. I sense the voice of God is speaking to you, and, like most men, you are choosing to ignore it."

Jacob looked into the piercing eyes of the wise man sitting in front of him. He could feel emotion beginning to well up inside but valiantly kept it from pushing to the surface.

Ezra saw Jacob's discomfort and turned his attention to Levi, who had been sitting quietly until now. Levi shook his head.

"Levi, my son, it seems you know the question I am about to ask," Ezra said.

Levi shifted uncomfortably under Ezra's gaze.

"You have seen what your good friend has seen but have not experienced the same burning in your heart. Is that true?"

Levi nodded.

"What do you think of Jesus of Nazareth?" The question was direct.

Levi answered truthfully. "He is a peaceful man. He is beloved by his followers, unlike any leader I have ever seen. He truly does perform miracles, as we have heard."

"You think of him as a mere leader, as in your legions and garrisons?" Ezra questioned politely.

"Well, no . . ." Levi started to explain.

Ezra interrupted him. "I don't blame you for succumbing to the bias of the culture in which you've lived most of your life, my son," he said kindly. "But it has blinded you to the refinement of the spirit." He paused, emotion welling in his voice. "He is the living Messiah, my sons. I can't even begin to explain that to you. I don't have the words. Jacob, God has caused you to understand more fully by speaking to your heart. Levi, you can ask for that same knowledge. It will come to you once you really desire it.

Don't just believe what you've seen with your eyes. It must be confirmed to your heart by the Spirit."

Jacob spoke. "Ezra, when was it confirmed to you?"

"I knew some time ago, even before I met you two. However, I allowed the voice of man to dissuade me from believing the feelings burning in my heart. After our journey, I decided to study the matter more fully. I felt there had to be more evidence. The more I studied, the more confused I became. The prophets spoke and testified of him. I, like my fellow Jews, had been deceived about the manner in which he would come. Jesus of Nazareth did not fit the interpretation we had invented. He is not the great military conqueror we imagined. He did not arrive on a galloping steed, swinging a flashing sword to vanquish our enemies. He came as a gentle wind proclaiming peace. His weapons are the knowledge of the heavens and the authority he has been given by his Father. He testifies of the prophets and the true gospel but is guarded in testifying of himself. I soon realized I would not find the answer in any of these scrolls." Ezra motioned toward the scrolls littering his abode. "There lies a wealth of prophecy, but not definitive proof." He turned his gaze back to Jacob. "My beloved Jacob," Ezra said in a tender voice. "Like you, I felt the necessity to seek the guidance of God in this matter."

"How do you know I sought an answer from God?" Jacob asked.

"Did you not?" Ezra looked at Jacob and smiled.

Jacob smiled weakly back.

"I know your heart, my son. It is what you would do. It is how you know the irrefutable truth of these things." Ezra placed a warm hand on Jacob's shoulder. "Amid this clutter of history, I cleared a space and knelt in prayer to God and told him how confused I was. I told him what I had studied and deduced. Then I asked him straightforwardly the desires of my heart." His voice wavered, and his eyes moistened with tears. "My sons, I can't describe to you the sacred nature of my experience. I have never felt so sure about anything in my life. Jesus is the promised Messiah. He is the Son of God, and he walks among us." Ezra's confession of faith seemed to give him strength. His face warmed with a broad smile, and his eyes twinkled with light. He extended his hands to Jacob, who took them in his. They gripped each other tightly, silently affirming their mutual knowledge.

A melancholy suddenly overcame Ezra. He lowered his head and dropped his hands heavily in his lap. "If it is true what you say, then he comes to Jerusalem like a lamb to the slaughter." He looked up at Jacob. "There must be something you can do?" he pleaded.

Jacob stood to stretch. "I will make my report to Pontius Pilate. I see no reason why Pilate would not take my report and admonition seriously. The power to punish with death lies only with Rome and not with the high priest or the Sanhedrin. I can't see him bending to their prejudice."

"Don't underestimate the power and influence of the Sanhedrin, my son. They are clever men who can make black look white and white look black. They twist the Law to suit themselves," Ezra said, struggling to stand.

Levi reached out to assist him.

"Thank you for lending me your strength," Ezra said, balancing himself on Levi's massive arm.

Jacob took Ezra's other arm. He could feel the frailty in his mentor's body. His search for truth had taken a physical toll, albeit self-imposed, but he was not weak in spirit.

"We need to meet with Pilate as soon as possible!" Ezra blurted out, his face lighting up with renewed energy. "We have no time to waste. We must get to him before those vipers from the Sanhedrin poison his mind." He rearranged his robe, tightened his sash, and adjusted his head covering. He reached for his staff and headed for the door.

Jacob and Levi watched him, smiling with affection, and followed him into the sunlight outside. Their pace quickened as Ezra marched purposefully down the road, with his two friends in tow.

30

Jershon called his family together. Days of melancholy had caused him much anguish, and the women in his household were suffering from what he could best describe as the pains of lost love. Sariah had become sullen and grumpy, snapping at the slightest provocation. Her mood was unchanging from day to day. Liora was disconsolate and withdrawn, doing her chores in silence and speaking little. The departure of Jacob had dredged up everything in her life that had gone against her: never having known her mother, the untimely loss of her brothers, and the death of her father. The usual sparkle in her eye was gone, and she walked with eyes downcast. She retired early each night and woke each morning with red, swollen eyes. His beloved wife, Naomi, suffered because of the sadness of her daughter and niece. She too was distant and quiet, her usual radiance subdued by sadness.

Jershon stood in the center of the house and called to his family. "I want you all to sit down and listen." He pulled up a stool and sat. Naomi sat in a chair next to him. She leaned affectionately on his shoulder and held his arm. Something had to be done to pull her family out of this darkness. She relied on her husband for a solution and hoped he would provide closure for the emotional wounds Sariah and Liora were suffering.

"I have come to a decision," he said with authority. "This family is suffering from a disappointment I cannot define. I feel we have misjudged and misunderstood the action of our friends. I can't explain why I feel so strongly about this, but we need to take action to arrive at an understanding." He paused for effect. "We will go to Jerusalem for Passover."

Heads immediately lifted, and the mood in the room brightened significantly. All eyes and ears were upon Jershon. "It is no small undertaking to take a family of our size to the Holy City, but we will prepare well and enjoy the time together. I have heard rumors that Jesus of Nazareth also travels to Jerusalem at this same time. That should provide some inspiration to each of you. There is a chance we might enjoy his teachings once again, and I surmise that if Jesus is going to Jerusalem, so are our brothers Jacob and Levi." Liora and Sariah's gaze were fixed on Jershon. "I call them brothers because in a short time they became part of our family, a very close part." He looked down at the two beautiful girls at his feet, feeling great compassion for them. "Among the crowds we will find them," he whispered. "This is not the end of the story. I believe the answers we seek to many questions can be found in Jerusalem. Let us prepare for our journey." He slapped his hands on his knees in finality.

Naomi wept and hugged him tightly. Sariah and Liora joined her. Jershon saw smiles on the girls' faces for the first time in days. He silently thanked God for the inspiration to take his family on this journey.

Lamech immediately asked how they could simply leave their nets. Jershon closed his eyes and lifted his palms in the air, halting any further objections. "The fish in this sea have been here for thousands of years; they will be here when we return," he said in resolute response.

The mood in the house continued light and happy as plans were made and executed for the journey. The fishing boat and equipment were secured onshore. It was decided that Lamech and Raisa would stay home, as traveling with the new baby would be difficult. Lamech would enjoy spending time with Raisa and their new son without having to rise early and fish every day and deal with the constant intrusion of a large family.

The next day they awoke refreshed and ready to begin the trek. Jershon offered a prayer for their protection and safety. They set off excitedly, walking along the dusty highway south. It would take them a few days to make the journey and, if everything went as planned, they would arrive in Jerusalem just before the Sabbath. Jershon had arranged for two donkeys to carry the family's supplies. David's donkey was brought along for Naomi to ride while the rest of the family walked.

Sariah and Liora walked ahead, each holding one of Esther's hands. Jershon led the donkey that carried Naomi. She smiled and leaned forward to touch her husband's shoulder. He looked back and relished the smile lighting her rosy cheeks.

"The girls seem to be much happier," Naomi said to him quietly.

"Yes, I'm pleased they have discovered some joy in our journey," responded Jershon. "I am hoping it will bring some closure for them."

"Do you really believe we will find Jacob and Levi there?" Naomi asked.

"They will find us," Jershon answered.

"But they do not know we are coming, and we don't know if they are there. How can you be so sure of that?" Naomi queried.

"God led them to us once. He will lead them to us again,"

Jershon answered confidently. Naomi believed his every word. Her faith had wavered recently, and she felt the oppressive melancholy promoted by the adversary. She offered a silent prayer for strength and faith. She trusted in God and trusted her husband. She was comforted by that knowledge, refusing to worry about the *how* of God's ways. She settled back and contentedly watched the girls chat in animated tones.

The second day on the road began early and without the same enthusiasm as the day before. Muscles were sore, and the animals were uncooperative. In trying to settle the young donkeys so he could pack up, David suffered a kick in the calf. He was all right, but a bruise rose, and he walked with a definite limp.

"How's your leg, David?" Jershon asked when the family stopped to eat their midday meal.

"We may see it turn a few shades of black and blue before it gets better," David chuckled, "but at least it won't leave a nasty scar like the wound on Jacob's leg," he said without thinking.

Liora overheard David's comment and shot a menacing glance his way. She quickly walked away to hide the tears welling up in her large eyes. Her emotions were still close to the surface. Naomi placed a comforting arm around Liora's waist, pulling her head into her shoulder as she began to weep. Liora believed her uncle's words and was euphoric and yet fearful at the thought of seeing Jacob again in Jerusalem. She loved him with all her heart and was confused beyond understanding by his abrupt departure.

31

Ezra led Jacob and Levi boldly to the palace of Pontius Pilate. They had to work to keep pace with him: he was on a mission. Jacob was amazed at the renewed vigor suddenly displayed by their wise mentor. They followed Ezra as they wove their way through crowds of people, taking side streets and narrow passages to avoid the shoulder-to-shoulder crush of visitors. It seemed every crevice on every street was filled with vendors hawking wooden bowls, brass cups and plates, incense, herbs, silks, tools, and even daggers and swords. Ezra greeted many acquaintances along the way and paused occasionally to converse briefly with some.

Upon their arrival at the palace of Pontius Pilate, Jacob saw a contingent of eight Roman soldiers outside the main entrance. He and Levi drew back to allow Ezra to go ahead without them. Ezra fearlessly addressed the soldier who appeared to be the captain of the guard. The Roman officer soon disappeared into the inner courtyard, leaving Ezra waiting outside holding his staff upright, his back straight, and his head held high. The officer quickly returned with a smallish man dressed in colorful and costly robes.

A conversation ensued that Ezra seemed to dominate. Jacob could sense the nervous movements of an outmatched diplomat as he made excuses for which Ezra obviously had no patience. Ezra then spoke at length with the captain of the guard, who suddenly gave Jacob and Levi a scrutinizing glance. Jacob could not hear the conversation, but he saw Ezra touch the breastplate and tunic of the large Roman he was engaging. He also motioned toward the captain's belt and short sword and gestured emphatically toward Jacob and Levi. An accord was finally reached, and the two curtly shook hands. Ezra spun on his heel and headed straight for them. The slender young diplomat was left shaking his head and making some explanation to the captain of the guard, who warily watched Ezra depart and then stared menacingly at Jacob and Levi.

"He is resting!" blurted Ezra. "Pontius Pilate will need his rest if the Messiah indeed comes to Jerusalem to observe the Passover," he said with disdain. "We are promised an audience with him first thing tomorrow morning. We will return to the house and prepare our case more thoroughly." Ezra walked off abruptly, leaving Jacob and Levi with unanswered questions and hustling to catch him. "We will stop briefly at the temple," Ezra called back to them. "There is something I want you to observe."

Soon they were at the crowded gates of the temple. Ezra passed through confidently. Jacob and Levi hesitated and then heeded Ezra's motion to join him. Ezra retraced his steps and approached his friends. "Your reluctance is without cause, my friends. This is the Court of the Gentiles." Ezra indicated the large space around them. "You are welcome here, no matter who you might be." Ezra smiled kindly.

Jacob was impressed with the fine stonework of the courtyard. He noted with irony how Herod, a murderous client-king of Rome, could be so generous in his treatment of the Jews he seemed to despise. Jacob had seen no better construction in Rome itself. The carving and placement of the stones was impeccable. But the beauty and serene elegance of the architecture was starkly contrasted with the atmosphere within the courtyard. It was a madhouse of people and animals. Vendors offered doves, goats, and white yearling lambs for sale as sacrificial offerings to the great Jehovah. Arrogant-looking men seated at tables exchanged all types of foreign coins for the half-shekel temple coin, the only coin accepted by the collectors of the temple tax. These proud, bejeweled men clad in rich robes shouted their competitive rates of exchange loudly, no doubt realizing a healthy profit from those who were eager to enter the temple to make their offering. Jacob thought the citizens of Rome displayed more respect and reverence for their gods than the people in this courtyard surrounding the temple of the Jewish God, Jehovah. It was like a strange and loud bazaar. Jacob half expected to see jugglers and athletes waging wrestling matches for patrons gambling in the corner. It was an incongruous scene. Ezra observed Jacob and Levi as they took in the spectacle before them. He was pleased to see hints of surprise and disgust on their faces.

Ezra moved close and spoke softly. "You witness firsthand the very reason Jesus of Nazareth cleansed the holy temple of this defilement. It was an affront to him and his Father, just as it is to you and me."

Jacob shook his head in bewilderment as he and Levi followed Ezra back outside the Court of the Gentiles. They walked some distance away, lost in thought, until Jacob asked, "Ezra, I saw you speaking with the Roman guard. What was that about?"

"I told them who you are," Ezra answered, smiling at his friend.

"You what?" Jacob exclaimed.

"I told them you are the great general Lucius Fabius Maximus.

There's no reason to hide any longer. You've come to the end of a long journey. Pilate knows who you are and will approve delivery of Roman clothing and arms first thing in the morning. Let's go home and get you cleaned up. It's time to restore you to Roman citizenship and your normal life." Ezra laughed and walked on.

Soon they arrived at Ezra's house, and their mentor spoke. "When I instructed the guard at the gate to furnish you with Roman clothing appropriate to your rank, the captain of the guard was reluctant to comply. I told him he could confirm your identity with Pilate himself. The wormlike little man was one of Pilate's aides who was in Caesarea at our first meeting. I didn't remember him, but he remembered us, and when he saw you two, he told the captain that what I was saying was true. They will supply you with clothing, breastplates, and weapons. You can bathe, shave off those beards that annoy you, and present yourself as the elite Roman citizens and soldiers you are when we attend Pilate's court tomorrow. I don't want any doubt that your report is genuine, and I'm afraid that your Jewish disguise weakens your presence. Besides, you will be returning to Rome soon."

Jacob listened without commenting. It would be hard for him to explain to Ezra what he was feeling, so he didn't. He simply thanked him.

32

At midday on the fifth day of their dusty and tiring trip, Jershon and his family crested a rise and saw the city of Jerusalem before them. They had passed many camps of travelers like themselves who were journeying to the city to celebrate Passover. The surrounding hillsides and olive groves were filled with tents and people and an ever-present cloud of dust. Jershon could not hold back tears. He was looking forward to celebrating Passover and making his offering to Jehovah at the temple. Overcome with gratitude and emotion, he leaned heavily against Naomi as she sat on the donkey. She tenderly pushed back his head covering and stroked his graying hair. Jershon was a good man, a holy man. He had always taken care of his family and been faithful to his God. Naomi loved him dearly, and she was grateful they had brought their family this distance. She was sure the experience would bind them closer together. She shed tears of gratitude as she thought of how good God had been to her family. They walked the last few miles to the city in high spirits and found a place to make camp with other worshippers outside the city.

The next morning, after they had eaten and fully organized the camp, Jershon led them into the city to explore. The family passed travelers from many nations, vendors hawking wares, and foreign sights and sounds that bombarded the senses of the humble family from Galilee. Naomi and the girls stopped at a tent along the way to admire colorful silk from the east that they had only heard about. The vendor let them handle the fabric and began a one-sided barter. Naomi smiled and would have nothing of it. Liora veiled her face with a piece of fabric, coyly turning her head from side to side. Sariah and Esther laughed. The vendor, sensing a sale was not to be made, quickly relieved Liora of the fabric and haughtily returned to his stool in the back of the tent.

The walk through the city was having the desired effect. The mood of the family was lighter, and they were excited to see what was around the next corner. David and Seth were drawn to a blacksmith shop, smoke billowing from the hole at the peak of the large open tent that provided the workers with some shade. The man working the metal had the typical strong arms of a blacksmith; however, David noted his lack of skill in bending the metal to his wishes. David could see immediately he was too impatient to heat the metal to make it sufficiently malleable. If this man was representative of a skilled blacksmith in Jerusalem, David thought, surely he could come here and make a decent living. David had learned from his father and brothers that metal could be worked more easily with sufficient heat and finesse than with simple brute strength. David had discovered early that blacksmithing was an art for a craftsman, not just a trade for strong men.

Jershon guided his family toward the great temple. He paused to offer a prayer of gratitude before entering the Court of the Gentiles. The irreverent atmosphere of people shouting and bartering took Jershon aback. It was more like a marketplace than he had expected. He shared a look with Naomi; they frowned and shook their heads. Jershon had heard stories of Jesus of Nazareth sweeping through the temple with a makeshift whip, tipping over tables, and driving the vendors out of the temple precincts. He had heard accounts of many things Jesus supposedly had done; he had discounted this story only because physical conflict seemed against Jesus's nature. But after experiencing the offensive scene in the temple for himself, he could see why the Messiah would clear the courtyard of the raucous crowd.

He turned to his family. "We are all tired from our journey. Let's go back to our camp and prepare for Shabbat. We will purify ourselves and give thanks in the humble confines of our tents." The family followed Jershon back through the busy streets and out the city gate to their camp. Jershon felt relieved to be outside the confining walls of Jerusalem. This was far from the simple life they enjoyed in Capernaum. He chided himself for thinking ill of his fellow Jews, but he could sense with every step the mocking glares of the puffed-up citizens as his humble family passed by.

Shabbat was observed simply. Jershon and Naomi lit traditional candles shortly before sunset, and Jershon offered a prayer of gratitude. His prayer included thanks for the presence of the Messiah and a request that they as a family would more fully understand Jesus's mission and how it affected them. The family enjoyed discussing their religion, the great exodus, the teachings of Moses, and their thoughts on Jesus of Nazareth. Jershon made a commitment that when he returned home he would study the writings of the prophets more diligently. Lately he had become complacent in his studies, but with the coming of the Messiah, he realized he would require additional inspiration and knowledge. His family was asking questions for which he had no response. Their questions were honest, and he should have the answers. He was humbled by his family's thirst for knowledge and their dedication to their faith. He promised himself and God that he would improve.

The Sabbath meal was plain but strengthening. The braided challah bread seemed more like a dessert. The family discussed the sights and sounds they had experienced already in Jerusalem. They talked of Jesus and the commotion at the temple that he surely would have condemned. They had heard rumors that Jesus was in the nearby town of Bethany and would soon visit the temple. David and Seth agreed to ask around to learn when and where Jesus would come.

33

Early on Friday morning, a burly and unkempt Roman soldier accompanied by a young boy leading a donkey loaded with two medium-sized bundles appeared down the street from the house of Ezra. He looked carefully at a small piece of parchment in his hand and surveyed the street up and down. He turned to the boy holding the reins of the donkey, and the boy pointed to Ezra's doorway. The surly guard rapped on the wooden door with the back of his hand. Presently Ezra opened the door and peered out.

"Good morning," Ezra said. "I assume you come with the delivery for my guests." The soldier grunted and turned to the boy, ordering him to untie the two packages. The boy quickly complied.

"May I see your guests?" the soldier slurred in a gravelly voice. "I know every Roman soldier in Jerusalem. I wasn't aware of the arrival of anyone new, and I am not accustomed to leaving weapons in the hands of Jews," he said with contempt.

Ezra, in his confident diplomatic tone, answered, "I assure

you my guests are worthy of the items you have brought. I thank you," he said dismissively.

The soldier straightened and placed the palm of his hand on the hilt of the short sword resting loosely on his left hip. "I deliver these packages directly to them or to no one at all," he said gruffly.

Ezra stepped out of the doorway onto the street, facing the soldier. He was in no mood to be intimidated first thing in the morning by a dirty soldier smelling foully of wine. "This matter is under the direction of Pontius Pilate," Ezra rejoined. "I suggest you leave the packages here and report to the prefect upon your return to the prefect's residence."

"This is a matter of the captain of the guard at Antonia. I *will* see your guests!" The soldier spat out the words in a loud voice. Curious neighbors and passersby started to gather. The boy set the packages behind the soldier and tended to the donkey once again.

At that very moment, Jacob stepped through the doorway, followed by Levi. They stood beside Ezra, towering over him and the Roman soldier. "Thank you for the clothing and equipment. That will be enough of your questions." Jacob glared at the soldier.

The soldier was noticeably perturbed by the apparent challenge to his authority. "And who are you to order me to do anything?"

Jacob was immovable. "I am a citizen of Rome, the general Lucius Fabius Maximus. I am here under the direct authority of the emperor Tiberius. This is Androcles, deputy commander of our legion. He is here by the same authority. We thank you for your delivery and ask you to leave us."

The soldier looked up at Maximus, gauging him carefully, his hand tightening on his sword. "You look like no Roman general I've ever seen," he said defiantly. He snorted and spat at Maximus's feet.

Before the spittle hit the ground, Androcles planted his large fist squarely between the soldier's eyes, dropping him to his knees before he collapsed face first into the dusty road.

"I don't know if that was necessary," Maximus remarked, turning toward Androcles, "but it appears you have convinced him, my friend." He chuckled quietly.

Androcles was expressionless as he lifted the bulky soldier and in one motion slung him on top of the donkey, which adjusted its hooves to balance the awkward load suddenly placed on its back.

"Take him back to the fortress," Androcles commanded the young boy, "and tell whoever sent him to have him bathe."

The boy nodded in fearful agreement and pulled the donkey harshly to get moving.

Maximus smiled at Androcles. "You still have a persuasive way about you," he joked.

They picked up the two bundles and went back into the house, leaving the onlookers speechless.

They unpacked the bundles to find Roman attire. In each was a clean white tunic and new sandals, two baldrics with narrow leather straps to go over their shoulder to hold the sheath for their swords, and a thicker *cintus* to fasten around their waist to hold daggers. They were also supplied with Roman short swords and daggers and two embossed leather breastplates. A pair of scarlet red *paludamenta*, or officers' capes, completed their uniforms. Everything fit perfectly. Both men opted to use the higher quality swords that had been given to them by Flacchus Aurelius in Capernaum.

Freshly bathed, clean shaven, and fully dressed in Roman

attire, Maximus and Androcles cut imposing figures in the small room of Ezra's home.

"Yes, I can see the general and his deputy commander," commented Ezra. "You indeed look the part."

Androcles smiled. Maximus untied the straps on his breastplate and adjusted it to a more suitable position. He seemed uncomfortable in his new clothing.

"It appears we are ready," Ezra announced. He was eager for their audience with Pilate. He was sure they would face questioning about the incident earlier, but Maximus outranked every Roman in Jerusalem and would have no trouble quelling any objections to their actions.

They opened the door to find a curious crowd still gathered in the street. The buzz of conversation stopped as Ezra walked out, staff in hand, followed by Maximus and Androcles. Dressed in their Roman attire they were even more imposing. The crowd stepped back in sudden fear. Ezra simply marched on with Maximus and Androcles following.

The streets and byways of the city were becoming more and more crowded with visitors, who made way for the two Romans. Ezra appeared to be as Moses, parting the sea of people with his staff. They approached a group of Roman soldiers loitering in a courtyard. Upon seeing Maximus and Androcles, they saluted by placing their forearms across their chests. Maximus and Androcles saluted back. The soldiers stared after them, not recognizing the two strange officers.

"That was odd," commented Androcles.

"Yes," responded Maximus, "I've become accustomed to being an inhabitant of this land, not a Roman legate worthy of a salute."

"Well, most of the residents of this city don't think us worthy of any recognition. I can almost feel the scorn these people have for us," Androcles added.

"If our friend this morning was any indication of the Roman presence here, it's no wonder," Maximus said.

They soon arrived at Pilate's place of residence. Ezra confidently ascended the few steps that led to the portico and announced himself and his two friends to the guards, who stood tall, holding long javelins at their sides. "We have an audience with the prefect. My name is Ezra, and this is the general Maximus and his deputy commander Androcles. Pilate is expecting us," Ezra announced.

The guards looked on without responding. One opened the large wooden door and disappeared into a courtyard. He returned in a minute with the same small man Ezra had talked to the day before. The man had his ever-present scroll and spoke animatedly, explaining that the governor was meeting with the high priest and members of the Sanhedrin on a pressing matter.

"Pontius Pilate requests your patience," the man said in an effeminate voice. "He has commitments that will take him to the dinner hour, and as you know, that is the beginning of Shabbat. Because the governor honors local traditions, he asks that you return the day after tomorrow." He looked at the scroll he was carrying. "He will have more time for your report then." The man raised his head and smiled blandly.

Ezra stood his ground. "There is nothing more important to the governor than the information we bring to him—*nothing!*" Ezra gestured with his staff for emphasis.

The slender man stiffened, his eyes widened, and he stepped backward slightly. The two Roman soldiers at his side tightened their grip on their javelins.

"I think it is presumptuous of you to imply that you know best what would be important to the prefect," the man said, his voice trembling slightly.

"In this instance I do," Ezra responded. Maximus wanted to

smile. He sensed Ezra had the upper hand, but Pilate's scrawny puppet held the key to the door.

In one motion, the scribe gathered his robe about him and said, "We will see you after Shabbat," as he sashayed through the wooden doors. The guards quickly shut them with a resounding slam and stood holding the javelins across their waists with two hands, discouraging further discussion.

Ezra turned in disgust and walked down the stairs ahead of them. Maximus looked at Androcles. They both shrugged and followed their mentor back into the streets of Jerusalem. They followed him for some time before he finally turned to them and said, "They are plotting his capture and death, those vipers!" he spat. Maximus and Androcles looked at him with furrowed brows, not fully grasping Ezra's comments.

"Whose death?" asked Maximus.

"The Messiah's," Ezra responded dejectedly. "Members of the Sanhedrin meeting with Pilate can mean only one thing: they know Jesus is coming, and they are preparing to have him killed." He walked on in silence, his head bowed.

BOOK V

APPROACHING PASSOVER

34

יום ראשון

Yom Rishon

Ezra was up early the first day of the week to prepare for what he hoped would be the last time for the meeting with Pontius Pilate. Maximus and Androcles donned their Roman uniforms. They were out early, but the streets were already full of people heading toward the temple. It was a curious phenomenon, which prompted Ezra to take a detour. Maximus and Androcles obligingly followed him down a narrow side street away from the main road. He stopped to talk to a man who appeared to be a friend of Ezra's. They spoke in animated tones, the other man gesturing in every direction. At one point they stood close and spoke in hushed tones. Upon finishing their short conversation, they embraced and the friend returned to his house. Ezra approached his two friends.

"He says it is rumored that Jesus of Nazareth has been staying with a family in nearby Bethany. Some of his disciples have preceded him into Jerusalem. Apparently he is preparing to come to the temple. My friend is a disciple and believes as we do; I trust his information. That is most likely the reason for the additional excitement in the air today." Ezra looked sternly down the street.

"When will he arrive?" asked Maximus.

"It is but a short distance from Bethany to Jerusalem. He could arrive any time before noon," Ezra answered.

"Will this affect our meeting with Pilate?" Maximus asked.

"No, I think it makes it timelier," Ezra responded. "Let's not tarry here. Let's go and make our report." He spun and walked with renewed vigor. Maximus and Androcles dropped in behind.

The same two guards stood at the palace doors. They recognized Ezra and the two Romans with him. Before being asked, the larger one opened the door and went inside, quickly shutting the door behind him.

As they ascended the steps the remaining guard said with unconvincing authority, "You are to remain here."

Ezra turned his back on the guard and looked out at the great city before him. He quietly remarked to his two friends, "You two are here because of Pilate's request to Tiberius, yet he treats you like dogs that have been sent to fetch a bone for which he has no use." Ezra struck his staff on the stone steps as he spoke. "I urge you to be bold with him. Tell him the truth. Hold nothing back. And be sure you tell him that the emperor and the senate of Rome await your report."

Ezra turned again to face the guard, who shifted his stance in obvious discomfort under the scrutiny.

The door to the palace suddenly opened, and the Roman guard stepped out ahead of the slender secretary who once again carried a scroll. He spoke curtly. "The prefect will see you now," he said, without looking directly at them.

Maximus admired the finely carved columns surrounding the

courtyard and looked upward to the bright blue sky. "I could almost believe we're in Rome," he remarked to Ezra.

"Well, you are *not*," Ezra responded tersely.

Maximus thought Ezra might be more opposed to the Roman occupation than he let on.

A wave of white came through the columns at the rear of the courtyard as Pilate and his entourage walked through the portico and onto the fine mosaic floor where Ezra, Maximus, and Androcles stood.

Pilate greeted them. "My friends," he said in a kind voice. "It is so good to see you again." He shook their hands, then stood back and looked at Maximus and Androcles. "General Maximus, you and your deputy commander look a little different from how you looked the last time I saw you." He laughed heartily. "Apparently you still have a penchant for tangling with your fellow soldiers, however." The report of the incident with the drunken guard had obviously reached his ears.

"I don't apologize," Maximus said forcefully as he stepped forward with his head held high. "It appears some soldiers in Jerusalem indulge too much in the local wine. Perhaps they need a reminder of Roman discipline and restraint," he said, confidently asserting his rank.

Pilate looked at him curiously, considering the intent of his statement. It occurred to Pilate that Maximus was a senatorial legate and thus outranked every Roman in Judaea. He decided against a challenging rejoinder. Instead, he retreated to the governor's judgment seat. A mixed group of Romans and Jews, including the secretary, stood by his curule.

Pilate decided on a friendlier tack. "Have you enjoyed our marvelous Judaea?" he asked.

"Yes, we have," Maximus responded. "It is beautiful and peaceful in many ways."

"Not as beautiful as the lush Roman countryside, I daresay," Pilate added.

"It is a different kind of beauty," Maximus said.

"Yes, different it is. And the people—how do you find the people?" Pilate questioned. "I hope less drunk on wine and less threatening than we Romans." Pilate again laughed out loud.

Maximus smiled. "They are a very peaceful people, hardworking and dedicated to their families and religion," Maximus responded.

"Ah yes, their religion," Pilate said with some contempt, "and a complicated religion it is."

"With respect, prefect, I would disagree," Maximus replied. "It is very simple. They have one God, Jehovah. And they are diligent in their obedience to his laws."

"Yes," Pilate interrupted, "it is hard to distinguish their religion from their government. But I disagree that they have but one God," he added. "They worship an ancient god—Moses, they call him. Then there is Abraham, the one they call *Father*. Recently they have paid homage to an itinerant preacher called John the Baptist. As powerful as this John was, he couldn't stop the effects of Herod Antipas's axe—his head came off like any other mortal's." There was again laughter, muffled this time, from the men flanking Pilate. "Now we have this Jesus of Nazareth going about claiming to be king of the Jews and the long-awaited Messiah who will conquer all their enemies. What have you learned about this Nazarene and his intentions?" Pilate settled back into his curule, crossing his legs under his long robe.

Maximus wanted nothing more than to say, "Yes, he is the promised Messiah!" But he knew that would destroy his ability to protect Jesus. "I have learned a little about their religion. Perhaps I should share that with you." Pilate waved his hand condescendingly, as if giving Maximus permission to continue. "Moses was a prophet, not a god. He received commandments directly from Jehovah in the form of stone tablets that he gave to the children of Israel. The commandments became known as the Law of Moses, which the Jews still adhere to faithfully. They were simple enough tenets when they were first received. The law has become complicated, as you have noted, by the interpretation and infighting of the Jewish priests and rabbis." This comment was met by a murmur among the Jewish authorities present. "Even the great Sanhedrin disagrees on the observance of the Law of Moses. They have changed it to control the people and serve their selfish purposes. It has become a political tool."

One of the priests objected. "With respect, prefect, this man knows little of our religion."

Maximus cut him off. "I know more than you think, sir," he said, addressing the priest directly. "The Jews call Romans heathens and idolaters, but have you been to your temple lately? Have you witnessed the commerce there? Romans show more respect and reverence in the temples of their gods! And your revered prophets—how many of your prophets have your people stoned and killed over the ages?"

The challenger said no more.

Ezra looked at Maximus approvingly.

Maximus continued. "This John the Baptist you speak of, Pilate, is related to Jesus of Nazareth; their mothers are cousins. As I understand it, John was considered a prophet like unto Moses, who was sent by Jehovah with the specific message that one mightier than he would soon come. That mightier one of whom John testified is Jesus of Nazareth—the Messiah." To this there was a boisterous objection.

Pilate held up his hand and asked pointedly, "Does the great general Lucius Fabius Maximus believe that this simple carpenter from Nazareth is the promised Messiah of the Jews?"

Ezra shifted uncomfortably as Maximus responded, "It is ir-relevant what I believe. I am just explaining what I have learned." Pilate nodded as Maximus continued. "Jesus teaches the people that the Law of Moses will soon be fulfilled, and he brings a new law. His message is of peace and brotherly love. Simply put, the law that Jesus teaches is more threatening to the Sanhedrin than Rome is. He does not promote rebellion. He is not collecting arms and forming an army to come against us. He heals the sick and afflicted and preaches a message of kindness. His detrac-tors are more concerned that he is wresting the allegiance of the people away from them."

"That is my concern too, General Maximus." Pilate sat up in his seat. "We want the people to give their allegiance to Rome."

Maximus chose his words carefully. "We Romans come here as a conquering army. I have been on more campaigns than I can count in which we subjected foreign lands to Roman ways. We tax them heavily and strip them of their wealth and dignity, then expect them to accept their fate without complaint. If Gaul were to invade Rome and be victorious, how well do you think any of us would accept that fate? Would we ever show allegiance to that conquering army?" Maximus spoke with passion. The hall was hushed, and a few of his detractors nodded their heads in agreement.

Pilate stared into the eyes of the powerful man standing be-fore him, digesting what he had just heard. "Your point is wise and well taken, general," Pilate said as he folded his hands pen-sively under his chin. "You almost sound as if you sympathize with the Nazarene and his *disciples*," he added.

Maximus did not respond.

"Ezra, you have been uncommonly quiet." Pilate directed his attention to his old friend. "What do you think?"

Ezra shifted his staff to his other hand. "Pilate, the general

has spoken well. He speaks the truth about the ways and senti-
ments of my countrymen. I think you should listen to him and
heed his counsel." Ezra turned again toward Maximus.

"General Maximus, have you witnessed any miracles? We
hear reports of a type of magic he possesses. Have you seen this?"
Pilate asked.

"I have been witness to what you speak of, but it is not magic,"
Maximus explained. "He heals without consideration to whether
the person is rich or poor. He does not brag about his actions nor
promote them or himself. He simply serves the people as they
come to him and then asks them to remain quiet about what they
have received at his hands. He looks for no payment or recognition for his works."

"Where does he profess to get this knowledge or power?"
Pilate asked.

"From his father," Maximus answered. "He says he receives
his authority from his father."

"The carpenter?" Pilate asked.

"I believe he is referring not to the carpenter Joseph but to
God," Maximus answered.

This statement brought a stir and loud objections throughout
the hall.

"So he claims that God is his father?" Pilate probed.

"God is the father of us all," Maximus stated boldly.

"Are you claiming that the God of the Jews is also the God of
the Romans?" Pilate said with a smirk. His men smiled.

Maximus looked at Pilate without expression, leaving no
room for doubt about his silent answer to the question.

Maximus proceeded boldly. "I sense you have been approached by the leaders of the Sanhedrin, defending their position and asking Rome to intervene by suppressing Jesus and
his teachings. They have likely portrayed him as a threat and

a hindrance to the rule of Rome here in Jerusalem." Maximus waited for Pilate's response.

"Yes, they have come as recently as yesterday with that very request," Pilate obliged him.

Maximus continued. "Their opinions and charges are without merit. They come from pure selfishness and greed. These men do not seek the good of the Jewish people. They seek preservation of their unrighteous power over the people."

Another murmur rippled through the assembled men.

"Are you defending the Nazarene? I hear the passion of an evangelist in your voice, general," Pilate challenged.

"You sent your good friend Ezra to Rome," Maximus said, gesturing toward his mentor. "Your request was given directly to the emperor Tiberius. Through the great senator Gaius Valerius, the emperor assigned me and my deputy commander, Androcles, to honor your request. You *will* take heed of my report. My words are the words Gaius Valerius would have me speak to you. My words are the words of Tiberius, emperor of Rome." Maximus paused for effect.

Pilate fidgeted in his chair and was clearly nervous. His men shuffled their feet.

Maximus concluded, "We report that Jesus of Nazareth, the Messiah of the Jews, is not a threat to Rome. It would behoove all Jews and Romans alike to heed his words." Maximus paused to let his statement sink in. "That is our report."

The room was veiled in silence. At that moment, the door at the front of the hall was thrown open, and a Roman guard entered. Pilate's secretary scurried off to meet him. The guard leaned down and whispered in his ear. The secretary swiftly turned, making a beeline toward Pilate. He whispered quietly in the governor's ear. Pilate's eyes widened, and he stood and addressed Maximus.

"Jesus of Nazareth approaches the gates of the city as we speak. A throng follows him, and thousands of curious pilgrims are gathering along the roadway to see him."

The meeting was over. Pilate bade his company follow him to the balcony on the roof of the palace, where they could get a better view of the city gates. Maximus grabbed Ezra and Androcles and all but pulled them out the front door.

They had only a couple hundred yards to walk to arrive at a place in the road where they could observe the entrance to the city. They stopped next to a short but wide wall which would give them a view over the heads of the people gathering. Maximus climbed up, and he and Androcles assisted Ezra to stand beside them. People were appearing from all directions, anticipating Jesus's entry into Jerusalem. An excited buzz ran through the crowd as the people were now four and five deep along the roadside in some places. It was reminiscent of the mob that would greet legions returning home from a campaign, but in contrast, there was a reverent and respectful nature to this gathering.

"They gather to greet and welcome their Messiah," Ezra commented, smiling. "This is the reason the Sanhedrin met with Pilate. They can't snatch Jesus off the street like the common criminal they claim him to be. His disciples by their very presence protect him."

A procession of men entered the gate. Maximus recognized some of them from Capernaum. Other Galileans who had traveled with Jesus accompanied them. Jesus rode in the midst of them on a donkey. Maximus thought he didn't seem to have the carriage of a conqueror, yet the people hailed him as a king, and he permitted it. They waved palms and laid their cloaks and palm fronds on the ground in front of him. Many bowed as he passed; some even knelt. A few reached out, hoping for a touch from his hand. He rode slowly on, meekly and gracefully.

Despite the throngs of followers entering Jerusalem, the only sound that could be heard was the clopping of the donkey's hooves on the narrow stone street and the shuffling of sandaled feet. Thousands of disciples followed Jesus into the city, kicking up clouds of dust in their wake. As Jesus drew nearer, Maximus could see deep lines in his face and sensed a profound sadness in his eyes. The crowd murmured quiet prayers and praise as he passed. Many wept tears of joy; some cried, "Hosanna to the Son of David." The procession passed directly in front of them, so close that Maximus could have leaned out and touched the top of Jesus's covered head. As Jesus passed, Maximus could feel tears welling up in his own eyes. He glanced at Ezra, who wept quietly. Androcles stood stoically.

The throng of people headed in the direction of the temple. Maximus thought this a relatively safe haven for Jesus. Ezra had told him that the Sadducees and the temple guard planned to arrest Jesus when he came into the city, but the number of his followers dissuaded them from making a public arrest. They would wait for a time when he was alone or with just a handful of his disciples. Maximus suppressed the impulse to step down, take the donkey by the reins, and lead it and Jesus through the crowd to the safety of the temple precincts. He wondered whether two powerful Romans escorting Jesus would actually protect him, or if the wheels of his destruction were already fatefully set in motion.

Maximus waited for an opening in the crowd following Jesus, then he jumped down off the wall. Androcles followed suit. They then helped Ezra down to the street. Without hesitation, all three men followed the crowd to the temple gates.

Upon seeing two large Roman soldiers of some import entering the gates to the Court of the Gentiles, the crowd parted and allowed them passage. Ezra stayed close behind his two friends.

The courtyard was filled with people and activity. Maximus noticed again the vendors of all sorts selling doves and animals for sacrifice and the moneychangers shouting to attract business to their tables. Having lost sight of Jesus, Maximus assumed that he had entered the inner precincts of the temple with his close disciples. He looked up at the towers of the Antonia fortress. It was filled with Roman soldiers looking down onto the courtyard and the temple, no doubt monitoring the bustle of activity. From the number of armed guards with javelins in hand, tensions were obviously high.

Ezra tugged at Maximus's elbow to draw his attention to the side of the courtyard below the stoa, where the Sanhedrin met. There, upon an elevated roof, stood a group of priests. "The Sanhedrin," Ezra said. Maximus could see the handful of men standing close together, talking animatedly. "The vipers collect in the pit and replenish their venom," Ezra remarked. Maximus knew that this group of men was far more threatening than the hundred or more armed Roman soldiers gathered on the wall of the Antonia fortress. But Maximus could only observe. He knew that his power and authority as a legate of Rome was meaningless in that environment.

"Let's go back to Pilate," Maximus said. "I'm sure he will have seen what we have seen, and condemning reports will be forthcoming." He led them back out into the streets of Jerusalem. Throngs of people were still trying to enter the courtyard to get a view of Jesus. Maximus and Androcles forged ahead.

Within a few minutes they were once again at the palace. Pilate had reconvened the discussion about Jesus with his advisors. They stopped their conversation when the three men entered.

"So, what is your assessment of *that*, my good general?" Pilate asked in a condemning voice. Pilate didn't wait for an answer.

"This Jesus of Nazareth enters the city as if he owns it." The prefect raised his hands. "The people acclaim him a king, and the accolades and his behavior are offensive to all." The same group of men stood by Pilate, waiting for Maximus's response.

Maximus thought for a moment, weighing his words carefully. "I see it differently," he began. "Jesus didn't enter like a king; there was no ornate palanquin, no royal chariot pulled by war horses and surrounded by an armed guard. I saw a humble servant of the Jewish God entering the city upon the back of a donkey. He wore the garb of a Galilean fisherman and was escorted by fishermen. They carried no swords or javelins or shields displaying the emblems of a foreign army. There were no weapons at all, except for the walking staffs carried by some worshippers coming to celebrate Passover."

Maximus continued. "He went directly to the temple to pray, not to the battlements." He feigned laughter. "I see no comparison to a conquering king."

Pilate rubbed his clean-shaven chin. "The temple *is* the Jews' battlement, general."

"Then their strategists must be the Sanhedrin, for don't they meet and make policy there? You listen to them frequently and are not afraid of their influence over the people. Or are you?" Maximus challenged boldly.

Another murmur rippled through the assembled advisors, a few of whom loudly voiced words of disagreement.

"I mean no disrespect, governor," Maximus added, sensing them allying against him. "But it seems to me that the intentions of Jesus of Nazareth are to bring order to the house of Israel. From what I have gathered, the Sanhedrin have now imposed laws of their own interpretation."

"What do you know of the house of Israel?" challenged one of the Jewish advisors.

"He has learned well," Ezra stepped in. "General Maximus speaks wisely," he added. "This is a factional religious conflict of no concern to Rome. I suggest that the rulers of the Jews in Jerusalem are much more prone to disagreement with Rome than are Jesus and his followers. Their charges against the Nazarene are claims of blasphemy within the realm of their unique beliefs, not charges of rebellion against Rome. What does Rome care about the religious beliefs of any of its subject countries? You don't enforce belief in your own gods or religion here; why would you try to monitor and enforce Judaism?" Ezra addressed Pilate directly.

That silenced the critics. "You make a valid point, my friend," Pilate said to Ezra. "And you have a better understanding of these issues than most, you being a part of the rulers of the Jews," he added.

"I am not a part of them," responded Ezra emphatically, "if you mean the Sanhedrin. I also deny any attachments you think I might have to the Pharisees or the Sadducees. They are at odds with each other and at war with themselves. Each group looks to you, governor, for rulings on specific points of the Jewish religion that are in their own best interest. With all due respect, my good friend, are the rulers of Rome prepared to interpret Jewish religious law? I think not." Ezra spoke with confidence while trying at the same time to be respectful of Pilate and the egotistical advisors surrounding him.

"But he stirs up the people," said a portly man in an ill-fitting robe. Others agreed.

"He preaches peace, gentlemen," Maximus said. "I have heard him. The people who are stirred up are his detractors, and then they turn to Rome for help. Their motivation is purely political and self-serving."

"Yes, it is a quandary," Pilate agreed. After a brief pause he added, "It appears no immediate action is warranted."

Some of the advisors murmured disagreement, particularly those who had made quiet promises to emissaries of the Sanhedrin.

Pilate continued. "We will keep a close eye on the Nazarene and his followers this week. Regardless of your logic, Ezra, it is not a good time to be making waves with any part of the Judaean government, Roman or otherwise. This Jesus is making waves but not the kind that warrants reprimand or punishment from Rome. I would prefer this issue be settled internally by the Jewish leadership and for me to be left out of the entire matter. For now, I will let it play out."

That was Pilate's decision. Maximus smiled at Ezra, and Ezra smiled back. Gaining the neutrality of Rome was a victory.

The three men took their leave, exiting into the busy streets of Jerusalem. There was talk about Jesus everywhere. Along the way back to Ezra's house, Maximus stopped to purchase a flagon of wine for the evening. For the moment the three were satisfied, but in his heart Ezra knew this wasn't the last battle they would have to wage on behalf of the Messiah.

◆　◆　◆

After a simple breakfast that same morning, Jershon and his family prepared to venture within the great walls of Jerusalem. It proved to be a difficult passage as the crowds were increasing in anticipation of the rumored arrival of Jesus of Nazareth. Seth and David flanked Jershon in front and asked him question after question as they walked. Jershon was enjoying their company and curiosity. The girls walked closely together, Sariah and Liora commenting to each other about every new thing they saw.

Naomi held Esther's hand tightly as they walked through the energetic city. The mood of the entire family had perked up.

As they turned a corner and passed under a large arch, a group of about twenty Roman soldiers marched toward them down the center of the street. They marched side by side, each carrying a heavy shield in one hand and a javelin in the other. The crowds, including Jershon and his family, quickly moved to the side of the street, hugging the walls of the buildings to let them pass. As they passed, one of the soldiers glanced sideways and caught Liora's eye with a leer that made her feel sick to her stomach. The sight of the armed and imposing soldiers made her reflect on how powerless her older brothers must have been against such a force. She held back tears of sadness and anger. As Liora continued to weave through the crowd of people all around her, Jershon's confidence that they might encounter Jacob and Levi in Jerusalem seemed more and more unlikely. She had little hope of a satisfactory reunion, anyway, and tried to put Jacob out of her mind.

After seeing a little more of the city, the family returned to their camp for their midday meal. Sariah sensed the decline in Liora's mood, and they shared a sisterly hug. Tears briefly leapt to Liora's eyes, and she held Sariah a little more tightly.

In the distance, David spotted a few men running along the road away from the city and followed them with his keen eyes. They disappeared as the road turned behind a hill. He kept his eyes on the spot and within a few moments was rewarded with the sight of rising dust as a group entered the valley, leading a donkey carrying a man in a white robe.

"It must be Jesus," David said loudly.

The entire family rose to their feet and looked in the direction David was pointing. People could now be seen following him into the valley, and more people were gathering on the side of the road as he passed. Liora and Sariah descended the hill toward the road leading into Jerusalem to meet Jesus. Liora and Sariah smiled at the Nazarene's passing by but did not join the crowds following him. Seth and David tucked themselves in among the crowd and continued behind Jesus into the city. The crowd was large but quiet and respectful. Liora and Sariah retreated to a rocky knoll to get a better view of the procession and noticed that many were waving palm fronds and placing them in Jesus's path as a sign of worship and respect. Tears welled in their eyes.

Within minutes, Jesus and his disciples passed through the gates of the city and disappeared from view. By that time the crowd was so large it was impossible for Liora and Sariah to move any further. Satisfied that Jesus had actually come to Jerusalem and believing they would likely have an opportunity to hear him teach again, Liora and Sariah returned to camp. Jershon, Naomi, and Esther had stayed behind and were captivated by the girls' account. They had watched the throng follow him, and Liora confirmed that what they had witnessed from the hillside was like the triumphant entry of a king entering his capital.

"David and Seth must have been caught up in the crowd entering the city," Sariah said.

"Those two like to be in the thick of it," commented Naomi. Jershon smiled.

The day wore on, and at dusk they saw a multitude of people streaming out through the eastern gates of Jerusalem. It was too far to see, but Jershon surmised it was Jesus and his apostles returning to Bethany for the evening. Suddenly concerned for Seth and David, he hoped they would soon finish their exploration of the city and return soon to camp.

❖ ❖ ❖

Seth and David held their ground on the side of the road as Jesus and his throng of followers approached. Their patience was rewarded, and they slipped in behind the apostles who guarded and accompanied Jesus. They squeezed through the large gates of the city as the crush of people narrowed to make the passage. Once inside the walls, the crowds pressed the edges of the stone-paved streets. David and Seth had to be assertive and sure of foot to keep up. It was an amazing scene. People on both sides of the road threw cloaks and palm fronds in Jesus's path. There was no cheering, just the reverent adulation of thousands of loyal disciples and the press of curious but respectful onlookers. People in every corner watched from windows and balconies and rooftops.

The crowd wound through the streets of the city before reaching a place where the buildings opened up to allow the passage of more people. "Let's head back," David said. "With all the people swarming into the city, it may take us a while to work our way back out of the gates." David and Seth moved to a niche in the wall that allowed them to stop and let people pass. Their eyes followed Jesus on the donkey as it moved up the street and approached a corner where he would be out of sight.

At the end of the street, just before it turned, was a wall about three feet high. A handful of people stood on the wall waiting for Jesus to pass. At one end of the wall, as it butted up to a large building, were two Roman soldiers beside an old man holding a staff. David stared curiously at the two soldiers. They were large men who appeared all the larger standing on the wall. As the dust of the crowd cleared, David got a better look and suddenly realized he recognized the two soldiers: Jacob and Levi. His stomach churned with excitement and sickness at the same time. He couldn't make sense of what he was seeing. He felt flushed with excitement, and then he felt angry. A thousand conflicting thoughts cluttered his mind.

He grabbed Seth by the arm, and they forced their way back into the moving sea of people, but the number of people funneling into the smaller street around the corner had caused the crowd to stop in its tracks. He focused again on the wall where Jacob and Levi stood, but now they were climbing down and assisting the old man. The press of people prevented David from moving forward, and he realized he'd never be able to catch up with them. David spotted an alley running perpendicular to the street and pulled Seth away from the parade of people. Seth ran after him.

"Where are you going?" Seth shouted.

"Just follow me," David shouted back, "and stay close!"

They weaved back and forth, dodging people, dogs, carts, and everything else that cluttered the swollen streets of Jerusalem. David finally turned onto a wider street that allowed them to trot side by side.

"Where are we going?" Seth asked again.

"To the temple," David responded.

"I thought you said we needed to get back. If Jesus is headed toward the temple, it will be impossible to move around there," Seth protested.

"I want to show you something," David blurted out.

Seth, excited by the adventure and intrigued by David's remark, quickened his step. Soon they arrived at the outer temple wall. Crowds were already gathering in anticipation of Jesus's arrival, but David and Seth had managed to arrive just ahead of the tidal wave of people. They found a spot at the top of the steps and stood against the massive wall that framed the entrance. The stone wall had absorbed the heat of the day and was warm to their backs as they leaned against it. Within a couple of minutes, the people began flooding through every street leading to the temple. The donkey Jesus was riding was led to the bottom of the steps, where he dismounted and began climbing the steps to the entrance.

Seth could see that David was not watching Jesus at all but was craning his neck left and right. "What are you looking for?" he asked.

"There," David finally said, pointing toward the sea of people approaching.

"Where? What?" asked Seth.

"There —over there," David said excitedly, "the two Roman soldiers walking with the old man. Do you see them?"

Seth squinted in the late morning sun and finally answered. "Yes, the two tall soldiers. I see them," Seth said.

"Do you recognize them?" asked David.

Seth shook his head, not sure what David was getting at. "No. I don't know any Romans," Seth said. But he kept looking until finally his brain told him what his eyes were seeing. "Jacob and Levi?" he said slowly.

"Yes," answered David. "I saw them earlier and wanted to be sure my eyes weren't lying to me."

David and Seth watched the trio ascend the stairs outside the temple and disappear into the Court of the Gentiles. They looked at each other, not knowing what to say or do.

David was processing a myriad of emotions. Seth was simply confused. "What does this mean?" he asked finally.

David shook his head. "Let's stay here until they return and follow them to see where they go."

"Why don't we just talk to them?" asked Seth.

"I'm not sure that is the wisest thing to do now," answered David. "Let's follow them wherever they go after this. I am sure there must be some explanation." But David could not think of one. *Were they really Romans?* He had a thousand questions. He decided to gather as much information as he could and then take it to Jershon. His uncle would know what to do.

David and Seth kept a keen eye on the gate, and in only a few minutes he saw the two tall Romans working their way back through the mass of people jostling for entry. David and Seth followed them discreetly. A ten-minute walk across town led them to the entryway of a large ornate building where two Roman soldiers stood guard. They saluted as Jacob and Levi approached, and the gate was quickly opened to allow them access.

David and Seth looked at each other in amazement. They chose a place where they could sit and lean against a wall but still keep an eye on the gate that Jacob and Levi had entered.

"I'm hungry," Seth complained.

"I am too, but this is more important than satisfying your endless appetite." David joked with Seth despite his bewilderment about the events unfolding before him. "We will eat soon enough."

"Father will be angry with us," Seth said after a few minutes.

"Yes, he will be angry, but he will forgive us when we tell him the purpose of our absence." Soon the soldiers guarding the entry reopened the large gates. Jacob, Levi, and the old man came out and descended the steps to the street where they stood talking. David could not hear what they were saying, but he nudged Seth and indicated they should pull their head coverings over their faces. He didn't want Jacob and Levi to recognize them. When the three men began walking away, David and Seth followed them at a safe distance.

Along the way Jacob stopped to buy wine. David and Seth made themselves inconspicuous in a vendor's booth nearby. Soon the three men continued on their way. The old man seemed to be in the lead, and within a few minutes they exited the northern gate of the city. David and Seth had to follow them more closely so as not to lose sight of them, but the three men soon reached a house near an orchard and entered it.

David and Seth memorized the location. "Let's head back now," David suggested.

Seth agreed. Not only was he hungry but he knew his mother would be worried and they would be in trouble with his father.

◆　◆　◆

"Where have you two been?" Naomi asked with relief when David and Seth reached the camp. "I thought something awful had happened to you. I was so worried."

"I'm sorry, aunt. It was my fault," David admitted. "I can explain."

Naomi was just happy for their safe return. It was getting dark, and the rest of the family had eaten the evening meal without them. "Let me warm the soup and get you some bread. Go wash your hands and faces. Your father is in the tent, anxious for your return. You can explain to him."

David and Seth obeyed Naomi and entered Jershon's tent. "I am grateful for your return," he said sternly. "Your mother and I were worried. This is a big city, and there are many people here from strange lands. We must stay together." Jershon finished his mild scolding, then smiled at David and Seth, who sat with their heads bowed. "What were you up to that kept you away so long?"

David began talking and didn't stop until he had relayed everything he and Seth had done and seen. Jershon sat, listening quietly, without asking a single question. When David finished his story, Jershon sighed deeply, and the three men sat in silence.

Finally Jershon spoke. "Let me talk to your mother about this.

Don't mention it to your sisters until I have done so." David and Seth nodded in agreement.

"Good. Now go eat, and promise me you will not stray off again." He smiled at David and Seth. Seth embraced his father tightly.

35

יום שני

Yom Sheni

onday's dawn was brisk, the bright sun rising to warm the cool earth. A layer of fog covered the bottom of the deep valley and would soon burn clear. The muffled noise of various camps preparing the morning meal echoed nearby. Jershon sat outside his tent, warming himself by the fire David had started earlier.

He watched with curiosity as a large crowd of people moved along into Jerusalem. He called his family together and pointed to the approaching crowd. "It appears Jesus of Nazareth once again comes to the temple," he remarked. His family stood watching as Jesus led his apostles and disciples in a spirited walk.

"They must have left Bethany before sunrise to be here so early," David observed.

Jershon grunted his agreement.

Because of the hour, the group was much smaller than it had

been the day before. Jesus and his hundred or so followers moved quickly to the east gate of the city.

"I wonder if he plans to teach at the temple all day. I'd really like to hear him," said Sariah. Liora and David voiced their agreement.

"Then go," said Jershon, giving them his blessing. "But I want you all to stay together. Please return by midday. I have an errand to run and will meet you here for our meal." He turned to Seth. "Son, I need you to remain behind with me to help with a project. You can join David and the others in the afternoon."

Seth was visibly disappointed. Naomi hugged each of the departing family members while her younger son sat dejectedly on a boulder near the fire. Jershon retired to his tent to ask God for guidance in his errand.

Not long afterward Jershon emerged from his tent, tightened the laces on his sandals, gathered his robe around his shoulders to guard against the cool morning, and picked up his staff. "Seth, let's go," he said as he began to walk toward Jerusalem.

"Where are we going, Father?" Seth asked as he scrambled to catch up with his father.

"I trust, my son, that you can remember the location of the house Jacob and Levi entered?" Jershon kept his gaze on the path ahead. "We will search them out and speak with them, but I don't want you to mention this to anyone."

Seth grinned when he realized why he had been held back. He was happy that his father trusted him as a guide and confidant. "You can trust me, Father," Seth answered with a certain amount of pride.

"I know, my son. Let's enjoy this fine day together." Jershon was excited at the prospect of seeing their friends again; he held no rancor toward them. His prayer had left him with a feeling of peace, and his heart was full of forgiveness.

They soon learned that Jesus had gone to the temple, and crowds were headed that way. Once they reached the city, Jershon and Seth were walking against the flow of people and had to work to avoid the anxious disciples trying to get to the temple to hear Jesus preach. Seth asked questions about the stonework of buildings they passed and wondered aloud where the vendors had acquired the many strange goods he saw in the markets along the way.

Jershon enjoyed talking and teaching his son. Their lives in Capernaum were filled with work: fishing six days a week kept them busy. He realized he needed to find more opportunities to expand his son's world. Seth was voracious in his thirst for knowledge. Jershon smiled at his son, invigorated by the conversation. Seth in turn was amazed at all his father knew of architecture, stone masonry, and the culture of curious strangers they encountered in Jerusalem.

The two passed stalls of tooled leather and colorful cloth from eastern lands. Seth was particularly interested in the shiny brass urns and other brassware being hawked by a man wearing a white linen robe and a bright red turban. The sights, scents, and sounds of the different languages being spoken were almost too much for Seth to take in. He drank in everything he saw.

Soon Jershon and his son exited the gate Seth remembered. He pulled his father's sleeve, guiding him down the main highway to a road he recognized. There were twists and turns, but Seth negotiated them as if he had passed that way a hundred times before. He stopped abruptly, holding Jershon back, and pointed to a sandstone dwelling with a tile roof standing near an olive orchard. Smoke rose from the house, a telltale sign that someone was home.

"This is it, Father," Seth said quietly. He waited for Jershon to take the lead. His father took a deep breath and with conviction walked ahead. He tapped on the weathered door with his staff. Seth stood anxiously behind. Nothing was heard from within the house. Jershon tapped again, this time a little harder.

Jershon thought he heard a rustling inside, then the door rattled and was pulled open, squeaking on its pivots.

"Yes?" A haggard older man appeared at the door. From behind his father, Seth recognized him as the same man he and David had seen with Jacob and Levi. Jershon looked back at Seth for confirmation, and Seth nodded his head.

"My name is Jershon. I am visiting with my family from Capernaum. This is my son Seth." Jershon stepped aside so the old man could see the younger man in full view. "We come seeking our friends Jacob and Levi. Do you know them?" Jershon asked kindly.

The visitors standing in his doorway suddenly had Ezra's full attention. He looked back and forth from one to the other before opening the door fully. "Please come in," he said. He bent over and cleared a path through the messy house. Scrolls, engravings, and parchments were stacked on every surface.

Jershon and Seth entered timidly and looked for a place to sit. Ezra, his arms full of scrolls, moved some cushions over with his feet. "Please sit down. Forgive me for the disorder—I have been doing some research." He went to the adjoining room and came out without the scrolls. "I am not a very good host," Ezra said apologetically. "My name is Ezra." He offered his hand to his guests.

Jershon smiled. "Thank you for inviting us in, rabbi." If Jacob and Levi were his acquaintances, considering all the scrolls and other artifacts in Ezra's home, their story was more curious than he thought.

"Just call me Ezra." He motioned for his visitors to sit on

cushions on a carpet that covered most of the room. A fire burned in the hearth, and the house was pleasantly warm.

"Why do you seek Jacob and Levi?" Ezra opened the conversation carefully. He contemplated the rustic-looking man sitting before him. From his Galilean clothing and calloused and scarred hands, he knew this must be the patriarch of the good family that Maximus and Androcles had told him about. Ezra was surprised at their appearance in his home but was glad to have a chance to meet them.

"They are friends of our family. We are fishermen from Capernaum. We were fortunate that they came to us when my oldest son was in great peril. They saved his life."

Ezra smiled. "That sounds like them. How did you happen to arrive at my door?"

"My son Seth and his cousin discovered them in the city yesterday. They followed you here." Jershon sensed that honesty would be best. "They were confused by the Roman clothing Jacob and Levi wore and were reluctant to speak to them. Instead, they found where they were staying and then relayed that information to me. You see, Ezra, in the short time these two men were with us, we grew to love them. Their parting was, to say the least, sudden and without explanation. But we hold no ill will toward them, in fact, just the opposite. My family and I came here for the holy days, not only to worship but in hopes of finding them again. I was hoping we could talk with them." Jershon waited for Ezra's response.

Ezra sensed the man sitting before him was kind and genuine and was already taking a liking to him. He rocked slightly on his cushion and exhaled deeply. "Yes, Jacob and Levi are my guests. They are not here at the moment. They have gone into the city— to the temple." Seth darted a concerned glance at his father. "I assume they will return when they get hungry. You see, I have a very good cook." Ezra chuckled.

"I have a good cook too." Jershon said, and the two men shared a smile. "Can you answer some questions?" Jershon leaned forward.

Ezra raised one hand slightly. "I'm sure you have many questions about our mutual friends. I would prefer, however, that you ask them directly and that they answer you directly. There is a logical explanation, and they are not hiding anything of a serious nature. I assure you these are two very good and sincere men."

"I have no doubt of that, Ezra," Jershon agreed. "I am sure it will come as a surprise to them that we are here, and they may be reluctant to see us. Can you help us arrange a meeting?"

"I don't think they will be reluctant—perhaps a little embarrassed, but not reluctant. From what they tell me they deeply regret the manner in which they left Capernaum and your family, but it couldn't be avoided. They hold you all in the highest esteem. But as I said, I will let them explain everything. I would be happy to arrange a meeting. Where are you staying?" Ezra asked.

Jershon replied, "I would prefer to meet them by myself, first. Would it be convenient to meet them here tomorrow?" he asked.

"I can certainly ask them. How would I get a message to you?" Ezra responded.

"Perhaps I can send my son back tonight or in the early morning. He can relay the time and place to me," Jershon offered.

Ezra smiled at young Seth.

"That would be fine. Young man," Ezra addressed Seth, who sat to attention, "why don't you return after breakfast tomorrow? I will have had a chance to talk to our friends by then and to make arrangements."

Seth looked at his father.

Jershon placed his hand on Seth's shoulder. "My son will be here at the time you've requested."

Seth beamed.

Jershon decided to change the subject. "I assume by all the scrolls that you are a teacher. Am I wrong?" Jershon asked.

Ezra smiled. "Yes, I am a teacher. My two best students are Jacob and Levi. We have discussed much, and they have learned much."

"But all this couldn't possibly have been only on their behalf." Jershon motioned to the myriad of material throughout the house.

"No, indeed it is not. I have been investigating an interesting matter on my own," Ezra said.

"May I be so bold as to ask what that matter is?" Jershon inquired.

Ezra contemplated avoiding the question but decided he could trust Jershon, so he answered, "Prophecies regarding the Messiah."

"You mean Jesus of Nazareth?" Jershon offered.

Jacob had told Ezra that the family were followers of Jesus, so he spoke freely. "Well, yes, if you believe Jesus of Nazareth is the Messiah." Ezra raised his eyebrows.

Jershon looked Ezra straight in the eye and said, "I do."

Ezra looked back. "Isn't it interesting?"

"Yes, very," responded Jershon. "We saw him arrive the other day. They greeted him like a conquering king. I know the animosity the rabbis in Capernaum have for him. His arrival here has to have greatly upset the elders and the Sanhedrin."

"I am afraid you're correct," Ezra answered. "They don't hold him in much esteem here. They are afraid. His teachings disrupt their stranglehold on the people. His miracles confirm his authority. Our ancient fathers prophesied of him." Ezra motioned to the scrolls surrounding them. "But I am afraid that as we speak they conspire to destroy him."

Jershon looked at Ezra with confusion in his eyes. "I'm not sure I understand."

"They seek his life," Ezra said. "As we sit here and discuss him, the Sanhedrin meets to contrive his death."

"Why?" Jershon questioned.

"He threatens them with his teachings. As wise as the rabbis and elders are, they can't see past their own ambitions. They are not students of the scriptures, and they are not ready to face up to that which has been prophesied about him. The writings are clear to any who are humble and whose heart is open to the words of the prophets. But the members of the Sanhedrin possess neither trait. They deny the truth that walks before them and desire to crush him with their stumbling feet." Ezra shook his head in sadness. He reached for one of the nearby scrolls and unrolled it.

"But they allow him to walk through the very gates of Jerusalem and teach in the temple. If they are convinced he is a threat and propose to do away with him, why do they hesitate to arrest him?" Jershon asked.

"Because they fear repercussions from the people who follow him. It is an interesting balance of power. But I fear the time is short, and they won't miss an opportunity to seize him."

Ezra held up the scroll to the light of the fire behind him. Tilting his head back and squinting his eyes, he read aloud, "'Rejoice greatly, O daughter of Zion; shout, O daughter of Jerusalem: behold, thy King cometh unto thee: he is just, and having salvation; lowly, and riding upon an ass, and upon a colt the foal of an ass.'" The words of the prophet Zechariah. I believe this prophecy was fulfilled yesterday when Jesus arrived. Did you see him?" Ezra asked.

"We saw him pass, and we witnessed the adoration of his disciples. It was exactly as Zechariah said," Jershon said.

"*I* saw him!" Seth blurted out.

"You did?" asked Ezra, smiling at the young man.

Seth gazed at his father sheepishly, looking for permission to enter the conversation. Jershon nodded his head in approval. "Tell us, my son."

"He rode upon a donkey. People threw palm fronds down in front of him. Some laid down their cloaks." Seth was excited and animated. "We followed for a short distance and were able to see everything. People reached out to touch him. They called him Rabbi, but also names like Son of David and Messiah. Some people were crying. Jesus smiled at them, bowed his head, and kept moving through the crowd. That is when David grabbed me by the arm and pointed to two Roman soldiers standing with you on a wall ahead of us. We lost you for a moment when you came down into the crowd, but David spotted you again, and we followed you to the temple precincts. We waited outside, and after a while you came out, and we followed you here. I couldn't believe the soldiers were Jacob and Levi—they looked so different." Seth looked straight at Ezra, who was listening intently.

Ezra chuckled. "Yes, my son, they do look different. But don't let that concern you. I assure you they are still very much the Jacob and Levi you know."

"We are happy to hear that," Jershon said, "and we are very anxious to meet with them." He gathered his robe and stood. "We should go. We have taken up enough of your time. You have been very kind." Jershon put out his hand to help Ezra stand.

Ezra shook Jershon's hand. He liked this rugged Galilean and his equally rugged son. He could see why Jacob and Levi had been drawn to them. He wished them well and told Seth he looked forward to seeing him early the next day to arrange a meeting with their friends. Silently Ezra hoped that Maximus and Androcles would be willing to meet with them, though he understood why they might not.

After his visitors departed, he retired to his scrolls and the warmth of his hearth, grateful for the interruption of unexpected company.

◆   ◆   ◆

Maximus and Androcles left early that morning and went directly to the Antonia fortress. When Herod the Great had built his massive temple, he had rebuilt an earlier Hasmonean fortress as a barracks and garrisoned it with his own mercenaries. Conveniently attached to the corner of the temple, it overlooked the temple courtyards. Now that Judaea had become a Roman province, the soldiers in the Antonia kept an eye on the Jewish leaders and rabbis to discourage rebellion.

From their position on the ramparts, Maximus and Androcles could see the countryside around them: the rocky hills spotted with trees and shrubs seemed to go on forever in the distance. Smoke rose from cooking fires, reminding them of the camps of the legion on campaign. They leaned over the wall, looking downward, and saw the crush of people approaching the entrance to the temple. Jesus led the crowd up the steps and into the outer courtyard. They lost sight of him as he entered the roofed porticos where the vendors were already beginning their day's business.

Suddenly they heard shouting and people running from the columns of the Court of the Gentiles. Jesus emerged with a makeshift whip, shouting something unintelligible, but his intentions were obvious. He had overturned the tables of the moneychangers, sending the coins flying over the stone courtyard. He had opened the pens of goats and cages of doves, setting them free. He shouted indignantly at the scattering vendors. Maximus

looked at Androcles curiously. This wasn't the Jesus they had observed in Galilee, this man who wielded a whip and scattered his
own people before him. The captain of the garrison in the fort
began to shout commands. Roman soldiers ran, preparing with
sword and javelin to descend the stairs to the courtyard. They
would quickly suppress any uprising. The Roman captain soon
joined Maximus and Androcles on their perch along with a slight
Jewish man dressed in costly robes.

"He throws them out," the Jew said calmly. "He says they de-
file the house of his father." He turned to the captain. "I don't
think this is anything to be concerned about. This is of more
concern to the priests of the Sanhedrin." He laughed dismissively.

"May I ask who you are?" queried Maximus.

The Jewish man looked arrogantly at Maximus and responded, "May I ask who *you* are?"

Maximus took exception to the man's attitude and answered
him boldly. "I am General Lucius Fabius Maximus. I am the
ranking officer here, and I would just as soon throw you off this
wall as listen to your impertinence."

The man looked at the captain of the guard for confirmation. The captain nodded. "I am an advisor to the prefect and an
interpreter for the garrison commander." His tone and manner
remained condescending.

Androcles seized the slight man by the shoulders and held
him up as if to pitch him over the wall. The man let out a high-
pitched scream. "We don't care who you are, you impudent little
weasel. Just tell us what's going on!" Androcles shook him once
before setting him down.

The man's attitude changed immediately, and Maximus and
the captain had to refrain from laughing.

The man collected himself and adjusted his robe before
speaking. "Frankly, I don't blame him," he said in a timid voice.

"It was becoming more like a marketplace than a temple. He is speaking Aramaic, this Galilean, and it is clear he is upset by the behavior of the temple merchants. 'My Father's house,' he shouts—that is an interesting statement," the man observed. "He will certainly raise the ire of the Jewish leaders. They share in the profits of these vendors, and he is disrupting their commerce."

The mayhem below died down as quickly as it started. The scorned merchants collected their belongings and left the temple precincts. The brief purging had been effective. The atmosphere calmed down, and Jesus discarded the whip. He quietly ascended the steps above the Court of the Gentiles.

The captain shouted to his lieutenants, and the call to arms within the fort ceased. Everyone who could find a place squeezed in along the high ramparts of the fort, intent on seeing Jesus's next move. Oddly, the Romans exhibited a degree of respect for this Nazarene. Most of the Roman soldiers had heard of Jesus, but few had ever seen him; they were all curious about this Jewish *Messiah*, as the people called him. They were commanded to watch his every move.

Jesus raised his hands in peaceful greeting and smiled, a different man than the one they had seen a few moments previous. The throngs of people in the courtyard began to press close to him. They brought their sick and afflicted to him. With his head bowed and speaking too softly for Maximus and Androcles to hear, he touched and blessed everyone who was pressed upon him. Sick children took strength and no longer lay lifelessly in their parents' arms. The lame abandoned their crutches and stretchers and walked away, restored to strength and vigor. The blind discarded the bandages that had hidden their eyes, and with their sight restored, embraced their neighbors and praised Jesus while kneeling to kiss his feet. He was healing them all.

The scene was reverently quiet except for the soft weeping of those who had received miraculous blessings at Jesus's hand.

Maximus glanced at Androcles in disbelief. He looked around at the Roman soldiers who were riveted, observing the miracles being, performed in front of them. Not a word was spoken. All eyes were on Jesus.

Maximus saw a contingent of Jewish priests looking down from their high place in the royal stoa. He sensed their vexation as they whispered among themselves. They watched as Jesus walked among the people in the courtyard, blessing all who reached out to him, healing them of wounds and afflictions, both inward and outward.

Maximus felt emotion beginning to well up inside him. The Court of the Gentiles was completely full of people sitting on the ground listening to Jesus. The sound of his voice carried magnificently as it echoed off the surrounding stone walls. It reminded Maximus of the time he had attended the amphitheater in Rome with his mother and sisters. How he longed to see them again. He wondered what his mother would think of Jesus of Nazareth. Because Maximus was much like his mother, he knew she would tell him to follow his heart. He cleared thoughts of home from his head and focused on the impressive teacher speaking to the multitude. He could hear him from where he stood—Jesus was telling a story. Maximus could not understand all the words, but he felt in his heart the burning warmth of the truth of what was being spoken. The sound of Jesus's voice pierced his soul. It was the same feeling he had experienced when he prayed in Capernaum.

Then he thought of Liora. He felt pangs of guilt for leaving her without an explanation. He wanted to talk to her, feel the warmth and tenderness of her presence, and hold her in his arms. He needed to talk with Ezra.

"Come on, my brother." He thumped Androcles on the arm. "It's time to go." He started down the stone steps.

◆ ◆ ◆

Seth assured his father he could look alone for David and the others at the temple. Jershon gave him his blessing, and Seth ran off enthusiastically.

Jershon contemplated what he had learned from Ezra. He was sure this revelation of Jacob and Levi's true identity was part of the explanation for their actions. It did, however, pose a problem for Liora and his daughter Sariah. He thought that perhaps it might be better not to pursue their friendship any longer. He surmised it was the same conclusion Jacob had come to, which would explain their abrupt departure.

Jershon enjoyed his leisurely walk through the city. There was so much to take in, and the people of different cultures who walked through the gates of Jerusalem at this time of year made it truly a spectacle. Jershon was Galilean, his coarse clothing reflecting his home and the manner of his livelihood. Content with his life in Capernaum, he never wanted to live in Jerusalem. He missed the smell of his home and the green shores of the Sea of Galilee. As he walked, he offered a silent prayer of gratitude for his humble state and his beloved family, especially Naomi. Tears filled his eyes as he thought of her and the blessing she was in his life.

He pondered his encounter with Ezra. He was intrigued with him and hoped to meet with him again before they left Jerusalem. Ezra seemed so well informed about Jesus and the movement around him. He frowned at the thought that the Jews in authority would want to do Jesus harm. There was so much to think about. He was glad his life was uncomplicated—or was it? He was anxious about the meeting with Jacob and Levi. He wondered how Liora and Sariah would take the news that they were Romans—Gentiles. Regardless of the outcome of that issue, he was happy his family had made the journey to Jerusalem. He would take Naomi with him to the temple tomorrow to make an offering. Today he would sit and rest and enjoy the clear blue day.

Jershon traversed the busy city, exited through the gates, and climbed the hill to the camp. Naomi was on her knees, making bread for the day. Jershon reached down to help her stand. He was normally reserved in his outward affection, but during his walk that morning he had reflected on the strength of this woman with whom he had the pleasure to share his life. She lived the life of compassion that Jesus taught, always sacrificing her own needs for the needs of others. He loved this woman beyond measure. He could not imagine life's joys and afflictions without her.

Naomi was surprised at Jershon's embrace and even more so at his tender kiss. She blushed, glad that their camp was isolated from public view. She loved this rock of a man dearly. He worked so hard all the time. She had been looking forward to spending a quiet afternoon with him, resting and talking of the children. They had so little opportunity to be alone and discuss the future, though it seemed to her that the future had become cloudy. So many things had changed.

"I have missed you," Jershon said as he held Naomi tightly.

She pushed herself away from him, smiling. "You've been gone but a morning," she said, holding his face in her hands.

"I've been away far too much." He kissed her again on the forehead. "Come into the tent, so we can talk for a moment." His tone was serious, and the look on Naomi's face betrayed her worry. Jershon assured her that all was well.

Quickly she finished making the bread and set it to bake. She washed her hands, wiped her face, and then joined her husband in the tent. She sat down and looked up at him expectantly.

Jershon wasted no time. He held Naomi's hand and announced, "David and Seth found Jacob and Levi." Naomi gasped. "Before you say anything, let me explain." Jershon squeezed her hand. "David and Seth were in the city yesterday and spotted them among all the people following Jesus—not because of their size but because they were wearing the uniforms of Roman soldiers."

Naomi's brow furrowed and tears began streaming down her face. She couldn't speak.

"There is a logical explanation, my dear," Jershon assured her, "though I can't tell you what it is. I mean, I don't know why they were dressed like that. My heart tells me it is because that is who they really are."

Through quivering lips, Naomi asked, "How can that be?"

"It is somewhat clearer to me now," Jershon said, looking at his beloved wife. "They came seeking Jesus. That is what they told us, and that part is true. We knew they were different when we met them, but our deep gratitude for saving our son and our hope of finding proper husbands for our daughters blinded our reason. They sought Jesus not to become disciples but, I surmise, at the command of Rome. Did it not make us wonder that they were strong and muscular like soldiers and wore the scars of battle? We ignored that, however, because of their kindness to us. They tried to avoid accepting our hospitality, but they were hungry after their exertions in towing in the boat, and then they became smitten with our daughters. We never gave them a chance to decline our invitation. They were well behaved and well mannered but lacking in knowledge of Jewish traditions." Jershon looked downward, still trying to grasp everything. "They left out of respect for all of us."

"Did you talk with them?" Naomi asked.

"No, but I have spoken with the man they are staying with in

Jerusalem, a rabbi named Ezra. He is a good and honest person. Out of respect for Jacob and Levi, Ezra would not divulge much but assured me that they are both good men." Jershon rubbed his tired eyes. "I believe Jacob realized the futility of continued residence in our home. They had so quickly become part of our family, and he could no longer pursue the charade with us."

Naomi began to speak, but Jershon held up a hand. "Let me finish. It is obvious, my good wife, that Jacob had fallen in love with Liora, and I believe Levi was experiencing the same feelings for Sariah. You of all people know the hearts of our daughters." Naomi nodded. "I'm sure it was an agonizing decision for them. You remember how they left so abruptly, and they seemed hurried and angry? For days we mourned over their departure, wondering what we had done to cause it. In truth, we had done nothing. I think I am correct in believing Jacob was angry only with himself and could no longer continue in his deception. He and Levi are honorable men who returned our love, and the only thing they could do was leave quickly without explanation. It was painful, but it was a simple solution for everyone involved. Jacob and Levi had to have known the prohibitions against a Jew marrying a Gentile. They were unwilling to make Liora and Sariah, and our family, face that decision. So, to shield us all, they left."

Naomi listened intently to her wise husband. Her red and swollen eyes reflected the sadness and confusion of her heart. Everything Jershon said made complete sense now as she reviewed the events of their experience with the two men. She felt no anger and sensed that Jershon was equally at peace. However, she still ached for the broken hearts of her daughter and niece.

"So you will meet with them tomorrow when you receive word from this rabbi?" Naomi asked.

"I have proposed a meeting, but now I wonder if it's a good

idea. Perhaps we should just let them go their way," Jershon sighed.

Naomi reached out to her husband pleadingly. "Don't you think we should at least talk to them?" she asked.

Jershon looked at her and shook his head. "If indeed they are Romans, what can we do? We cannot marry our daughters to them, regardless of how much we would like it. The Law is explicit in this," he said sternly.

Naomi looked away. "But we are followers of Jesus. Does that change anything?"

"We are of the blood of Abraham; they are not. I have heard Jesus teach nothing of intermarriage. I can't comprehend bending that commandment," Jershon responded.

"Six months ago you couldn't imagine going against the mandates of the Sanhedrin, but by accepting Jesus as the Messiah, we have ostracized ourselves from them," Naomi reasoned.

"The feelings of our hearts cannot rationalize or change the knowledge of what we know to be true. I can't talk of this anymore. I am a simple fisherman." Jershon threw his hands in the air. "I cannot understand or interpret the ways of God, but we can't go wrong if we are obedient to what we know to be right."

"I believe he sent them to us," Naomi said with conviction.

"Perhaps he sent them to us for his own purposes—not ours—and surely not as husbands for our daughters." Jershon had grown exasperated and stood. "I need some fresh air."

"I love you, my husband," Naomi said to his back.

He turned and looked down at her, "Woman, I love you too, but please don't ask me to rationalize the impossible." He smiled at her and exited the tent.

Jershon walked a distance away from the camp and sat on a large stone overlooking the great city, now hazy with the dust of thousands of pilgrims within its walls. He turned his head sky-ward and, closing his eyes, quietly prayed.

"O God, I raise my voice to thee in humility. I am a simple fisherman that thou hast blessed beyond my ability to receive. I am grateful for my beloved Naomi and the children that thou hast sent to us. I cannot comprehend all thy ways, but I try to be an obedient servant. Thou hast blessed us with the presence of thy Son, and I truly believe it is he that walks among us. These are troubled times, confusing times. I have prayed long and hard for my sweet Sariah and Liora to be properly espoused. Two men have come into our lives that at first seemed sent from thee. Now their appearance is a puzzlement. The selfish desires of my heart conflict with thy commandments, yet, how can I deny the good-ness of these Gentiles? Are not all men equal in thy sight? Thy Son has come and given us a new message of compassion and brotherhood. Yet the Law has been clear to the seed of Abraham for generations, and yet, as the world changes around us, it be-comes foggy. The Gentiles rule our people and impose hardships upon us. Is this because of our stubbornness? Are we as a people being punished for our disobedience? Rabbi Ezra tells of how the chief priests of the Sanhedrin seek the life of thy Son—how can this be? Please grant me wisdom, and if I should make the wrong decision, may the punishment lie with me and not my children."

Jershon was overcome and fell to his knees. A dam of emo-tion broke. He leaned on the great stone and shed the heavy tears of an overburdened father, tears held back for years trying to be strong in the face of many challenges and weaknesses.

◆　◆　◆

Naomi didn't question the long absence of her husband. She knew he was wrestling with God. She was energized with the news of the discovery of Jacob and Levi yet confused at the same time. She pondered the ramifications of Jershon's revelation about them—to no avail. She went about completing the baking of the bread and the preparing of the afternoon meal.

It wasn't long until she heard the animated voices of her children as they approached the camp. She gave Sariah and Liora particularly affectionate hugs, causing them to look at her strangely. "What happened today?" Naomi asked as she stirred the kettle of soup in the hot coals of the fire.

"It was so exciting," Sariah blurted out. "Jesus taught in the temple. We were able to get close to him. Mother—it was so wonderful!"

"He healed people, Mother," added Seth. "He healed a blind man and made another walk that had been carried to him. I wouldn't have believed it if I hadn't seen it with my own eyes."

"And there was a child." Liora began to speak but then emotion flooded her tender soul, and she wept and spoke in a subdued voice. "A small child held in the arms of his father. You could see the little boy was so sick, his face as pale as ashes. Jesus took him up in his arms and shed tears as he held him. He placed one hand on the child's head and whispered something in his ear that no one could hear. We were close enough to see the boy suddenly become alert in his arms and struggle to sit up. Jesus held him to his chest, and the boy laughed. Jesus handed the boy back to his father, and the boy jumped down, out of his father's arms, and ran back to Jesus and hugged his legs. It was the most incredible scene." Liora wiped the tears from her soft cheeks. "We experienced marvelous things today."

Naomi looked compassionately at her niece and embraced her again. "You all must be hungry. Come, eat." Naomi handed wooden bowls to each of them.

"Where's Father?" asked Seth.

"He will be along shortly," Naomi answered. "He has taken a short walk."

They ate and talked of the events of the morning and all the sights they had seen. As they finished the meal, Jershon walked toward them. Naomi could see he was tired and drawn. She stood to greet him. "Sit down, and let me get you some food," she offered.

Jershon declined and went straight to the tent to lie down, claiming he was too tired. She had never known him to take a midday nap. She knew he was struggling, as she was, with the news of Jacob and Levi. Naomi would check on him later.

The afternoon turned into evening, and the talk about the day's events in the temple continued. Jershon emerged from the tent to eat the evening meal but was noticeably subdued. The family talked of how much they missed Lamech, Raisa, and the baby.

Shortly before sundown, Jesus and his followers could be seen leaving the city for their trek back to Bethany. Jershon wondered how much longer the members of the Sanhedrin would let him roam freely. He believed Ezra's statement that surely they had intentions to seize him.

As everyone settled in for the night, Seth quietly approached Jershon. "Father, what time should I leave to see the rabbi?"

Jershon sighed heavily, pondering what to do. Seth waited expectantly for him to make a decision. "Leave just after sunrise, before everyone is stirring. I will make your excuses. I am not ready to share with everyone the reason for your absence. Come directly to me when you return."

Seth smiled at the responsibility granted him and hustled off to bed. Jershon would have a difficult time sleeping through the night.

◆　◆　◆

Maximus and Androcles arrived back at Ezra's just as Zilpah, the young cook and housekeeper, was setting out the evening meal. They greeted Ezra and waited for him to join them around the low table. They waited respectfully for Ezra to finish his prayers before beginning to eat.

"I had two interesting visitors today," Ezra began.

"Let me guess," Androcles said. "Pilate and his impish secretary." Androcles laughed, and Maximus grinned with a mouthful of greasy lamb.

"No, two visitors of much more importance and interest," Ezra said.

"Pray tell, rabbi," Maximus inquired.

"A fine Galilean fisherman named Jershon and his son Seth," Ezra answered.

Androcles choked on the wine he was drinking, and Maximus dropped a chunk of lamb meat onto his plate. They looked at each other blankly, then stared at Ezra, expecting further explanation.

It was Ezra's turn to laugh. "I thought that might interest you. What fine men they are," he added casually.

Maximus and Androcles remained speechless. Ezra drank deeply from his goblet, dragging out the suspense.

Maximus tried to speak. "How did they . . . when did they . . . what . . . " He was tongue-tied.

"The family has come to celebrate the Passover. Young Seth and his cousin David spotted you during the commotion when Jesus first came into town. They followed us here but were afraid to approach you. It appears you have changed." Ezra grinned at the two Romans who shared his table. "Wisely, they returned to their camp and informed their good father. Jershon and Seth knocked on my door early this morning. We spent a pleasant morning together. I can see why you became attached to them;

Jershon is a wise and hardworking man and has raised a good family. They are every bit as good as you described them."

"You met the entire family?" Maximus asked.

"No. One does not have to meet the entire family to know of their goodness once one has met their father." Ezra smiled. "You have made a good choice of friends," he added.

Maximus shifted nervously. "They kind of chose us," he said.

"That is how Jershon explained it as well. He admitted he didn't give you much of a choice to decline their invitation. And I assume that if his daughter and niece are as beautiful as you have said, then I fully understand the difficult decision you made to part company."

"You're not making this easy on us," Maximus said.

"No, it is not an easy thing. I could sense Jershon's reluctance to meet with you, but he is sending Seth back in the morning to invite you to do just that."

Maximus and Androcles were unable to eat. "What did you tell him?" Maximus asked.

"Nothing. I felt it was up to you to tell him your story," Ezra answered.

"But he knows we are Romans," Maximus exclaimed.

"Yes, he does, but he doesn't know the reason for your disguise. He believes you are honorable men, and he spoke highly of both of you. He was sure that there was a logical explanation for your sudden departure. But I sensed reluctance on his part to pursue further contact. I feel there is a chance his son will not come."

"I wouldn't blame him," Maximus said and took another bite of lamb. Suddenly it didn't taste as good as it had earlier. His mind was flooded with so many thoughts of Liora that he lost his appetite entirely. "I'm going to take a walk," he said. He was out the door before Ezra or Androcles could say anything.

Androcles looked after him and smiled at Ezra, then resumed his meal as if unaffected by the news. What Androcles hid well was the churning of his own stomach as he thought of Sariah. He had never had a relationship with a woman like her. Like Maximus, he had lived a life of campaigns and battle. Yet he had talked with her about their having a family and his working as a blacksmith. He had started to think of himself as something other than a warrior, and it was an appealing thought. He didn't want to go back to Rome. He didn't like Jerusalem, either, but life near the Sea of Galilee had occupied his mind since they left. Androcles began to be excited about seeing Sariah again. He would not let Jershon or Maximus stand in his way. He grabbed a large piece of meat and bit it vigorously. Ezra looked on in amusement.

36

יום שלישי

Yom Shlishi

Tuesday morning Seth was up early in anticipation of his errand. If he was lucky, he might get to see Jacob and Levi.

Jershon soon emerged from the tent and joined Seth by the fire he had rekindled with hot coals left from the night before. Disheveled from a long night of prayer and disquiet, he had come to the conclusion that Jacob and Levi needed an opportunity to make peace with his family. He was impressed that the two men were vexed by their deception, which had prompted their abrupt departure. If nothing else, a meeting would be an opportunity for them to clear their conscience and move on. The subject of Sariah and Liora was closed, however. The Law was clear. He would meet Jacob and Levi with Seth and David and then inform the girls. It would serve no purpose for Sariah and Liora to have further contact with Jacob and Levi. They would have to understand.

Jershon gave Seth his blessing and sent him off with

instructions to arrange a meeting at the house of Ezra later in the day and to say that he would be coming with Seth and David only. He reiterated to Seth the importance of keeping their meeting secret for now and admonished him to go straight there and come straight back. Seth ran off excitedly. Jershon smiled after him but soon became apprehensive about seeing the two men again and even more so about informing Sariah and Liora. He absentmindedly added some wood to the fire.

Seth jogged down the hill into the valley and moved quickly along the main road to the gates of the city. He was soon at Ezra's doorstep. Winded from his run, he took a minute to catch his breath. He leaned over, hands on his knees. He wanted to see Jacob and Levi but was afraid at the same time. After a moment he stood, but as he raised his hand to knock, the sun-bleached door slowly creaked open, and Ezra appeared in the doorway.

"Come in, my son," Ezra said with a wide grin. "There are a couple of men here who would like to see you." Ezra opened the door wide for Seth to enter. Seth hesitated, then stepped out of the bright sun into the dim room. It took a second for his eyes to adjust to the lack of light, and then he spotted two large figures standing at the back of the room—two large Roman soldiers. He stood wide-eyed as the figures came into focus. They were Jacob and Levi but clean-shaven and in Roman uniforms.

"Hello, Seth." He recognized the deep voice of Levi, the man with whom he had spent time fishing. Seth finally shook off his fear and strode over to him, embracing him and burying his face in the leather breastplate covering Androcles's chest. Androcles laughed and embraced Seth warmly with his massive arms.

"Hello, Seth," Maximus said. "This must seem very strange to you." Seth turned and embraced Maximus. Seth stepped back, not knowing what to say. "Are you alone?" Maximus asked.

Seth found his mouth was dry. Though tongue-tied, he

managed to stammer, "Yes, I have come with permission of my father to meet with you—I mean, to arrange a time he can meet with you." Seth kept staring at the two very familiar yet different men.

"We are excited to see your father, Seth. We want a chance to explain this," Maximus said, placing the palm of his hand on his breastplate. "It has to be confusing, but I assure you we are the same friends you knew in Capernaum." Seth smiled but his discomfort at seeing his friends as Roman soldiers was obvious. Maximus spared him further speech. "Tell your father we will visit you after the evening meal, if you will tell us where you are camped."

Androcles shot a questioning look at Maximus.

Maximus continued. "We have a meeting soon with Pontius Pilate. We are glad you came early, or we would have missed you."

Ezra stepped up. "My son." He placed his hand on Seth's shoulder. "Maximus and Androcles need to leave right away."

"Who?" asked Seth.

Ezra shook his head. "Jacob and Levi will be late if they don't leave immediately. Have some breakfast with me, and give me directions to your camp. I will be sure they are relayed, and they will meet with your family as they said." Ezra looked at Maximus and Androcles, excusing them with a nod.

Androcles and Maximus hugged Seth again. "It's good to see you, Seth," Androcles said. "We have missed you." With that he and Maximus donned their belts, swords, and daggers. Seth looked on nervously.

"All will be well, my son," Ezra said, squeezing Seth's shoulder. Sensing the young man's apprehension, Ezra guided him to a place at the low table.

Maximus and Androcles went out the door without saying

more and disappeared. Seth relaxed and greedily ate the good food that Ezra offered. They spoke of the great crowds in Jerusalem and the interesting events at the temple. Seth asked many questions, but Ezra skillfully avoided any additional explanation or talk of Maximus and Androcles. Seth explained to Ezra the location of their camp but said his father wanted to meet with Jacob and Levi alone first.

"I am sure that is the case, Seth," Ezra agreed. "But in talking to Jacob and Levi, I know they want to meet with your entire family, and I think that is the better option."

Seth shook his head but didn't argue and indicated he would relay the message to his father.

Ezra sensed that Seth would like to stay beyond the time Jershon would be comfortable with, so he moved him along and wished him well as he showed him out of the door. Seth ran off, his hunger satisfied.

◆ ◆ ◆

Maximus and Androcles entered the familiar courtyard of Pilate's palace and were immediately directed to a comfortable room furnished with luxurious chairs. They seated themselves and waited, taking in the wealth displayed in rugs and tapestries adorning the floors and walls. Candles in golden candelabras lighted the room.

"The taxes on the poor seem to be serving the empire well," Maximus said caustically. A servant entered the room with a tray and two goblets of wine that he served with deference to the two guests.

"My good General Maximus and Androcles," Pilate said with affection as he entered the room.

Both stood to greet Pilate, who appeared to be in an affable mood. "I will miss these daily meetings when you return to Rome." Pilate sat down in a large chair. "I am glad we have a chance to speak privately." The servant returned with a plate of bread and fruit and was dismissed with a quick wave of Pilate's hand. "It seems my conversations are always in the presence of advisors and emissaries from the Sanhedrin. I must apologize for my behavior on your last visit. They expect me to be a hard-liner on issues of importance to them, when frankly I believe it is prudent to seek the perspective of both sides."

Maximus shot a quick glance at Androcles as both sensed Pilate was more amenable to their report than they had expected. "Tell me what you have learned, gentlemen. I trust you have continued to follow the Nazarene?" Pilate asked.

"Yes, we followed him to the temple and witnessed some interesting events," Maximus offered.

"Tell me," Pilate encouraged. "I have the high priest's version. Now I would like to hear yours."

"We stand by our original assessment, prefect. Jesus is not a threat to Roman rule," Maximus began. "However, he did startle us with his behavior yesterday. We saw him confront the money-changers and overturn their tables. He created quite a stir, cracking a makeshift whip and herding the merchants along like unruly cattle." Maximus smiled. "But after speaking with Ezra, we understand his actions a little better. The merchants had made the courtyard of the temple seem like a bazaar, a marketplace, with their banter and offerings. Androcles and I felt the same ourselves when we visited the temple for the first time the other day. Ezra explained that Jesus was offended on a previous visit at the lack of respect shown for the temple, throwing out the moneychangers and admonishing them, as the Nazarene put it, 'make not my Father's house an house of merchandise.'" Maximus waited for Pilate to respond.

"Yes, I had heard about that incident some time ago as well as his purging yesterday, and that defines the issue the Sanhedrin has with the Nazarene. I have no quarrel with a man clearing the temple grounds of rapacious merchants and vendors. I would not want a carnival in my own courtyard, but his statement about the temple being the house of his father raises the hackles of the chief priests of the Jews. They call that blasphemy, which is a serious crime to them. To my way of thinking, Herod's temple stands where Solomon's temple once stood. Jesus claims to be a descendent of the house of David, who was Solomon's father. So under those circumstances the Nazarene's claim would be appropriate. But it is generally understood by the Sanhedrin that Jesus claims to be the Son of the Jewish God himself. They take issue with him about that assertion. Everything I have heard leads me to believe that he does not refute the claim—and therein lays the quandary." Pilate furrowed his brow and scratched his chin.

It was obvious to Maximus that Pilate had done his research and given great thought to this question.

Pilate continued. "If someone came to Rome and claimed to be the literal son of Jupiter, we would laugh him off as a sick man. Unless he performed some remarkable actions, he would be dismissed as no more than a lunatic. But this Jesus seems to be an intelligent man. In fact, these miracles—did you witness the miracles reported at the temple yesterday?" he asked Maximus directly.

"Yes, we did. From the walls of the Antonia fortress we saw unexplainable miracles." The room fell quiet as Pilate listened to Maximus's accounts of Jesus's healing.

"This is perplexing to me. How do you explain this?" Pilate asked sincerely.

"It is perplexing to us as well," Maximus responded.

"Do you believe he is the Son of God?" Pilate asked candidly.

Maximus hedged. "I know only what I have seen, and my

opinion of the Nazarene remains unaltered. He is not a threat to Rome, only to the leaders of the Jews." He felt an immediate pang of guilt for not admitting truthfully what he felt about Jesus and what the answers to his prayers had told him.

Pilate sighed deeply. "It presents me with a serious problem. The Sanhedrin fears him and clamors for his punishment, but he has not broken any law of Rome. And yet he displays a power and a confidence that cannot be ignored. I fear I won't be able to ignore him much longer, general. Soon I will be forced to make a judgment."

Maximus stood to make his point. "Prefect, Jesus is not a criminal. His people misunderstand him, and he does nothing but *good* for them. I hope you will judge wisely."

Pilate likewise stood, and the three men exchanged farewells. "Thank you for coming today. Please keep me informed of future events. I fear this week will not end peacefully."

Maximus and Androcles took their leave. As they left the palace, Androcles said, "Anyone else would have taken you for a disciple, my brother."

"I am," Maximus said firmly and walked toward the temple.

◆ ◆ ◆

Seth arrived at the camp and found his father. Jershon, with a subtle motion of his finger, reminded his son to be quiet about his errand until they could speak privately. Soon Jershon led his son to the olive orchard nearby, where they sat, and Jershon asked for his report.

"I saw them, Father—Jacob and Levi. They have shaved their beards and wear breastplates made of leather and brass. They look so different dressed as Romans," Seth began energetically.

"They are Romans, my son. Let us not forget that," Jershon

said. Then, coming straight to the point, he asked, "So when can we meet with them?"

"They are coming here, Father," Seth replied. "They will be here after the evening meal. I told them where we could be found."

Jershon turned his face skyward. "I wish you had not agreed to that, Seth," he said quietly. "That is not what I wanted." He shook his head.

"But they had to leave for a meeting with someone whose name I can't remember," Seth said defensively. "They said they would be gone most of the day and wanted to see our whole family. Ezra said they would explain everything to us." Seth reached out for his father's arm. "Father, they are the same. They are still our friends," he added, pleadingly.

"They are still our friends, but they are not the same." Jershon adjusted his robe. "Have you forgotten that your cousins Nehum and Hanan were slain at the hands of Roman soldiers? How do you think this change in Jacob and Levi will affect David and Liora?" he asked with soberness.

Seth considered his father's comment. "You have always taught us to respect all men and not be judgmental. Jacob and Levi have proven to us that they are good men. The Romans who killed my cousins were bad men. That doesn't mean that Jacob and Levi are bad men."

Jershon gave Seth an approving smile. "You have wisdom beyond your years, my son." He placed his hand affectionately on Seth's shoulder. "You are right. We should not judge them. We will listen to their story. I'm sure it will prove to be an interesting one."

Nevertheless, Jershon's stomach churned at the thought of Jacob and Levi meeting with the entire family. *How will Sariah and Liora react? How will David react? What will Naomi say?*

Where will this lead? Jershon was plagued by a myriad of questions. He would let them come, hear their explanation, and then let God be his guide. Fishing had taught him patience. It had also taught him that sometimes you do your best and come away disappointed, but that shouldn't cause you to waver from proven methods. He would be obedient to his knowledge and his convictions. Reminding Seth to stay silent on the subject of Jacob and Levi, Jershon and his son returned to the family. As their patriarch, he would find the right time to break the news of their pending visit.

The afternoon couldn't pass fast enough for Seth; it progressed too fast for Jershon. It was well after the midday meal, and he still was silent on the subject of Jacob and Levi. The others had gone once again to the temple. He remained behind with Naomi, enjoying the mild day and quiet conversation with his wife.

Naomi finally summoned the courage to speak candidly. "What troubles you, dear?" she asked as she sat close beside him, leaning comfortably on his shoulder. Jershon caressed her cheek and ran his fingers through her graying hair.

"Is it that obvious?" he said.

"Only to me," she reassured him.

He decided to be forthright. "Jacob and Levi will visit us after our meal this evening. I sent Seth early this morning to arrange a private meeting with them, but they wanted to speak with all of us. That rather changes things."

Naomi gasped. "I wish you had told me sooner; I would have made some sweet cakes." Naomi began bustling around the camp.

"I'm afraid our lack of sweet cakes is the least of our concerns," Jershon replied.

"Nonetheless, we want to be good hosts." Naomi began to assemble ingredients.

Jershon was already lost in thought. He wished he could meet with them first. Worried that their meeting with the whole family at once would turn out badly, he sighed and fiddled with the fire.

"Are you making sweet cakes, Mother?" Sariah asked when she and the others returned from their visit to the temple. "Are we expecting guests?"

Naomi nearly dropped the pot she was carrying.

"Yes, we are," interjected Jershon. "Let me speak with you all a moment." His voice was serious, and everyone assembled quickly. "I have news of Jacob and Levi," Jershon announced. "They are coming to visit us."

Liora gasped audibly. Sariah let out a faint giggle, then reached to hug Liora. David scowled at the announcement.

"I want to prepare you for their visit," Jershon said, looking at each one to gauge the reaction. "The other day David and Seth spotted our friends in the city. They were among the crowd following Jesus to the temple when he first arrived. They weren't immediately recognizable because they were dressed as Roman soldiers. In truth, they *are* Romans."

Sariah looked at him, dumbfounded. Liora lowered her head, her head covering shielding her eyes from his view, but he could see the tears streaming down her face. "I know this news comes as a shock, but in itself, it explains some things we all suspected. Seth and I met with their host here in Jerusalem. He is a wonderful man, a rabbi named Ezra. He spoke highly of both of them and assured us that they were the same good men we had come to know in Capernaum. He deferred any further explanation to them, thinking it wise for them to tell us their story directly. I was unsure if it was prudent to meet with them, knowing the tender feelings some of us hold in our hearts."

He glanced again at Liora and Sariah, who were now both silently weeping. "Our family has had bitter experience with Romans." He sat silent for a minute, pondering what to say next. "I believe Jacob and Levi deceived us about their true identity, but I don't believe they deceived us about their kindness. That, I think, was genuine."

Jershon reached for Liora's hand. "Seth met with them this morning. He says they look the same, except for their clothing, and they have shaved their beards, which must have been an irritant to them." His attempt to interject some levity failed. "They will be here shortly after the evening meal. For myself, I'm anxious to hear their story. I can appreciate that it will be strange to see them as Romans; I'm not sure what to expect myself. But if we can believe their friend Ezra—and I do—they will be the same men we came to love. I know this may be a difficult reunion. I caution each of you to reserve judgment."

Sariah went to her mother, who hugged her tightly. Liora joined them and Naomi hugged her as well. The three women departed into the seclusion of the tent.

"David, you have been most somber since you sighted our two friends. I think I understand the reason. I would ask you, especially, to reserve judgment, even though the sight of Romans inspires harsh feelings. We should judge no man by the actions of others, no culture by the actions of a few. There are bad Egyptians, bad Assyrians, bad Samaritans, and bad Romans; there are even bad Jews, my son, but I believe that mankind in general is good. Misguided leaders and occasionally too much wine lead men astray."

Jershon continued. "We have not spoken openly of these things before, but perhaps we should in the future. We are isolated in Capernaum. We lead a simple life and are protected from many of the failures of the cultures that surround us. We are exposed only to the inconsequential failings of our neighbors. However, Rome has touched our lives through their occupation of our land and the taxes they levy. That is a harsh infringement and makes it easy to judge all of Rome and its citizens by the same measure. That is wrong. Forgive me for stirring up tender feelings, my son. Our beloved Nahum and Hanan were slain by drunken soldiers, bullies who were weak men prone to violence. Jacob and Levi are men of strong character but their natures are not violent. I am hoping our meeting with them reinforces that judgment."

"My beloved David." Jershon stood to address his nephew. "Open your heart to our friends, allow them to explain. I believe that perhaps they can help you heal your anger, particularly Levi."

They embraced, and Jershon held the quivering shoulders of his muscular nephew.

The meal passed quietly, and the camp was cleaned and tidied. Each was caught up in his or her own anxiety about seeing Jacob and Levi again. Jershon was not one normally to pay much attention to such details, but he noticed that the girls had changed into clean robes and brushed their hair. The sweet cakes had finished cooking and were wrapped in cloth to maintain heat and moisture. Jershon was amazed at how Naomi could make a simple camp seem like home. Seth was vigilant, keeping watch on the road below, looking for two Romans. The sun was setting and the evening was beginning to cool, prompting Jershon to don his thick outer robe and throw additional wood on the fire. Soon it was dark, and their vision was limited to the orange glow thrown from the dancing flames of the fire.

Jershon saw two men walking slowly along the trail near their camp. They were still in the shadows, but their robes seemed to identify them as Jews. Blankets were draped over their shoulders and heads for warmth.

"Jacob . . . Levi . . . is that you?" Jershon called out into the night. There was no answer, but the two men proceeded cautiously toward the camp.

"Jershon?" It was Jacob's voice. Everyone stood and looked at the two men who entered the light of the campfire and pushed back their head coverings to reveal their clean-shaven faces. They stood hesitantly, gauging the group and their reaction. Naomi walked over to greet them, giving each a warm embrace and leading Jacob closer to the fire. Jershon gave them both a welcoming embrace. Esther unabashedly ran to Levi, who swept her up in his arms and swung her around; she screeched with delight. Seth was next, embracing Jacob and playfully boxing with Levi, who laughed heartily. Liora and Sariah stood apart, each smiling broadly but withholding any outward show of affection. David remained seated by the fire.

"Come, sit," Naomi ordered. "I hope you have some appetite left. We have made sweet cakes." She motioned to Liora and Sariah to serve them.

The young women went into the tent to fetch the cakes. Jacob tried to look at Liora without drawing attention. He caught the side of her smooth face in the light of the fire. Her eyes sparkled and her hair shone, but she would not make eye contact with him. He momentarily forgot that there was anyone else sitting around the fire. He watched her enter the tent and come out again a moment later. She walked straight toward him and bent to offer him the cake. He looked straight into the dark pool of her eyes. Liora smiled shyly and lowered her eyes, not wanting to meet his searching look.

"Thank you," Jacob managed to squeak out of his dry mouth. Liora smiled again but didn't speak.

Jershon was glad the two had not worn their Roman clothing.

He broke the tension by bringing attention to their lack of facial hair. "I see you have rid yourselves of the traditional beards."

"Yes," responded Jacob, "we have," as he rubbed his chin and smiled. "There's nothing traditional about us any longer." He tried to make a joke, but it fell flat, which made him even more uncomfortable, but he decided to plow forward. "We owe you all an apology and an explanation."

"Yes, you do!" David said tersely. Jershon shot him a cautioning glance.

"Yes, David, we do," Jacob answered. "First of all, let me apologize with all my heart for our deception. When we arrived in Capernaum, it was not our intent to prey on an unwitting family. It all happened so fast and so innocently. We could not refuse your gracious hospitality, and the next thing we knew we had become part of you. Let me assure you, our feelings and actions while we were with you were not a deception—they were genuine." He glanced at Liora, hoping she would understand what he was saying. "You all became part of us—both of us," as he motioned toward Levi. "It was necessary to leave, but I can't tell you how difficult it was. We have been guilt-ridden ever since for not being honest with you that day. I am so grateful we have the chance to meet and clear this up." Jacob fidgeted uncomfortably, hoping he was making sense. He wanted to take a bite of the cake, but his mouth was so dry he was afraid he would be unable to talk afterward.

"Seth, bring Jacob and Levi some wine," said Jershon. Jacob was grateful for the chance to collect his thoughts. Seth returned with a goatskin bag full of wine and two wooden cups that he handed to each of them and then filled generously. Jacob took a large gulp.

"Thank you," Jacob said. "This is harder to put into words than I thought it would be."

"Proceed honestly, Jacob. You are among friends; we hold no animosity," Jershon assured him.

"Thank you, Jershon." Jacob put the cup down as his hands shook. "We are Romans," he confessed. "We came here on assignment in response to a request of the prefect of Judaea, Pontius Pilate, and under direct command of the emperor Tiberius." All eyes were upon Jacob. He continued courageously. "My real name is Lucius Fabius Maximus. I am a Roman general and command a legion." Maximus chuckled at what he revealed next. "Ironically, I am the highest-ranking Roman officer on Judaean soil. And this is my good friend, Androcles. He is my deputy commander. We have fought together for Rome since we were younger than Seth. It seems like a lifetime." Androcles nodded in agreement.

Maximus continued, "We haven't known peace for most of our lives. Your family, Jershon, has given us a view of the world and a respite we have seldom known. We are indebted to you and envious of what you have." He looked at Jershon with admiration. Jershon met his glance, and the old man's eyes began to fill with tears. "We come from families similar to yours. My father is a senator in Rome. My mother and two young sisters work a small farm north of Rome because they refuse to be caught up in the conceit of the empire." He turned to Naomi. "You would like my mother, Naomi. She is a great woman." Now Maximus's eyes were filling with tears.

Maximus turned his attention to David. "Androcles comes from a good family. He grew up like you, David, wielding the hammer of a blacksmith. His talented father taught him the trade, and his skills were refined with the help of his three older brothers. I understand your anger, David, and you also, Liora, at this revelation." The very sound of his voice saying her name caused Liora's heart to leap. "Your anger at Rome is understood by us both. Roman soldiers took the lives of your brothers.

Androcles, show them your amulet." Androcles hesitated and then pulled the leather cord from his breast, holding up the lump of gold.

"Marauding Gauls murdered Androcles's family. The Gauls attacked his family and burned his home to the ground. This amulet was taken from the charred remains of his mother." Maximus paused to let the reality of his story take hold. "We know about evil men. We know the horror of war and the scars a conquering army leave on a people and their country. I don't agree with what Rome is doing here, but perhaps we can have that conversation another day. Androcles and I are sick of the lives we have led. We are tired of the wars and the killing. We have learned so much in our short time here, and much of that has come as a result of our time with you."

Maximus took another long drink of wine. "I have gotten off the subject." He looked around; everyone was staring at him open-mouthed. No one spoke, so he continued. "Some months ago Pilate sent a messenger to Tiberius, requesting that emissaries from Rome come to investigate an upstart Nazarene named Jesus. Pilate thought Jesus might be building an army that could prove detrimental to Roman rule. That messenger was a good . . . no . . . a *great* man named Ezra." He turned to Jershon. Jershon concurred with a nod of his head. "My father, knowing my restless discontent, was responsible for my being assigned as one of those emissaries. I am responsible for Androcles being here." He turned to his friend.

Androcles responded. "I was angry with him for making me come along. But he is weak and needed protection." Androcles's humor broke the tension, and everyone laughed a little nervously. "But I will be forever grateful for being asked to come to Judaea." Androcles smiled at Sariah.

Maximus dropped the blanket from his shoulders as the

warmth of the fire took effect. "The plan was to pose as Jews to better enable us to follow Jesus unnoticed. It was an interesting transformation."

Maximus told them of the voyage from Ostia by ship, the Egyptian captain Akhom, the pirate attack, and the long days sitting on deck cross-legged with Ezra, learning Jewish ways. He told them about arriving at Caesarea and the encounter with the Roman soldiers and their journey to Capernaum with the caravan led by Alhasan. Some parts of the narrative made everyone laugh; others made them gasp with fear and wonder. Each one gained a renewed respect for the bravery and courage of Maximus and Androcles.

"Fate brought us to Capernaum on the shores of the Sea of Galilee just as help was needed. We had no intention of staying with anyone. Our plan was to blend in with Jesus's disciples and follow him from place to place. But it became harder and harder to separate ourselves from your hospitality and kindness—and your good cooking, Naomi." Naomi blushed with the unexpected compliment.

"Our discussions with your family were enlightening. Androcles and I have not been part of a family in the past decade and more for any length of time. We talked about leaving your home several times, and we should have done so before the bonds became so deep and complicated." Maximus stole a quick glance at Liora. She looked angelic sitting by the fire, shadows dancing off her deep olive-green robe and white head covering. He wanted to talk with her privately, perhaps take a walk, but circumstances would not permit. All the better, for he knew how Jershon would feel about anything that might draw them closer together. Ezra had made it clear what the Jewish law was on that subject, and his heart pained him, even though he also knew that

Roman law and custom forbade a citizen to marry someone who was not also a citizen of Rome.

"The longer we stayed, the harder it became to leave. We never meant to deceive you. We apologize again if we have caused you any pain. We would be grateful if you would let us repay you for your hospitality."

Jershon raised his hand in objection. "Don't insult us with an offer to compensate us for the love we showed you. The feelings were genuine on our side too, my sons." Jershon's use of the familiar form of address caused Maximus to smile despite his embarrassment about the offer.

"You have had a most interesting journey. We would certainly like to hear more." Maximus's heart leapt at the thought that they might be invited back. He had resigned himself that after their meeting tonight they would say a good-bye, and that would be the end of it. He had mixed emotions about continuing any association with Liora, because it could not lead to happiness for either of them, but now that he was with her again, he was not ready to turn his back on his feelings quite yet.

Liora stood to refresh Maximus's cup of wine. She leaned toward him, her back to the fire. He raised his cup and breathed in the scent of her closeness, his gaze welded to her eyes. Maximus sensed they had a private space for about two seconds. *I love you,* he mouthed. Her composure suddenly weakened, and she lost her balance. Maximus reached out to catch her, placing his strong hand on her delicate shoulder. The touch sent a warm shock through his entire body. He wanted to hold her close, even if it was for just a moment. She steadied herself and pulled away. Her smile and the tears forming in her eyes told him she felt what he felt.

"Are you all right?" he asked.

"Yes, I am fine now." She smiled, acknowledging his whisper.

"Would you like some more cake?" she asked. The sound of her voice racked his heart. He suddenly knew he could not leave this woman. In the brief time they had spent together, something had happened between them to form an unbreakable bond. She had somehow become part of him—and he of her. He was going to need Ezra's help. He didn't know how he would make it work, but he could not go on without her.

"Are you all right, my dear?" Naomi bustled over to help when she saw Liora stumble.

"I am fine, aunt," she answered, but Naomi heard the trembling in her voice and saw the tears in her eyes. She had watched Sariah flirt with Levi, and she sighed in resignation. A complex ache welled in the heart of a concerned mother on behalf of her children.

Jershon leaned forward. "Tell me, Jacob, what was your report to Pilate today about Jesus of Nazareth, if I may ask?"

Maximus took his eyes off Liora and answered. "We have met with him twice and reported the same thing: Jesus is not leading any revolution that Rome should be concerned about. Unfortunately, the Sanhedrin seeks his arrest. They have been meeting and pressuring Pilate daily."

Jershon hissed through his teeth. "Those vipers are still looking out for their own skins."

"Yes, they are," Maximus answered.

"How much longer will they let him walk the streets freely and teach in the temple?" Jershon asked.

"They plot against him as we speak," Maximus continued. "I suspect they will arrest him any day. I don't know what their reason will be or the charges, but we seem to have Pilate's ear at the moment, and I believe he will not have any part of it. They may ban Jesus from the temple, or from Jerusalem for that matter, but I don't think that will have any effect on his teachings, and his followers increase daily. That is why the chief priests of the Sanhedrin seek to quiet him. The Jews are more passionate about listening to the teachings of Jesus than they are the teachings of the local rabbis—and that disturbs them."

"He passes near here each day early in the morning and late in the afternoon. They say he is staying in Bethany," Jershon commented.

"Yes, I understand he has friends there," Maximus answered.

"Levi, what are your thoughts?" Jershon turned the conversation to Androcles.

Androcles was startled as he had been looking at Sariah the whole time. "Yes, the sweet cakes were delicious, Naomi—thank you." There was a pause, and then everyone laughed together as they realized he had not been paying attention at all to the conversation.

"I see you have other things on your mind," Jershon said with a grin. He was well aware that the connection had once again been made between the two men and his daughter and niece. He was regretting this meeting but was glad to see the light come back into the girls' eyes. "You two should probably be getting back. It is getting late."

Maximus took that as their cue to leave. He felt so much better having told them the truth, but he wasn't sure whether anything had changed. He couldn't think how to ask for another invitation to visit, so he wished that someone would invite them back, yet he sensed reluctance in Jershon's tone. He knew Jershon was grateful to have the matter of their departure cleared up, but that didn't change the fact that Maximus and Androcles were Gentiles. That divide could not be crossed.

Maximus stood. He extended his hand, but Jershon instead gave him a warm embrace. Then Jershon turned to Androcles and embraced him warmly as well. Naomi gave an affectionate hug to each.

"I am glad we were able to see you again to explain a bit," said Maximus with some finality.

"We are too, Jacob," responded Jershon. "It was good to see you both." He could not think of anything else to say.

David reluctantly shook hands but did not say a word. Seth hugged each of them as if they were lost brothers and playfully slugged Androcles, who shoved him away.

"We will see you again, won't we?" Naomi asked, looking at Jershon for confirmation. Everything became so quiet they could hear the flames of the fire licking the cool night air.

Jershon sidestepped the question. "I'll walk with you, my sons," he said as he led them out of the light of the camp.

"I'm glad we had this chance to talk. Everything is much clearer now," Jershon began. "Although I am not sure where we go from here," he said with honest doubt in his voice. "It is very complicated."

"I agree with you," answered Maximus. "But I will be frank with you, Jershon, now that there are no secrets between us." Maximus shuffled his feet nervously and took a deep breath, gathering his thoughts, then blurted out, "I am in love with Liora."

Jershon looked at him tenderly. "That is obvious, my son, and it is obvious she feels the same way about you. Though I now understand the reason for your leaving us so abruptly in Capernaum, I also know it troubled you deeply to do so. The anguish my daughters felt was no less." He turned to Androcles. "Sariah told Naomi and me the things you talked about in private, and it appears you feel the same way about her as Jacob feels about Liora."

Now Androcles was shuffling, but he answered strongly. "Yes,

Jershon, I do. I promise you that although our talks were intimate, in no way has my behavior been in conflict with your ways."

"I trust that they haven't, my son. That was never in question," Jershon assured him. "I have seen the respect with which you treat our entire family. I must apologize for David's coolness, however. He is still struggling with your being Romans, as you can understand. When his brothers were killed, it was especially difficult for him. He had worked closely with them and his father for years."

"If anyone understands that, Jershon, it is I," said Androcles. "I would have a hard time not taking immediate revenge on any Gaul I happened to meet in the street—peaceful or not."

"Then you understand the need to be patient with him. Especially since he is aware of Jacob's feeling toward his sister. He is quite confused." Jershon struck his staff on the rocky path where they stood. He looked at both of them with compassion. "But I can't possibly let this continue. You know that."

"We do," answered Maximus, who started to speak.

Jershon held up his staff, not unlike the way Ezra had signalled for them to hold their tongues while he taught them. "I need to converse with my God," he said, bowing his head with fatigue. "We have become followers of Jesus. His teachings are new, and Jesus says he fulfills the old Law of Moses. I am not sure what he means by that." He tapped his staff nervously. "The purity of our race has been foremost in our teaching." Jershon's eyes began to fill with tears. "I do not have the wisdom of your friend Ezra. I would like to talk with him before I make a decision. Would you ask him on my behalf if he would meet with me tomorrow? I can send Seth in the morning to confirm a time."

Maximus took Jershon's arm as the strong Galilean seemed suddenly feeble. "I am sure he would be pleased to meet with you. He is a wise man; we have learned much from him. He spends most of his days studying and could use the company. In fact, it would do well for him to get out. Send Seth mid-morning, and Ezra can return with him to your camp. Your whole family should know him."

"That would be good," Jershon said. "I will arrange some time to speak with him alone as well."

"Then it is settled." Out of great love for Jershon and a sudden hope for the future, Maximus gave him another affectionate embrace.

Jershon smiled and looked at the two men he loved. "Be well, my sons. We will figure this out." He walked slowly back to the camp, wiping the tears from his eyes.

37

יום רביעי

Yom Revi'i

Wednesday dawned cool. Maximus was up early and took a short walk. He found a quiet place some distance from the city and sat to ponder the events of the previous night. Jershon was hard to read; he was being cautious with his words. Maximus had felt a surge of relief when he and Androcles left after revealing the truth about themselves and discovering that his feelings hadn't changed for Liora, nor hers for him. He was still unsure about the future and didn't want to think the worst, but his common sense told him not to hold too much hope for a happy outcome. Besides, there was more than just Jershon's family to consider. He was glad Jershon had suggested a meeting with Ezra. Not that he thought Ezra would be able to dissuade him from following Jewish law, but perhaps there were some exceptions to the law that Jershon wasn't aware of.

Maximus had processed life both with and without Liora ever since leaving her in Capernaum. He had concluded that he would never find someone like her. The few women he had come to know in Rome all had expectations of him that he knew he could not meet. What they didn't know was that he was far removed from the Rome they thought he supported. He would never live an elite lifestyle in the city, and he had no interest in associating any longer with those in power. He was tired not only of the fighting but tired of the politics too.

Rome seemed like a distant memory to Maximus. He looked at the simple robes he wore and realized how much he enjoyed being an ordinary man. He thought back to the days in Capernaum, working hard and helping out—that was what he wanted. He was through with generalship and all the responsibility that came with it. He was through with the senate's imperialism and the campaigns that were placed on his shoulders. The pain of separation that he felt was for his mother and sisters, not Rome.

In the distance, he saw farmers beginning to work the fields and orchards. Tradesmen and pilgrims filled the roads into Jerusalem. The city was awakening. He stood, shook the loose leaves from his robe, and made his way back to the house. He had a busy day ahead.

Maximus returned just before Seth arrived. Ezra had protested mildly the night before when Maximus asked him to go with the young man in the morning, but Ezra knew meeting with Jershon was important to both Maximus and Androcles. He had a pretty good idea why, so he withheld serious objection. He spent too much time in the house, anyway, and needed to get out among people again. If nothing else, the walk would do him good.

Seth eagerly knocked on the door, and after a warm greeting, Ezra gathered his cloak and staff, and the two set off together.

Maximus and Androcles did not discuss the events of the previous night. Androcles had been quite close-mouthed about

Sariah, anyway, and it ultimately didn't matter to Maximus what Androcles was thinking of doing. Each man would have to come to his own decision. Surprisingly, it was Androcles who broached the subject.

"What are you going to do, my brother?" he asked.

"About what?"

Androcles laughed as he donned his leather breastplate in preparation for the day. "About Liora."

Maximus parried. "What are you planning to do about Sariah?"

Androcles's response caught Maximus by surprise. "I plan on living a long life with her in Capernaum, working as a blacksmith."

Maximus stopped lacing his sandal and stared up at his life-long friend. "You never cease to surprise me."

"I'll bet you the rest of your gold aurei that you do the same. You'll find a way to be with Liora and make a life for yourself, although I don't see you as a fisherman." Androcles laughed.

Maximus continued dressing. "No, you're right. I was thinking of becoming a member of the Sanhedrin instead," he said.

They both laughed.

Maximus sat disconsolately, leaning forward with his elbows on his knees and his hands folded. "What's the answer, my brother?"

"It will work out," Androcles answered confidently. "I don't know how, but it will work out. We've fought many battles together with the odds stacked against us—this one is no different. Don't give up, Maximus." Androcles put his hand on his friend's shoulder. "Victory is within our grasp. Fight hard, and at the end of the day, the laurel wreath will be ours."

"They're not laurel wreaths, you numbskull." Maximus shook his head dejectedly.

"No, and they are not the enemy—and we never conquered anyone that afterwards we gave our hearts to," Androcles said with a grin.

Maximus chuckled. "You think yourself a great philosopher, don't you? But, we are fighting the long-held traditions of an unbending culture, my friend. They may be insurmountable."

"Their culture is changing as we speak. Their laws are being challenged, and their world is being turned upside down. The Nazarene is our ally in this," Androcles said as he secured the belt around his waist.

"I don't know if the gospel Jesus preaches includes Jewish women marrying Gentile men, especially Roman soldiers," Maximus said.

"Perhaps, but I think that's about to change as well." Androcles opened the door to leave.

"God has given you the power of ten men, Androcles. You never run from a fight—you keep slashing until you have won. I will trust you on this one," Maximus said and followed him out the door.

"Which god do you speak of?" Androcles asked.

"That's another problem we have." Maximus followed his friend as they began the trek to Pilate's palace.

◆ ◆ ◆

"General, commander." Pilate seemed fatigued as he greeted the two soldiers. "I have news I find troubling."

Maximus looked at Androcles warily.

"Good morning, sir. I'm sorry you're troubled. How can we help?" Maximus said with a slight bow of his head.

Pilate pursed his lips together, then said flatly, "Make this Nazarene go away." A low murmuring chuckle rose from the group of advisors and scribes surrounding him.

Maximus wisely refrained from comment but rather kept his attention on Pilate, waiting for an explanation.

"Ever since he has arrived he has been nothing but trouble." Pilate waved his hand in disgust.

"In what way, governor?" Maximus probed.

"I have a constant stream of Jewish rabbis and priests and other authorities knocking down my door with complaints: Sadducees, Pharisees, Herodians. These contentious factions have united against this Nazarene as if they were all long-time friends. He has managed to unite them in purpose as Rome never could. Surprisingly, they look to us for relief from one of their own." Pilate shook his head. "It is incredible to me." He rubbed his temples with his hands, as if seeking relief from a headache. "Last night I received a disturbing report. Apparently, prior to his kingly arrival the other day," Pilate rolled his eyes in mockery, "Jesus was in Bethany. While he was there he restored the life of one Lazarus, brother of two of his beloved friends, Martha and Mary. It has been verified that indeed this Lazarus had been dead four days. Jesus had his sepulcher opened, and the man walked out in his burial wrap. Is it not enough that he restores sight to the blind, heals the lame, and cures the leper, but now he must raise the very dead? It makes me shiver to think of it." Pilate clutched his robe tightly to his chest.

The room was quiet, but Maximus knew Pilate expected some comment. "That is most curious. I have witnessed healings with my own eyes, both in Galilee and here at the temple. It amazes me too. But with respect, governor, as I've been told by Ezra, the Jews have laid hands on their sick and afflicted for years with the intent of healing. Now the prayers to their God are answered before their eyes. They have proof of his love and power, yet they attempt to refute it and desire to have the perpetrator of these miraculous acts, Jesus of Nazareth, put in shackles. That is even more troubling to me," Maximus offered.

Pilate scratched his chin. "You make an interesting point, my friend. Nevertheless, it causes them concern—fear, I suppose. If this Jesus can call down the power of the gods to perform the healings of which we have evidence and now even raise the dead, can he harness that same power to make the sky rain with fire to vanquish his enemies?"

Maximus considered his response. "He isn't that kind of man. He teaches peace and forgiveness and is not vindictive or malicious."

"Then why do the leaders of the Jews clamor for his arrest, Maximus?" Pilate countered.

"On what charges?" Maximus asked honestly.

"High treason," Pilate answered.

"How does he commit treason?" Maximus asked skeptically.

"My sources tell me he claims authority from his father; intimating he is the son of their god and some sort of king," Pilate answered. "In turn, Jesus accuses them of being hypocrites because they neither know nor practice the Law. He offends his own leaders in public, and from what I understand, he does a pretty good job." Pilate smiled, causing muffled laughter from his surrounding sycophants. "He confounds them at every turn, challenging their very authority in a way they can't argue. They come to me beaten and angry, looking to me to be the great defender of their faith. I find that ironic."

"It is ironic," Maximus agreed. "From occupier to defender. Pilate, you must be proud. You have come full circle here in Judaea, gaining not only the Jews' respect but also their confidence. My report to Rome will state as much." Maximus continued. "My advice, governor, is to continue to lend a sympathetic ear, keep your door open, and withhold judgment. On occasion, especially in time of war, some of my soldiers would descend upon me with complaints about the undue hardship of the campaign. I listened to them but never agreed with them. The next day we would go into battle, and those who were not committed to the task at hand usually fell by the sword—their own doubt destroyed them. In your case, the enemy is coming to you confessing their doubt. Listen with a kind and caring ear, but don't agree with them—let their own doubt destroy their will. You will win on two fronts—both Rome's and Judaea's."

Pilate looked admiringly at the powerful soldier standing before him. "Wisely stated, my son. Spoken like a true general. You have the analytical skills of your father, I see. Thank you for your insightful counsel." Pilate stood, causing a stir among the crowd surrounding him. He turned to the aide at his side. "Tell them to prepare our midday meal quickly. Maximus, you and Androcles will dine with me." It was more of an order than an invitation, and Maximus was not inclined to refuse.

◆ ◆ ◆

Seth led Ezra to the family's camp. He greeted Jershon and Naomi cordially and was introduced to David. He was led to a makeshift bench in the form of a thick olive branch balanced on deftly placed rocks at each end, and he sat gratefully.

"Age is getting the better of me," Ezra said as Naomi offered him a cup of wine. "Thank you." He took a generous gulp and wiped beads of sweat from his forehead. Two young women and a girl emerged from the tent in front of him and approached.

"These are my daughters, Sariah and Esther, and my niece, Liora," Jershon said proudly. Ezra struggled to stand, then faced the three girls and in turn took each one by the hand. "I see what has the good legate and his deputy commander so agitated." Sariah giggled, and Liora bowed her head and blushed. Ezra turned toward Naomi. "God has blessed you with a beautiful family. I am sure you are proud."

"Yes, we are, rabbi," Naomi responded. "Our oldest son, his wife, and their new son remained in Capernaum. It's been only a few days, but I miss them greatly."

"I am sure you do." Ezra took his seat again, still feeling light-headed from the uphill walk.

"Are you all right, rabbi?" Jershon asked.

"Oh, yes. I'm just a little tired from the hike. I have been pre-occupied as of late and have not gotten out much. The walk and the fresh air were exhilarating. My studies have given me great strength of soul, but I'm afraid they have made the body weak." He gladly accepted more wine from Naomi.

"Tell us about your studies, rabbi. I was interested in your comments when we met, and I am sure my family would like to hear, if I may be so bold."

"It is fine to ask, but please, call me Ezra. I am not worthy to be called rabbi."

"Jacob and Levi spoke highly of you as a great teacher, so I assumed . . ." Jershon's voice trailed off.

"They are good students and good men. You have made a great impression upon them." Jershon smiled, and Ezra contin-ued. "I have been studying the writings of the prophets and their words testifying of the Messiah. By your reverence and attention, I take it this is a subject of interest," Ezra observed.

"It most certainly is," Jershon answered. "Would you be will-ing to share with us what you have learned?" he asked.

Ezra looked thoughtful. His bushy gray eyebrows almost en-tirely covered his closed eyes as he spoke. "The prophecies have pointed toward Him for centuries. The words are very clear."

"Is Jesus of Nazareth the Messiah?" David blurted out impatiently.

Ezra lifted his head, opened his eyes, and looked straight at David, weighing his answer carefully. "I think each one of us needs to discover that for himself," he responded.

"But you said the scriptures you study are clear. Do you believe Jesus is the Messiah?" David asked again. Jershon bristled at his nephew's impertinence.

Ezra smiled at David. "The scriptures are not always clear to those who fail to read them with proper humility. It seems the prophets want us to search these things out for ourselves and come to a prayerful decision." Ezra looked David squarely in the eye. "David, from my perspective, the Messiah walks among us. Everything I have studied supports that conclusion. His powers are self-evident, and his love and charity toward all men is unquestionable. I believe if you have chosen to follow him, you have made a wise decision."

Ezra paused and then continued. "Jacob said to me that you are believers."

"Yes, we are," Jershon answered without hesitation. "We first heard him months ago in Capernaum and have since had other opportunities to listen to him teach. Liora, Sariah, and David followed him to Bethsaida recently and saw and heard wonderful things."

"That must have been an enlightening experience," Ezra said to Liora.

"I will never forget those days, rabbi. They are burned in my memory and my heart," Liora answered softly.

Ezra had known why Maximus insisted on his meeting with Jershon and his family. His intentions regarding this beautiful woman were clear. Now, as Ezra listened to her and observed her, he understood more fully why. Her skin glowed like a pearl in the sunlight, and her long brown hair framed her face, which projected an indefinable radiance. She spoke as softly as a summer's breeze and moved with the grace of a girl he had known years ago—the girl he had made his wife, she who by the will of God had left him too soon. *If Maximus loves you the way I loved her, no one should stand in his way,* he thought, holding back a tear as he thought of his beloved Miriam.

"I assume you have questions regarding my two Roman students?" Ezra lowered his head covering and brushed his unkempt hair out of his face. He could see all eyes were upon him. "Jacob told me last night that he and Levi had told you everything. I have come to know these two men well, and they speak nothing but truth. They are good men. In fact, I have not met men with such integrity in all of Jerusalem. They have become like sons to me. They seek only to do their duty. Their mission here will soon be complete, and it will be hard to see them go." Ezra spoke in a melancholy tone. He did not want to lose his association with them, but that was out of his hands.

Jershon spoke. "We were grateful when they came to us; they probably did not tell you, but they saved my sons and me from destruction on the sea. Their sudden departure was confusing, but we all feel better about things now that we know the truth. We are dismayed too that they will soon leave us for good."

"Then don't let them."

Ezra's response caught Jershon off guard. Ezra, sensing his puzzlement, continued. "I know full well why I am here, my brother," he said to Jershon affectionately. "Perhaps we could take a little walk and have a few words privately."

When Ezra stood, he stumbled slightly, and David quickly grabbed his arm to steady him. "Thank you, David. You have the strength of Levi."

"We are both blacksmiths," David said with a smile.

"You are?" Ezra asked.

"Yes," David said with pride.

"Your grip is like the iron you work," Ezra commented. "A man with iron muscles must develop a soft and forgiving heart to temper the great strength he possesses."

David gave him a perplexed look.

Ezra was fully aware of the manner in which David and Liora had lost their brothers. He had given Androcles the same counsel, knowing anger was a millstone around his neck in the form of a gold amulet. He was sure David wore the same millstone around his heart. He hoped the young man would ponder his words.

Jershon took Ezra's arm and led him away from the camp. "Let's walk over here. There is a grove of olive trees whose shade awaits us. I've brought some wine we can share." Jershon held a small goatskin sack in his other hand. The two men walked some fifty yards away in silence and came to a grassy area beneath two large trees. Jershon helped Ezra sit down and sat down opposite him.

"You have a beautiful family, Jershon," Ezra said.

"Thank you. God has blessed me," Jershon answered. "And you, rabbi, what of your family?" he asked.

Ezra stared blankly across the valley toward Jerusalem. It was a magnificent sight from their perch on the hillside. "My wife died many years ago."

Jershon instantly regretted his question as Ezra's eyes clouded with tears.

Ezra continued. "I have a son in Alexandria, whom I don't see often . . . I need to change that."

"I'm sorry, rabbi," Jershon apologized. "I didn't know. Jacob told us of your son—a merchant in Egypt, I believe? I only assumed . . ."

"He is adopted," Ezra interrupted. "God was kind to me shortly after I suffered the devastating loss of my wife. He brought me Benjamin." He told Jershon the story of how the young Egyptian boy had come into his life and of how he had taken him under his wing and taught and tutored him. He told of Benjamin's turning from idolatry and accepting Jewish teachings and the Law of Moses, a fact that deeply interested Jershon.

Jershon sensed that this was a story Ezra had not shared with many people. He was honored by the show of trust. "Thank you, Ezra, for telling me. You have been blessed with a son who has brought you much joy." He smiled at his new friend.

Ezra leaned forward. "Let me come to the reason I think Jacob and Levi desired that I meet with you. I know you are asking yourself whether they would convert to Judaism, and if they did, would that conversion allow you to give permission for them to marry your daughter and your niece."

Jershon was surprised by Ezra's frankness and could not respond.

Ezra continued. "I cannot answer that complicated question or even give you much guidance. We of the house of Israel are under strict covenant. It is in our nature; it is who we are. The Law is our life, and it dictates our decisions in everything we do."

He leaned against the gnarly olive tree at his back. "I have heard it reported that Jesus talks of fulfilling the Law of Moses. I have pondered the meaning of those words, Jershon, and they confuse me. I, like you, am convinced that Jesus is the promised Messiah, the Son of David, even the very Son of God. I am a student of the Law and consider myself a relatively intelligent man, but I do not understand the deeper meaning of his teachings. If the Law of Moses is fulfilled, what will take its place? Does that change the covenant Jehovah made with our father Abraham and the house of Israel? Can Jews and Gentiles alike be followers of Jesus and his law? If so, does that mean we are both part of a new covenant, one that gives us the right to intermarry with those of like thinking but not of similar bloodline?"

Ezra sighed and shook his head. "It is almost too much to digest. This is what I have been studying so diligently lately, and this is the question the Sanhedrin struggles with. This is what keeps them discussing the Law late into the night. This is what fuels their desire to be rid of Jesus." He paused. "I don't have a good feeling about how all this is going to end."

"Do you mean the interpretation of the Law?" Jershon asked.

"No, I mean the life of the Messiah," Ezra answered. "But let me speak of our friends Jacob and Levi for a moment, for that is the real reason we are here talking together. I have never met finer men. I am not inclined to like Rome or the Romans and what they have done to our people. However, Rome is wise in that they let us govern ourselves, with only a few exceptions. They definitely have their hand in the taxation of our people, but they let us worship and govern ourselves by our established law. Rome does reserve the authority to take the life of a person convicted of a capital offense, even one convicted by the Sanhedrin under Jewish law. The chief priests therefore seek to convict Jesus of a capital offense and then have Rome decree his death. Our friends Jacob and Levi have met each day this week with Pontius Pilate, the prefect of Judaea, to dissuade him from siding with the evil-minded Sanhedrin and pronouncing a death sentence upon the Messiah. As you now know, Jacob and Levi are here by the decree of Tiberius, emperor of Rome, at the request of Pilate himself to advise him in this matter. They are doing their best to defend Jesus, but the pressures of the Sanhedrin are likely too strong for Pilate to ignore. I fear that soon he will succumb to their pernicious request to render a judgment of death on the Nazarene. Jesus comes to Jerusalem like a lamb to the slaughter."

Ezra shook his head. "Our friends are both good men, and in

this struggle, they are on our side. Jacob, in fact, has become a disciple. He fights with every bit of power and influence he has to prevent a tragic end. His character is flawless, and his intentions are pure. You could not find a better husband for your niece. I echo the same feelings for Levi. I am not sure of his feeling for Jesus, but he fights for him with the same zeal."

Ezra looked squarely at Jershon, who was listening intently. "I envy you your family, my friend. Being a father is not for the faint of heart. You and Naomi have done well for yourselves. You have the love and respect of your children, and I am sure they will eventually see wisdom in whatever decision you make."

Jershon smiled. "You are most kind. The problem with loving my children as I do is giving in to them when I shouldn't." He looked away into the distance. "But in this case I am torn, yet I shouldn't be. The conditions of the Law are black and white. Yet why do I feel things are changing?"

"I sympathize with you, Jershon," Ezra said. "The changes attendant on the coming of Messiah are hard to comprehend. He is not what we Jews have historically expected. He comes not with the steel sword of the liberator but with authority and righteousness in fulfilling the Law of Moses and giving us a higher law, a gospel of kindness, forgiveness, love for our fellow man—and service. He teaches a gospel that requires even more work and devotion from its converts, and it focuses on a personal relationship with a loving God. He does not limit his teachings or his healings to Jews. Some Gentiles have even reached out to the Messiah. I think the Abrahamic covenant as we understand it remains in force, but I have pondered prayerfully our bloodline and the purity of our Jewish family. I have observed the actions of the leaders of the Jews, and I question their purity. On the other hand, as I share experiences with men like Jacob and Levi, born Gentiles of Roman blood, I see purity in its truest form."

The two patriarchs sat in silence for some time. Finally, Ezra added, "I think as we profess our belief in Jesus and accept him as the Messiah, that act purifies us and by God's reckoning makes us all partakers of the covenant as followers of Christ, no longer divided by such labels as Jew and Gentile."

Tears welled up in his eyes. His studying and praying had culminated in belief nurtured by faith. Originally a rushing in his ears and a burning in his bosom. Now it manifested itself in tears of joy like those flowing freely down his deeply lined cheeks.

The warmth of witness overtook Jershon as well in the form of silent tears. He too felt an inward joy at knowledge and light being once again confirmed to his soul.

◆　◆　◆

Maximus and Androcles endured the meal with Pilate. The constant babble of his court sickened Maximus. They were pitiable in their condescension toward the Jews and the inflated opinion they had of themselves and Rome. Their wine-soaked banter was full of derision for everything Judaean. Maximus found it hard not to contradict their ignorance but knew it would bring no good. He looked for the first opportunity to excuse himself and return to the more comfortable surroundings of Ezra's humble home.

"The longer I stay here, the less Roman I become," Maximus said as they arrived at Ezra's house.

"I agree. It's time to leave Jerusalem," Androcles answered.

"That's not what I meant." Maximus immediately began to change into his woolen robe. "I have become more Jacob than Maximus."

Androcles eyed his friend warily. "You talk as if you have made a decision."

"I talk like one who values the lifestyle of a simple fisherman over that of a general fighting for causes he no longer believes in." Maximus sighed as he sat down on a wooden stool and put his head in his hands. "Did you listen to them today?" he asked Androcles.

"Yes."

"No, did you hear what they were saying? They think themselves superior in all things. They even think themselves above you and me when in fact we outrank all of them in Jerusalem. They have lost touch with reality. They don't care whether Jesus lives or dies. To them he's a bother and a distraction to their indulgent lifestyle. I don't understand." Maximus threw up his hands.

Androcles remained standing. He chose his words carefully as he sensed the passion behind Maximus's feelings. "My brother, we were sent here to advise Pilate and report back. We have advised him. Let's go back to Rome and report."

Maximus leapt to his feet. "No, I am going to see this through!" he said belligerently.

"See what through?" Androcles asked.

"We need to stay and protect him," Maximus said.

"Protect Jesus of Nazareth?"

"Yes."

Androcles tried to reason with his friend. "That's not our mission, Maximus. That's not what we were sent here to do."

"It's what I *have* to do!" Maximus responded.

"If you chase the enemy into their own dark forest, you have to know that's a tactical disaster," Androcles cautioned his friend.

"This is not war," Maximus responded.

"You're making it a personal one," Androcles replied.

Maximus sat back down, realizing his deputy commander was right. Androcles was just trying to keep his general from making a fatal error.

"So what do I do?" Maximus asked.

"We go. We've made our recommendation to Pilate. We collect the horses, return to Caesarea, and catch the first available ship to Rome. It is done. After we meet with Gaius Valerius and perhaps the emperor himself, we make our own decisions about returning to Capernaum."

Maximus squirmed uncomfortably. "I don't want to leave until I see this through. We will stay through the Jewish Sabbath."

"This is more about Liora, isn't it?" Androcles posed.

"Perhaps it is equally about her," Maximus answered honestly. "Never have I felt so helpless, Androcles. I give orders; people obey them. I change the course of a battle and perhaps of history, yet I feel helpless to make any difference here."

Androcles sat down on a chair to face his friend. "We weren't sent here to make a difference. We were sent here to observe and report, my brother."

Maximus looked Androcles squarely in the eye and, with great restraint, said, "Jesus of Nazareth and a beautiful Jewish woman from Capernaum have changed that."

They sat in silence until the door suddenly opened; it was Ezra, a little out of breath. Maximus helped Ezra sit, and Androcles poured some water into a cup for him.

"Are you all right?" Maximus asked as Ezra threw off his head covering and wiped the sweat from his brow.

"I am fine, my son. What a glorious day I have had." He smiled as he took the cup of water from Androcles and drank deeply. "What a wonderful family you have befriended."

"You met with them?" Maximus asked anxiously.

"Oh, yes, my son, I met them. You have chosen well." Ezra took another drink.

Maximus looked at Androcles, who shrugged his shoulders.

"You have chosen two beautiful young women from a worthy family." Ezra looked at them both and smiled.

"I don't understand," Maximus questioned.

"My good general, surely you weren't this blind on the battle-field—or you, either, commander. There are two women camped not far from here whose hearts are broken because the men they love have left for another campaign. Go to them. Leave your swords for good. Collect them in your strong arms and make the life for yourselves that you long for. You will receive Jershon's blessing. Now go. I need to rest." He walked to his bed to lie down.

Maximus and Androcles stood speechless. They heard his faint voice from the back room once more, "Jacob, Levi, go . . . go now." Then all was quiet.

❖ ❖ ❖

Seth was the first to spot them approaching and hurried to greet them. Jershon embraced both men, heartily welcoming them as his sons. David, with some reservation, shook their hands as they entered the camp. Naomi was hard-pressed to hide her happiness. Sariah was unreserved in her embrace of Androcles. Timidly Liora approached Maximus.

"You have returned," she said as she looked up into his eyes.

"I have returned for you," Maximus whispered as he reached out his hand. They embraced affectionately.

The evening was filled with animated and happy chatter. Sariah sat close to Androcles, and Liora sat next to Maximus. Her reserve and proximity were intoxicating. It was all Maximus could do not to take her passionately in his arms.

Jershon stood. "My sons, may we have a word in private?" He walked away, expecting them to follow, and headed for the place where he had spoken with Ezra earlier in the day. Maximus and

Androcles followed, and the three men sat down under a large olive tree.

Jershon wasted no time. "I assume you both know I met with Ezra today?"

"Yes," Maximus and Androcles answered in unison.

"Did he tell you of our conversation?" Jershon asked.

"He said you had talked of us," Maximus said, reluctant to elaborate.

"The feelings my daughter and my niece have for you," he chuckled, "are quite obvious. My question is, What are your intentions?"

"Intentions?" Maximus asked.

Jershon continued. "I don't expect you to be familiar with our customs, some of which I find tedious myself, yet there are certain protocols to be followed in arranging a marriage." Maximus and Androcles squirmed at his words. Jershon sighed, and it became clear he was having a hard time conveying what he wanted to say. "These are confusing times," he continued. "I know you as fine young men. I understand all that has happened and why. What I struggle with as a father and uncle is how to justify my daughter and niece being courted by two men not of the covenant of Abraham—and Romans at that. Even though they are two of the finest men I have ever met."

"Jershon," Maximus replied, "we have a job to complete. I think it would be premature to make any decisions beyond what Androcles and I came here to accomplish in the first place. This is a volatile time, and he and I seem to be at the center of the battle. That is not unfamiliar territory for us. But this is a different kind of battle. Despite our experience in war, we are finding it difficult to influence the outcome. In fact, the closer we get to the center of the storm, the more we realize how powerless we are. This battle seems headed toward a predetermined outcome, and I greatly fear the consequences."

"You speak perceptively, my son. Will your further involvement take you from us?" Jershon asked.

"Not in the way you are thinking," Maximus answered. "We would like to continue our association with your family, especially with Liora and Sariah, but we must remain vigilant throughout the rest of this week. Our mission requires us to observe. We can only do that by monitoring the movements of the Nazarene and remaining close to Pilate." He looked Jershon in the eye. "Your enemy is not Rome but your own leaders who stir up evil because they fear losing power and control. They will not be satisfied until they have brought about their dark conspiracy. I don't think we can stop it, but we have to document it."

"You speak of Jesus," Jershon said sadly. "Will they arrest him?" he asked.

"I'm afraid it's well beyond that, my friend. They seek his life," Maximus said soberly.

"Surely they won't just murder him?" Jershon said with concern in his voice.

"They will bring some charge against him that will precipitate his death," Jacob answered.

"But I understand that the prefect retains the power to take life under the law," Jershon said.

"Yes, that is true," said Jacob. "That is why we are staying close to Pilate. We don't want him swayed by members of the Sanhedrin. Ezra calls them vipers, and he is right."

"But if he truly is the Son of God, surely he has the power to stop it." Jershon put up his hands in frustration.

"You would think so," acknowledged Maximus, "but it seems he won't. I don't know why. His death appears inevitable, and yet on some level it must be acceptable to him or he wouldn't have come to Jerusalem. I don't understand it."

Maximus had succeeded in directing the conversation away from Liora and Sariah, but his heart was suddenly troubled as he thought of the innocent Nazarene being pursued by wolves. He stood abruptly. "We must go, Jershon. We will return soon, rest assured, and we will talk of more happy matters." They bade him good-bye, embracing him affectionately, and left him pondering the things they had discussed. Jershon had even fewer answers now, and he realized he had very little to tell Sariah and Liora, who would certainly quiz him on his return.

◆ ◆ ◆

It was late in the afternoon when Maximus and Androcles returned to Ezra's home. "I think we should change into our uniforms and return to Pilate to get an update of Jesus's movements and see what the Sanhedrin are up to. The battle lines are being drawn, my brother," Maximus said firmly.

Ezra was studying his scrolls. Zilpah had prepared the evening meal, so they ate with haste and departed, barely speaking to Ezra, who was engrossed in his studies. They returned to Pilate's palace.

"My friends, we meet again." Pilate greeted them as they entered the courtyard. "You left so abruptly earlier I thought we had offended you."

"We had other matters to take care of," Maximus replied. "Have you met with the members of the Sanhedrin?"

"You just missed them," Pilate said. "They were here not an hour ago."

"Why did they grace the court of the prefect?" Maximus quizzed.

Pilate laughed. "They never grace my court. They come

complaining and asking favors. They wanted to know if we knew the whereabouts of the Nazarene. I told them we had heard he was in Bethany and that if he came back to Jerusalem we would certainly be aware of it, as he seems to attract a lot of attention. Even absent he causes them grief. I'm beginning to like this Jesus." He laughed and those around him laughed as well.

Maximus managed a weak smile. "Do you know where the leaders of the Jews have gone?" he asked.

"I believe to the home of Caiaphas, the high priest. They plan to arrest the Nazarene if he returns. Apparently they have spoken with one of his disgruntled followers and are striking a deal to arrest him quietly. How they will manage this I don't know. He is followed by thousands everywhere he goes. Go to the house of Caiaphas and inquire yourself. I will have one of my men show you where he lives." Pilate waved a dismissive hand.

A short, quiet man timidly moved forward. "Would you like me to take you to the home of Caiaphas?" he asked, his eyes on the floor.

"No," Maximus said bluntly and turned to go. Androcles followed him. The sun was starting to set as they reached the steps outside the palace. Maximus looked out, his brow furrowed in deep thought.

"What do you have in mind?" Androcles asked. He knew this look of stern conviction on Maximus's face. It meant he was making a strategic decision.

"You are right, Androcles," Maximus said as he looked off to the orange glow of the western horizon. "We wait. As you say, it would be foolish to chase the enemy into the darkness of their own forest."

38

יום חמישי

Yom Chamishi

E arly Thursday, Maximus woke before the sun came up. He donned his robe and head covering and decided to visit the temple. His walk toward the temple was unhindered by the pushy crowds that were certain to fill the streets within a couple of hours.

Ezra had told him the previous night that the temple would be filled early with people making their Passover offering. It would be crowded, noisy, and dusty, a place to be avoided. Maximus had asked Ezra if he thought Jesus would visit the temple today. Ezra thought not. His presence would make for more confusion and, out of respect for the people who had journeyed long distances to make their offerings, he would most likely stay away.

At this early hour, the Court of the Gentiles was quiet; the gates to the inner precincts were shut. The sky reflected a dark blue hue just before it gave way to the yellow of sunrise. The outlines of the buildings and walls of the city were coming into focus. Shadowy figures darted here and there on early-morning errands.

Maximus was uneasy. This was not the kind of battle he was accustomed to fighting, and he felt powerless against the rising tide of the enemy. He couldn't just sit around and wait for something to happen, but he wasn't entirely sure anything would happen. Maximus smiled to himself at his obsessive concern for the potential arrest of a common Jew. That it took so much space in his thinking was foolish, yet this Nazarene had affected him like no other man ever had. Yet he couldn't just find him, walk up to him, and say, "I'm a legate of Rome. For your own protection, come with me." He almost laughed out loud at the thought. A man who could heal the blind and raise the dead probably had no fear of arrest. If the Jewish authorities were able to arrest Jesus, would he subject himself to it? They could have taken him anytime in the past few days when he was at the temple. But as Ezra had noted, the leaders of the Jews feared that confronting him in public could cause an uprising. That's the last thing Pilate wanted and something the chief priests preferred to avoid. They wanted to do it quietly and without notice so there would be no questions, or worse, revolt.

It appeared the Jewish leaders were reaching the point of no return; the outcome seemed inevitable. Maximus hoped he had influenced Pilate enough that he would refuse to render a death sentence. That would be reckless. But he had the uncomfortable feeling that to retain their power, the Sanhedrin would settle for no less than the Nazarene's death. In their minds, they were thwarting an eminent threat to their control. He shook his head in frustration.

It was beginning to be light when Maximus arrived back at Ezra's house. Androcles appeared in the doorway. "I heard you leave but wasn't fast enough to follow you. Is everything all right?" he asked.

"Yes, everything is fine. I needed to walk, just as we did on campaign," Maximus responded.

"Well, when you used to walk, it was before making decisions about strategy prior to battle. You would return and lay out the plan to us. So, what is the plan?"

"There is no plan, Androcles. But we're not going into battle, and surely Jesus will stay away from Jerusalem today. Why don't we go for a ride on the horses and get away for a while? I feel cooped up in this city. It's no different from Rome with its walls, narrow streets, and plague of humanity. Maybe later we can visit Jershon again."

They walked to the tent of Tamur, who was happy to see them, and retrieved their horses. They rode westward, encountering a secluded stream in which to bathe.

"Have you considered what you might lose if you resign your rank and stay in Judaea?" Androcles finally ventured.

"I wouldn't lose anything. For most of our lives, Rome has sent us into battle, Androcles. There was never a guarantee of our survival. In fact, we have beaten the odds. I am taking my life in my own hands for a change. I will complete my duty to Rome, but I will not remain Roman." Maximus's tone was unequivocal.

Androcles could not refute his friend's reasoning, nor did he care to argue. Maximus was right; to this point they had both given their lives to the whims of Rome. His thoughts turned to David and blacksmithing, recalling bittersweet memories of his days as a young boy with his father and brothers in the forge. He saw himself pounding steel by a hot fire, sweating, but with a smile on his face. Blacksmithing was hard work, but he would never have to go to sleep at night wondering if he would die by the sword the next day. Yet he was torn by it all. His heart was telling him one thing, his mind another.

"I have followed you into the darkest battles with the odds heavily against us. I have slept in the cold and in the mud by your side. I have walked thousands of miles of hot and dusty roads under your command. Why would that change now?" Androcles said in a calm voice.

"I am not commanding you to do anything. If you follow me, you do so of your own free will," Maximus responded.

"Then I *will* myself to follow you once again, general." Androcles splashed water in Maximus's face.

"*Jacob*," Maximus corrected him. "This time you walk freely with *Jacob*—still your friend and brother."

◆   ◆   ◆

Ezra greeted Maximus and Androcles on their return from their afternoon in the countryside. "I have received word from two sources. The Sanhedrin has been gathered the entire day at the home of Caiaphas, the high priest. It appears they intend to arrest Jesus soon, perhaps tonight. Another source tells me the Nazarene and his closest associates may return to Jerusalem this evening." Ezra returned to the scroll he was reading.

Maximus looked at Androcles. "Let's visit Jershon. We can watch the road from there." Androcles nodded his agreement, and they were off again.

"Welcome, my sons," Jershon said as they entered the camp. "You will join us for our evening meal?" Jershon stated more than asked.

"Thank you, yes, if it wouldn't be too much trouble," Maximus responded. He noticed that Sariah was already talking quietly with Androcles. Liora was helping Naomi. She gave him a warm smile, which made his heart pound in his chest.

Jershon told them of his journey to the temple that morning to make an offering and of the crowds in the city. "Too many of them come to be seen of men, I fear. Humility seems to be lacking among my people," Jershon observed. "I will be glad to be back in Capernaum soon." With Jershon's words, an uncomfortable quiet settled over the small camp.

Soon everyone gathered around to partake of the meal. Liora knelt beside Maximus. He could feel her warmth next to him.

As they began to eat, a lighthearted conversation ensued about Roman baths. It was a sign to Maximus that they had been fully accepted into this family, despite their differences. Jershon was almost jovial as he kidded Androcles about his shaving. It was a wonderful evening with easy talk and intimate familiarity. Maximus felt at home.

After the meal, Maximus helped Liora clean up. They whispered quietly and sought chances to touch shoulders and hands. Jershon and Naomi seemed comfortable with the interactions between Androcles and Sariah. They were sitting so close to each other that a sharp sword couldn't have passed between them.

Maximus was enjoying Liora's company and her confident and soothing voice as she spoke; he could listen to her talk all night. Then Liora said matter-of-factly, "We will be leaving soon, Jacob."

Maximus looked deep into her eyes. "Yes, I know."

Placing her warm hand on his forearm, Liora looked up at him and boldly asked, "Will you be coming with us?"

Maximus was shaken. How different this was from the quick decisions he made in battle. He felt helpless to answer this beautiful woman's simple inquiry. "I can't answer that yet," was all he managed to say as he looked away from her. She left her hand on his arm and leaned on his shoulder. The feel and scent of her hair was intoxicating.

He closed his eyes and breathed deeply. "I want to answer you," he continued, "but we still have much work to do in the next couple of days. I can't guess what that will bring. Has your uncle set a specific day for your departure?"

"He said we would stay through the Sabbath and leave the following day." Liora put her arm through his.

Maximus placed his rugged hand on her smooth cheek and whispered in her ear. "Let's just enjoy our time together now and not worry about tomorrow. I love you, Liora. That won't end in two days."

Liora smiled, still leaning her head on his shoulder, and held back tears. Maximus put his arm around her, pulling her close.

The two must have crossed some line in their behavior because Jershon said suddenly, "Jacob, Liora, come join us by the fire."

Maximus was reluctant to release his hold on her, but Liora stiffened at her uncle's voice and quickly obeyed, pulling away. Maximus followed, and they sat together on the ground near Naomi, who smiled kindly at them.

"We are grateful you have joined us, my sons," Jershon began. "Jacob, you said you had work to do in the next couple of days; can you share with us the nature of your work?"

Maximus began to explain cautiously. "Our interest is to see a peaceful Passover here in Jerusalem. Although Rome rules in Judaea, it is done loosely. The people are free to come and go as they please, and normal life carries on." Maximus did not want to get into a political debate. "Pilate and the leaders of the Jews do not want anything to happen that could spark revolt or rebellion. The presence of Jesus of Nazareth poses a dilemma, however. It is not Rome that objects to the teachings of Jesus. It is not Rome that fears he is a threat. That is what we came here to determine; we have made our report to Pontius Pilate, and I believe he agrees with us. However, the Sanhedrin and the Pharisees and Sadducees may spark a conflict. The chief priests have been pestering Pilate ever since Jesus arrived in Jerusalem. Jesus is plaguing *them,* not Rome. Our work is to assure that Pilate stays his hand and is not swayed by the accusations of the Sanhedrin."

"What exactly do you mean by 'stays his hand'?" Jershon asked.

"The leaders of the Jews seek to arrest Jesus on charges of blasphemy, which I understand is a capital offense under Jewish law. But blasphemy is no crime under Roman law, so the chief priests would have to make a false charge of treason, which does warrant capital punishment under Roman law. The Sanhedrin may clamor for Jesus's death, but Pilate alone holds the authority to execute the sentence. He may release him with a flogging, or jail him for a time, but I don't think sufficient evidence can be found to warrant a sentence of death. Rome gains nothing by aiding in the death of an innocent man," Maximus concluded.

Liora looked up at him, admiring his intelligence and his ability to clarify a difficult subject.

"This seems like such a dark and serious subject," interjected Naomi. "Can we talk of something happier?"

"You are right, my good wife," Jershon agreed. "We should be talking of happier things—like our new grandson!"

"Oh, I miss him so," exclaimed Naomi. "I am so anxious to return home."

Liora leaned into Maximus as melancholy with the thought of leaving him overcame her. "Everything will turn out all right," he whispered.

Liora took comfort in the reassurance of his voice. She felt safe in the embrace of his arms. She was startled when he suddenly moved away from her and stood up.

All evening Maximus had kept one eye on the road into

Jerusalem from the east through the Kidron Valley below. It was late and few people were on the road. He noticed a group of nine or ten men walking quickly down into the valley toward the city. He was too far away to make out faces but close enough to recognize the shape of two of the large fishermen from Galilee that were close associates of Jesus. Then he spotted the recognizable figure of Jesus, wearing a white head covering, walking briskly with them. Maximus wished he could run down the hill and warn them not to go into the city, but instead he just watched as they reached the city wall and entered the gate that was left open during Passover.

It is beginning, he thought. He wondered if he and Androcles should follow them. They wouldn't be going to the temple this late. They were most likely staying someplace for the evening and would remain there through the Sabbath.

"The Nazarene?" It was Androcles's voice behind him.

"Yes, it appears so," answered Maximus.

"Should we follow him?"

"No, he will surely be out of sight before we could catch up to him," said Maximus. "Let's just enjoy the evening here. We can go back to Ezra's later." They returned to the campfire and sat down. Maximus announced that they had seen Jesus returning to the city.

"Is he safe in Jerusalem?" Jershon asked.

"No, I don't believe he is," Maximus answered. "He is in the company of his trusted men, but he is brave to return to Jerusalem, given the mood of the leaders. He obviously does not fear them."

"Surely lookouts have seen him enter the city, just as you did, and followed him to his destination," observed David.

"Perhaps you are right, David," said Maximus. "We will have to wait till tomorrow." But Maximus was thinking like the general he was, calculating the danger Jesus was in all the time and what he could possibly do to intervene. Liora sensed his aloofness but assumed he was contemplating her departure and their separation. She had no idea she was the farthest thing from his mind at that moment. They all talked until well past dark, when Jershon announced it was time to retire. They said their good-byes, and Maximus and Androcles promised to return before the Sabbath.

The two Romans walked into the darkness, far enough away from the camp to talk without being overheard. On the side of the hill above the Kidron, they talked late into the night about Liora and Sariah, returning to Rome or not returning to Rome, and doing what they could for the Nazarene.

Unexpectedly, a group of men exited the east gate of Jerusalem. Once again, Maximus and Androcles could see but not be seen. In the light afforded by the stars, they agreed it was the Nazarene and a handful of men.

"He leaves untouched," Maximus said with noticeable relief. But the small group did not follow the road to Bethany. Instead the men followed a path that led into a thick grove of olive trees a few hundred yards from their position on the hillside. Maximus and Androcles stared at each other. Were they spending the night there or taking a different route back to Bethany? It was too dark to see exactly where they had gone.

It was well past midnight. They were both exhausted, and they decided they should just sleep where they were. They had spent too many nights recently on soft beds of new straw. A night on the hard ground might help them think more clearly.

Maximus lay awake processing the day's events. Androcles was soon snoring. Shadows moving in the distance beyond his sleeping friend caught his attention. Maximus could see another group of men emerging from the city, walking down the hill into the valley, and proceeding up the hill in the same direction he had seen Jesus go earlier. He shook Androcles, who sat up grumpily. Maximus motioned for him to look in the direction of the men, a few of whom carried torches and lanterns. It appeared some members of the Sanhedrin accompanied them.

"They go to arrest the Nazarene," Maximus said quietly. They watched as the men disappeared into the darkness of the grove in the distance. They could make out the lights of the torches, compromising the group's position in the grove of trees, but it was too far to see what was actually happening.

"Let's go!" said Androcles as he stood.

"No, let's wait. Surely they will take him back to the city. We can drop in behind them without being noticed and follow them."

Androcles agreed this was a better plan. They kept watch on the grove. Within a few minutes, the glow of the torches began to move toward the city. He stood and Androcles joined him, and together they followed the path to the valley. The group marched quickly toward the city gate, and Maximus and Androcles fell in at a safe distance behind. They could see Jesus in their midst.

"Where do they take him?" Androcles whispered.

"I don't know. If nothing else, we should inform Pilate of the arrest. If they seek Jesus's death, they will ultimately have to come to Pilate." Maximus walked quickly ahead.

39

יוֹם שִׁשִׁי

Yom Shishi

Maximus and Androcles reached Pilate's palace in the early hours of Friday morning. In the dark they could see a guard sitting at the side of the gate. His lack of movement told Maximus he was asleep. The group they were following had obviously not come this way.

Carefully Maximus gripped the guard's javelin and then kicked him. "Get up, you lazy swine. Is this how you guard the property of Rome?" Maximus shouted.

The guard awoke and stumbled to his feet, as Maximus wrestled away his javelin. Thinking he was being assaulted by two Jews, he reached for his short sword. Maximus deftly placed the tip of the javelin under his chin. "Not a wise move, my friend." The guard released his sword and stood up straight. "Go awaken Pilate. We need to see him immediately."

The guard, by then coming out of his stupor, recognized Maximus and Androcles and turned to comply with his request.

As the men entered the courtyard, another guard approached them with a lantern.

"General Maximus requests an audience with the prefect," the now-penitent guard said to his fellow soldier.

The soldier carrying the lantern raised it to better see the faces of Maximus and Androcles. "This is highly irregular."

"So is sleeping on duty," Maximus retorted. "At least under my command. I should have you both flogged." His rank was known by now among the garrison in Jerusalem, and they, at least, afforded him the respect he deserved.

"I'll get him right away, sir." The soldier hurried off.

Maximus handed the javelin back to the guard. "Return to your post, and try to stay awake. A group of people will be coming this way, and we want to be told the moment they arrive."

The guard took the javelin from Maximus and walked quickly out the gate, securing the lock. Maximus was sure the soldier was now standing at full attention outside the large wooden door. Androcles chuckled.

"What's this all about?" Pilate said as he emerged from the shadows in his sleeping robe, wrapped in a blanket. His hair was disheveled and he lacked the bearing of a noble Roman. "Why was I awakened at this unseemly hour?" He rubbed his face and eyes, focusing on the two large men standing in front of him. "General Maximus?" he asked with uncertainty.

"Yes, it is I," answered Maximus, stepping forward.

"Is there trouble?" Pilate asked with apprehension.

"I'm not sure. They have arrested the Nazarene."

"Who has arrested him?" Pilate asked.

"It seems members of the Sanhedrin have taken him, with the help of the temple guard." Maximus explained what he and Androcles had observed earlier.

"Where have they taken him?" Pilate asked.

"We thought they might bring him here, but they have not arrived. I do not know where they have gone. We thought you should know."

"Yes, yes," Pilate commented, still groggy. "Thank you, but I don't see cause for such alarm. Certainly nothing will be done at this hour. I'm going back to bed." Pilate dismissed them.

Maximus shrugged, and he and Androcles headed for the gate. Outside the palace, they heard a commotion down the street. A group of people, now led by Roman auxiliaries, was headed their way. Maximus and Androcles stepped aside as the guard at the palace gate stood taller and took a more menacing stance than he'd had a few minutes before.

Maximus could see it was the same group he and Androcles had spotted outside the city. Four guards led the procession, and following closely behind were members of the Sanhedrin. To the rear, escorted by the temple guards, was the Nazarene. His hands were bound and his feet hobbled. His face was drawn and hollow, but his demeanor was calm. The soldiers at his side held him by the sleeves of his robe. Maximus had seen many prisoners in his day. Most had been beaten into submission before they reached him, but all were arrogant and defiant in his presence. In his meekness, Jesus stood confidently magnificent among his captors.

One of the Sanhedrin stepped forward to address the guard at the gate. "We seek an audience with the prefect."

"For what cause?" asked the guard, who was wide-awake now and exercising his authority.

"We need the ruling of Rome. We seek his judgment on an accused criminal," said the high priest loudly. His voice echoed off the surrounding stone walls in the early morning quiet.

The guard turned slightly to look at Maximus as if seeking advice. Maximus ignored him, leaving him to act on his own.

Intimidated by the Sanhedrin and the presence of Roman soldiers he recognized, he opened the gate to the courtyard and disappeared inside. Maximus and Androcles remained in the shadows.

A few minutes passed before the guard returned. "Pilate will see you," he announced as he opened both gates wide to let the group enter.

The soldiers in front began to move forward, but the members of the Sanhedrin remained in place. A spokesman came forward, saying, "Our traditions are different from Pilate's. If we could ask the prefect to come outside to meet with us—it is the Passover, and we are forbidden to be in the presence of leavened bread." The guard stood still for a moment and then retreated into the courtyard.

Maximus whispered to Androcles, "They come seeking the punishment of an innocent man, yet they can't be in the presence of leavened bread because their religion prohibits it? Ezra was right—vipers and hypocrites."

The guard soon appeared with three other guards from inside the palace. They stood two by two on either side of the gate. Pilate's assistant appeared next and behind him was Pilate, now dressed in a fine robe, his hair combed. "You seek an audience with the prefect," boomed Pilate. "You had better have a good reason to request my presence at this hour."

A priest stepped forward. In the moonlight, Maximus now recognized him as Caiaphas, the high priest. He motioned to the guards to bring Jesus forward. The temple guards roughly pushed him to the ground near the bottom of the steps at Pilate's feet.

Pilate looked down at the prisoner kneeling at his feet and asked the priests, "What charges do you bring against this man?"

"If he weren't a criminal, we wouldn't be here," Caiaphas rejoined.

Pilate stood indignant. "You talk in circles, Caiaphas. If you bring me a prisoner at this hour of the morning, I expect you to have proper charges. If you have no charges, then go. Charge him by your own laws!"

Caiaphas threw up his hands in frustration. "This man has committed high treason. He is a threat not only to Judaea but also to the peace of Rome." Caiaphas looked at Pilate. "You know it is not within our power to punish any man for a capital crime that deserves death. It requires not only your voice but your hand."

Pilate was taken aback by Jesus's calm, majestic appearance. "So you seek his death? On what act of high treason do you base your charges?" Pilate spat back.

The high priest quickly answered, "He claims he is king of the Jews!"

Pilate stared down at Jesus and asked, "How do you answer your accusers, Nazarene?" Jesus made no reply. Unbeknownst to Pilate, Jesus had already answered his accusers directly at the home of Caiaphas not long before.

In his wisdom, Pilate turned his back on the frothing crowd that had begun to assemble. "Bring forth the accused," he said to the soldiers standing beside Jesus, and he returned to the courtyard that served as Pilate's hall of judgment. Pilate was confident that the members of the Sanhedrin would not follow.

Maximus and Androcles followed Pilate into the courtyard. Two soldiers seized Jesus by his arms and dragged him up the steps and through the gates. A few Jews in the crowd followed, apparently not bothered by the breach of Passover protocol that so concerned the chief priests. Maximus recognized a couple of them as Jesus's close associates.

Once alone with Jesus, Pilate stood face-to-face with him. "These are serious charges they bring against you, Nazarene. What do you say to defend yourself?"

Jesus stood tall and quiet, not offering a word.

Pilate was taken aback by his self-discipline and silent maj-
esty. With some trepidation he looked Jesus directly in the eye
and asked, "Are you the king of the Jews?"

Raising his head, Jesus answered quietly. "Do you believe I
am king of the Jews? Or are you just repeating what others have
told you?"

Pilate shook his head in frustration. "I am not a Jew. Your
own people have brought you here for my judgment. What have
you done to raise such ire in them?"

Jesus looked at Pilate and in a soft voice answered, "My kingdom is not of this world; if it were, then my servants would fight
to have me released."

Pilate threw up his hands. "So are you a king then?"

Jesus answered, "Thou sayest that I am a king. To this end
was I born, and for this cause came I into the world, that I should
bear witness unto the truth. Every one that is of the truth heareth
my voice."

Maximus was amazed at Jesus's bearing and demeanor under
the eyes of his accusers. He was impressed at the bold and calm
manner in which he answered Pilate's query. Here was a chance
to plead his case to the official who could release him, yet he did
not do that. Instead, he affirmed his identity and mission.

Pilate again threw his hands in the air in frustration. "What
is truth?" he sighed. He returned to face the accusing Jews waiting outside and exclaimed for all to hear, "I find no fault in this
man."

The priests, scribes, and elders of the people voiced their
disapproval loudly. Jesus was taken back down the stairs and
once again forced to the ground by the soldiers. Maximus and
Androcles followed and removed themselves to the shadows.

Caiaphas spoke, raising his voice fiercely above the rising

cries of the crowd. "But, sir, he stirs up the people against us, from here to Galilee."

Pilate scratched his unshaven chin and asked, "Galilee? Do you say this man is a Galilean?"

"He and his men have been doing their evil in Galilee and have come to Jerusalem causing trouble and seeking more followers," answered Caiaphas.

Pilate was pleased at this news. "Herod Antipas is the ruler of Galilee. Take the accused to him for judgment." With that Pilate turned, gathered his robes about him, and left the stunned crowd in silence.

Caiaphas was not deterred. He turned to the growing crowd and announced, "We will take him to Herod Antipas for proper justice." The crowd cheered, and the procession continued through the streets of the city.

Maximus and Androcles followed in the wake of the boisterous crowd. They walked with the disciples of Jesus who stayed quietly in the background.

When the throng arrived at the steps of Herod's residence, the sun was adding definition to the gray shadowy walls within the city. Maximus, having been told of the usual habits of Herod Antipas, expected he would be found in a drunken stupor. Maximus was not wrong. Herod was unkempt and even from a distance it was obvious he was suffering the effects of too much wine the night before.

When Herod saw Jesus, he was amused, for he had wanted to meet him. He had heard rumors of his miracles and thought this would be an opportunity to persuade Jesus to perform some magic for his pleasure. Jesus remained silent. He had nothing to say to the murderer of his cousin John the Baptist. To Caiaphas, Jesus had answered the Jews, and to Pilate he had answered Rome. Further defense was unnecessary.

Herod, flustered by the silent Jesus and in an effort to please the crowd, energetically questioned and cajoled the prisoner before him, to no avail. He then resorted to derision and mockery. In the end, he told his soldiers, "Array the prisoner." Herod's men appeared with a beautiful robe and with derisive mockery, ceremoniously draped it around Jesus's shoulders.

"Take the king of the Jews back to Pilate, and thank him for sending him to me. Let Pilate pronounce Rome's judgment; I see nothing to reprimand." The priests and scribes again loudly voiced their contempt for Herod's inaction.

Herod dismissed the assembly and stumbled back into the quiet of his residence. Maximus shook his head in disgust. His report to Rome would include a condemnation of the degenerate client-king.

The nest of vipers squirmed back to Pilate. Maximus and Androcles ran down a side road to get ahead of them as the crowd of gawkers was becoming large and unruly. Some spat on Jesus; others ridiculed and mocked him. Maximus and Androcles slipped through the gate, wanting a word with Pilate before he was summoned outside again.

Maximus and Androcles were escorted into Pilate's presence. "Gentlemen, won't you join me for breakfast?" Pilate motioned to nearby seats at the table.

"Herod Antipas has found the Nazarene innocent and sends him back to you. They are probably at the gates now," Maximus said.

Pilate sighed. "So what do I do?"

"You release him. Set him free," Maximus declared. "He has done nothing."

A guard appeared. "The priests seek you again, sir."

Pilate stood wearily and walked toward the gate.

The mob was three times as large as it had been and swelling by the minute. As Pilate stepped onto the portico, the voices of the crowd rose in vehement slander and accusation. He knew he would be forced to make a decision.

Caiaphas ascended the steps to stand before Pilate. "We demand justice upon this criminal!"

"As I said before, I find no fault in this man," Pilate replied.

"Pronounce Rome's verdict and punishment on this man who proclaims unlawful kingship," Caiaphas said calmly, quietly.

Pilate had begun to respond when Maximus stepped forward. He was disturbed that no one spoke on behalf of Jesus, a custom in the courts he knew, and he felt compelled to defend him.

Maximus stood squarely in front of the chief priest and in a low but powerful voice said, "I ask you—what evil has this man done? You bring false accusations from false witnesses that ring hollow to intelligent ears, and then you seek out Rome to punish him. Shame on you—*coward!*" At this, the chief priest took a step back, speechless before this imposing man who seemed to have found favor with Pilate.

Maximus continued. "In branding him a blasphemer, you blaspheme and perjure yourselves. You are all *hypocrites!*" He pointed to the group of priests and rabbis standing together. "This man is more than a king."

Maximus leaned forward, lowering his voice further and speaking sternly to Caiaphas. "The title 'king of the Jews' is a shadow of what his title truly is. He is your *Messiah!*" It was all he could do to keep from smashing his fist into the smug face of the high priest.

Androcles stepped forward and drew Maximus back. Maximus spat defiantly on the ground at the feet of Caiaphas. The high priest took another step back from the man seething before him. He looked to Pilate for protection.

Pilate stepped between Caiaphas and Maximus. He had no interest in inciting the mob to violence.

Pilate turned to Maximus and said quietly, "Your passion for this Nazarene is enviable, but I question its wisdom." Pilate felt he had come up with a solution and said to Maximus, "It is the custom for the governor to release a prisoner as a show of mercy during Passover. I will offer the people a choice between the Nazarene and the murderer Barabbas. Surely the people will release Jesus."

Pilate put his hand on Maximus's shoulder and turned back to face the crowd. Maximus turned his back on them all.

Pilate called before him the chief priests and the Jewish leaders present and gave them an ultimatum. "I have interrogated this Jesus and found nothing wrong with what he has done. Herod also declares his innocence. The Nazarene has done nothing to warrant the death penalty you seek."

Jeers and epithets came up from the gathered crowd. Pilate raised his hands to silence their indignation. "You have a custom among your people to release at Passover an accused criminal. Choose you between Barabbas, whose crimes are known unto you, or this Jesus that is called the Christ."

The members of the Sanhedrin soon dispersed themselves amongst the murmuring crowd, talking quietly to many.

Pilate became impatient at the delay and repeated his ultimatum. "What is your decision?"

The shouts of *Barabbas* began quietly and grew until the crowd in unison chanted his name.

"What should I do with this Jesus?" Pilate asked the crowd.

"Crucify him!" they shouted.

Pilate, his emotions frayed, made one last plea: "What has he done worthy of death?"

"Crucify him, crucify him!" came back the shout from the hostile crowd.

Pilate saw that further defense of the Nazarene could cause a riot. He sent for a basin of water and washed his hands as a symbol. Then he turned to the crowd and said, "I am innocent of the blood of this just person: see ye to it."

Pilate was incredulous at the decision of the people. Surely the chief priests had poisoned them. He purposely avoided the scathing looks of Maximus and Androcles. He was sorely troubled as he gave instructions to the guards. That very morning his own wife had warned him to have nothing to do with Jesus, for in a dream the previous night she had suffered greatly because of the Nazarene and knew he was innocent. Nevertheless, Pilate instructed the soldiers to scourge Jesus.

Maximus and Androcles could not watch as the soldiers stripped Jesus of the robe and whipped him unmercifully. They hurried from the palace and walked quickly to retrieve Ezra. Surely he would know what to do.

After the scourging, Pilate led the smitten and bloodied Jesus forward. He was clad now in a purple robe and wearing a crown of thorns that had been roughly crushed onto his head by the guards. Rivulets of blood streamed down his face.

"I present you the accused," Pilate said to the crowd.

The shouts from the chief priests and elders again rang out in the early morning. "Crucify him, crucify him!"

"Go and crucify him, then, but I find in him nothing worthy of crucifixion," Pilate weakly repeated, attempting to assuage his own guilt.

But the Jews answered Pilate. "He has made himself out to be the Son of God, and by our law he ought to die."

Pilate felt a great fear come over him and attempted once more to intervene. He turned to Jesus and quietly asked, "Who are you and where did you come from?" But Jesus again remained silent. Wholly exasperated, Pilate said, "Don't you know I have the power to crucify you or release you?"

Jesus looked directly at Pilate and answered, "You have no power over me. These who accused me have the greater sin."

Pilate saw that it was useless to defend the Nazarene further. The crowd was now accusing him, because of his delays, of being disloyal to Caesar. He turned Jesus by the arm toward the accusers and said, "Behold your King!"

"We have no king but Caesar!" shouted back the chief priests.

Reluctantly Pilate released his grip on the prisoner, retreated to the curule, his official judgment seat, and bade the guards take Jesus away.

◆ ◆ ◆

Maximus and Androcles pushed open the door to the house harder than they'd intended, startling Ezra as they entered. He was up early, holding a piece of bread in one hand and a scroll in the other.

He looked up at his two friends, who looked agitated. "My friends, you didn't come back last night. Is everything well?"

"They have arrested Jesus. Pilate, at the bidding of the Sanhedrin and because of his own weakness, has allowed him to be crucified. What should we do?" Maximus asked in a calmer voice than he felt.

Ezra put down the bread and lowered the scroll. "It is written," he said in a sad voice.

"What do you mean, 'it is written'?" Maximus asked.

"The ancient prophets foretold the Messiah's coming and his death at the hands of his own people. There is nothing we can do. If he is to be crucified, then Rome has dictated the sentence.

Surely if Pilate has spoken, it is done." A tear appeared in the corner of Ezra's eye. "Who was present?" he asked.

"The high priest Caiaphas and members of the Sanhedrin," Maximus explained. "There were many elders and rulers there. The crowd was a mixture of Jews, even Jews from other lands. The rabble grew as the morning progressed. They were offered the choice to spare Jesus or a man named Barabbas. They chose Barabbas, so the murderer goes free, and Jesus goes to die." Maximus paced the room. A rescue would be risky, but he felt confident he and Androcles would prevail. Plans and strategies began forming in his mind.

"Be calm, my son," Ezra said. "It is written. There is nothing you can do—or should do. It is God's will." He spoke with knowledge and a force of wisdom that Maximus was unable to contest. Ezra understood the Messiah and his mission. If Ezra asked them to let events take their course, as much as Maximus might want to disagree, he had no real basis to intervene other than his passion to fight for the innocent. It was an infuriating set of circumstances.

"Where will they take him?" Androcles asked.

Ezra thought for a moment. "Outside the city gates to a place called Golgotha, the place of the skull. It is there the Romans execute criminals."

The thought that Jesus would be crucified like a common criminal sickened Maximus. He looked at Androcles, and in one motion they headed out the door.

"Wait," Ezra called after them. "I'll go with you."

The three men reached the gate exiting the city before the mob did. It was still early and people were beginning to move about the city. The Sabbath would be upon them at sundown, and people were making last preparations for Passover. Soon a commotion of people and dust came toward them with Roman

auxiliary soldiers leading the way. Behind them was a man bearing a large crossbeam on his shoulders, followed by two others
bearing similar crossbeams. Jesus walked behind them, covered
in blood, dirt, and sweat, looking not unlike soldiers Maximus
had seen after a fierce battle. A crown of thorns had been pushed
into his scalp. Sweat and dried blood caked his face and arms.
Close behind him were crowds walking and talking almost in a
manner of celebration, both those who had accused the Nazarene
and borne false witness and others who had maligned and deni-
grated him with their words and disrespectful actions.

Among those near the end of the procession were some of
Jesus's disciples, identifiable from their despondent demeanor.
Three women in particular drew Maximus's attention. Two of
them held up an elderly woman, who wept openly and appeared
wont to faint as she trudged sorrowfully along.

Ezra, Maximus, and Androcles joined the procession.

Not far from the great walls of the city, the well-traveled road
forked right and began a steep incline up a rocky hill. The way
was dusty and the going slow as the multitude of people walked
single-file to negotiate the narrow path.

At the top of a low hill was the place of crucifixion. The
crowd dispersed, sitting on the rocky ground where laborers had
dug three holes. Some gathered large rocks to aid in propping up
the crosses once they were lifted into place. Maximus didn't recognize the soldiers assigned to carry out the crucifixion. The captain in charge barked orders and stood drinking wine that spilled
onto his sweat-stained tunic and armor. A coarse and hairy man,
he displayed the scars of battle. The soldiers were indifferent to
the suffering of the three prisoners in their charge. Inflicting further pain by nailing them to crosses would suit them fine.

Maximus watched as Jesus was grabbed roughly by his arms
and his body stretched out on the cross that was lying on the

ground. Two soldiers held him down: one grabbed his hair and knelt with his knee on Jesus's upper arm. Another soldier knelt with a knee pressing on his forearm. The burly captain took a spike in one hand, a hefty hammer in the other, and with cold detachment dropped the hammer heavily on the end of the spike. Jesus did not cry out—the women cried out for him. More blows drove the spike through his flesh and into the rough timber of the cross.

Maximus, who had seen unimaginable cruelty and heinous wounds in battle, could not watch. Androcles twitched with every strike of the hammer. Once Jesus's hands were secured, the two soldiers crossed his feet over a board serving as a foothold. The captain of the guard took a larger spike out of the bag and placed the tip on the top of Jesus's foot. Repeated blows forced the spike through both feet and into solid wood. Further blows to secure the spike broke Maximus's heart. A wooden placard was then nailed to the post above Jesus's head. It carried an inscription that Maximus could not make out from his vantage point.

With the prisoner secure on the cross, four soldiers positioned the bottom of the cross at the edge of one of the holes. They lifted it by the crossbeam, sliding it into the hole where it hit bottom with a jarring impact, causing Jesus's body to bounce and rack. Maximus could only imagine the pain he was suffering. The soldiers straightened the cross and secured it with rocks and dirt to keep it upright. They repeated the action two more times for the prisoners being crucified alongside the Nazarene.

The women Maximus had seen earlier huddled together in quaking sobs near the base of the cross on which Jesus hung. Androcles placed a comforting arm around Ezra, who wept openly. The clouds above them darkened ominously.

The crowd, spurred on by the priests, continued to mock the dying Nazarene, shouting up at him, "If he is a king and the chosen of God, let him save himself as he did others." Even the Roman soldiers mocked him and offered him a vinegar-soaked sponge on the tip of a reed.

Maximus was incredulous at the cold-hearted contempt the people and their leaders demonstrated. He looked at the heart-rending scene of the Nazarene hanging from the cross, thick, dark blood dripping from the piercings of the spikes through his flesh. His head hung down, tilted to one side with his bearded chin resting on his chest, his stomach distended because of the awkward position in which he hung. The Roman executioners sat near the cross, making a sport of dividing the clothing of the three criminals.

Jesus's head slowly lifted as he opened his bloodstained eyes and looked upward. He spoke something in Aramaic. "What does he say, Ezra?" Maximus asked.

"He talks to his father . . . he says . . . 'Father, forgive them; for they know not what they do.'" Ezra watched in grief and disbelief. Maximus could only wonder at the strength of a person who could forgive anyone for the cruel and unjust punishment he had been caused to endure.

An older woman stood and, in anguish, moved nearer to the cross. A man Maximus thought was one of Jesus's apostles from Galilee helped her.

Ezra leaned over and said, "His mother."

What torment it would be for a mother to see her son treated as Jesus was that day. The woman's shoulders shook in agonizing sobs. The young man with her tried comforting her, to no avail.

Jesus looked down from the cross and, seeing his mother weeping, charged the beloved apostle next to her with her care.

The apostle put his arms around Jesus's mother, and the two wept silently together.

Maximus thought of his own mother and the tears she surely

had shed as he left for each campaign. But she had never had to see him tortured.

After a time Jesus raised his head to the heavens and spoke loudly, *"Eloi, Eloi, lama sabachthani?"* Maximus looked to Ezra for interpretation.

"He speaks to his Father again," Ezra said. "'My God, my God, why hast thou forsaken me?'" Ezra translated.

The skies darkened further with more than just menacing clouds. The sun was blotted out, and a palpable fear overcame all present. Many fled to escape the darkness and the impending storm.

Jesus cried out once more in a loud voice, "Father, into thy hands I commend my spirit." He closed his eyes and bowed his head, drawing one last breath and then sagging limply upon the cross. Maximus had known victims of crucifixion in Rome to hang on the cross for days. It was unusual that Jesus would die so comparatively quickly. At the very moment his head bowed in death, the earth rumbled and quaked. Maximus had experienced earthquakes in Rome; earth tremors always caused him fear. The timing of this quake caused fear for another reason. *He truly was the Son of God,* Maximus thought. *If this powerful God is vengeful, he could overturn the entire earth.*

Maximus saw a priest talking to the captain of the guard. As they spoke, the captain reached for a cudgel he had brought with him. He walked to one of the other malefactors and slammed it against the man's leg. The bone cracked audibly, and the thief screamed in anguish. The captain did the same thing to the other thief, and a second scream rang out.

"They break the legs to hasten death before the beginning of the Sabbath," Ezra said with contempt.

The captain approached Jesus, who was hanging lifelessly on the cross. Androcles stood to prevent the cruel act of breaking the Nazarene's legs. The captain looked up at Jesus, discarded the cudgel, and waved to one of the other guards, issuing a command. The guard brought a spear, which he drove into Jesus's side. Blood and a clear fluid spurted from the wound. Jesus did not quiver. He was dead.

The sky had turned a dangerous shade of black. Never had Maximus seen day turn to night so treacherously or so quickly. The scene took on a surreal look in the glow of the soldiers' torches. The priests slithered away, not wanting to infringe on their piety about Passover and the Sabbath. Only the three women and a few faithful disciples of Jesus remained.

The soldiers worked quickly. Fearful of the threatening sky, they removed the rocks and dirt, lifted the cross with Jesus on it out of its hole and dropped it onto the ground. They pushed the other two crosses back and forth until they fell to the ground; one thief landed face down, causing great laughter among the drunken soldiers.

Maximus watched as a soldier leaned over the body of Jesus and tried to pull his hand up through the spike without removing it from the crossbeam. He was watching so intently that he didn't notice Androcles move forward. Suddenly, Androcles was pushing the drunken soldier to the ground. The guards chose not to challenge him for interfering with their work.

Androcles reached down, grabbed the top of each spike with his muscular hands, and worked them back and forth until they loosened. Then he pulled them gently out of Jesus's flesh. He did the same thing at the feet. When he finished, he began to weep silently. The weeping turned to sobs. He looked down at the crucified body of the Savior—the blood, the torn flesh, the gaping wound in his side, and the crown of thorns. He read the inscription on the placard above his head: "Jesus of Nazareth the King of the Jews."

Androcles clutched the amulet around his neck. He thought of the cruel death of his innocent family, cut to pieces and left to burn in the rubble of their home. He shed tears he had held back for too long. He was flooded with an avalanche of emotion. *This man did not defend himself against his wicked accusers,* Androcles thought. *He did not fight back or call upon an army of supporters. Most improbable of all, he forgave them. How do I become a great warrior like this man?*

As he knelt next to the Savior's broken body, Androcles could feel the burden of hatred and vengeance being drained from his soul. It felt like warm waters pouring over him, washing him clean. He released the amulet and smiled inwardly at the thought of his father, mother, and brothers and how he remembered them in life. He would never again remember them in death.

The guards picked up the two thieves by their arms and legs and dropped them roughly on the litters that had been brought to carry the bodies to the burial ground. Androcles bent down and, with strong arms under Jesus's shoulders and legs, lifted him. He felt as light as a small child in his arms. Androcles cried openly as he looked into the face of the Savior. His countenance was peaceful—he was finally at rest from the pains that had been inflicted upon him and that he had suffered so willingly.

Androcles felt lightning surge through his body; his heart burned in his bosom. This was something he had never felt before. He remembered Maximus's being unable to explain the feeling of powerful warmth that had coursed through him when he prayed. *This is what Maximus must have felt,* Androcles thought. With the warmth still burning in his chest, Androcles looked into the face of Jesus and said, "I now believe. Truly you are the Son of God."

With the utmost care Androcles laid the body of Jesus in the litter in a dignified manner. A group of Jewish men covered the body in a fine linen cloth and reverently carried him away. Androcles wiped the tears from his eyes. He clutched the amulet around his neck, lifted it to his lips, and kissed it tenderly. It would no longer hang like a millstone around his neck as a token of hatred and revenge against the insensitive cruelty of men. It would become a reminder of love, forbearance, and forgiveness. When he touched it in the future, he would think of his beloved family and Jesus of Nazareth, the Son of God.

"Brother." Maximus stood behind him. Androcles turned, and they embraced warmly. Ezra joined them, and the three men wept in a soulful embrace.

◆ ◆ ◆

They escorted Ezra back home. It was now late in the afternoon, and the darkness was abating. Not a word was spoken during the short walk. They entered the house and stood, not knowing what to do.

Maximus straightway gathered his meager belongings, placed them in a satchel, and slung it over his shoulder.

"You have a plan?" Androcles asked.

"Yes. We will spend the Sabbath with Jershon and leave with them for Capernaum tomorrow. Let's collect the horses and go now. Ezra, why don't you come with us, at least to their camp for the day?"

Ezra slowly shook his head. "I am tired. I would like to rest and ponder these things and do some more studying." He sat dejectedly. "Will you return?" he asked feebly.

"Of course, rabbi. I will return soon." Maximus smiled warmly at Ezra.

Androcles packed his satchel and stood waiting. They each embraced Ezra affectionately.

Ezra asked, pointing to the Roman garb stacked in the corner, "What shall I do with your clothing and armor?"

"Let the guards at the Antonia fortress have them. We have no further use for them."

Androcles nodded in agreement.

"The swords?" Ezra asked.

"Those least of all," said Maximus.

40

יום שבת

Yom Shabbat

Jershon's camp bustled with excitement at the appearance of Maximus and Androcles with their horses. They both appeared sorrowful and exhausted. Jershon cautiously asked about the bloodstains on Androcles's robe. That led to a recounting of the night's vigil and the crucifixion of the Savior. Everyone in the family wept as Maximus related the story.

Liora sat close to Maximus, her hand holding his without objection from her uncle. Sariah was held in the strong arms of Androcles.

"We knew something terrible must have happened when the sky blackened and the earth quaked," said Jershon. "We were in fear of our lives." He paused. "What do we do now?"

Maximus looked at Androcles, who smiled. "We are returning with you to Capernaum tomorrow."

Naomi gasped, covering her mouth with her hands. Liora clutched Maximus's arm more tightly.

He continued. "We desire to become part of your family, Jershon. We have experienced things the past few weeks that were entirely unexpected. We couldn't have imagined their effect on us, and we are treading on unfamiliar ground. I love your niece with all my heart. I don't know how this will work, but I desire to marry her. I have not known anyone like her in all the world. I came by request of Tiberius himself to Judaea on an unrelated errand, and I encountered the woman of my dreams." Liora looked at Maximus with tears of joy in her tender eyes. He embraced her warmly.

"I too want to become part of your family, Jershon," Androcles said. "I love your daughter. My life has been forever changed by the events we have witnessed in recent days. Capernaum is not Rome, but Rome has nothing to offer me in comparison to a life with Sariah in Capernaum. I have no family . . ." He hesitated, holding back tears. "You have become my family." He tightened his grip on Sariah's hand. She leaned into him affectionately. He looked at David. "David, I know a few things about the trade of blacksmithing. If you agree, I would propose a partnership, as neither of us is a very good fisherman." Everyone laughed out loud, and David smiled broadly.

Jershon was silent. The reality of what had just taken place was too much for him. All he could do was lift his hands in a welcoming gesture to the two Romans who sat before him. He caught Naomi's eye—she was weeping tears of joy.

The Passover meal was prepared and eaten solemnly. Little was said. The sadness of Jesus's crucifixion weighed heavily on each of them, bringing with it unanswerable questions and an unsure future for the new disciples. Despite the somber mood, Liora could not hide her joy at Maximus's announcement. She and Naomi beamed at each other across the fire.

It was the most unexpected time in the most unexpected place. Liora leaned against Maximus's shoulder, looking up at him with loving eyes. He smiled down at her, and her heart melted.

EPILOGUE

Maximus and Liora stood at the rail of the ship as it pulled away from the wharf at Caesarea. Maximus had grown accustomed to the robes of the Jews, but as he rubbed his clean-shaven chin, he vowed he would never grow a beard again. He pulled Liora close and kissed her lightly on the lips. She smiled up at him, wondering when she should tell him of the new life now growing in her womb. She wrapped her arms around his waist and held him tightly. She had never been so happy in her life.

"I've always loved the smell of the ocean," Ezra said as he joined them at the rail. The land continued to fall away as the sails filled with the fresh offshore breeze. Ezra placed his hand on Maximus's shoulder. "We embark on yet another adventure together, my friend—hopefully without pirates or high priests this time," he chuckled.

Maximus grimaced, not wanting Liora to worry about pirates.

Ezra had put on weight and was active again. His face was flushed, and his gray hair blew haphazardly in the wind. He had told Maximus of the incredible events after Jesus's death—his resurrection and appearance in the flesh to his apostles. Some of the apostles had returned to Capernaum and resumed their lives as fishermen, although Maximus understood they were now preaching the gospel of Jesus Christ not only in Judaea but also in other lands. Ezra had confided quietly to Maximus a dream he had had of his deceased wife, Miriam.

Akhom barked loudly to his crew. The Egyptian mariners scampered about the deck, obeying the captain's orders to pull ropes and trim sails. The ship took a course southwest toward Alexandria en route to Rome.

Akhom and Maximus had had an emotional reunion the day before and shared the evening meal. The Egyptian captain barely took a bite of his supper as he listened incredulously to Maximus's tale. "Your big friend—does he want a job on my ship? I could use a man like him," Akhom had asked. He exploded with laughter when Maximus told him Androcles was married to a lovely Jewish woman and content to work as a blacksmith in Capernaum.

The ship was at full sail, and the white water pushed ahead of the bow as it cut through the waves. Maximus and Liora gazed at the distant shore. Liora squealed as cool spray from the surging ship engulfed them. Maximus held her tightly, shielding her from the water and smiling as he looked down at her. How pleased his mother was going to be.

THE END

ACKNOWLEDGMENTS

Marian, my beloved wife and a true disciple of Jesus Christ, has been an inspiration in more ways than she will ever know. I thank her for believing in me and assuring me I could be an author before I became one.

NOTES

Page 102. "The Ten Commandments": see Exodus 20:3–18.

Page 103. "Thou shalt not kill": Exodus 20:13.

Page 104. "Thou shalt have no other gods": Exodus 20:3–5.

Page 107. "From my father": John 10:32.

Page 126. "Suffer the little children": Mark 10:14.

Page 132. "Behold, the days come": Jeremiah 23:5.

Page 134. "Therefore the Lord himself": Isaiah 7:14.

Page 144. "I see men": Mark 8:24.

Page 245. "not found so great faith": Matthew 8:8–10.

Page 276. "king of the Jews": see Matthew 2:2; Luke 23:30.

Page 282. "*Immanuel*": Isaiah 7:14.

Page 284. "I will hide my face": Deuteronomy 32:20.

Page 284. "perverse generation": Deuteronomy 32:5.

Page 286. "What do you think": see Matthew 22:42.

Page 315. "one mightier": Mark 1:7.

Page 320. "Hosanna to the Son of David": Matthew 21:9.

Page 340. "Rejoice greatly": Zechariah 9:9.

Page 344. "My Father's house": John 2:16.

Page 361. "make not my Father's house": John 2:16.

Page 414. "We seek an audience": see Luke 23:1–7; John 18:28.

Page 415. "What charges": John 18:29–32.

Page 417. "Are you": John 18:33–34.

Page 417. "I am not a Jew": see John 18:35–36.

Page 417. "Thou sayest": John 18:37.

Page 417. "What is truth?": John 18:38.

Page 418. "When Herod saw Jesus": see Luke 23:8–11.

Page 420. "no fault": Luke 23:14; see also vv. 13–25; John 18:38.

Page 421. "It is the custom": John 18:38–40.

Page 422. "Crucify him": Luke 23:21; see also vv. 13–24.

Page 422. "I am innocent": Matthew 27:24.

Page 422. "I present you": John 19:4–13.

Page 423. "Behold your King": John 19:14.

Page 427. "Father, forgive them": Luke 23:34.

Page 428. "*Eloi, Eloi*": Mark 15:34.

Page 428. "Father, into thy hands": Luke 23:46.

Page 429. "Jesus of Nazareth": John 19:19.